Freya

MATTHEW LAURENCE

[Imprint]
MAKE YOUR MARK

NEW YORK

[Imprint]
MAKE YOUR MARK

A part of Macmillan Children's Publishing Group, a division of Macmillan Publishing Group, LLC

FREYA. Copyright © 2017 by Rovio Entertainment Ltd. All rights reserved. Printed in the United States of America by LSC Communications, Harrisonburg, Virginia. For information, address Imprint, 175 Fifth Avenue, New York, N.Y. 10010.

Library of Congress Cataloging-in-Publication Data
Names: Laurence, Matthew, 1982- author.
Title: Freya / Matthew Laurence.
Description: First Edition. | New York : Imprint, 2017.
Identifiers: LCCN 2016015264 (print) | LCCN 2016042638 (ebook) |
    ISBN 9781250088178 (hardback) | ISBN 9781250088185 (ebook)
Subjects: | CYAC: Freya (Norse deity)—Fiction. | Goddesses, Norse—Fiction. |
    Magic—Fiction.
Classification: LCC PZ7.1.L382 Fr 2017 (print) | LCC PZ7.1.L382 (ebook) |
    DDC [Fic]—dc23
LC record available at https://lccn.loc.gov/2016015264

Our books may be purchased in bulk for promotional, educational, or business use. Please contact your local bookseller or the Macmillan Corporate and Premium Sales Department at (800) 221-7945 ext. 5442 or by e-mail at MacmillanSpecialMarkets@macmillan.com.

Book design by Ellen Duda

Imprint logo designed by Amanda Spielman

First Edition—2017

10 9 8 7 6 5 4 3 2 1

fiercereads.com

Steal this work and you shall find
that gods aren't always fun or kind,
for those they hate the most by far
are thieves of books in which they star.

For Danielle, Helen, Scott, and all the
other marvelous mortals in my life

1

TWILIGHT DREAMS

I live in a mental hospital. I'm not actually crazy; I just like it here. The Inward Care Center has a lot going for it. They give you clean clothes and neat foam slippers, feed you, and protect you, and nobody questions the bizarre. I can feel safe here. Sure, it's all low-grade construction, dull white walls, and linoleum. Everything smells like pine oil cleaner mixed with a hint of cigarettes, and the only breeze comes from sterile air-conditioning. But I don't live here for the scenery. I live here because it's the only place I have left in this world, the only place where they'll *believe* in me.

You see, I'm a god.

There you go again, thinking I'm crazy. I'm not, I swear. I go by Sara Vanadi. They used to call me something else entirely, of course, pious lips and tongues caressing the perfect syllables of my name alongside countless prayers, but that doesn't matter anymore.

They don't believe in the old titles any longer, so why should I keep them? All that's left of my heyday are scattered myths and a blur of faded memories. Don't trouble yourself wondering who I was. Today I'm just a girl who wants to stay safe and hold on to the last embers of belief that she can find.

"Hey, how are you?" a baritone voice asks, interrupting my daily pity party. It's the staff supervisor, Elliot Russom. He looms over me like a mountain—used to play football before he joined the Inward Care Center—but he's a softy at heart. "I'd like you to meet our newest psych tech."

I look up from the little house I'm building out of Uno cards and into a pair of bright blue eyes. They belong to a cheery guy with a shock of auburn hair he must've spent hours getting to look perfectly tousled. Or maybe he just woke up with it, in which case he has my sincerest envy. He also looks way too young to be chasing a career in a place like this. Wonder where his life went wrong. "Hi," he says in a bright voice. "Nathan Kence. So nice to meet you, um . . . ?"

He wants my name. For the briefest moment, I want to give him the true one. I want him to look at me with adoration and respect, to make me feel like the goddess I once was. *Was, was, was.* The longing surprises me. It's been a while since I've felt that ancient ache for what I've lost. But I'll never have it again, so I say, "Sara. Nice to meet you, too, Nathan," and hold out my hand.

He shakes it, seeming perplexed. Elliot smiles—that disoriented look on Nathan's face is exactly what he wants. "You're wondering why she's here, aren't you?" he asks.

It's a common source of confusion. After all, I don't look like I belong in a crazy house. I seem young and happy, like I should be out babysitting or studying for tomorrow's chemistry test. My clothes might be castoffs donated to the ward—a too-large T-shirt decorated with the message *Give Blood* and faded jeans—but there's a healthy body under all that. One might even think I'm a bit on the curvy side, but what can I say? They liked their ladies a little thicker back in the day, and I was supposed to embody that ideal. No one could have predicted the body-image apocalypse to come.

Now Nathan looks embarrassed, but he has no need to worry—there's a reason why Elliot brings new staff to meet me first. "It's okay, Nate," I say, smiling. "I'm an educational prop."

Elliot rolls his eyes; I'm trampling all over his script. "Sara is the nicest girl you'll ever meet," he says, pretending he hasn't heard me. "But she's here for a reason, so there are two things I want you to understand. First, not everybody who gets committed is an angry lunatic, and second, don't make assumptions about our clients based on how they look."

My smile widens and I laugh. "Aww, Elliot, am I that misleading?"

He gives me a happy bounce of his eyebrows. "Why don't you tell Nathan who you are?"

I clear my throat and fix my eyes on the new hire. Mine aren't the sharp, striking blues he lucked out on, but they're still a captivating forget-me-not hue. They go perfectly with my silky gold hair—almost as if someone planned it that way. "Well, Nate," I begin in a sunny, clear voice, "I'm over a thousand years old. I was born in mankind's dreams and empowered by his beliefs. I'm a goddess."

His eyes widen and he grins. "I've always wanted to meet a god. So, is Sara your real name? Would I know you?"

Oh, I like him. Most new hires give me a nervous look and say something along the lines of "That's nice!" when I tell them what I am. He actually has a sense of humor.

"You've probably heard of me, but I don't give out my true name anymore."

"Well, of course not," he says. "Don't want to get mobbed by the paparazzi wherever you go."

I love it when they play along. "If only," I say, heaving a dramatic sigh. "Belief gives me strength, and doubt takes it away. If I told you who I really am, you'd know exactly who to disbelieve in, and then I'd be just a bit weaker for it."

Nathan looks at Elliot, who shrugs. "She's never told me, either. As far as we're concerned, she's Sara."

"Sara it is. Well, whoever you really are, I'm glad we met," Nathan says.

I'm about to tell him something similar when Carolyn calls to us from the nurses' station. "Ms. Vanadi? You have a visitor."

"I—I *do*?" I never get visitors. Nobody knows I'm here. This must be a mistake. "Excuse me," I say to Nathan, who nods and follows Elliot on the rest of the tour.

I sidle away from my table in the dayroom, careful not to disturb my growing house of cards. As I head for the main room, I catch a bit of Nathan and Elliot's chatter from behind me and smirk at its content.

". . . just seems so young," Nathan is saying. "Happy, too. Fit right in at glee club, y'know?"

"Like you're any older?" Elliot replies with a deep chuckle. "I think she's at least eighteen. She has to be, otherwise she'd be on the juvenile ward."

Ha. If they only knew, right?

I walk up to Carolyn with a spring in my step, pleased to hear the centuries have been good to me. She's busy filling out patients' charts but breaks into a smile as I get close. I tend to be on everyone's good side. It's kind of my thing. "There you are. You can head into the cafeteria. I'm so glad someone's actually come to see you."

"Um, me too," I say, eyes flicking to the double doors on the other side of Carolyn's station. My unexpected visitor lies just beyond, probably sitting patiently in one of the center's cheap plastic chairs. "Do you know who it is?"

"No, sorry. Bill just stuck his head in to say there was someone here for you, that's all."

"Okay, thanks." I give the doors a wary look, then square my shoulders and head toward them. Why do I feel so nervous all of a sudden? There's nothing to be afraid of. I'm a forgotten god in a hand-me-down T-shirt and foam shoes, after all. Who's going to mess with *that* combination?

The moment I push through the doors, I spot my mystery guest. There are several visitors in the cafeteria today, friends and family occupying half a dozen wide tables, all chatting with loved ones of questionable mental health. Bill waves as I walk in, then goes back to his newspaper. There's only one thing out of place, and I'm certain he's here for me: a man in a dark gray suit, sitting at an otherwise-empty table.

He looks up, fixing me with his dark brown eyes, and I freeze.

It's not a conscious choice—I feel like a startled deer. He's . . . *dangerous*. A steady sense of menace rolls off him like a wave of heat, a lifetime of cruel experience at odds with the twenty-to-thirtyish years he looks to be around. Part of me wants to hide under a table, but I crush the impulse. Abandoned or not, I'm still a *god*. Who does he think he is, scaring me like that? I march right over to his table, pull out a chair, and sit in front of him.

"Hi there!" I say, sickly sweet.

A slow smile oozes onto his face. It's creepy on a calculated level, like he's spent a lot of time practicing it in front of a mirror. "Ms. Vanadi?" he asks smoothly.

I resist the urge to shudder. I swear, everything he does is unsettling. "That's me!" I say, keeping up the overly cheerful voice.

"Of course it is," he says. "But why deal in half-truths? After all, we're about to become close friends."

There is no earthly way I will *ever* become this man's friend. And this is coming from a god built around the concept of friendship, among other things. "Wonderful!" I say. "But I'm not quite following you on the 'half-truths' bit. I'm Sara."

"And yet you were committed here for claiming to be something . . . *more*."

I want to go. This guy freaks me out on so many levels. But I plow ahead, hoping he'll decide to leave if I play the vapid cheerleader just a bit longer. "Well, of course I'm something more! I'm a god of—"

"Love," he says, tongue darting between his lips as he draws out the word. The way he says it makes my skin crawl.

"Um, yeah. Been over my charts, huh? Are you a doctor?" I know he's not. A real doctor would be talking to me in the day-room, or maybe one of the dormitories. A real doctor wouldn't make people want to shriek if he reached out to touch them, either—and I know I will if this guy so much as lays a finger on me.

"Of course not, Ms. Vanadi. And feel free to drop the act any-time. I know who you really are. Or should I say *were*? My name is Mr. Garen. I'm here to extend an offer."

Oh, crap.

Is he lying? I'm so bad at telling—a trusting girl by nature, in fact—that I just assume he is. He seems the deceitful sort, anyway. "This is new," I say, trying not to let my worries show. "Most people have trouble believing they might be talking to a god!"

He sighs and reaches into his pocket. "I see you'd prefer to make this difficult. It's so rare I need to prove myself," he says as he searches. "You people tend to be chatterboxes. Are you afraid of me, sweet—ah!" He withdraws his hand, fingers closed tightly around something, and raises it over the table. He eyes me to make sure I'm paying attention, then opens his fist to release its contents. My brow furrows in confusion. It's a crumpled ball of fabric, maybe satin. There are dark stains on it, as if someone used it to clean their hands after rummaging around in a bag of potato chips.

I give him a puzzled look. He motions at the ball, encouraging me to open it and examine its contents. I hesitate, then reach out with questioning fingers, curious. Just before I'm about to touch it, I get a flash of hideous imagery, a split-second vision that sends my hand shooting back to clutch at my chest.

Blood. Cracked skin and suffering. Flesh caught between long teeth. Pain, dismemberment, and death, all inflicted with a sadistic glee that takes my breath away.

"It's a piece of Ahriman," the man explains, sweeping the ball of fabric off the table and back into his pocket. "A particularly foul Zoroastrian god we're keeping under lock and key. He's not a very big fish in this day and age, but he still has enough believers to make him quite the threat. Every part of him carries the taint of destruction, as you can see."

I'm too shocked to say anything. I can't remember the last time I've felt the presence of divinity. He's not lying. He knows exactly what I am.

The oily smirk returns. "I represent an organization of . . . *concerned citizens*, let's say. We deal in deities, Ms. Vanadi. We contain or destroy those who would do harm, and recruit the rest. You were once—"

"What I was is none of your concern," I say, putting on my best angry face. "I don't have a clue how you found me, but I have not meddled in your affairs, and I expect you to extend me the same courtesy."

He spreads his hands and makes a token effort to look apologetic. It's about as insincere as you can get. "I'm sorry, Ms. Vanadi, but you really are quite rare. I could go into all the nice perks you'll receive, but let me break it down a bit more simply: Join us . . . or die."

My mouth drops open. He's threatening me. He knows who I am and he's actually *threatening* me. I don't think this has ever happened before.

"Spare me the vengeful-deity act," he says, waving a hand to dismiss my ire. "I've seen it all before. Here's the deal, 'Sara.' We're well aware there's precious little anyone can do to put you down permanently. You still have a handful of believers here and there, and they'll put you back together, won't they?"   .

I cross my arms and glare at him.

"Of course they will," he says, answering his own question. "So this is what will happen: Accept my offer, and we'll see to it you have all the believers you need. You'll be a true god again, not some stray begging for scraps. Deny me, and we will make the world disbelieve you out of existence."

My heart drops into my stomach. I dearly hope he's lying now. Is it even possible? Sure, disbelief hurts, but it would take the concentrated doubt of thousands to erase me entirely. That means convincing all those people I exist, and *then* getting them to think I *don't*. Sounds pretty damn hard to me. "How on earth do you plan to do *that*?" I say, aghast at the idea.

He chuckles, and my anger returns. I really wish I had something heavy to smash that grin off his face. "Oh, you of all people should know how cynical today's masses can be," he says. "I won't get into specifics, but do you honestly think we can't find a few skeptics out there to point at you?"

I have to kill this man.

He's right, of course. This is why I don't give out my true name. Nobody *believes* anymore, and if this little "organization" of his has the means, then it could be the death of me. I need to strike first. My options are limited, though. My power is low. All I can do at this point is meddle with body chemistry, and getting this scumbag to feel attracted to me is about as far as you can get from my goal.

"That's it?" I say, deciding to stall for time. "I walk out of here with you for the vague promise of worshippers?"

He shrugs. "It's usually all I need to say. You're a rather desperate lot, these days."

I have to fight to keep from wincing at that. Of course I miss the age of legends, when whole pantheons rose and flourished. I miss my friends, and I miss being loved. But not enough to turn my back on what *we* believed in. This man seems to be forgetting that my kind valued freedom and rebellion, that we were a rough-and-tumble bunch who would rather die than follow orders from smug bootlickers like him. If he thinks he can buy my servitude, he has another think coming.

"The world's changed, and we can't follow," I say. "Look, I'll level with you: I don't want to work for you, and I don't want to die, either. I just want to be left alone. My time is past. I've been in this hospital for . . ." I pause, trying to count. The Inward Care Center has been my life for so long I've seen the staff go from pagers to cell phones.

"Twenty-seven years, by our estimates," the man says. "I assume the workforce hasn't caught on thanks to your talent for emotional manipulation."

"Whatever," I say, reddening. He thinks he has all the answers. I really do hate this man. "I'm not going anywhere, Mr. Garen."

He gives me a sour look, then sighs. "You don't want to be on one of our teams? Fine. We have other uses for gods. But despite what you believe, you *are* coming with me. We'll just have to go about it the hard way."

He gets up and fishes around in his pocket again, but instead of the little satin ball of nightmares, he retrieves a long, thin piece of metal. It flashes briefly in the light of the overhead fluorescents, and I see it's a large needle. Bill glances up from his paper and frowns when he notices the object. I can tell he's about to say something—shoelaces aren't even allowed on the unit, for safety reasons—but before he can open his mouth, Garen holds out his left index finger and stabs it.

Instantly, the room goes silent. Every client and visitor sprawls onto the tables, limbs askew. Bill slumps forward in his chair and begins snoring. Beyond the double doors, I can hear clatters as staff and patients alike tumble to the floor. Garen just smiles, pockets the needle, and sticks his finger in his mouth to keep it from bleeding on his nice suit.

He's just put the entire care center to sleep.

"Doesn't work on immortals, of course," he mumbles around his finger before pulling it out and looking it over.

"So what does that make you?" I ask when I find my voice. The calm in it surprises me.

"Oh, I'm no god." He gives me a nasty grin. "I *did* say we had other uses for you."

Okay, on *that* unbelievably sinister note, it's time to leave. *What's the plan, Sara?* I look him over, wondering if I can take him. Ordinarily, I'd assume I could. I can do more than hold my own in a fight, and like he said earlier, we gods are remarkably hard to kill. I get the feeling I might need a bit of an edge this time, though. He knows too much about me already, and I'm probably not the first god he's tried to recruit. I hate to admit it, but I know exactly what's needed here. It's painful, but in my weakened state, it's the only option.

Time for a little trip down misery lane.

See, I can't make people love me—not really. Love is as much a mental and emotional state as it is a physical one, and the latter is all I can touch: body chemistry and mood. Still, that's a rather fertile playground. This man strikes me as a fairly loveless individual, but even monsters can feel loss. So I concentrate, reaching out to him with the little spark of power I have left, and push at his brain chemistry. It's exhausting, but worse than that, it *hurts*—I'm supposed to inspire love and adoration, not despair. What I'm doing goes against the very core of my being.

Garen frowns and shakes his head, trying to clear it. His face loses its disturbing, superior cast, breaking down into confusion. "What are you—?" He puts a hand on the table to steady himself before staggering away from it. I think he's trying to glare, to reassert himself, but he keeps stumbling on the sadness I'm pouring into his brain.

Either he's hiding something or I'm weaker than I thought. Maybe it's both, because he should be on the ground right now, crying for his mother, instead of looking a little tipsy. There's no way I can keep this going much longer. Hell, *I'm* starting to tear up from the sheer effort of it all.

Luckily, my pantheon has a solution for problems like Garen: Hit them again, and *harder*. While he's distracted, I launch myself up, sending my chair clattering away. I leap onto the table and run across it, gathering what little speed I can in two footfalls before throwing myself into the air, pulling my legs up, and sending both knees crashing into the man's chest. The air goes out of him with a *whoosh* and he topples to the floor. He seems dazed, but I refuse to give him the chance to retaliate. I lean back, grab one of the nearby plastic chairs, and bring it down on his head with a savage *crack*. His eyes roll and he goes limp.

This is the part where I'm supposed to run. The bad guy's unconscious, and everything's clear for me to make my getaway. Well, how stupid is *that*? I feel this is one of the many poor lessons Hollywood teaches today's young women. You don't leave an enemy behind, not when you have the upper hand.

I raise the chair high above and bring it down again, bouncing Garen's head off the floor with the strength of the blow. Blood spatters onto the dingy linoleum. Again. A grim smile begins working its way onto my lips. He's still breathing, but I figure another hit or two should be enough to—

Garen's body contracts, sucking into itself. Fabric, skin, muscle, and bone flow like water into a drain, spiraling down into nothingness. He's gone in an eyeblink, a blast of air rushing in to fill the void with a sound like a suction cup being torn off a window. There's nothing left of the man but a bloodstained floor and a dented chair.

His empty seat clatters to the linoleum, dropping from my nerveless fingers, and I lean against the table for support. Oh, this is *very* bad. He's been saved by some sort of contingency magic, his friends will no doubt be back in force to finish the job, and . . . and I have to be gone before they return. *Gone.* The thought stabs me, fills my heart with a thunderous jumble of grief and fury. This isn't *fair*. I've lost everything a hundred times over, been reduced to a shell of a goddess in an asylum, and now I'm about to fall even farther. What, I haven't been humiliated *enough*?

I scream and kick over the table where Garen made his offer, where he changed everything, and stand there for a moment, seething. Then I shake my head. It's done. I want to sit and pout, to rage against the injustice of it all, but centuries of experience are screaming at me to leave, and I'm inclined to listen. I may be fickle, but I'm not stupid. I spare a moment to glare at the spot where Garen vanished, then dash over to Bill and unclip the keys from his belt. Around here, if you have keys, you can do anything.

I push out of the cafeteria and nearly trip over Nathan. He and Elliot must have been finishing up their tour beside the nurses' station. Lucky me; I'm not sure if I remember how to drive a car—twenty-seven years in a mental hospital!—so I'm going to need a chauffeur. Deciding whom to take is easy. I might be a lot stronger than I look, but Elliot's a giant, and there's no way I'm getting him out of here without a forklift, so I bend down and haul our newest psych tech off the floor. He groans as I toss him over my shoulder. I think Garen's sleep spell might be wearing off.

By the time I've made my way out of the Inward Care Center, fumbling with Nathan and more stupid locked doors than I can count, he's starting to wake up. Good, I was getting tired. This little journey has made me realize I'm nowhere near as strong as I used to be.

"Whazzit?" he mumbles as I jog into the parking lot.

"Which car is yours, Nate?" I say, pulling him off my shoulder and giving him a shake.

He rubs his head, trying to banish the last bits of sleep. "Silver Toyota Camry, why—wait, what's going on?"

I grab him by the shoulders, stare into his eyes, and give him my best smile. "You're about to rescue a god, Nate. Now, get me out of here!"

He frowns, fully awake now. "What, no, I'm—it's Sara, right? What are we doing out here? No, we have to go back inside! I just started this job and—"

I flood his brain with as much happiness, love, and desire as I can manage. His look of confusion slips away into puppy love. It would be adorable if I weren't so pressed for time. "Oh," he murmurs, a dreamy expression returning to his face. "'Kay."

I hand him his keys and he wanders over to his car, unlocks the passenger side first (what a gentleman!), and lets me in. Then he enters, starts the engine, and pulls out of the lot. "Where to, Sara?" he asks with a silly smile.

The question stops me in my tracks. After twenty-seven years, the hospital has become my world. I'd never considered where else I might need to go, and now all I know is it's the one place I can't stay.

"I don't know, Nathan," I say, the words filling me with terror. "I really don't know."

2

THE NEW WORLD

We go to his apartment, of course.

It's the only idea I have. For almost thirty years, my only window to the outside has been a limited supply of television and movies, and they're quite clear on the first step: Everyone runs to the guy's apartment first, and *then* they make a plan. So that's where we go. I almost feel guilty for picking the clichéd choice.

The first thing Nathan does when we get inside is hug me. "You're *amazing!*" he says, still heady from a brain full of pheromones, dopamine, and serotonin. (You can learn a lot about the science of attraction if you hang around doctors for a few decades.)

I smile, but it's a sad one. He doesn't really love me—not with his heart. You'd think it wouldn't matter, but the empty adoration I've forced on him is against everything I stand for. I live for displays of true, genuine love, not this forgery, so I release my hold on his mind and try to bring him back to normal. It doesn't take long. One moment he's bouncing off the walls, giddy at just being around me, and the next he's cooling down, steadying himself against his kitchen's Formica countertop. A frown replaces the inane grin, and he starts to realize what happened.

"Wait, why are we here?" he says, looking around. He turns to me, eyebrows shooting upward. "Oh, crap, we have to get back to the center! It's my first day!"

"Well, we kind of can't do that, Nate," I reply, hitching my shoulders in a bashful shrug. "Sorry."

"Oh god," he says, really seeing me for the first time, putting two and two together. "I kidnapped a patient. I am so fired. Oh, no no no, this is all kinds of fired and sued and arrested and—" He starts heading for the door, but I move to block him.

"Calm down," I say. "You're not in trouble. I kidnapped *you*."

"What?"

"And I really am a god." Might as well slip that one in. It's not like it's going to make him any *more* bewildered.

He laughs and holds up his hands. "Sure you are, um, Sara? It *is* Sara, isn't it? Why don't we get in my car and head . . . out?"

I roll my eyes. "I'm not letting you take me back to Inward, Nate. Now, look, what do I need to do to prove to you that I'm a god?"

He pauses for a moment. "Go back to the center with me?" He says it with such hope I can't help laughing.

"Nate, calm down. I'm not going anywhere until you start taking me seriously."

He begins to pace. I can see this isn't exactly what he was expecting when he went in to work today. "Sara, please," he says. "I need this job, and it's going to look really bad when they find out I snuck a beautiful crazy person out of the facility, drove her home, and can't even remember how it all happened."

He doesn't realize it, but the little compliment he sneaks in next to "crazy person" really makes my day. It's hard to look nice in an old T-shirt and a pair of jeans, particularly after decades in a place where the "hairdresser" is more concerned with lice than style and the only makeup is already on the nurses' faces. I sigh and say, "Nate, I'm a goddess of love. The reason you can't remember what happened is because I was messing with your head."

He gives me "the look." I'm used to it by now—it's the one that says, *Aww, how sweet. You really believe all this, don't you?* To his credit, though, all he says is "I'm not sure how well that'll hold up in court, Sara."

That gets him another eye roll. I don't care how "creative" or "open-minded" people claim to be now. Time was, you could do something inexplicable and tell someone it was the result of divine power, and they'd believe it in a heartbeat. Now they just chalk it up to science and sleight of hand. Or drugs. "Back in my day . . ." I say under my breath. Well, those days are gone. I have to play the hand I've been dealt, and right now that hand thinks I'm adorably insane. I decide to try a different tack.

"Okay, Nate, how about this: I'm going to sit down on that chair"—I point at a metal folding chair next to a beat-up card table—"and you sit on your little futon over there, and I will make you fall in love with me. If you don't think I've done anything after five minutes, I'll go anywhere you like. Deal?"

He glances at the couch, then back to me. "Deal," he says, trying very hard to keep his face neutral. It's clear he still thinks I'm nuts, but at least he's being nice about it.

He moves over to his futon, sits, and gives me an expectant look. I plop onto the metal chair, lean forward, and begin ratcheting up the affection between us. It takes a little longer than the fire hydrant of desire I unleashed in the parking lot, mostly because I want to leave him aware and in control this time and partly because I'm just plain exhausted.

His eyes widen in surprise and his mouth drops open. He looks at me with a delightful sense of perplexed attraction, and I can see he gets it. I stop what I'm doing to his head. "Apologies sound better with chocolate," I say, giving him a knowing smirk.

He laughs, seems like he's about to say something, then closes his mouth and marches into his little kitchen. There's some rustling, and after a moment he returns with—*Yes!*

"Do you have any idea how long it's been since I've had one of these?" I exclaim, holding out my hands.

"I am very sorry I doubted you," he says, dropping a Toblerone chocolate bar into my eager grasp. I used to *love* these things. For some reason, the presence of almond nougat and honey folded into chocolate seems perfectly calibrated to strike at the joy centers of my brain.

"Apology accepted, mortal," I say with a grin, tearing open the bar and biting off a succulent triangle.

"So you're *really* a god?" Nathan asks. "Not just, I don't know . . . a psychic superhero or something?" He's not fully convinced, but at least he's not rushing to get me into a straitjacket anymore. I can work with that.

"You guys and your fantasies," I say around a mouthful of chocolate. It's just as good as I remember it. I decide to count it as an offering in my name, the first in a *very* long time. "Here, I'll prove it to you. Get me a knife."

"Um, pass?" he says with a frown. I wait a moment, then give him an unamused look when he stands his ground. Okay, he may be open to the idea that I'm telling the truth, but part of him is still clearly unwilling to arm someone he met in the loony bin.

"Worried I'm one of those teenybop serial killers you keep hearing about?" I ask, setting the chocolate down and heading for the kitchen.

"Well, no, but—wait. Seriously, you don't need—!"

"Your skin does look *very* fashionable," I say, rummaging through his knife block. "Ah, perfect."

I pull out a large chef's knife, noting it's one of the few things in this apartment that isn't a bargain brand. I add *Takes pride in his cooking?* to the short list of things I know about Nathan, then sit back down across from him, grinning as I see he's gotten very still. "Don't be a baby," I say, giving the air a few lazy swipes with the knife. "You should see what I can do with a long sword."

Before he can react, I draw the blade across the tip of my left thumb. He winces and holds up his hands, saying, "Hey, no! Stop. Don't do that!"

I just smile and hold my thumb out at him. "I don't have many believers left," I say, directing his attention to the injured digit. "But the ones I *do* have don't think of me as a goddess with a cut on her finger. So I change to match their beliefs. Watch."

Hundreds of years ago, the wound would have started to heal

before I'd even finished making it. Now it takes almost a full minute. Still, for those who don't know any better, it probably seems very impressive. Bit by bit, the cut stitches itself closed, a few dainty drops of blood oozing out before it seals itself completely. There's not even the barest hint of a scar; it's like the gash was never there in the first place. I wipe the remaining blood on my T-shirt (an act I find vaguely ironic, considering the message on it) and raise an eyebrow at Nathan. "Well?"

"That's . . . that's incredible," he says, sounding suitably awed. "I mean, you could just be some *regenerating* psychic superhero, but still. Not something you see every day." He stares at me for another few seconds, then shrugs. "Okay, maybe you *are* a god. Whaddaya say we roll with it for now? Hot damn."

"You're taking this rather well."

He grins, eyes alight. "Are you kidding? This is just about every childhood daydream of my generation come to life. So which god are you, really? There's a *way* higher chance I'll believe you now, I promise."

I barely resist telling him—the urge to gain a new worshipper is so strong—but I can't yet. We're not safe here. It won't take a genius to figure out where I've gone and with whom, and telling Nathan all about myself is a long story that can wait for a safer place. I make a little hurt sound and shake my head. "Not now, Nate. I'm in danger. Actually, I think we both are."

"We?"

"Probably, yeah. Sorry." I really do feel bad about it; he seems like a nice guy, and not someone who deserves to be thrown into the middle of some supernatural struggle, but much like my past,

21

now is not the time to focus on this. "Someone's hunting me, and since you helped me get here, I think pretty soon they'll be after you, too."

"Oh," Nathan says, digesting this. Then he laughs, and it's that crazed sort of sound you make when you're not sure if you should be amused or appalled. He glances around the utilitarian apartment, at the ID clipped to his waistband, and shrugs. "I have to tell you, Sara, this is probably the best excuse I've ever had for taking a day off. The first day of my first grown-up job . . . and apparently also my last."

I laugh with him. It *is* a bit ridiculous. "Glad I could help you play hooky."

"So, who are you running from?"

No point in keeping him in the dark there. I quickly describe Garen and his nasty organization. When I'm done, Nathan nods and says, "Yeah, I don't blame you for wanting to get the hell away from *that*." He pauses for a moment, then bobs his head as if he's made some internal decision. "Well, can't let a nice goddess like you make a break for it on foot. Where do you want to go?"

It's the question that's been running through my head since we got here. I lean back in my chair and grab for the chocolate again. "Truth is, Nate, I have no idea. I've been at the Inward Care Center for twenty-seven years. I don't have anywhere to run."

"Twenty-seven?" he barks, surprised. "You don't even look old enough to drink."

"I *did* say I was over a thousand. Not bad for a millenarian, eh?" I say, gesturing at myself.

He taps his forehead. "Aah, right. Goddess. I guess you don't age." He frowns as a thought hits him, then gives voice to it. "How come nobody at the center noticed? Your records must have admittance dates."

I shrug. "I can tweak how people feel about me, like I did to you. Seriously, it's not like I'm a hazard to myself or others; they wouldn't normally keep me in a place like that. My butt has 'outpatient care' written all over it."

"I guess that makes sense," Nathan says. "So you're on the run, you have no place to go, and, lemme guess, you have no friends to call, since all your contacts are twenty-seven years out of date."

"Right in one."

"I've got plenty of friends in town," he says. "And family up in the Maryland-DC area."

I shake my head. "Can't be anyone connected to you, either. Nowhere they'll know to go looking. I need a nice, permanent place to lie low."

"Permanent, huh? That makes things difficult. I'm your classic starving artist, and something tells me you weren't drawing a paycheck in the hospital."

"No, and all my things, well . . ." It hurts to admit I have nothing left, not even my necklace. If it glitters, it calls to me. I adore bling of all types, the more unique and precious the better. Just a quirk of mine. I have a lot of them, too. As a figment of humanity's imagination given form, my thoughts, desires, and motivations will always be a little larger than life. "I don't even have proper clothes anymore," I finish, looking down at my bedraggled cast-offs. He thinks I'm beautiful? In *this*?

Nathan frowns. "C'mon, you look great."

Don't get me wrong, I still appreciate his words, but I want to *feel* great. How I *think* I look is just as important, and right now, outside the Inward Care Center, I'm starting to realize how unflattering this outfit really is.

I think he can tell I'm unconvinced, because the next thing he says is "Well, I can try to get you something on the way to wherever you're going. I wish I'd kept some of my ex's clothes, but I, um . . ."

He stops, and I cock my head, curious.

"Kinda burned them," he mumbles, embarrassed.

I laugh at that, and he seems grateful my reaction is one of amusement instead of criticism. I don't think he quite grasps the whole "god of love" thing just yet. I've seen every relationship, every kind of heartbreak and affection possible. Even if it didn't last, I'm just glad he had that kind of connection, that experience. It means there was love and passion there once, and I choose to focus on that. It's my nature.

"Anyway, you still need to figure out where to go," he says, clearly trying to steer the conversation elsewhere. And he's right—we're no closer to a plan of action.

"Okay, so clothes can wait," I say. "But money shouldn't be a problem. I might not have glittering riches anymore, but you still have banks, right?"

"Right . . ." Nathan says slowly.

"Then I'll just ask for some over-the-counter handouts. I can be *very* persuasive." I wink at him. "So that will give me the means to get wherever the hell it is I'm going."

"Sure is nice to be a god," he murmurs, thinking. "Money's no object, then? We could always get you a hotel room somewhere far away."

I shake my head at that. "Too public. Hotels have a pretty high turnover on guests, and I'd stick out soon enough. I need someplace more secluded."

"Some kind of cabin-by-the-lake deal?"

This is the part where he finds out gods are rather particular. Oh well. Had to happen sooner or later. "No, no, I need to be somewhere I can interact with people, maybe even gain a new worshipper or two."

"Wait, so it can't have too many people because you're worried you'll get discovered, but it can't be empty, either." He pauses. "Is your true name Goldilocks?"

I like this guy. "Got the hair for it, don't I?" I say, giving my blond tresses a fluff. "Sorry, but it's just how I'm wired. If I didn't care, I could bury myself underground and wait a few years for the heat to die down."

"You don't need to eat?"

"Or breathe, or any of that stuff. Immortality and all that. I enjoy doing both, though, so I'd really prefer not to go with the whole 'shallow grave' approach. It's kind of like how you don't *need* to have a job, listen to music, or fall in love, but you'd rather not go without."

"Gotcha," Nathan says, thinking. "Man, a mental hospital really *was* a good idea."

"Thanks. They'll probably be watching them now, though," I say, feeling a little dejected. I'd been rather proud of the scheme, back when I committed myself. Now that path is closed to me. The next time I see Garen, a chair's not going to be nearly enough to satisfy my bloodlust. I eat another piece of chocolate and contemplate murder.

"Old folks' home?"

"Boring."

"Island resort?"

"Not bad, but dangerous if they find me—I'd have nowhere to run."

He snaps his fingers. "Hey, are you against hotels because they get a lot of visitors, or because you'd get noticed more easily in a place like that?"

"Not following."

"What I mean is, are you okay with getting lost in a crowd?"

"Oh. Well, yeah, of course I am. Gods are pretty social by nature. We like being around you little dreamers."

"So a lot of people is a good thing, so long as you don't get noticed?"

Where's he going with this? "That's what I'm saying, yeah."

"Then how about a theme park?"

A what? Geez, when was the last time I went to one of those? Maybe that World's Fair back in Chicago? How long ago was *that*? "You mean the places with roller coasters and rides and such?"

"Exactly," Nathan says. I give him a puzzled stare, not feeling up to speed just yet. "This is Orlando," he explains. "It's practically the tourist capital of the world. Get a job working at one of the parks, and they'll never find you."

I like the "never being found" part, but I still feel like I'm missing the full picture. "Okay, but where would I live? They close eventually, right?"

"Employee housing."

"Worshippers?"

"Several million starstruck, impressionable children a year." He holds up his hand and begins ticking items off on his fingers. "Safety in numbers, anonymity like nowhere else, and believers aplenty. Beat that."

I get it now, and he's *right*. I love this idea. The only way Garen could have found me the last time was through my files; a patient who's been claiming she's a god would probably raise a few red flags. I can start all over in one of these parks—a new life in the most unlikely place.

"Nathan, it's perfect," I say. "Let's do it."

He shares in my joy for a moment, then something clicks behind his eyes. Slowly but surely, his smile fades. "Wait. 'Let's' . . . as in let *us*?" he says in a wary voice.

I fight to hide a grimace as I realize just how much—intentional or not—I've asked of him with that little word. "Oh. Yes . . . ?" I say, feeling awkward.

"I mean, I want to help, but, um, *all* of it? Together?" he asks, clearly uncomfortable with the drastic pileup of change my presence will bring. "This isn't just a road trip anymore, is it?"

I shake my head sadly. "It's a new life, Nate." I'm really starting to like this guy, but I don't want to rip him out of everything he's built here (not that it actually looks like much) or endanger him more than I already have. Seriously, divine follower isn't the safest of career picks. "You don't have to come with me, you know. It might not be too late to act like we never met. I could knock you out and leave you in the bushes back at the Inward Care Center. Tell them

I stole your car—I can probably teach myself to drive again—and that will be the end of it."

Nathan considers this for a moment, looking around his rental apartment as he does. The place isn't exactly a disaster, but it's obvious a guy's been living here alone. Mail is piled on the counter, plates are climbing their way out of the sink, and the carpet's begun to gather a nice collection of stains. I can sense the conflict taking shape in his mind, fear of the unknown warring with the thrill of adventure, disenchantment with his current lot in life, and, to my embarrassment, a little leftover adoration for yours truly.

"Screw it," he says at last. "You know why I needed that job? Because it's the only one I could get. Nobody's hiring Web designers fresh out of high school, and it's not like a degree will do me any good. My girlfriend's gone, my mom kicked me out as soon as I graduated, and my friends are all in college or busy getting jobs wherever they can, too."

He looks me in the eyes and smiles. "Following a goddess . . . That's pretty much like following your dreams, isn't it?"

A silly grin creeps across my face. "The wildest ones, Nate. Bring whatever you need, and let's start that new life."

He nods and begins dashing around his apartment, gathering his most important possessions. It takes a depressingly short amount of time. Minutes later, we're back in the car, pulling out of his complex's parking lot and heading for the highway. As the place disappears behind us, I feel like I'm waking up. I should have done this years ago. Leaving Inward isn't as scary as I thought it would be—it's more like I'm coming out of retirement, shaking off three decades

of dust, and taking the first steps down a new path to glory. It's definitely not what either of us expected when we got up today, but
somehow, I think we're both happier for it.

The future calls to me, and for the first time in years, I don't
know what it holds.

3

FALSE LIVES

Getting a fresh start is just as easy as ever. The Social Security office isn't where it was back when I needed a new identity for Inward Care, but Nathan has one of those ridiculous smartphones with all the answers, including the new location. He seems a little sad he'll need to ditch it to keep my pursuers off our trail, but I assure him we'll get an even better one soon enough.

I know the idea of creating a brand-new life at the drop of a hat these days seems impossible. It's certainly gotten harder, I'll give you that. There was a time when it was as simple as walking to a new village and giving a different name to anyone who asked. Now society's managed to put all sorts of roadblocks in place. Forms, numbers, licenses, birth records—it's enough to make your head spin. I've never bothered to learn any of it. I just do what I've always done:

march straight into the place where they hand out those IDs and make a new friend who knows how to get me everything I need.

Nathan seems stunned by how simple it is. He still has all those roadblocks in his head, a lifetime of movies, books, and experiences telling him just how hard it is to disappear, how many hoops you have to jump through to bypass the system. What he doesn't realize is that all those obstacles were put in place by *people*. I understand technology has made things faster and more impersonal, but in the end, it all comes down to the decisions of another human being, and with a touch of my talents, any one of them would bend over backward to give me what I want.

The clerk lovingly slips me new Social Security cards, explaining the next steps we'll need to take to get driver's licenses and such. We spend the rest of the day racing all over town, collecting new forms of identification and forging new lives for ourselves. Nathan spends a while obsessing over what his new name will be, but I don't particularly care about mine. I still intend to go with Sara for those close to me; I've had this one for hundreds of years, and I'm not about to change it outright. Even so, I need to pick something, so I snag a set of names off some street signs: Amelia Robinson. That should be fine.

By the time we stop for the night in a luxury hotel downtown, I'm completely drained. I haven't had to push myself like this in ages. I barely have enough juice left to persuade the clerk at the front desk to set us up with a complimentary room, and even then it's something of a struggle.

"Couldn't get the suite," I mumble unhappily as we make our

way upstairs. I find myself leaning heavily on Nathan, concentrating on just putting one foot in front of the other.

He laughs and throws an arm around my shoulders, propping me up. "I think you did just fine, my goddess," he says with a cheesy grin. I'm too weary to elbow him for the silly line, though I dearly want to.

When we get to our room, I collapse onto the bed. Sure, I don't *need* sleep, but there's nothing like peaceful rest to recharge. I'm dimly aware of Nathan climbing into the other bed, and then I'm out like a light.

Glorious, vivid dreams come to me, like they always do. A charming doctor in Germany once told me they were expressions of my subconscious, filled with symbols he could interpret to reveal my innermost hopes and fears. What he couldn't know was that it'll never work like that for me. I *am* the dream. My kin and I, we're humanity's wishes and nightmares given form.

And so when I sleep, I dream of you. All of you.

In my dreams, I see what the human race thinks of love and beauty, fertility and magic, vanity and war. I see whole continents of insecurity and doubt, a world wrapped in worry. It's a strange development. The anger, the mistrust, the violence . . . of course they sadden me, but they've always been there; man has killed man since the beginning of time. It's the anxiety that's new, that sense of reservation.

Where is the confidence, the pride? At every turn, you underestimate yourselves. But I suppose it's not surprising, not if you consider what's happened to the world since my heyday. Now that you have a global audience, you can measure yourselves against the best among you. The most beautiful people, the smartest scientists, the greatest musicians . . . all of them are just a news article away, ready to tell you that no matter how good you are, there will always be someone better.

I wish I could tell you it doesn't matter. I wish I could hold you close and tell you that you will be loved for what you do, that you are incredible and unique. I wish you knew how much you were needed, how much I miss you. I wish. You dream of desires and hopes, and that is why I dream of you—because you are *my* desire and hope.

I wake refreshed and wistful, the Florida sun streaming through cracks in the curtains. The ache has returned in full, that longing for worshippers and lovers, high priests and hopeful peasants. There's so much hurt out there, so many prayers I could answer, if only their owners believed someone was listening again. I cram a pillow over my head to shut out the light and sigh into the mattress. Things were stable back at Inward. I'd managed to find a way to balance my cravings with reality and shut out the pain of yearning for what once was. Now that I've left that little safety net behind, it's all creeping back. Maybe this wasn't such a good idea.

Then again, it's not like I had much of a choice.

"Sounds like someone's awake!" Nathan's voice cuts into my musings. I don't care what time it is; he sounds far too chipper for any morning hour. "I guess you're ready to rise and shine at last."

There's a clink and a gurgle, and I crack open an eye as I recognize the sound of coffee being poured. The smell wafts through the room, and I groan and disentangle myself from the little nest I've made of my blankets. I love coffee. It always perks me up, which I find a bit odd, considering my divine nature. I couldn't begin to tell you how it works.

"Lots of sugar, no cream," I mumble, rubbing one eye and stretching.

"Thy will be done," Nathan says after a moment, bringing a steaming cup to me. "I took advantage of room service, too. Want anything? Toast? Eggs? Waffles?"

It's been far too long since I've had breakfast in bed, not to mention having it hand-delivered by a cute guy. I could get used to this. "Yes to all three. Eggs, buttered toast, and definitely the waffles," I say, taking a sip of my coffee.

"Coming right up," Nathan says, moving to the tray. There's a buffet of food here, far more than either of us can eat. I get the feeling he's having a bit of fun with an unlimited budget. I watch as he puts my meal together. He's wearing a shirt and a pair of boxers, letting me get a better look at him. Just out of high school would put him in his late teens, though his high cheekbones and five-o'clock shadow could let him pass for a few years older. He's certainly no gym rat, but he has an athletic look that implies he at least attempts to exercise on a regular basis. Cute. Not exactly my type, but cute. I look down at myself and wonder who I am to judge anyone at this point: I'm still in the *Give Blood* T-shirt and ill-fitting jeans from Inward.

"So," Nathan says, bringing over a heaping platter of food, "you ready to tell me who you really are?"

I dive into the meal with gusto. I have no idea what happens to the stuff inside my body, but just like sleep, it helps me recharge. "Sure, why not?" I say around a mouthful of eggs. I can't imagine wolfing down several servings of food makes the most dignified participant for this sort of discussion, but now's as good a time as any.

"Ready when you are," Nathan says, plopping onto his bed and looking at me with curiosity.

I wash things down with a slurp of coffee, clear my throat, and turn to him. "Well, you understand the whole 'god of love' thing, right?"

"Yep," he says, nodding. "So who does that make you? Aphrodite?"

I make a disgusted sound. "That simpering, oversexed tart? *Please*. Don't make me vomit."

"Okay, okay," Nathan says, holding up his hands. "Then who are you?"

I draw myself up and straighten my back, trying to look at least halfway regal. It's probably undercut by my ridiculous appearance (I don't even want to *think* about how my hair looks right now!), but it'll have to do. "I am the daughter of the wind and seas, the giver, the flaxen, the Lady of the Slain. Lover and warrior, wielder of the sacred mysteries of seidh, most glorious of all goddesses." I pause, pleased by his rapt attention, then deliver the answer he's been waiting for: "I am Freya."

"Freya," he repeats, nodding slowly. My high and mighty posture fades as I watch desperation race across his face. He's clearly ransacking his memories, frantic to make a connection. "I—um, yeah! Freya! Huh!"

"You have no idea who I am, do you?" I ask, incredulous.

He at least has the good grace to look embarrassed. "It *sounds* familiar. I mean, I took a classical mythology class in college, but it was all Greek all the time."

I roll my eyes. "I *hate* those guys. When did they hire a PR firm?" I sigh. I guess it's not his fault—there's a reason I don't have worshippers, and I can tell he's kicking himself for not knowing me. "Asgard?" I prompt. "Yggdrasil? Valhalla?"

"Oh!" he says, clearly thankful for the hints. "Norse! Okay, yeah! I totally know those myths. So you're, uh . . ."

"I am of the Vanir," I say with a wistful smile. "Love is my domain, yes, but so, too, are war and beauty, fertility and death, sex and gold. I might not have made the headlines like some of my kin, but I am the greatest of them, for in the world of men, what shapes life more keenly than the touch of a lover . . . or the edge of a blade?"

"Wow," he whispers after a moment, looking suitably impressed. "You know, it's going to sound like a pack of lies after I blanked on your name, but I really do know some stuff about Norse mythology. Always thought it was the coolest, too."

A heartfelt grin immediately cracks my divine facade. "Well, thank you, Nathan. I'm glad you got a chance to find out you were exactly right."

He returns my smile, and in that moment, I feel his belief spark to life within me. I know he's had doubts ever since I told him I really was a goddess, but like all insidious thoughts, they were hidden on the edges of his mind. Now that he has a name, a cause to focus on and truly consider, he's dragged those suspicions back into the light and found them wanting. Behind those bright blue eyes of his, I feel the last nagging shackles of disbelief crumble and rejoice in their demise. He *accepts* me. It's a wondrous thrill, gaining his trust like this, one made all the more spectacular by the current scarcity of my worshippers. Whether he realizes it or not, Nathan has just joined the painfully exclusive ranks of my followers, and for that, I am endlessly grateful.

"So where are the rest of the gods?" he asks, clearly unaware how deeply he's just bound his fate to mine. "You know, Odin, Thor, Loki . . . all those guys?"

"Oh, so *those* you know?" I say with a laugh.

He gives me a nervous grin. "Marvel. You can't pick up a comic or hit the theater these days without running into one of them."

"Ah, yes," I say, remembering a few fun movie nights at Inward. "So how come *I* never got to be a superhero? Who do I talk to about that?" I wave a hand. "Never mind. You were asking about my kin?"

"Yeah, are they still around? I mean, if they're all famous, wouldn't that make them stronger?"

I give my head a forlorn shake. "Fame isn't always a blessing. Everyone thinks of those three first, but there are reasons for that . . . and, sadly, it's part of why they're gone." I frown as ancient memories bubble to the surface, some rather embarrassing. "Actually, I'm not all that broken up about Loki. I'm glad that slanderous little pest is dead."

"What happened to them?"

"Ragnarök," I say simply.

"The end of the world? Wait, that actually *happened*?" Nathan asks, eyes wide.

"No, no," I say with a giggle. "But their deaths were foretold, and people believed in those prophecies. Remember, we are what you *make* of us, and, well, you decided some of us would die. Any god not mentioned by name in the telling of Ragnarök survived, but those unfortunate enough to get top billing—like my poor brother, Freyr, for instance—were disbelieved into oblivion." I pause, thinking. "Well, 'disbelieved' isn't the best word. More like 'killed by conviction.' The end result is the same, but there's a difference in how it happened."

"I think I get it. That still leaves a lot of gods, though."

I nod. "Dozens. Many of them faded away completely, of course, overwhelmed by disbelief or injured badly without the worshippers needed to regenerate them. All my knowledge is decades out of date, but I know Frigg is still around. Nice lady—the ultimate mom. Used to be a midwife, then a nurse, but I think she runs a bakery now. Sif's a marriage counselor. Bragi did a lot of poetry, and I think he became a newspaper columnist. Hel's alive, too, I'm pretty sure. Used to be a nice girl, but the myths changed her in a bad way. Don't know where she ended up. Baldur got resurrected—always liked that part—and I think he went into politics. There are probably others, too, but we all drifted apart after the believers dried up, so I can't be certain who else is left."

"Gods among us," Nathan says softly. "How cool is that? There are others, too, right? Greek, Egyptian, Hindu . . . ?"

I shrug. "Sure. If they managed to hold on to their believers, they're still around. Some of them are going to be *way* more powerful than me, too, since they actually have real religions and worshippers. Jerks."

"Well, how many do you have left?"

"You don't want to know," I say with a grimace. "I'm a minor player at this point. Let's just leave it at that."

"Okay. So have you met gods from other pantheons? I mean, like, have you ever run into Shiva? Or Jesus?"

"Oh, absolutely," I say, smiling at the memory. "Incredibly kind man. I can see why he gets all the attention these days. Actually came to visit us, back when we were just starting to fade. Apologized for what was happening, said all he ever wanted was for people to be decent to one another. I get the impression he doesn't always approve of what others do in his name, you know?"

"Yeah. It's something of a running joke on the Internet," Nathan says, rolling his eyes. "Bump into any other big names?"

I sigh. "Well, I used to run into gods a lot more often back when my pantheon actually mattered. After our fall, I'd just hear snippets of news—so-and-so is mad about what Zeus did to their wife and such. Now I'm completely out of the loop."

"Huh," Nathan says, digesting this.

"Yeah . . . you haven't exactly hitched your wagon to a rising star," I admit, feeling a little uncomfortable as I do. Why did I just tell him that? I feel a stab of fear begin to work its way through my guts. Now that he knows what a joke I am, I'm worried he'll decide I'm not worth the trouble. It's not that I can't make it on my own, but to lose a new believer so soon . . .

"Sara, I couldn't care less how you rank in comparison to a bunch of random old gods," Nathan says, cutting into my thoughts. "Where are those other deities and what have they ever done for me? You're *here*, turning my life upside down, and I couldn't be happier about it."

Just like that, the fear vanishes, and I laugh at how much I've underestimated this guy. "Oh, I bet you say that to all the pretty goddesses."

"Just the ones in blood-donation T-shirts," he says, laughing with me.

"Argh," I groan, grabbing a pillow to cover myself. "After breakfast, you're taking me shopping."

"Actually," he says, pulling a hotel notepad off the nightstand, "we should really map out our day. We've got IDs now, so what's next?"

"Clothes, cash, a new car, and jobs," I say. "In that order."

"Sounds like a plan," Nathan replies, writing the items down on his little pad with a hotel pen and tearing off the sheet.

I finish my breakfast while he takes a shower and gets dressed. Once he's done, I switch with him, heading into the bathroom. It's annoying, laying out my ratty clothes and knowing I'll just have to get back into them again, but I tell myself this is the last time. The shower feels great. Inward wasn't bad by any means, but a white-tiled community bathroom and stall isn't my idea of luxury. They even have those fancy little shampoo and conditioner bottles here, which gives me a chance to do something about my hair. When I finally step out of the shower, I feel a thousand times better. Going back to my revolting rags (and those awful slippers! Ugh!) diminishes the feeling a little, but I refuse to let myself dwell on it. I have places to go and things to buy.

Nathan drives me around town to every fashion hot spot I can remember, gleefully racking up credit card debt on plastic he's going to abandon in a few hours. As soon as we begin our shopping in earnest, I'm struck by how out-of-touch I've gotten. The mall, for instance, is like nothing I remember. I'm used to low-ceilinged, crowded shopping centers and dingy food courts. The Mall at Millenia soars, its two levels opening across beautiful halls cast in glossy marble, steel, and glass. The central atrium is ringed in digital monitors, broadcasting shots of fashionable people and beautiful scenery while hordes of well-dressed teens, tourists, and business-casuals dash in search of merchandise. Where are the skater punks and dead-eyed shoppers? There isn't even an arcade to be found, and the restaurants actually look appetizing.

Most of the government offices I visited yesterday didn't seem all that different from what I remember of the eighties, but outside the public sector, things have gotten *slick*. I'm liking this modern world. Now I need to up my style game to match it.

Unfortunately, my first few attempts aren't . . . well informed. Apparently, oversize tops, leggings, off-the-shoulder sweaters, and acid-washed jeans are no longer in vogue. Not yet in the loop on that, I plow ahead with misguided stubbornness, managing to cobble together some truly hideous outfits and marveling all the while at the small selections available. Nathan doesn't even say anything about them at first, the traitor. We make it through a few stores before he finally cracks.

"How about this one?" I say, modeling another too-big shirt. "I think it needs a lot more jewelry to really shine, but—what?"

"I'm sorry," he says, clearly holding back laughter. "I thought you might be going for ironic at first, but I really should have said something sooner."

"Ironic? What's wrong with this?" I say. "The jeans are even pre-ripped! How cool is that?"

He tries to say something else, but it comes out as some kind of gargle-snort.

I make a frustrated sound and turn to a well-dressed guy going through a nearby rack of clothes. "Excuse me? Sir?" I say, getting his attention. I gesture at my new outfit. "What's your take?"

He looks me up and down. "It's not Throwback Thursday, hon," he says at last, then returns to his own shopping.

My mouth drops open. I return to Nathan, who's sporting a rather telling shade of red. "How much has changed?" I ask. "Is it my hair? I know it needs volume, but once you tease it out—"

"Oh god," he chokes. "No, no, I can't do that to you. Big hair is over. Like, *way* over. Haven't you been watching television? Movies?"

"It was a mental hospital, not a hotel," I snap. "Sure, we got some new releases, but there were just as many reruns from the library. Do you have any idea how many times I've seen *Flashdance*?"

"You poor thing," he says, trying to compose himself. "C'mon, let's get you some fashion magazines or something."

He leads me out of the store—*after* we return most of my purchases—and I spend the next hour or so flipping through a half-dozen issues of the latest magazines, pausing every now and then to glare at him over the tops of the pages.

"All right, *fine*," I say at last. "I think I get it now."

"Ready to try again?"

"Yes," I say, a sullen teenager. Then my smile returns. "But you're going shopping, too. I've seen what trendy guys are wearing. Graphic T-shirts and unfitted jeans from Old Navy aren't exactly hot, either. Get yourself something nice. *Hon*."

He looks down at himself. "I, but . . ."

"You let me buy scrunchies, Nathan! *Scrunchies!*"

He fakes a wince at that and holds up his hands. "Too cruel. All right, fine. I guess that's fair. Meet you at the food court in an hour?"

"Make it two," I say. "I have three decades of fashion horror to unlearn."

He laughs at that, then waves as he heads off, making a beeline for J. Crew. I suppose there are worse places to start. As I go from store to store, it strikes me that there's a bit of a gender gap in terms of outfit difficulty here. Nathan doesn't seem like he'll have much trouble finding something decent, but is it just me, or is everything that's halfway stylish these days meant for starving stick-girls? It's surprisingly difficult to find something that looks good and actually fits my hips. If I weren't the divine embodiment of beauty, I might start thinking my hourglass figure wasn't attractive. As it is, I just feel a little flabbergasted at the lack of good selections.

My foam shoes are long gone, but I supplement the pale rose flats I used to replace them with a variety of heels, wedges, and sandals. I eventually gather a halfway decent selection of jeans, skirts, and dresses, as well as sweaters and shirts that actually stay on my shoulders. I even pick out a few upscale pieces in case I need to class it up, and once I've finished spending a king's ransom on new outfits, I decide to show off a little and change into one of them.

It was a real relief when I ditched my awful Inward clothes a few stores ago, but as good as getting rid of those hideous castoffs felt, there's something even better about slipping into designer labels and date-night makeup. I choose tight jeans with a creamy off-white top, using the women's restroom as my changing closet and applying some lipstick in the mirror. *There, much better.* I think it might come off as a little *too* nice for a random day at the mall (especially on someone who looks like they might still have to ask their parents' permission to stay out late), but considering how long it's been since I've worn anything approaching "decent," it feels right.

Nathan's eyes pop when we meet in the mall's food court. I do a little twirl for him as I walk up. "Actually look the part now, don't I?" I say, flashing him a winning smile.

"I'll say," he murmurs, looking me over with obvious glee. I get the feeling I'm drawing eyes from all corners, and that suits me just fine. After all, vanity's part of my portfolio, too, and centuries of human hope, desire, and lust have crafted me into a rather fitting package for it. I feel bad for the mortal women with similar measurements, though. The bras alone cost a fortune.

Next, we hit a series of banks on the outskirts of the city. I cover my hair with a scarf and put on an enormous pair of dark sunglasses before heading into each one. With a touch of my gift, nobody will question the outfit—it's for the cameras, and the people watching their footage whom I can't affect. Nathan waits off-property in the car while I go inside, make senior management fall madly in love with me, then ask for a donation. Minutes later, I'm walking out with wads of cash. It's never a lot, just a few thousand each time, but it all adds up. I'm a little concerned Nathan may be having second thoughts about all this blatant thievery, but because we're in a bind and gods don't do cheap, there seem to be few legal solutions. Hopefully, it's not weighing too heavily on his conscience.

After a few hours of highly compliant robbery, we have more than enough to buy a new car. While I could charm a salesman at any dealership and get him to give one to me for free, that's something that gets recorded. Someone will eventually realize an entire car just got handed away. Since Garen's probably smart enough to look for reports of big-ticket items being turned into party favors, I don't want to link Nathan or myself to a four-wheeled red flag.

We end up getting a Honda CR-V, which is almost entirely Nathan's decision since I don't have a clue about cars and he's always wanted that particular type, apparently. We get a *very* good deal on it, and any surprise the dealer might have at being paid in full—and in cash—is banished by his overwhelming affection for me. It's getting late in the day as we begin transferring our purchases to the new car, and I'm definitely feeling the strain from all the romantic manipulation I've had to perform. Still, things are a lot better than they were a day ago, when I was reeling from having to torment Garen to distraction. I think the strength of Nathan's belief is really helping. The confidence I feel from my new look probably has something to do with it, too.

Once we're done loading up the CR-V, the sun is beginning to set. "They'll be closed for the night," Nathan says, looking at our list. Everything's crossed out but the *New jobs* entry.

"That's okay. It's been a pretty full day anyway," I say, glad to put this last task off until tomorrow.

"We need to hit the DMV and get a new license plate for our car, too."

"Sounds good," I say. He nods and adds the task to the list. "For now, though . . . dinner?"

"Thought you'd never ask. I'm starving," Nathan says, holding a hand to his stomach in mock pain.

We settle on an upscale steakhouse. I immediately focus on the filet mignon, my mouth watering at the thought of high-quality beef for the first time in decades. Nathan's wavering between a burger or pork chops when I give him a troubled glance. "What?" he asks, noticing the look on my face.

"Go with the burger," I say in a neutral tone.

He sets his menu down and looks at me. "I've got another lesson in the care and feeding of deities coming, don't I?"

I smile. "Sorry. Pigs are sacred to me."

"No kidding?"

"I used to ride into battle on an enormous boar. He had golden bristles." I sigh. "I miss him."

Nathan's quiet for a moment—awed, I assume, at the image of a beautiful Norse warrior goddess charging enemy lines atop a massive battle-pig. Then: "Wait . . . does this mean *no bacon*?"

He seems so appalled at the idea I feel like I've just stolen his puppy. "Um, if it helps, that wasn't exactly a big menu item back in the day," I say, trying to smooth things over a little.

"Eesh. Talk about your sacrifices. Okay, well, burger's on the menu for tonight, then. Anything else I should know?"

"Hmm. I'm a fan of cats, but I don't see them showing up in restaurants very often, so you're probably in the clear there."

"Don't hurt pigs, pet cats," he says to himself. "I guess I can work with that."

"Glad to hear it," I reply. The waiter arrives soon after, and we place our order. We chat absentmindedly for a bit as we wait for the food to arrive, until I decide to turn the question back on him. "So what do I need to know about *you*, Nate? What's your story?"

"Me?" he says, seeming surprised that I'm asking.

"Well, yeah. If we're going to start this new life together, I'd like to learn more about you."

"Okay." He smiles. I think he likes the fact that I'm interested in hearing more. "Only child. Grew up an army brat, so we moved around a lot. Didn't have many friends, but it gave me a chance to focus on computers. Went to high school here in Orlando, graduated a year ago, and took about that long to realize the freelancing gigs I can get don't quite pay the bills, and nobody's hiring full time."

"Which is why you started at Inward."

"You got it. Between that and making websites on the side, I figured I could start paying bills and, y'know, eat. Not perfect, of course, but it would only be until I built up my portfolio and finally got a job somewhere permanent."

"Makes sense. And you said you were a military kid, right? I approve. Which of your parents was in the army?"

Nathan hesitates, and it seems like he's having a small internal debate. Then he sighs. "My dad."

"Not a happy subject?"

"Well, no, I mean—my dad was awesome. I stuck with him after my parents split up. Mom was a flake. Still is. But my dad, it was like he was trying to win Father of the Year every second. We did everything together, when we could. He was away a lot, but when he came home . . . it was really good, Sara," he says with a distant look in his eyes.

"Past tense," I say softly.

"Yeah," he says, leaning back in his seat and looking gloomy. "He went out on deployment, didn't come back. Well, we got him back, but . . . you know what I mean."

I nod, saying nothing. I know all too well what he means. War never changes.

"It happened back in high school, and it's just . . . it's like I never got a chance to know him. Hell, I didn't even get a chance to say *good-bye*. I wanted to grow up and make him proud, make him laugh, but I'd . . . have settled for good-bye."

"Oh, Nathan," I say, reaching across the table for his hands. He clasps mine, and I look into his eyes. They dart away, but not before I notice them shining in the dim light of the restaurant. Poor guy. I know his loss—I've seen it countless times before and been just as powerless to do anything about it.

But that's not quite true anymore. He's a worshipper of mine now, and that *means* something. I don't want to give him false hope, but he seems so dejected I feel I have to say something. "Nathan, I need you to understand I can't do anything yet," I say, lowering my voice. "I'm far too weak. So take this with a grain of salt . . . but your father was a warrior, and that matters a great deal."

He looks back at me, confused.

"I'm the Lady of the Slain, Nathan. Half of those who die in battle belong to me."

There's a moment where he just frowns, and I worry I've offended him. Then a look of comprehension dawns, and he fixes me with this fantastic expression of joyful hope. I glance over his shoulder and notice the waiter heading toward us, bearing our food. I smile, both for Nathan's sake and my stomach's, and I'm about to continue telling him exactly what I can offer when fear rips through me like a knife.

Just over the waiter's shoulder, I can see a man standing in the entrance of the restaurant, scanning the crowd. The dark gray suit is the same. His patrician features, seemingly locked in a self-confident sneer, show no signs of the damage I inflicted a day ago. I can even make out those frightening, intense brown eyes of his as they dart back and forth incessantly, searching for *me*.

Garen is here.

4

RAZOR'S EDGE

"What? What is it?" Nathan asks. The terror engulfing my body has obviously registered on my face in some way.

Garen moves a little farther into the restaurant, and his eyes slide down to some device in his hands. It looks like an oversize version of Nathan's cell phone. Is that what he's using to track me? But how—

I gasp and glance back at Nathan. *The phone.* Of course. He hasn't gotten rid of it yet—used it to find this restaurant, even. I want to be annoyed at him for not being careful enough, but first I need to figure out what to do about my gray-suited stalker. I look up again, and my jaw drops in dismay. I'm too taken aback to be certain, but I think I might've even released a small squeak of alarm.

Garen's looking right at me, that oily grin of his creeping across his face as he moves forward. The waiter stops by my table, and even half a restaurant away, I can see Garen glancing at our order, appraising it, and then looking back at me with a smug expression, as if to say, *The filet? Nice choice.* Then, while the waiter moves to set Nathan's plate down in front of him, I watch as Garen smoothly extracts a long sliver of metal from his pocket.

The needle. He's about to put the restaurant to sleep. *I can't let that happen.*

I lunge up, bolting out of my seat. My stomach screams in outrage as I wrench the serving platter from the waiter's upraised hand, hurling my dinner away. With one smooth motion, I whip the metal disk around and send it tearing through the air on a tight arc.

Garen's expression changes in an instant to one of surprise as the platter crashes into him, knocking him back and sending the needle clattering to the floor. I don't waste a second, snatching my steak knife from the table and dashing across the restaurant. Dumbfounded waiters and shocked patrons blur past me, screaming and shouting as I pick up speed.

I leap into the air at Garen, knife upraised, closing the last fifteen feet between us in one giant bound. I'm literally an eyeblink from plunging my blade into the man's heart when he brings up his wrists, locking them together in an X. I catch a moment's glimpse of metal bands covered in delicate silver filigrees on his forearms before there's a staggering flare of light. A brilliant golden explosion catches me in midair and sends me flying away like a piece of paper in a gale. There's a brief flash of the entire restaurant as I rocket backward before colliding with the far wall with enough force to splinter it. I topple to the floor, dazed and winded, hair spreading onto the tiles around me like a golden net. The steakhouse is spinning; I can barely roll myself onto my back.

Distantly, I'm aware of more screams and stamping feet as the restaurant's patrons panic and run. Glass litters the floor from shattered windows and drinks, crunching under panicked footsteps. There's a ringing in my ears, and I can't seem to get my bearings. Then Garen looms over me, looking down with that awful smile of his. "Fool me once, shame on you," he says, kneeling and flicking me in the head, right between my eyes.

I moan and try to bring up an arm to bat him away, but succeed only in flopping around like an infant. Garen chuckles and extracts a syringe from his jacket, an antique thing of brass scrollwork and handblown glass. He holds it up to the light, and I see it's filled with some sort of pale milky fluid. He taps it, then looks back at me. "Fool me twice, shame on—"

There's a resounding *clang* that cuts him off midsentence, his head shuddering as if he's just experienced a very brief and personal earthquake. I have the perfect view as his eyes cross and he tumbles to the floor beside me, unconscious. Nathan's standing there, panting, a dented serving tray clutched in his hands.

I smile, still dazed, and manage to cough out, "Get me a knife."

By the time Nathan returns with another steak knife, I've managed to pull myself up to a kneeling position. He places the weapon in my hand, and I feel my fingers wrap themselves tightly around its handle. No more messing around with chairs and bludgeoning. I am going to stab this evil freak right between the eyes, split his skull open, and make confetti out of his—

His limbs twitch and lurch inward, spiraling around his torso for the briefest moment before his body folds in on itself and disappears. My knife crashes into the tile right where his head used to be. Garen's gone again, his form compacting into a pinprick before winking out. I toss the blade away from myself in a fury, unleashing a litany of Nordic curses as I do.

"Damn, was that him?" Nathan asks.

The question brings me out of my rage, and I bite off the rest of the insults as I turn to look at my savior. "Yeah," I grate, still angry. I take a breath and compose myself. "Yeah, that's Garen—and you just saved me from him. Nathan, I could kiss you." Part of me thrashes to the surface, obviously energized by the recent battle, saying *Oh yes please do you realize how patiently I've waited*, and bathes the room in desire before I can cram it back down.

He grins, clearly pleased with himself, and, in a stroke of brilliance I suspect isn't entirely his own, says, "What's stopping you?"

I laugh at that and find my footing, levering myself back to a standing position. The warrior goddess in me screams that we should be running, that this isn't the time for romance. The urges of beauty, vanity, and love call to me as well, though, telling me just how long it's been, just how pathetic my available dating pool has been lately. They win out in the end.

"Not a damn thing," I reply, throwing my arms around him and covering his lips with mine. I clutch him tightly, pressing our bodies together for several warm, wonderful seconds before I pull away. Nathan has a faraway, almost mournful look on his face, as if he's just been rudely awakened from a rather pleasant dream.

I feel a sense of delight bubbling within me and realize I've just had my first real kiss in almost thirty years. And I call myself a god of *love*? I'm about to kiss him again and start making up for lost time when I finally manage to get a hold of myself. We need to get out of here. Garen recovered far too quickly from our last encounter, and I handed him a much worse beating that time. The sooner we make our way onto the open road and toss that stupid phone of Nathan's, the better. I glance at him and see the dreamy look has faded along with my unanticipated wave of desire, bringing him back to the reality of the shattered restaurant. He looks confused, anxious, and—surprisingly—embarrassed. I think he wouldn't normally have kissed me out of the blue like that, and now he's wondering if he's made things awkward. Well, no time to worry about that now.

I grab Nathan by the hand, and I'm about to lead him outside to join the panicked crowd of fleeing diners and staff when I notice a glimmer at my feet. The syringe. I waver between leaving it, destroying it, and taking it, before finally deciding on the latter. If Garen thinks it can put down a god, it might be useful. I scoop it up with my free hand, drop it into my bag, and hightail it out of the building, joining the crowd of shocked onlookers and staff.

From the chatter around us, most of them seem worried about bombs, gas leaks, and so on, but a few begin darting glances my way, no doubt recognizing the girl who got launched over their heads in the initial blast. I start edging Nathan through the swarm, taking care not to look too suspicious, but when I spot the flash of police lights in the distance, I drop that approach, grab his hand, and make a dash for our car.

"How did he find us?" Nathan asks as we peel out of the restaurant's parking lot and onto a back road before the cops can cordon the place off.

The question brings my annoyance back in full force. "Your stupid phone is how. I told you to get rid of that thing."

He pulls it out of his pocket, cradling the glossy rectangle of metal and glass in one hand as he keeps the other on the steering wheel. Seeing him so obsessed with the trinket simply irritates me even more. "It's just a *phone*. Destroy it now, or I will."

Nathan sighs. "But I have all my contacts on here. Let's hit a store first so I can at least transfer them to a new one."

"No!" I shout, thumping the dashboard. "Do you realize how quickly he found us before? And now you want to go and make a record of the transfer? Get. Rid. Of. It."

He hesitates again, so I grab it out of his hands. "Hey!" he barks.

But it's too late. I start lowering the window, ready to chuck the thing onto the pavement.

"Okay, okay! Stop!" he says, slowing down the car. "We need to get it wiped, whatever we do. They might be able to recover stuff from it that'll lead them to us."

That halts me. I raise the window with a reluctant tap of my finger. "Fine. How do we do that?"

He shrugs. "Take it to a store?"

I narrow my eyes at him. "We can't just mangle it beyond repair?" This is, incidentally, the traditional method of solving problems in my pantheon.

Nathan stops the car and looks at the phone in my hands, then at me. "All right, yeah. That ought to do it, too."

I glance out the window. Strip malls and occasional houses. "Great. Find me an empty lot," I say, still holding on to the phone.

In a few minutes, we drive up to a sandy parcel of land with a sign proclaiming it to be the planned site of a sprawling mixed-use commercial and residential complex. Considering the weathered look of the place, I get the impression that some economic issues have put a prolonged hold on the construction. I get out of the car and stalk into the undeveloped land, looking around.

"Here we go," I say, spotting what I've come for and moving toward it.

"What are you doing?" Nathan calls out, following me.

"Putting an end to this device," I reply, showing him the large rock I've found. It's not the cinder block I was hoping for, but it'll do.

"Well, just make it quick," Nathan says. "Don't want the poor thing to suffer, after all."

I roll my eyes at that, then turn and place the phone on the ground. I raise the hunk of rock over my head and bring it down onto the gadget with crushing force. The screen cracks. It takes a few tries, but eventually I manage to bash the thing into oblivion, pieces of circuitry and glass flying everywhere. All the while, I imagine what I'm really hitting is Garen's face. It's surprisingly cathartic. A field of splintered phone fragments surrounds me when I'm done. I toss the rock away and stand back up.

"Better?" Nathan asks beside me.

"Much," I say. "Now, let's get something to eat. Killing phones is hungry work."

We head back to the car. "Can we risk staying in this city?" I ask as we get in, concerned that Garen's finding us at a restaurant instead of, say, an international airport might lead him to assume we're not fleeing for safety in foreign lands.

Nathan shrugs. "I don't think he's seen anything so far that would tip him off about our plans. Plus it doesn't seem like the government's on his side or anything—it's not like he can put your picture in front of cops and federal agents. The first time he found you, it was probably because of a whole bunch of research. Just now it was a cell phone. A poor, innocent cell phone."

I stare at him.

"Okay, not ready to joke about that just yet," he murmurs. "Point is, Garen strikes me as a reactive sort—he probably has a lot of gods to deal with and limited resources. He'll follow up on a lead when he comes across it, but canvassing an entire city doesn't seem his speed."

That makes sense. If he really had a bottomless budget and government connections, after all, he'd have brought a SWAT team to the restaurant, not a pair of magic bracers. "All right," I say, nodding. "Orlando it is."

We end up hitting a late-night taco place with a giant mustache for a sign in the heart of the downtown area. If there's the slightest chance Garen is canvassing upscale steakhouses, this should be as far as we can get from one. Nathan gets a giant quesadilla, I settle for an assortment of fish tacos, and we split an order of nachos. It's not my poor lost filet, but it's still quite delicious. Our conversation is casual, focusing on the things we purchased and our plans for the next day. Subjects like his father, Garen, and even our kiss are set aside. On that note, I'm pretty certain I prompted that moment; my powers can get away from me when I'm keyed up. At least he's not taking it badly—things don't feel awkward. I wonder if I should apologize, or at least try to explain what happened, but it seems like we're already past it and I don't want to be the one to bring it up.

We spend the evening in another free hotel room and then head out bright and early the next day on our errands. Nathan's credit cards, old driver's license, and phone have been destroyed. With his Camry abandoned in a parking lot, everything tying him to his old life is gone. Our first stop is the DMV, where we find out we'll need to wait forty-five days for a new license plate for the car—and it needs to be mailed to our home. Our current IDs only have a fake address on them, but we manage to persuade them to mail the plate to a PO box we set up at the downtown post office the day before.

That just leaves the job. Nathan and I pull up outside the Walt Disney World Casting Center in the early afternoon. There had been some discussion on which park to go with, but Nathan assures me my ideal career is here, not at Universal. I take his word for it. That, and I have encyclopedic knowledge of Disney's entire archive—the Inward Care Center didn't allow R-rated movies, so family-friendly films were on almost every day. I saw a *lot* of Disney, let me tell you, and I liked pretty much all of it, except maybe the one about Hercules. Talk about whitewashing the past. *None* of the Greek gods were that nice, not even Hades.

The obstacles arise as soon as we walk through the doors. It's quickly made clear that becoming a face character is normally a difficult task. They hold mass auditions for roles like that; I need references, relevant experience, blah, blah. I barrel through it with overflowing amounts of love and adoration. It seems like I have to charm a *lot* of people, too. There's a pretty extensive bureaucracy at work here, and as soon as I have one level completely convinced I'm the most deliriously amazing hire they could ever hope for, I need to move up to their manager so I can get something on such short notice.

The process takes the whole day, and along the way, we learn that Nathan was wrong about the employee housing—it's only available to college interns. My new friends at the casting center are only too happy to inform us that there are apartment rentals that cater directly to Disney's workforce, however, so Nathan takes the CR-V and leaves partway through to get us a place.

By the time he returns a few hours later, I have just about everything squared away except our mailing address, which he provides. He informs me he's put down a security deposit and paid a month in advance at one of the nicer apartment complexes in the area, right near a central bus line to the parks. I start training in a few days as a face character—a princess, of course—and from everything they've said so far, I'm cheating. A *lot*. There's no way a brand-new addition like myself would be allowed anywhere near such a prestigious role, as they're usually reserved for professionals and longtime cast members. Everyone wants to be one, and vacancies are incredibly rare.

Pulling this off has taken a lot out of me. I might be feeling better since my "escape" from Inward, but I'm still far too weak, especially considering how much I've been relying on these meager powers. Abusing my birthright is just as effective here as it was elsewhere around town, and it's really becoming clear to me just how hard it would be to get anywhere in this society without it. I need to get stronger, and fast. If you think about it, my only marketable skill is getting people to fall madly in love with me. Without it, I have a hunch that the battle between my hunger for belief and need for safety would end up getting me in a lot of trouble.

Well, more than it already has, I guess.

In the end, the final stumbling block is, like most of life's challenges, clothing-related. Princess dresses only go up so many sizes, and I'm hovering right around the cut-off point. I'm also pushing five seven, which is the upper height requirement. My new friends here assure me it'll be no trouble at all, but I have a feeling their wardrobe department is going to hate me soon enough. After signing a huge stack of documents and confirming my training session times, I'm finally done. Nathan and I walk out, carting a pile of documentation and pamphlets to the car.

"So what do you think?" he asks as we drive to the new apartment.

"Seems like they're dead set on preserving the 'magic'—if I didn't look like a princess already, well . . ."

"All the love bullets in the world wouldn't keep the heat off you?"

"That's about the size of it, yeah," I say before silently mouthing his turn of phrase to myself. *Love bullets?* "I'd probably have had to spend a good chunk of each day 'convincing' people that I should be allowed to work there. Yech."

"Good thing that won't be a problem. And you're much prettier than any princess I've ever seen."

"Flattery will get you everywhere," I say, grinning.

"Oh, I'm counting on it," he replies.

You know, I think he has a bit more self-confidence than I gave him credit for. Of course, I might just be rubbing off on him. I tend to have a variety of interesting effects on people if they're around me long enough. Think of it as a bit of "divine overflow"—aspects of my personality tend to bleed into my surroundings, particularly when I'm using my abilities.

"That's the spirit," I say. "I might make you my high priest." That would mean he'd be my chief worshipper and expand my power by his belief alone.

Nathan laughs, and I can't help but join him. I'm in a good mood. This new job feels like it'll be a breath of fresh air, and the danger posed by Garen and his organization seems a thing of the past. "So how's the pay for your priests?" he asks.

"Terrible, but the benefits? *Spectacular.*"

"Any chance of a little immortality in that package?"

Kid, give me the worshippers I deserve, and you'd be amazed at what I can do. "There might be a taste," I say in an even tone. I'm still wary of getting his hopes up, so I decide to change the subject. "In the meantime, though, what are you going to do? I don't think I can rush you through casting as easily, especially with my powers as weak as they are."

"I thought about that. We're not really short on cash right now, and it seems like you can just get us more whenever you feel like as long as we're careful. With that and the small paycheck you'll be drawing, I figure I can focus on Web design."

"Fine by me," I say. "Just remember, gods of love and beauty have expensive tastes."

"I seem to recall they're also very good at getting free stuff."

"True enough," I say, hiding my discontent. I won't say anything yet, but eventually, I'd prefer not to have to use my gifts to weasel complimentary goods and services out of people. It's not because it feels immoral, either—it's more that the deific side of me rebels against the notion I am somehow undeserving of such gifts in the first place. The idea that I have to use my powers to trick mortals into giving me what I desire is an insulting one. Centuries of abandonment have muffled those urges, but every now and then, the ancient, battle-scarred goddess within me stirs. I'm smart enough to repress those feelings, to keep them from meddling with the reality of my situation and making things worse, but each time I'm forced to act as if I'm not the god I am, it rankles.

So for now, I keep it to myself and do what I must to persuade those around me to give what I want . . . all while knowing it should be mine by rights.

The apartment Nathan has chosen is prefurnished, and it's not half bad. Certainly better than Inward. "We'll need to have the cable and Internet hooked up," Nathan says as we get situated. "And get ourselves a phone plan together. But it's pretty nice, isn't it?"

"It is," I admit. "Let's try to keep it that way, too. Can you arrange some sort of local maid service to come by every week or so?"

He gives me a questioning look. "I saw your last home," I explain. "We're not living like that. I might be adrift in the modern world, but I'm still a goddess. We don't do chores."

"Wouldn't dream of it," he says, giving the only right answer. Smart boy.

We settle into a comfortable routine over the following days, putting things in order so we can begin our new lives. My thoughts of

Garen grow distant as it seems our precautions have finally given us a measure of peace. Nathan gets himself a replacement phone and a new computer, dumping all his important files onto it from an external hard drive he brought with him. I end up with a phone, too, but it takes hours before Nathan's able to teach me the ins and outs of the little gadget. It helps when he does some research on Norse mythology, then comes back and has me think of it as a digital Mímir. Odin once enchanted the head of a decapitated seer of the same name to whisper wisdom and counsel to him. It all clicks into place after that.

And suddenly my phone, my "Mim," becomes a link to the sprawling knowledge of the Internet. I've heard about this vast information network from the television at Inward, but nothing has really prepared me for the sheer scale of the thing. It's all available here, anything and everything. Whatever I desire is instantly at my fingertips, a schizophrenic world of facts and entertainment, education and debauchery. I'm addicted in a heartbeat, to the point where I have Nathan get me a computer of my own so I can browse without the constraints of my Mim's tiny screen and keyboard.

The days left until my first training session pass in an eyeblink. Through the Internet, I can see the latest fashions, learn what the world thinks of my kin and me (not much, unfortunately, beyond comic books and fantasies), and stare openmouthed at the incredible diversity—and perversity—of its pornographic archives. No wonder we've been left to rot in the past. The Internet is the new god of humanity, and why not? It can provide anything for anyone. Why pray to me in the name of beauty and fertility when millions of websites with enticing ads can promise all you'd ever want and more?

They seek you out, after all, while I sit here and wait for you to come to me.

It's troubling, what I'm beginning to understand here. I see now why we've faded. Our pride, our power, our distant strength—they've all been twisted over the years into crippling flaws. Humanity created us to answer its prayers, to protect bodies and souls alike. Now you've grown up, put us away like old toys, and built our successor. Worse, it's our better by far, because it's something you can see and touch and identify with. This realization of mine is a sobering one, but I'm no fool—I can smell the opportunity here, the chance to claw my way back on top. I can offer *real* magic—true power amid a downpour of deception. With my gifts and the global audience the Internet could give me, I might just be able to turn the world on its head.

It's food for thought, anyway. For now, I have a job to get to.

The training materials and classes are downright adorable. I was more concerned with just being a princess in general, so I left it to my friends at the casting center to pick which one I'd be. They chose Cinderella on account of my blond hair, blue eyes, and fair skin, and an opening at the Magic Kingdom, and while I suppose I could be a little annoyed they didn't give me Elsa (I mean, a Scandinavian princess? *Come on!*), at this point I'm just happy to have a role.

With my character decided, all my time goes into studying how to act like a proper handmaid-turned-princess for boys and girls of all ages. I learn how to write her signature, interact with kids, stay on message, deal with unruly guests, and, in general, keep the magic alive. It's absolutely spellbinding, to be honest. A thousand years ago, you people were praying to me for victory in battle, strong boys, and fertile wives. Now you've created these elaborate fantasy worlds and built an empire around them. I'm hooked and can't help wanting to learn more. The whole process takes several days, and at the end of the Traditions class, I get my cast ID, which gives me free access to the parks. Spectacular.

Finally, there's the on-site costume fitting. I enter the park through one of its hidden employee entrances after Nathan drops me off. The entire place was built over a network of tunnels, loading docks, warehouses, and utility rooms, turning what was once the ground level into a subterranean city. It's all in the service of immersion, a clever bit of engineering, and foresight to hide the machinations of the park from its guests. I'm given a brief spiel about the ins and outs of the corridors, then sent to get fitted. I soon find I was right about the costume—I narrowly manage to fit into Cinderella's biggest gown, and even then it's uncomfortably tight on me. Luckily, I get it into the heads of the staff that they should take pity on me and have some special alterations made, setting aside a dress that'll be all mine.

There's a bit more training, more costume and makeup tests, and even a few short character quizzes. Finally, the day comes when Nathan drops me off at the park and I'm actually going to go out there and perform in public. My heart is pounding. Adrenaline sings in my veins, and it feels like I'm about to go into battle, not sign autographs and smile. I'm sent to the dressing room to get ready. As soon as I arrive, I'm ushered in front of a long mirror, where dozens of princesses and face characters are transforming themselves from cast members into living legends. I'm soon stuffed into my outfit, long white gloves are pulled past my elbows, my hair gets bundled up underneath a wig and light blue headband, makeup's applied, and I'm ready to go.

As I make my way out of the dressing room, I'm paired with a character host who'll assist me with visitors and make sure I can focus on my job. I'm giddy with excitement, all set to begin my first day in earnest. We're both sent topside, emerging in the bright Florida sunlight. A beautiful castle that's apparently mine looms in the distance. Brilliant flowers bloom in carefully manicured beds, children and families dash over freshly cleaned paths, and bright colors and enticing architecture call to my eyes from every direction. I follow my guide in a daze, ready to begin winning hearts and spreading magic. I have a brilliant smile plastered on my face—one I intend to hold all day. From listening to some of the chatter back in the dressing room, the constant grinning begins to sting after a while, though I doubt it'll ever be an issue for me. Who knew I'd be using my superhuman stamina and pain threshold to play the perfect Disney princess? Considering how hot it is outside, it's even better that I don't sweat.

It's a short distance to the character-meeting site in the courtyard of my castle, but as I walk, I notice something odd about the park. There's a crackle of energy in the air, and an odd tickle begins to run up my spine. My smile almost slips as I realize with a shock what I'm sensing: it's the unmistakable scent of divinity.

There's a god here, somewhere.

He's powerful, too. I'm positive it's a "he"—there's a vibrant sense of masculinity to the aura, a certain distinctive charge that pulses on the underside of reality. I'm trespassing in someone's domain. Would he even consider a gnat like me a threat? I need to find this god and let him know who I am, and soon. Maybe he can tell me more about Garen, or at the very least, tell me how he got so damn powerful in the dry, faithless desert our world has become.

I give my head a little shake, trying to focus on the task at hand. There'll be time later; I can return as soon as my workday has ended and snoop around. I carefully arrange my character and her background in my head as I settle in. In no time at all, my host begins shepherding eager families into a line to meet me.

"Cinderella!" a young girl in braids shouts as she gets close. She can't be older than six. She's clutching an autograph book to her chest and giving me this gleeful, breathless look.

"Well, hello there!" I say happily. I notice her parents just beyond, standing at the front of the line. Their faces carry an odd blend of hope and worry—this is obviously something their daughter has been looking forward to, and I understand they dearly want it to go well.

The girl beams at me, then gets a hesitant look. She's not sure what she should do next. I kneel in front of her and hold out my arms. Excited, she rushes forward and wraps me up in a hug. I feel a rush of confidence stir inside her mind, mixed with—

"I love you," she whispers, holding me tight. And she *does*. This girl has formed a bond with this character as strong as any parent or caregiver could hope for, and here I am, in the flesh, justifying its existence for her. But that's nothing compared to what happens next, because just like that, a tiny flare of energy hums to life in my body, and I realize this girl actually *believes* in me.

For the second time in minutes, the integrity of my smile is threatened by a staggering realization. The only difference is that, this time, it's coming from within. How is this possible? She's never heard the name Sara, let alone *Freya*. What prayers for a Norse goddess could she have unleashed by thinking about *Cinderella*, of all things?

"I love you, too," I reply softly. Then I draw back and look at her. I search for clues, some sign behind her eyes that could point to how she knows who I truly am, and find nothing. "Are you having a good day?" I ask, at a loss.

"Mm-hm!" she hums through a smile, closemouthed. Then she seems to remember the autograph book in her hand and thrusts it out at me. I unclip the retractable Sharpie from the book, open it to the first blank page, and sign my character's name with a flourish.

I raise myself back to my full height and hand the pen and pad to my assistant, who takes it to the girl's mother at the front of the line. Her father pulls out a large digital camera, and I pose for pictures with the little girl, who happily clutches my side the entire time. The belief she has for me is real—I can feel it. But *how*? She just thinks I'm a Disney princess. *That's* who she loves, not some ancient goddess from the howling North.

Then it hits me.

The girl loves *me*. She believes in *me*. I've never thought about it like this before, never considered that someone's direct belief in me, no matter the guise, could count. It seems like it shouldn't work. *She* clearly thinks she's hugging Cinderella, after all. But whatever mystical scales balance the fortunes of the gods, they don't see a difference. Her belief is strong, and it's currently being channeled straight at me, a creature born to catch it. The spark is small, of course; she obviously hasn't dedicated herself to a lifetime of worship.

What's important, though—incredibly, insanely important—is that there's *something* there.

The next child is a little older, maybe eleven, and while she's obviously happy to see me, the belief is missing. The same is true for the following three kids, but the fourth, a little boy, has that same glimmering spark of adoration the first girl did. My mind whirls with the possibilities. Sure, they're not all would-be followers, and even when they are, it's just a distant flicker of belief. But it all adds up, and it's not like I'm in a hurry. Every day I'm here, I'm going to get just a little bit stronger. I can feel it.

I'm going to be a god again.

5

A LOVELY WAR

I close the door to our apartment behind me and lean against it, breathless with delight.

"And she's back!" Nathan says from the kitchen. Something sizzles under his care, and I realize he's cooking dinner. "How was work?"

"*Incredible*," I squeak.

He comes out into the hall to meet me, and I see he's wearing an apron designed to look like a tuxedo. I shoot a puzzled look at it, my earth-shattering discovery momentarily forgotten. "As long as you're bringing home the bacon, so to speak, I figured that left me to deal with dinner," he explains, gesturing with a spatula at his outfit.

"You'll spoil me," I say, pushing off from the door and giving him a friendly hug. "Good plan."

"Well, try it first," he says over my shoulder. "Worse comes to worst, there's always takeout. You're in a good mood—everything go well at the park?"

"Better than well," I say, pulling back to look at him and grin. "Ridiculously, wonderfully better."

"That's great!" he says, breaking into a big smile. "Let me finish this stir-fry and you can tell me all about it."

"A stir-fry?"

"Yeah," he says, heading back to the kitchen. "They had buy-one-get-one on mushrooms at the store."

"I can't remember if I've ever had a stir-fry." My diet at the Inward Care Center was always pretty bland—burgers, pasta, lasagna, that sort of thing. Before that, I tended to stick with the foods from my homeland. Fresh fish and savory meats, sharp dairy and sweet-and-sour jams. I'm making myself hungry just thinking about them. Still, no harm in trying something new. "But there's a first time for everything."

In a few minutes, we're sitting at our dining room table, munching on a serving of vegetables, chicken, and rice. It's not bad. I find myself liking the sauce he's made more than the actual food he's put it on, though—reminds me of some of the marinades we'd pair with fish. I can tell that what he's made isn't the effort of an amateur. There's talent here, whether I'm the best person to appreciate it or not. "This is good," I say. "Where did you learn to cook?"

He gives a halfhearted laugh. "My dad."

"Of course," I murmur.

There's a moment's pause, and I'm worried we're about to sink into silence. Then he speaks up again, obviously trying to move the conversation to happier places. "So tell me your big news!"

71

I snap my fingers. "Yes, thank you. Almost forgot!" I put down my fork and a gleeful look settles onto my face. "It's the kids—they believe in me!"

"Of course they do! I'd buy you as a princess any day."

"No, no, you don't understand. They *believe*. It's like I'm this kind of living proof their hopes and dreams are real, and when they realize that—when they have me standing there in front of them, *proving* them right—there's this surge of reassurance and conviction from them. It empowers me, Nathan. It's like gaining a tiny piece of a worshipper every time."

"Well, go, you. But how does that even work?" Nathan asks. "They can't know you're actually Freya, so how—"

"I have no idea," I say, shrugging. "She wasn't praying; I know that. As long as it's heartfelt, I can hear any prayer in my name, no matter the source, so it must be something else. I never really thought about how we get our powers, to be honest. All I ever knew was that the more believers I had, the stronger I'd be. You people . . . you're magic on a very fundamental level, so deep you can't even tell, but I know we wouldn't exist without you."

"Wild."

"I just wish I knew more about it. How it works, why it makes us thrive or wither." I pause. This line of thinking is leading somewhere I've never even cared to go, and I'm not entirely sure why. It's the most obvious question, now that I think of it—yet it's taken this long for me to bring it up? "How it gave me life," I say, feeling my curiosity grow by the second.

"Hm. We need an instruction manual," Nathan mumbles, thinking. "Well, here: What's your first memory?"

"Now, *that* is going back a ways," I say, screwing my eyes closed and trying to remember. After a minute of effort, I open them, sighing in frustration. "Nothing there. It's all too ancient. When my strength fled, most of my memories went with it. I can barely recall what I was doing a few centuries ago, much less the moment of my birth."

"Worth a shot," Nathan says, nodding as if he didn't expect me to remember. I get the feeling he can't recall much about his first days, either. "Then let's think about it from a different angle. People have to believe first. And it's obviously not just about believing something is real even when it's not. Cinderella's not a god, after all."

"Right," I say, bobbing my head. "I'm with you so far."

"So something in *how* they worship you matters. Whatever it is, it gives you the edge you need to survive, to fortify yourself—and that something is missing from other fictional creatures. For some reason, you and your kind are made to grow, to feed on our belief and—"

"*Catch* it," I say. "That's what I did today. They sent it out to me, and I caught a piece, kept it for myself."

"It's like you're stealing the mail."

"What?"

"Silly expression," Nathan says, waving a hand. "It's like they're mailing care packages to someone they love—like Cinderella—and you're opening them and nabbing a few cookies."

"Pretty much."

And those cookies, oh, how delicious they are. Even the vaguest promise of belief fills me with a ravenous hunger. We pause, digesting this analogy of Nathan's, and I eat a few more forkfuls of the stir-fry. Maybe it's just the vegetables he used. I'm more of a beet-root, carrots, and cabbage kind of girl, and there are water chestnuts and snap peas and all kinds of weird stuff in here. It makes me wonder what his background is—what kind of heritage he calls his own. Then my thoughts bounce from there to something far more interesting to me, and because gods are nosy things, I don't stop to wonder if it's a topic he'd rather avoid.

"Hey, Nathan?" I ask. He looks up, curious. "That ex of yours—what happened there?"

He blinks at my directness, then sets his fork down. "Uh, well, we broke up . . ."

"And some fire was involved . . ." I add.

"Ha, yeah, that—not my finest moment," he says, looking uncomfortable. "She just—ugh, do you really want the whole story?"

I give him a look. It says, *Duh. God of love, remember? I eat this stuff up.*

He sighs. "All right, here goes. Her name was Hannah. We met in high school. She was also into design, and she was really, really good at it. We hit it off, turned serious, were together for a while." He turns wistful as he speaks, and I get the sense the memories he's unearthing are happy ones. "Then we graduated. She stuck with me, even though her parents would've sent her to college. Knew there was no way I could afford it and didn't want to separate us. We both started freelancing, looking for work."

Regret starts replacing the pleasure in his mind. "Remember how I said she was good? Well, she kept getting better. Got a *great* job in no time. Yay, right?"

"I'm guessing there was a catch."

"Had to be." He picks up his fork again, gives his food a half-hearted stir. "It was in another state. Dream job, of course. Couldn't be anything less, could it? So there was no way I was standing in the way of that. I wanted her to take it, wanted her to kick ass and rule the world . . . but I had friends and job leads and an apartment and a life. I wasn't ready to leave."

"Long-distance relationship?"

He snorts. "For something like three months. All those leads fell through, friends got jobs or moved away, and here I am, with absolutely no good reason to stay."

"Why did you?"

He makes a helpless gesture with his hands. "Right?" he says, exasperated. "I guess I wanted to make it on my own, just like she did. What, was I going to follow her to an even bigger city and fail there, too? What was she going to see in *that*?"

Ah, there's a classic for you. "Felt like you wouldn't be equal? Worried things would always feel off?" I ask.

"I loved her," he says, and the quivering spear of pain that lances his mind in that moment tells me a part of him still does. "I couldn't take the . . . the *risk*." He groans. "Stupid. I didn't want to risk los-ing her, so I lost her. *So stupid.* Couldn't pick myself up, walk out the door, and take a chance."

"She broke it off, or . . . ?"

He frowns. "Sort of. I'm still not sure. There was a huge fight. Surprised the webcam didn't melt. She didn't get it, I didn't get it, and we were both *really mad about it.* In the end, I convinced myself it was better for her if we weren't together. She caught on, got furious I'd made that kind of decision for her. Told me I was treating her like a child."

He looks up at me, embarrassed as I've ever seen him. "That was around where I burned her clothes. On camera."

I wince. "Seemed like a good idea at the time?"

His eyes widen and he shakes his head. "I don't know if there's *ever* a time where that's a good idea. I think I was riffing off the 'child' comment. 'You want childish? Here's—'" He rubs his face with his hands. "It went downhill after that."

"I'll bet."

He gives his bowl an idle tap. "I hope she's happy. I mean, the whole thing would hurt a lot less if she'd been a bitch and I hated her, but you can't always be that lucky, I guess."

I nod. "There's always next time," I say, smiling. Then a thought occurs to me. "Is that why you were so eager to toss it all away and follow some random goddess out the door?"

He laughs. "I'd like to think I played a *little* hard to get."

"Really? I've had longer arguments with you over pizza toppings."

That just gets me more laughter, and I'm glad for it. I'd hate to think I ruined a perfectly nice dinner with my prying.

"You might be right," he says at last. "I spent so long beating myself up about the whole thing maybe I was primed to take a chance." He looks me in the eyes, and I see the gratitude there. "Whatever the real reason, Sara, I'm glad I did."

Aw. Corny little sweet-talker. I hope I'm not blushing. "Me too, Nate," I say, and we return to our meals. The conversation drifts back to idle thoughts and pleasantries for a few minutes, until I realize there's another bit of important news I haven't shared.

"Oh! Hey!" I say, brightening up. "Totally slipped my mind— got another bombshell for you."

"What's that?"

"When I was in the park today, I felt the presence of another god."

He gets an impressed look on his face. "You get all the adventures! Could you tell who it was?"

I shake my head. "No, but he's strong. I'm going back to look for him on my days off."

"Are you going to try to team up?" he asks.

"I doubt it. Unless they're from the same pantheon, gods don't tend to ally with one another. We don't play nice."

He shrugs. "All competing for the same believers, I guess," he says.

"Yeah, exactly," I reply. "It's literally life or death for us. But this god might know something. He's clearly managed to hold on to his power all the way into the present day, so it would be a good idea to at least talk to him. Besides, I want him on my side. If he decides I'm a nuisance, well, I don't want him to blow my cover and force us to move again."

"Hell no," Nathan says, seeming indignant at the thought. "Not after all our hard work. Plus there's all that new belief you just found."

"Absolutely! I had a handful of hour-long shifts today, and from those alone I feel like I managed to gain more strength than I did in *years* at Inward."

"That's great, Sara!" Nathan says, sounding pleased. "I wish I had some news of my own on that level, but all I've done so far is update my website and begin working on a few new designs for my portfolio."

"You, my high priest, are doing everything I could hope for and more," I say gratefully, pointing at him with my fork.

He grins at the compliment. Then the smile slides away, replaced by a rather serious expression. "Hey, Sara?" he says softly.

"Mm?" I say around a mouthful of stir-fry.

"That, um, kiss back at the restaurant? I'm sorry about that. I think I might've given you the wrong impression. I mean, I like you, but I'm not the kind of guy who tries to get into the pants of every woman he meets."

I frown. "It *does* take two, Nathan."

"Right, yeah, but it's just—" He sighs, clearly trying to find the right words, and I decide to help him out.

"Look, Nathan, I'm over a thousand years old," I say. "I'm not a pampered teenager, regardless of how I look. I actually *did* like the kiss, too. It's been a *really* long time. But you're right; it probably wasn't exactly your decision."

He gives me a calculating look. "You're going to be trouble, aren't you?" he asks, smiling.

I offer a halfhearted shrug. "Comes with the territory. Look, it was a charged moment and that part of my brain was feeling frisky. I probably short-circuited your sense of restraint. Was nice at the time, but we *are* on the run and we did just meet—I know you didn't mean for anything to come out of it, and neither did I. I've been meaning to bring it up, but then there was that thing with the phone and getting this job and . . . it kind of got lost in the shuffle."

"So it's okay," he says, seeming relieved.

"Absolutely," I say, a little taken aback. "What kind of cheesy romantic comedy do you think this is? 'God of love' does not mean 'needs a date now.'"

"Can't stand those movies," he says. "I'm glad I don't have to live one, either."

"Careful, priest," I say, narrowing my eyes. "Just because I don't live by the rules of awful chick flicks doesn't mean they're not a guilty pleasure of mine."

He quirks an eyebrow at that, then laughs. "Fair enough," he says, still smiling. "You know what? I'm just going to wing it."

"Most sensible thing you've said all night," I say, eating some more of his stir-fry.

We both chew a few more bites in silence before he speaks up again. "I researched you, you know."

"Oh?"

"Read everything I could about you online."

Oh geez. I've been through a few of those sites myself. As you'd expect, they all get a few things right, but nobody has the whole picture. People seem to like thinking of gods as people with superpowers, but we act in some decidedly inhuman ways, and each of us is just a bit different in how we do it. Far too many, however, appear to dwell on the fact that I have a reputation for being beautiful and promiscuous. Really, Loki, thank you *so much* for that one. "Please tell me you didn't spend much time on the more . . . risqué sites," I say.

He pauses, then picks the safest—if unlikeliest—option. "Can't say I found any."

"Mm-hm. Well, what *did* you find?"

"All sorts of stuff. It's hard to tell what's real and what's not."

"Big things are usually true," I say, "but they tend to get the details wrong."

"Actually, the big things were what I was curious about," he says. "You're the god of love, beauty, fertility, magic, and war, right? Those are the main things you cover?"

"Yes. Add vanity to the list, too, actually."

"All right." He stops, thinking that one over. I see a look of understanding in his eyes that tells me he realizes that particular specialization of mine is probably going to bite him in the ass one of these days, but then he shakes his head and dismisses the thought. "So two questions, then," he continues. "First, what does 'magic' mean? I've read the myths, but what can you do with it?"

"Right now, not a whole lot," I say, feeling embarrassed to admit it. "But in my heyday, I could enchant entire armies, raise the dead, bring down castles, invoke prophecies, curse my enemies . . . you name it. I'm a master of seidh, which is a kind of Nordic sorcery. Taught it to Odin, actually. He got more into the divination side of things—foresight, scrying, prophetic visions—but I was always the best at charms and enchantments."

"Except you've been weakened over centuries, so you can't use it as well," he says, looking as if he sympathizes with my plight. I think he might be starting to get the barest inkling of what I've lost.

"Don't remind me," I say miserably, digging around in my stir-fry for more meat. "The only thing I have left is the concept to which I'm closest: love."

"Lucky thing, too. I doubt we would've accomplished much otherwise."

"Don't sell yourself short," I say. "You've done a great job driving the car."

"Should add that to my résumé," he says, laughing.

I smile, glad to be reminded he has a sense of humor. It's something of a requirement for spending time around gods (we tend to be jerks). "So what was your second question?"

"Oh, right," he says. "Well, there are other gods out there who cover things like love, beauty, war, and so on. What do you do when you meet them? How do you divide things up?"

"We usually try to kill each other," I say matter-of-factly. His eyes widen, and he seems a little taken aback by that. "I'm serious—gods from separate pantheons don't really get along, but ones who share portfolios are instant rivals."

"Have you ever—"

"Infuriating pretenders," I hiss, mashing my stir-fry. Just the thought of it is bringing back all sorts of unpleasant memories. "I swear, I will wring Aphrodite's scrawny, powdered neck if I ever see—"

"Okay, question answered," Nathan says, holding up his hands. "Forget I asked."

"Sorry," I say, shaking myself. "Touchy subject."

"I can see that," Nathan says, a curious look on his face.

"What?" I ask. "What are you thinking?"

"Oh, just kind of interesting to watch the warrior side of you surface," he explains. "Same thing happened back in the restaurant, with Garen. One moment you're all sweetness and light, and the next you're flying through the air with a steak knife."

"You'll probably see shifts like that happen a lot," I say. "We're all bad at regulating our emotions, though some gods are worse than others. Besides, the bastard made me throw away a perfectly good dinner. How else was I supposed to react?"

"Well, what do you say we make up for it, then?" he asks, leaning back in his chair. "Actually finish that dinner properly."

"Nathan, are you asking me out on a date?" I ask, pretending to be coy. After our conversation a few minutes ago, I know he's not, but it's fun to try to push buttons.

"Believe it or not, two people of opposite genders *are* allowed to eat at a restaurant together and not be in a relationship," he says, lowering his voice as if it's confidential information.

"Teach me more of this modern land, oh great and worldly Web designer," I say, chuckling.

"All good things in time," he says, affecting a haughty tone. "So where do you want to go?"

"Actually, let me handle that one," I say, a place immediately popping into my head.

"Got something in mind?"

"Well, there's a steakhouse at Epcot that's supposed to be amazing. Heard some cast members talking about it."

"The universe *does* owe you a filet mignon."

"Damn right it does," I say with a fierce nod. "I should be able to get us both into the park pretty easily, but for the restaurant, you're supposed to have reservations six months in advance."

"Ouch."

"Yeah, but I have a few tricks up my sleeve. Leave it to me."

"Oh, I've got faith," Nathan says, polishing off the last of his stir-fry.

I think back to the flare of belief he gave me the instant I told him who I really was, and smile. "I know, Nathan," I say softly.

The next day, we head to Epcot late in the late afternoon, intent on doing some sightseeing while we're there. The scent of divinity is here, too, and I think it might be even stronger than it was back at the Magic Kingdom. I'm immensely curious about this god. What could he be doing here? After spending a few hours touring the park, we arrive at Le Cellier Steakhouse, just in time for our seven o'clock dinner reservation. We are almost late, and would have been if Nathan hadn't managed to drag me away from the Norway Pavilion. I'd been begging for just five more minutes, but he insisted, telling me the Canada Pavilion was still a good walk away. I swear I could spend the entire day in that little slice of Scandinavia; it's just so delightfully *kitschy*. You have all these adorable shops and bakeries, a replica stave church, and even a cute little *Frozen*-themed ride in Viking longships, all of it staffed by Norwegians in charming folk costumes. I couldn't stop grinning the entire time. Imagine if someone took your centuries-old home, added some of the most memorable aspects of its culture—aspects you had a direct hand in creating—and then made a theme park attraction out of them. I'm honestly flattered. Just thinking about it makes me want to go back. It's great.

Le Cellier, however, has filet mignon, which is an attraction of a different sort. It's been twenty-seven years since I had one of these, and I refuse to wait even one more day. The restaurant's interior feels warm and inviting. It's decorated to appear like an old wine cellar, with pale stone arches stretching between wood-paneled columns and low chandeliers hung beneath pine ceiling beams, all bathed in a dusky candlelit glow. We introduce ourselves to the hostess, who takes my name and, after a moment's wait, has a server usher us to our table. I don't even need to "persuade" her to do it; at this point, the magic's already been done.

Heady from my discovery of new believers the day before, I decided to see if I was capable of a minor spell or two. It wasn't anything fancy—just a little tweak to the restaurant's reservation list for the following evening. The effort put me down for the night, too. If I was being honest with myself, I'd admit I'm probably not ready for witchcraft just yet, but I was far too excited to listen to any voices of reason. Even gods are allowed to lie to themselves, after all. Besides, poor decision or not, it worked.

We soak in the atmosphere at our table, perusing our menus while we wait for our waiter to return. There it is, front and center. Mushroom filet mignon. Done. I return my menu to the table with a defiant slap, immensely pleased with myself.

Nathan chuckles. "Hard decision?"

"Oh, just the *worst*," I say, scrunching up my nose.

"You look beautiful, by the way," he says, setting his menu aside for a moment to look at me.

"And you look quite handsome," I reply. "If you were a god of dapper, we'd be a matched set."

He looks pleased with himself, glancing at his charcoal-gray jacket and the pale purple dress shirt underneath, its top button artfully undone. "If only. Think of the great and mysterious gifts I could grant to the well-heeled," he says.

"Never misplace your cuff links again," I say.

"Wrinkled suits will be a thing of the past."

"Shoes always shiny," I add.

He grins, then makes a face. "God, I'm the lamest deity ever. Good thing I've got you around to make me look cool."

I laugh, enjoying the comparison. In my new outfit, with this fancy atmosphere, my ego is only too happy to agree. I'm in a strapless pale pink dress cinched at the waist by a black satin sash. Judging by the way his eyes keep slipping, the combination works on me.

The waiter shows up before I have a chance to do more than beam at the compliment. He takes our requests quickly—the filet for me and the medallions of beef tenderloin for Nathan. "Now, where were we?" I ask as the man heads off to put in our order.

"I think we were busy praising each other's good looks."

"I think you're right. Does that make us shallow?"

He shrugs. "You're a god of vanity and beauty. Pretty sure it's required."

I'm about to respond when I'm unexpectedly cast in shadow. "A god of beauty?" a high, mirthful voice exclaims from above. "Well, who else would use magic to make a reservation? But you are not Aphrodite, I see."

I turn and look up to take in this strange interruption. It's a tall, young man in a crisp, tailored white suit with matching shoes that practically gleam with polish. His entire outfit is slick; besides a vivid red tie, it's all various shades of white and cream that somehow work to draw your attention up to his face. His skin is pale and glossy and his features have a sharpened, almost feminine beauty that seems at once alluring and treacherous. His long black hair is set in luxurious curls, neatly gathered in a wide ponytail that spills down his back. Rich brown eyes flash with good humor and a touch of euphoric madness.

In short, he's the boy you warn your daughters about.

"What's this? House wines? We can't have that," he says, seeming aghast at our selection of drinks. He snaps his fingers and our glasses instantly go bone-dry. Then he reaches over the table, moving his hands as if he's cradling something, and suddenly there's an ancient bottle of wine between them, a deep red liquid spilling from its mouth into the empty glasses. He pours our new drinks with practiced ease, then nods with a predatory smile. "Much better," he says, more to himself. Then he fixes me with those insane eyes, taking me in as if I'm a drink to be guzzled. "Mmm, very nice, but if not my dear Lady of Cyprus, then who are you?"

I'd like to think I'm pretty sharp, but even a complete idiot could tell you this is my god. The air practically shimmers with his divinity, and the strength of that trick he performed with our drinks sent shivers racing down my spine. I decide there's no point in playing dumb. "I have many names," I say in my best warrior-goddess voice. "But you may know me as Freya."

"My lady," he says, snatching my hand off the table and bending fluidly at the waist to plant a kiss on my skin. His lips tingle with the promise of endless—and mindless—pleasure. I decide in that moment that this is an incredibly dangerous man. "And you, dear sir?" he asks, turning his head away from my hand to look at Nathan. The way he's bent over my fingers as he says it, along with the feral grin that pulls back his girlish lips, makes it seem like he's a savanna predator hunched over a kill.

"Nathan Kence," my companion says flatly, not offering a hand.

"A pleasure," the man says, drawing back and straightening. "But where are my manners? I have not yet introduced myself." He puts a hand on his chest and strikes what is possibly the most self-involved pose I've ever seen. "I am the Liberator, the undying source of epiphany and *ecstasy*"—he gives me a meaningful look as he draws out the word—"of wine and merriment, laughter and madness. I am and will always be your most devoted servant, Lady Freya, for I am Dionysus, and what is happiness without love? Bliss without beauty?"

He pulls a chair over to our table and sits down in one smooth, catlike motion. "Long has it been since a fellow immortal graced me with their presence, and longer still since one of such exquisite loveliness *entered* my domain," he says, raising a hand to summon a waiter. I don't like the way he emphasized the word *entered*—it's perverted, and leaves nothing to the imagination. There's no subtlety to this man.

Nathan rolls his eyes. I'm glad we're on the same page.

Our waiter arrives quickly, chest heaving as if he's dashed across the restaurant to make it to our table. "What can I get for you, Mr. Nyce?" he asks breathlessly.

Dionysus fixes the man with a snakelike stare, and those chiseled lips part to hiss a single word: *"Everything."*

The waiter backs away at once, leaving for the kitchens. Dionysus turns to me, ignoring Nathan completely. I give my friend a look that pleads for patience. I hope he realizes I'd like nothing more than to snub this shameful man and return to our lighthearted conversation. I can't do anything overt, though; I must tread very carefully here, because this is not only a powerful god, but a perilous one.

"So how shall I address you, then?" I ask, trying to maintain my sense of dignity and power. "These mortals obviously do not know you as Dionysus, and there are appearances to maintain."

"Feh," he says, giving a lazy wave with one manicured hand. "Right now, the only appearance I care to discuss is yours . . . but I would never dream of denying the request of one so attractive. Save 'Dionysus,' then, for more *private* surroundings. Here, I am known as David Nyce."

"Of course you are," I say, wishing I could roll my eyes at him, too. At least the fact that he's ignoring Nathan has given my companion free rein to poke fun. "Sara Vanadi. And you've already met Nathan, my high priest and most trusted companion."

"Sara. Such a sweet name," he says, not even looking at Nathan.

Okay, I officially hate everything about this: Dionysus, the situation he's put us in, the "conversation" he's leading . . . It's all incredibly uncomfortable and hazardous. He's taking everything I say as an excuse to flirt, and the pitiless chaos that squirms beneath his perfect suit is giving me some really dark suspicions about how he treats rejection. I need answers, and I need him to think of me as more than a love puppet.

"Indeed, Mr. Nyce," I say. "I am honored by your presence and grateful for your company. We have much to discuss, however, for I have been without the companionship of a god for far too long." I tap Nathan's foot as I say all this, hoping he gets the message that I'm doing my best to wrangle this bundle of off-kilter divinity and lust beside us, and to just stay calm.

"Ooh, too true," Dionysus says. "What a sad, empty world it is without the presence of fellow gods. Everything's better when it's *filled* with the divine."

I suppress a shudder. "On that note, Mr. Nyce—how did you get here? And how have you become so strong in this doubtful world?"

He laughs a high, crazed titter. "You wish to know my secrets? Well, why not? But I assure you, I have far juicier ones I can share. Perhaps in a more . . . intimate setting?"

"Perhaps," I say. *Ew, ew, ew!*

"I can only hope—ah, wonderful!" he says with manic glee as our waiter sets down a few appetizer dishes on the table. He reaches for a platter of cheeses and fruits, grabs a handful, and stuffs them into his mouth. "*Mmmf,*" he says, rolling his eyes in delight. Nathan and I take the opportunity to exchange a look. The silent message that passes between us is clear: *What. The. Hell.*

After Dionysus finishes chewing, he turns back to me and clasps his chin in one hand. "Now, where was I? Oh, yes—secrets. Well, I discovered these delightful parks by chance one day. Imagine my shock when I noticed the magic in the air, the *fun* to be had. These places cannot, of course, hold the most meager candle to the festivities of my forgotten cults, but those are sadly long gone from this world. Even still, the merriment, the laughter, the excitement—it's always here, every day of every year, bubbling up from millions of dear little mortals. I had to take part. So I invested all my energy, wealth, and time, climbed their ridiculous corporate ladder, and insinuated myself into their system." He pauses to demolish a plate of ravioli. I notice that no matter how ferociously he eats, he never seems to stain his lips, drip something onto his clothes, or put even one hair out of place.

"Spectacular," he says, smacking his lips. He drains his glass of wine—a glass I didn't even realize was on the table until he reached out and took it—and continues his story. "You see, I recognized long ago that I didn't need worshippers. Filthy things, really. No, what I needed was *strength*. They're not one and the same, you know. More worshippers will keep you whole, keep you in whatever form they decide is most pleasing to them, but more *belief* . . . aaah . . . that will give you power, raw and pure."

"But worshippers believe. That's what they give you."

"*Anyone* can believe," he snaps, his eyes glinting. "Worshippers, they're like . . . like *shareholders*." He says the word with utter disdain. "Sooth, they'll give you money, but they want to control you, to shape your beauty to match *their* vision. No! I won't have it. I am *perfect* as I am—and how could they presume to improve on perfection?"

I have a few ideas on where to start, I think, wanting so badly to say it. But I manage to hold my tongue. He's on a roll now, anyway. I think he likes the sound of his voice.

"Ages past, I realized I could draw strength from any sort of gaiety or celebration, and all I had to do was have a hand in it. Whatever mystic force empowers us, it sees such events as offerings in my name and grants me a small measure of strength for it. So *what* if those revelers aren't cavorting with the word 'Dionysus' on their tongues? Why would I want their worthless praise? Or their pathetic ideas of what I should be to them?"

I think I get it. Merrymaking has the same effect on him as the belief of the kids when I'm in costume. "So you made sure you'd have a hand in running the parks, and when people have fun in them, you get a little bit stronger for it?"

"Intelligent *and* beautiful," he says, sighing. "How could anyone ask for more? Yes, that's it exactly. It's the barest fraction of a drop every time, of course. Each of these 'tourists,' they offer a mere pittance of strength, a grain of sand, if you will, but when they come in their millions—ah, how it does add up—power enough to fill the oceans."

"And you say you haven't seen another god in years?"

He shrugs and tosses a few pieces of steak tartare into his mouth. "Can't say I've gone looking for them, really," he says, chewing. "Then again, if I knew *you* were out there, my dear, I'd never have stopped searching."

Ugh. Sure, once he actually *starts* talking about a subject, he never shuts up, but getting him to focus on one is like herding cats. Hungry, perverted cats. Still, maybe I can use his seemingly unstoppable needs to my advantage.

"I'm so glad to hear it," I say, looking at him with wide, appreciative eyes, "because I'm in trouble, and I think you're the only one who can help."

"I am yours to command, my lady," Dionysus says. He downs another glass of wine, then flashes a gleaming smile at me.

My lady? Where does he think he is? Actually, I don't care at this point. He can say whatever he wants, as long as he's on my side. "Good," I say, thinking about how to phrase this next part. "You see, I'm being chased."

Nathan gives me an amused look. I think he's both impressed by how I've decided to handle our recent problems and pleased by how quickly Dionysus is falling for it.

"Unwanted suitors? I can understand why men would dog your every step."

Stop it with the flirting! I want to scream. Instead, I suppress it and just say, "Not quite."

"Then you are being hunted? There are true villains who wish to harm you?"

"Yes, that's it exactly."

Dionysus frowns, and I can see the madness flicker in his eyes. "I won't have it. Tell me who your pursuer is, and I will see to it that their screams echo in your ears for as long as you desire."

Gotcha. "There's an organization obsessed with gods," I say softly. "And one of its members is tracking me. I've had to start a new life here to escape him. Kill him for me, and I will . . . *reward* you."

"Give me a name," Dionysus croons. "And very, *very* shortly, all that will be left to do is enjoy your *abundant* rewards."

I pause, then spit it out like a curse. "Garen."

His frown deepens and, for a moment, I fear I've said something wrong. Then he lets out another high-pitched laugh, and I realize he's just committed the name to memory, like pinning an insect to a specimen case.

"It will be done," he says softly.

6

ALL'S FAIR

"What the hell just happened?" Nathan asks as we exit Disney property. We were both silent on our way out of the park—worried, I think, that Dionysus might hear us somehow.

I sigh and fiddle with the car's air-conditioning controls. "We met our god."

"And wasn't *that* a barrel of laughs. Are they all that psychotic?"

"No, he's a special case. I mean, did you see how he talked about his worshippers? That's insane. It's not how things are supposed to work, Nate."

Nathan frowns, his eyes on the road. "So what are you really planning on doing? I can tell you don't want to touch him with a ten-foot pole, and if he manages to do what you asked, well . . . I don't get the impression he's the type who handles rejection very well."

I shake my head. "Not in the slightest. He's a mad dog, Nathan. Setting him on Garen was a way to distract him for now, but I'm going to have to put him down, and soon."

"You gods play rough," he says, grimacing.

"No, that's not what's happening here. This isn't your typical deific spat. Dionysus has gone off the deep end, and he needs to be destroyed before things get any worse. Look at him—he's not playing by the rules anymore. He's gone centuries without real worshippers, and now all his boundaries are gone."

"Well, yeah, he's nuts and I wouldn't miss him, but . . . you also said he's really powerful. I don't want you getting hurt, Sara. Can't we just go somewhere else? Ditch him like we did Garen? I mean, sure, he's crazy, but are you sure that's not how he's always been?"

He's starting to babble a bit, and I can see he's really concerned. It's heartwarming. I've missed having friends who truly cared about me like this, and if I weren't in the middle of plotting deicide, I'd give him a hug for reminding me what I've gained. As it is, though . . . "I can't leave this to fester any longer," I say, trying to let him see how worried I am. "You don't understand what Dionysus *is* now. He's a god without constraints. He's struck out on his own, without the need to please anybody. At some point, he's going to completely snap and do something *really* bad."

"Wait, like what? What are you talking about?"

"Think of it like this: We're the products of humanity, right? We live to serve, because answering your prayers gives us strength. As we grow, your beliefs shape our personalities and appearances. Well, Dionysus doesn't serve you—not anymore. He's figured out a way to get strength without answering any prayers. He runs an amusement park, not a religion. One of these days, he's going to decide he doesn't need to hide what he is, and the second he does, he's going to try to rule you."

Nathan thinks it over, clearly weighing his desire for short-term security against the future danger of a rampaging god. "You're sure about this?" he asks at last. "Do you really have to destroy him?"

"I'm a god of war as well as love, Nathan. I've seen empires rise and relationships prosper. Without fail, whether you're talking kings and queens or husbands and wives . . . *every* time someone stops needing an ally or stops seeing the value of someone who was once their friend, it's only a matter of time before they try to take advantage of them."

"So he's a cancer," Nathan says. "That's what you see when you look at him? A god gone rogue, about to kill its host if he's not killed first."

"Nail on the head, Nathan. That's why we can't leave."

"This is officially the weirdest night out ever."

"And I *still* haven't gotten my filet," I say, folding my arms—a goddess denied. Nathan and I excused ourselves long before our dinners arrived, leaving Dionysus to devour his meal and plot murder. I thanked him for his assistance and bravery, and then we high-tailed it out of there.

"Well, where do you want to go? It's getting late and I'm starving."

"Me too. Maybe that Mexican place downtown again? It's open really late."

"Their nachos *were* amazing," Nathan says, his face taking on a wistful cast at the memory.

"I think it seems right. It can be our go-to spot whenever our dinner gets ruined by uninvited guests."

"Man, I hope this doesn't become a thing."

"It just might," I say, pulling a playful grimace. "Who knows how many other weirdoes are out there?"

"Ugh, please no. Whatever happened to having a normal life?"

"I think you signed it away the second you struck out with me, mortal."

"Hah. Should've read the fine print, eh?" he says, chuckling.

He's clearly joking, but I can't help feeling a little worried that maybe, deep down, he really does feel sorry for joining me. I know I haven't quite brought him the fun and adventure I'd intended. It's that thorn of doubt that pushes me to ask the question that's been dogging me for the past few days. "Are you starting to regret following a god, Nathan?" I force it out lightheartedly, but underneath the mirth, I'm petrified by what his answer might be. I'd really miss him.

Nathan takes a moment, seeming to seriously consider the question. Then he looks at me out of the corner of his eye and breaks into a friendly, incredulous grin. "Sara, I've made my share of bad decisions, but I can honestly say you're not one of them."

I think I smile for the rest of the night.

Compared with the revelations and encounters of the previous week, the following one is downright dull. Every day I hit the park in my character outfit, reveling in the little morsels of belief offered up by the guests. When I have free time, I spend it on the Internet, researching gods of every type imaginable. Once Nathan realizes I've spent more time at Inward than he's been alive, he starts to understand just how much of the modern world I've missed. When he finds out the only movies I've seen since I committed myself in the early nineties have all been rated PG-13 or younger, he balks and institutes a movie night, trying to catch me up on almost three decades of R-rated entertainment. My favorite film is still *The Princess Bride*, but after a few evenings of cinematic carnage, more adult fare manages to work its way up the list.

The park's open late on weekends, and I work a few evening shifts to pick up some extra belief. Honestly, I'd do this job for free as long as I was assured I would get more power out of it. I feel stronger than I have in centuries, and it's all from just a week. Imagine what I'll be like in a month. Hell, what about a *year*? Blessings upon the genius who built these parks. If I ever find your spirit in my wanderings, I will ensure you are brought to a place of honor in my vast and beautiful hall of Sessrúmnir.

I change out of my costume, carefully placing it back on the rack to be cleaned. I catch a glimpse of a clock on the wall of the locker room and grimace—it's getting late. Nathan should be by to pick me up soon, if he's not already waiting. My daydreaming probably had something to do with the minutes' slipping by so quickly. It's been ages since I thought of my homeland. It must be the power returning to me, sparking all kinds of forgotten feelings and memories as it does. I dress in a daze, focused on the events of centuries past. Lost in thought, trying to think of the last time I had the power to visit my house or the glorious fields that were my domain, I barely notice his approach until he's right behind me.

"Now, now," his voice says beside my right ear, a seductive whisper. "You shouldn't have gone to all the trouble of getting dressed."

I whip around with a gasp. Dionysus is there, leering at me, and I realize the dressing room is suddenly empty—the handful of princesses and other cast members who were here moments before are now missing.

He moves closer, eyes racing up and down. "An obstacle easily removed, thankfully." He reaches out, pushing aside my top and twining a finger around my bra strap with a practiced motion before I can reply.

"Stop that!" I say, swatting his hand and backing away.

He pauses, insane eyes twitching with confusion. "Words I'm not very used to hearing, I must confess," he says. "Usually, women implore me to do just the opposite."

"What have you found of Garen?" I ask, glaring at him.

He narrows his eyes at me. "All business? That's behavior hardly becoming of a goddess of love, isn't it? I offer you pleasures unparalleled among the mortals, and you can't even hide your revulsion."

Uh-oh. "We had a deal, Dionysus," I say, trying to keep him from going any further down this path. "One dead mortal for anything you desire."

"Ah, yes, our deal," he says, drawing closer. Longing and madness crackle around him like a storm. "Well, it just so happens I found your mortal."

What? So quickly? No, no, that's impossible! I thought I'd have more time to get stronger. If he's telling the truth and Garen is dead, that means I need to act now. But how on earth do I deal with a superpowered madman? I'm still too damn weak. This could turn very ugly, very fast.

"He told me so many interesting things, too," Dionysus says, beginning to pace before me.

Tell me you didn't give him a chance to talk, I scream in my head.

"Wasn't very hard to locate, either, loaded down as he was with mystic trinkets and the stench of the divine. I had to admit, I was curious about his obsession with you. And his answer, well, it was so very shocking I had to see if it was true."

"What did he tell you, Dionysus?"

"Ah, ah, ah, that's Mr. Nyce to you, *impostor*," he says, glaring at me.

I take a step back. Okay, this is going from bad to worse to some kind of ultrasuck faster than I thought possible. "I don't understand," I say, trying to seem fragile and nonthreatening.

"He said he found you in an asylum," he grates, crossing his arms. "That you had stolen the spark of the divine from Freya, killed her in the quest for immortality, and were planning to do the same to me."

"*What?*"

"I challenged him for proof, and he said all I had to do was ask for your affection. A true god of love, he said, would never deny a kindred spirit. If you were *truly* the embodiment of adoration and fertility, you would welcome my delicate attentions with open arms." He pauses, and the heat of his rage intensifies. "And you *did not*."

"Dionysus, he would have said *anything*—"

"It's *Mr. Nyce!*" he screams at me, eyes ablaze. He looks away for a moment, then turns back, seemingly at peace. The change is so abrupt it's terrifying. "Perhaps. Mortals can be slippery. So I told him I would speak with you, and if he was lying, he *and* his allies would know the true extent of my rage."

"Ask me anything," I say desperately. "Or better yet, take me to him. We'll see what he has to say for himself."

"No, I think not," Dionysus says in a high-pitched melodic voice. "I think you will give me what I want, and then I will make my decision. *Convince* me, 'god of love,' that you are capable of satisfying the desires of the divine, and I will believe you."

Well, isn't this a messed-up scenario. I either sleep with this scumbag, or he kills me. Or turns me over to Garen. Or some other equally unwelcome thing. Whatever. It's lose-lose, regardless. There's never a question what my answer will be, though. You do not make demands of my pantheon. We are elemental—the freezing winds, the tongues of flame, the endless sea—and we will not be chained, not by words and not by deeds. He seeks to make a servant of *me*, to flaunt my very nature in the name of his twisted lust?

I spit at his feet. *"Argr hóra,"* I curse at him, lips curled with loathing.

He looks down at the gobbet of my saliva, glistening between his feet, and then back at me with a baffled expression. He doesn't seem entirely clear on how strongly I'm rejecting his advances, so I follow up with a stinging slap across his left cheek, putting all my not-inconsiderable strength into it. His head whips to the side and he sways back a step. *That* should get the message across.

And it does. He turns to me and a bestial scream rips out of his throat. "How *dare* you?" he shrieks, features contorted with rage, before he shoves me through the wall.

It's like being kissed by an avalanche. His arms smash into my chest with brutal force and send me sailing backward, crashing through the masonry behind me to fall, limbs askew, in the utility corridor beyond. My hair is caked in plaster and flecks of paint, and the air is filled with the sound of clattering debris. I cough and lever myself up on one arm to watch as he pushes his way through the hole I've made.

"I asked nicely," he says, a deranged tone in his voice. "And you throw it back in my face?"

Groaning, I push myself to my feet. "You do not presume *anything* of me. You are a miserable—"

He screams and launches a fist at me. He's not a fighter, though, telegraphing the move ages in advance. I watch, adrenaline slowing the world around me to a crawl, as the muscles in his right shoulder contract, pulling his arm up and around to deliver a punishing haymaker to the side of my head. I'm more than fast enough to dodge it, ducking to one side and feeling the whoosh of air as it shoots past my left ear.

And then I'm running flat out, bolting down the corridor in a panic. I need to get away from this man, put some distance between us before he slaughters me. I'm not prideful enough to think I can take him in a fight, not on a single week of belief. He's had years to overcharge himself in these parks. The hallways zip past me as I run with all the speed a daughter of the wind can manage. I rocket under banks of fluorescent lights and snaking ductwork, watching the walls carefully. Where *is* everyone? I know it's after hours, but these hallways are usually packed. The lack of people is so stark and unprecedented it's chilling. I don't have time to reflect on it, though. I'm somewhere under Fantasyland, and if I can just get my bearings,

I can get out the back and into the outdoor loading zone. These tunnels aren't too hard to navigate normally, but when you have a crazed god on your tail, everything becomes a little more difficult.

I don't dare look back for fear of slowing down, but I can only hope he's not as fast as I am. I'm so focused on speed that when I skid around the corner and have to come to a complete stop, I almost pitch forward into a maintenance cart. I blink and cock my head to one side, not understanding what I'm seeing. There's a wave of crimson liquid rushing toward me from down the hall, crests of white foam dancing on its surface. It's so unexpected, so out of place, I'm unable to react before it crashes into me, sending me barreling back down the corridor I came from.

At first I think it's blood, but then, as it tumbles me around and gets in my mouth, I realize it's wine. Dark, luscious red wine. He's hit me with a tidal wave of merlot. I'm jostled and bounced in the flow for several seconds, caroming off pipes and who-knows-what-else in my unexpected surfing trip through the underground corridors of Disney. The wall of liquid eventually peters out, depositing me unceremoniously in the middle of the hall, drenched in the stuff. I sputter and hack, streams of liquid pouring off my hair to pool around me in a new red lake that ripples on the corridor's floor.

I pity tonight's cleaning crew, if they even still exist. Maybe Dionysus did something to make everyone just . . . vanish? Is that powerful? I try to get my bearings, wiping at my eyes and jostling my bag as I do; somehow, it's still on my shoulder. Coughing through wine-infused ropes of hair, I watch with growing horror as a pair of gleaming white shoes marches toward me through the puddles, not a speck of red staining them.

A hand grasps me roughly by the arm and tugs, hauling me upright. "What a mess you've made of yourself," Dionysus says with a sneer. He lets go of my arm with a little shove, sending me staggering back. I barely maintain my footing. "Now I will simply take what I want, and when I am done with you, this 'Garen' can have whatever scraps remain."

Well, that's wonderful. He's gone for a combination order of evil. I'll be damned if he's going to manage any part of it without a fight, though. I fumble in the bag at my side, turning away so he can't see what I'm doing and trying to make it seem like I'm cowering.

He reaches out and grabs me by the hair, attempting to pull me close. In that instant, I whip out the syringe I stole from Garen at the steakhouse, aiming to plunge it into his neck. His eyes widen as the metal barb punctures his skin, but he snaps his head back and twists, knocking it out of my hand before I have a chance to inject him with its contents.

The syringe clatters to the floor, and Dionysus kicks my legs out from under me, sending me toppling to the ground beside it. Before I can even reach it, he's on top of me, pinning my arms to the wine-soaked concrete. He smirks at me, and his eyes dance with delirium and delight. Since I can't wipe that smile off his face with my fist, I do the next best thing and spit in one of those wild eyes of his. He grimaces, then backhands me. Stars explode in my vision. He's unstoppably strong—not the best tactician or fighter, but he doesn't really need to be. With one arm free, I try to grab for the syringe again, but my head feels cloudy and I can't seem to control my movements very well.

Then there's a little scrape and a flurry of movement. I realize someone else is beside us in the same moment Dionysus does, but it's too late for either of us to react. I squint my eyes and try to focus on the blur of motion, and with a thrill of happiness, I realize it's Nathan in the split second before he stabs Dionysus between the shoulder blades with the syringe. The enraged god spins to focus on my devoted follower, batting his hand away. He pushes at Nathan unsteadily, more in confusion than anything else, but it's still enough to launch my friend off his feet.

Before Nathan can crash into the wall behind him, vines rip out of the floor and ceiling and snatch him in midair. The plants grow like lightning, sprouting broad green leaves and bunches of swollen red grapes as they ensnare him. It's almost too fast to be believed. In a matter of moments, he's caught spread-eagled in the middle of the hall, grapevines locking his arms and legs in place.

Dionysus gets to his feet and starts walking toward Nathan. "Her little high priest, I see. Come to save the day?" he mocks. "All you've done is force me to ponder which of you I should hurt first so the other can *watch*."

I launch myself off the floor, almost slipping in the wine, and punch him in the back, right on the plunger of the syringe, which is still sticking out from between his shoulder blades. "*Watch this*," I hiss in his ear as the liquid enters his body.

He doesn't even have a chance to turn around. He takes a staggered half step to the side before collapsing on the wine-pooled floor. The vines around Nathan immediately go slack, dropping him beside the unconscious god. I grin with satisfaction as Dionysus's immaculate clothes become stained at last, the red seeping into them and—I hope—ruining the fabric.

"Someone's been watching too many action movies," I say, helping Nathan to his feet.

"Oh, hey, you know, just picking the roommate up from work," he mumbles, sounding a little dazed. He reaches out and touches my arm. "Are you okay?"

"Chauffeur *and* knight in shining armor. I hauled the right psych tech out of the crazy house," I say, reaching up to pull a few stray leaves from his hair.

He grins at that, then nudges Dionysus with his foot. "Well, he's not so tough. I mean, *grapevines*? Talk about amateur hour."

I laugh, silently thanking whatever twists of fate brought us together. "Nathan, you are the most wonderful Web designer I've ever met," I say, hugging him.

"Hah. And you've met how many?"

"Shh. Best not to dwell on that," I murmur, soaking up the hug. To be honest, I feel a little shaken—it's been a very long time since I fought one of my kin, and I've never felt so outclassed. I have to get stronger.

Though I badly want to rest, I have no idea how long Garen's poison will last, especially on a god as powerful as Dionysus. "Come on," I say, breaking our hug. "Let's figure out what to do with him."

Nathan sighs as he moves beside me. "Well, isn't there supposed to be a cryogenic vault somewhere nearby we can use to freeze him?"

I elbow him lightly in the ribs and bend down to pick up one of Dionysus's arms. Carefully, I pull him onto my shoulders in a fireman's carry, then return to my feet with a groan. I might be stronger than I've been in centuries, but he's very heavy. Nathan seems impressed, though.

"Remind me never to piss you off," he says, taking a little step back.

"I promise the beatings will be gentle," I grunt from under Dionysus's weight.

We move toward the loading dock exit I was trying to make a break for earlier. "Where *is* everyone?" Nathan asks as we pad through deserted hallways, leaving ripples of wine in our wake.

"He must've done something to clear them out. He's supposed to be the life of any party, so maybe he can be the death of them, too. How'd you get here, anyway?"

"I got tired of waiting for you in the parking lot. Then I noticed the employee buses had stopped running, so I decided to leave the car and jog over to the tunnel entrance."

"You're not supposed to do that, you know." Disney's pretty strict about that sort of thing.

He shrugs. "Yeah, but it felt like the thing to do. Something was just . . . *off*. I didn't like the feeling, and then, when I saw what looked like blood pouring out of the back doors, I went inside for you."

I nod. Since he's my closest worshipper now, it looks like we're starting to link up a bit. It's not surprising. He probably got a twinge of emotional feedback from me as I was freaking out earlier. It's likely what protected him from whatever compulsion Dionysus used to clean the place out, too, and thank goodness for that. I wasn't entirely sure how I was going to get out of that one.

"Do you need any help carrying him?" Nathan asks.

"Nah, I'm fine," I say. He's very heavy, but I feel like Nathan's already done enough for me tonight.

"Okay. What do we do with him, anyway?" he asks as we near the exit to the loading dock.

"Eh. We'll figure something out. Maybe bury him in concrete. See how he likes one of those fate-worse-than-death endings."

We step into the warm night air, and for a moment, there's silence. Then floodlights kick on, blasting the entire place with piercing white beams. An all-too-familiar voice rings out from a megaphone. "How thoughtful. Saved us the trouble, I see," Garen says from somewhere beyond the brilliant lights. I can practically hear the sneer as he speaks.

There's no time to react. Darts whistle out of the blinding glare, embedding themselves in our bodies and injecting their poison instantly. I try to run, to get away or at least save Nathan, but there's no time.

The world spins, and the dazzling floodlights give way to blackness.

7

A DIFFERENT SPEED

I'm dimly aware of a little cut being made on my finger.

The world around me is flexing, its proportions zooming up and down. It feels like someone's locked me in a Tilt-A-Whirl for a week. Patches of blackness swim in and out of my vision, and I can barely keep my eyes open. I'm lying flat on my back, strapped to some kind of gurney. Actually, "strapped" isn't the right word. "Manacled" or "welded" would be more fitting. Thick bands of shiny metal restrain me, encircling my ankles, wrists, chest, and waist. Fluorescent lights shine from above, illuminating an immaculate room covered in little gray tiles. There's an IV bag filled with that same milky white fluid hanging just above my left shoulder, a tube snaking down from it to a cannula embedded in my arm.

"Thirty-seven seconds," a girl's voice says the moment the cut on my finger finishes closing up. It sounds intelligent and somewhat awkward, as if its owner should be pushing a taped pair of frames up their nose as they speak.

"What? She should be at least a minute plus," I hear Garen say, sounding baffled.

"That's how long it took, sir."

"Where's she hiding her believers, then? All our estimates put her at quasideity status."

"I just run the tests, sir," the voice says in a long-suffering tone.

"*Hmph*. Well, maybe she'll be ready to talk once she's awake." I'm aware of him moving beside me, adjusting the flow from the IV. "I'm getting something to eat," he announces when he's done. "Contact me if she wakes before I get back."

And then he's gone. A moment later, another face swims into focus. It's a teenager, I realize with a stab of surprise. This girl can't be older than—well, older than I look, actually. What's she doing here? She has a somewhat horsey appearance, exaggerated by an unfortunate habit of leaving her mouth a little open. Her thin, lengthy face is coated in a heavy spray of freckles, and her hair is brown and flat, tucked behind her ears and pulled into a ponytail. A pair of thick black glasses perch on her nose, and she's wearing a white lab coat stamped with a symbol that looks sort of like a sun with a crack running down its middle. An ID badge clipped to the coat's left breast tells me the girl's name is Samantha Drass.

"Poor thing," she mumbles as she checks her clipboard, a faint nasal twang in her voice.

"Seen worse," I whisper.

She jumps back, pale green eyes widening. One hand shoots to the matte black transceiver at her hip, but she hesitates, drawing closer and peering at me. "How in the world are you awake already?" she asks, seeming immensely curious.

"I don't know. Light sleeper?" I squeak. It's really hard to concentrate, even though the haze is starting to part.

She makes a note on her clipboard. "I think we need to up your ratio. Or get a fresher halāhala batch in here. For a deity of your grade, you should've been out for another hour at least."

"Sorry to disappoint," I say, blinking and trying to clear the mists out of my head. Whatever they've been pumping into me is noxious beyond belief.

"It's okay, just bad intel on our p—" She stops, frowning, and checks her clipboard again. "Wait, you're acting odd."

"I am?"

"Well, Garen and his goon squad hunted you down and drugged you. Most gods in your position wake up all angry, cursing at me, promising all kinds of vengeance." She pauses, then lowers her voice. "They're very mean."

I have to admit, part of me really does want to put a fist through this girl's abdomen and tear her spine out through her stomach. That bit about refusing to be restrained? Yeah, it's still true, and the Nordic warrior maiden within me rages at the notion that anyone would have the gall to try. Whatever. Those thoughts aren't helpful, and maybe it's all those years of neglect, or maybe it's all the happiness and love I've been feeding off lately at the parks, but right now I'm not finding it very hard to ignore that arrogant, infuriated voice within me. Besides, something tells me this girl isn't here because she likes torturing gods. She doesn't have that same aura of maliciousness that clings to Garen. She seems . . . innocent.

110

Let's see if she's guilt-ridden, too. "I'd never hurt anyone," I lie, trying to get my eyes to water. "I just wanted to be left alone. I'm a god of *love*. Then . . . then these people *attacked* me!" Lip quiver, go!

She frowns and looks back at her clipboard, seeming very confused. There's probably a threat assessment field on there about me filled with large, scary letters that say *EXTREMELY DANGEROUS* or *WILL WEAR YOUR INTESTINES AS A SCARF* or something similar. "That's not supposed to happen," she says, baffled. "They're supposed to offer to recruit you first."

"Well, they did, but I s-said I didn't want to go." Sadder! Eyes full of tears!

That seems to make her even more confused. "Oh. But didn't they tell you about the believers? We give you believers if you work for us, you know."

I nod miserably. "I don't want them, not after all these years." Now, *that's* a lie for you. "It's not our world anymore, Samantha." She looks surprised for a moment at hearing her name, then glances down at her name tag and makes a little noise of comprehension. "I wanted peace and quiet," I continue. "That's all. But they wouldn't take no for an answer"—I gasp, choking back tears—"so here I am."

"That's *terrible*," Samantha says, seeming distraught. "I don't know if we've *ever* had a god refuse our offer before." She pats me on the shoulder. "This is just a big misunderstanding—I'm sure of it. I'll talk to my father and make sure everything gets straightened out."

"Oh, thank you," I say, grateful as can be. Inwardly, I'm thrilled. This girl obviously has no idea what Garen's been up to. The part about her father is even better. Maybe he's high-ranking enough to make this a huge mess for everyone involved. Ha! Loki's not the only god who can manage a bit of deception now and then, is he? Take a bow, Sara.

"Is my friend okay?" I ask, deciding such concern can only help my cause at this point.

"I'm not sure," she says. "I remember hearing you came in with two others, but I don't know where they went."

"His name's Nathan," I say, trying to sound fragile. This is actually pretty hard to keep up. "He's very important to me. I just want to make sure he's all right."

"Of course. I'll go check. You wait right here," she says. Then she pauses to take on an embarrassed look as she realizes I don't have much of a choice. "I'll be right back," she finishes quickly, darting out of the room.

I sigh and try to get comfortable. It's difficult to move. If I could shift a bit more, get a little momentum to rock the gurney to the floor, that might be something. As it is, I'm almost completely immobilized, and things are *still* a bit woozy from that junk in the IV drip. What did she call it? Halāhala? I wish I had my Mim right now so I could look that up online. My eyes dart around, searching for my bag, but it's probably been deposited wherever they've taken my clothes. I'm no longer in my T-shirt and jeans, swathed instead in a backless white hospital gown. At first I think it's covered in little blue polka dots, but on closer inspection, I realize they're actually tiny flowers. How nice.

It would be great if I could do something while she's gone, maybe pocket a scalpel or loosen my bonds in some way, but I'm at a loss. The nasty combination of deity-level restraints and this damnable poison has left me helpless. I can't recall the last time I've felt this way, and hope I never have to again. Ten minutes later, Samantha returns, clipboard clutched tightly in the crook of her left arm.

"Good news!" she says. "Your friend Nathan is fine—he's in a holding cell a floor down. He'll be out for another day or two from the halāhala, but there won't be any permanent damage."

Phew. That makes me feel better. But another *day* or two? What *is* this stuff? I'm awfully curious about something that can put down a deity. "Halāhala?" I ask.

"Oh, it's a *very* nasty poison," she says, grimacing. "We have a pseudo-Shiva in our primary facility who manufactures it for us. Really strong. We have to dilute it heavily."

How unhelpful. I could've told you it was some kind of toxin, and now she's left me with even more questions. "Primary facility?" I ask, deciding location is the most important thing to find out right now. "Where are we?"

She's about to answer when a nasty voice cuts her off. "None of your business," it snaps from just beyond my view. Samantha squeaks and spins around. "Was I not clear on being contacted the second she regained consciousness, Ms. Drass?" the voice says through clenched teeth. Garen. *Great.* Thought I'd have more time before he came back.

"I did—I mean, she just woke up, sir!"

"Get out of here," he says harshly. She gives a glum nod and leaves, shoes tapping on the tiles as she scampers out of the room. Garen saunters into my view, head turned to watch Samantha go. As soon as the door shuts, he looks back at me.

"Didn't just wake up, did you?" he asks, smiling. He might be a despicable person in general, but I think it's that oily smirk of his

113

I hate the most. I entertain thoughts of peeling it off with a morning star as I reply.

"It's just so comfortable here I can barely keep my eyes open," I say sweetly.

"Right. Look, I'm going to cut to the chase. We want you to work for us. We want you to help our company with your divine powers and join extraction teams to help capture other gods. Oh, and we have all kinds of awful things we can do to you if you don't. What's it going to be?"

Really? He already knows what my answer will be at this point, so why is he even bothering to ask again? Then it hits me—this isn't his decision. Someone else wants me on board. It's not Samantha's doing, either, even though she mentioned speaking to her father; this has been in the works for a while, probably before I even arrived. I laugh. "You spend weeks hunting down this insignificant goddess, almost getting your head caved in *twice* for your trouble, and after all that, you're forced to ask for her help. Again. It's almost like they don't care that I tried to kill you, isn't it? *That* must sting a little."

For a moment, a look of supreme frustration dances across his face. It's gone in a flash, that familiar smirk returning so quickly you'd miss the change if you blinked—but I don't miss much. "The way you dealt with Dionysus, coupled with your unexpected strength, has caused my higher-ups to reevaluate your usefulness." He leans closer. "But we both know it's pointless, don't we?"

"Oh, I don't know about that," I purr. "What are the benefits like? Do I get dental?"

His grin shifts slightly, becoming more rueful than anything else. "You're bound and determined to be a thorn in my side, aren't you?" he asks.

"I'm certainly bound," I say, wiggling my fingers from underneath my wrist restraints.

"Okay, it's time for you to take this a little more seriously," he says, rubbing his forehead. "Allow me to be a little more upfront about what we can do here."

"Please do. I love a good story."

He glares, then begins to pace around my gurney, taking a leisurely circuit in and out of my field of vision. "We make and break deities, 'Sara,' and we have it down to a science. We know what makes you tick, how belief can build, shape, and obliterate you." He pauses, and his smile grows. "Did you know you're not *really* a god? Not like you think you are, anyway. You're a living figment, a bit of walking, talking, neural chaff. Some of the lab boys have started calling you cognivores." He makes a face. "I prefer 'parasites.' Feeding off us for centuries, living in your own little fantasy lands, sending out missionaries to get you more to eat. But it's never enough, is it?"

"Is this going somewhere?" I ask, bored already. He's taking the facts and twisting them, viewing me through a hateful lens of his own making. Of course we owe our existence to humanity. We yearn for your beliefs, but we also *work* for you. I want to bless my worshippers with romance, beautiful children, and victory in all things. We aren't your masters; we're your allies.

Garen shakes his head. He knows it's pointless, attempting to convince me, but he has to try. "We know how you're *made*," he says, running a finger down my arm. I squirm in revulsion, trying to jerk away from his touch. "We can help you—that's really not a lie. It's all about belief, after all, and we've gotten very, very good at brainwashing. We have our own in-house buffet of dreamers, all hooked up and ready to think you into Valhalla. Want to be able to breathe fire? Fly on golden wings? Give us a few weeks."

"What?" I gasp, suddenly very serious. He can't mean this. It can't be what it sounds like.

"You're a smart girl. I'm sure you get it. It's basically the same thing you do, isn't it? Take society's scabs and force them to believe in whatever you want? We're just a bit more . . . *precise* about it. We can improve our stable of allied deities, weaken our enemies, and even hothouse our own custom gods. Just takes brainpower, direction, and time."

He pauses, looking down at me and savoring the growing comprehension in my eyes. I'm horrified by the concept. If what he's saying is true, then this place is an abomination. These people—they've turned the very act of faith into an assembly line. I wonder if it's really happening here, what he's saying, but I already know in my heart it must be. For all our power and mystery, the mechanics of our divinity are remarkably straightforward: Believe in us, and we will answer. We will act as you think we should, provide the services for which you pray, and make your hopes our own. With such a simple foundation, of course it's *possible* to twist it, to peel it open with a scalpel and muck around with questing fingers . . . but to actually *do it*? Blasphemous.

"No, not the same," I hear the ancient battle-maiden in me say. "Not the same at *all*."

"So high and mighty!" he barks. "Oh yes, we're bad people, aren't we, toying with the divine like it's an Erector set. But *think* for a

116

second, will you? What we do is orderly, fixed. You just run around without a care in the world, gobbling up belief wherever you can find it. Ever stop to think that maybe we'd be better off without you? Maybe we don't want to have to pray for our scraps, for our capricious god to favor us over our enemies. *You*, little parasite, invite chaos. Pain and misery follow in the wake of all your kind, every last religion sowing pandemonium in the name of salvation. We are dedicated to ending that torment, and we want you to help us do it."

I'm about to start cursing him, his parents, and every child of his lineage out to the fortieth generation when he grasps me by the shoulders and leans into my face.

"Don't throw this chance away, Freya," he hisses. "Join us and help make things better. We're not out to kill your kind. We just want to take you out of the equation—to make this a rational, serene world. You can live forever, for all I care, so long as you do it without endangering everything we've built."

He's so close I can smell his lunch on his breath, see his pulse throbbing through the skin on his neck. "Gods are a disease," he whispers. "A plague on humanity. Help us cure it."

My first thought is to lunge forward and tear out his jugular with my teeth. My second is that he's insane. Humanity *made* us. We were brought into this world to help you prosper, not self-destruct. But I refuse to let myself fall into that trap. If I start thinking my enemy is mad, I risk underestimating him. And these people *are* my enemy—of that I have no doubt. They seek to rob mankind of my gifts and bind me in the process. We have as much right to freedom as any creature, to say nothing of the fact that our existence is—and will always be—dedicated to aiding our creators.

So Garen is wrong. And yet . . .

I cannot dismiss his words. The conviction that burns in him must be reflected in the organization he represents, and if I am to destroy it, I have to understand what they are trying to accomplish. These people are *very* well prepared, dedicated heart and soul to their task, and backed by a ruthless combination of technology and divinity. So I must try to keep an open mind, to *appreciate* what drives them, so that one day I may ravage them utterly.

In just a few short moments, my goals have expanded from a simple act of revenge against one man to the annihilation of an entire conspiracy. That's why my answer must be what it is. Anything less, and I jeopardize my chances of achieving this brutal aim.

"Okay," I say in a soft, compliant voice. The battle-maiden in me screams for blood, and it takes all my strength to hold her down, placate her with the promise of future carnage and retribution.

Garen blinks and pulls back. "What," he says in a flat voice. Not a question.

"Okay," I repeat. "I'll join you."

He narrows his eyes, and there's an odd tic to his features, as if he's just had a wrench thrown into his brain's gears. "Never. You're lying," he says.

Of course I am, Garen. But you have no way to prove it. "Doesn't really matter, does it?" I reply. "I'm sure this is all being recorded. What will your bosses say if you label me a threat and lock me away, when all the evidence says I am willing to cooperate?"

"They'll believe—" He stops. That smirk of his is completely gone, and I get the feeling he's furious.

"They need me more than they need you, don't they? No matter how many years of faithful service you've given them, you're just not quite what they're looking for, are you?"

He bites his lip, and I can tell I've hit him where it hurts. This, then, is Garen's weakness—the button I can push to send him over the edge: He hates gods with an all-consuming passion, and yet they will always be valued more highly than him. Years of loyalty, consummate skill, tremendous work ethic, and *none* of it matters. He knows it, and now I know it, too.

"Thank you, Freya," he says at last, spitting the words at me. "Finemdi Corporation appreciates your willingness to cooperate."

Finemdi? That's it, then—the name of the organization I'm going to devastate. It's Latin, I think, or maybe Italian. I can understand the language of any prayer I receive, but this isn't Garen's native tongue and he's using it as a proper noun, so I don't know for sure. Another task for my Mim, I suppose.

Garen walks to the side of the gurney with the IV drip. "We will have more information for you shortly. For now, please rest." The words are friendly enough, but I can tell by the way he says them in that strained, hateful voice that what he really wanted was for me to refuse his offer.

He adjusts the poison's flow, and I start feeling woozy almost at once. The blackened haze begins to return, and the room starts shifting. Then he leans close, putting his lips no more than an inch from my ear. When he speaks, it's in a voice so soft even I can barely hear it.

"I know what you're trying to do," he whispers. "You can't hide it forever—it's your nature. I'll be waiting for you to snap, Freya. And when you do, I'll be there to end you."

I can't even respond. I'm unconscious before he leaves the room.

HANDLE WITH CARE

This is the strangest meeting I've ever attended.

I'm sitting in a slick conference room, leaning my elbows on a large, oval-shaped wooden table in its center. A chipper, clean-cut young man who introduced himself as Adam Carraway is standing at the front of the room. He's happily chattering before a large drop-down projector screen, giving a PowerPoint presentation to me . . . and Dionysus.

The god of wine, merriment, and sexual harassment is sitting across from me. Every now and then, I stare daggers at him, wishing my divine portfolio included the ability to make someone's head explode. Of course they'd try to recruit him. And of course he'd be taken in by Garen's offer. He's a vain, self-indulgent harlot obsessed with power—it would be stupid to assume anything else. His presence has made this a remarkably tense experience, and I find myself lapsing into a daydream about new ways to maim him every other minute.

That anxiety has been making it kind of hard to concentrate, as well. Adam's already moved past the short history of Finemdi, which I sort of blanked out on. Something about an organization of philosophers and statesmen coming together around the time of the American Revolution. What I mostly remember is feeling relieved their history didn't involve Leonardo da Vinci or the Freemasons in some way. I've seen a lot of movies and read a *lot* of books, and I am so very tired of seeing them pop up everywhere. From hell's heart I stab at thee, scriptwriters.

Now Adam's moving on to gods in general. Apparently, we're ranked within the organization based on our strength, ranging from lesser to greater deities. They also have a "bottom of the barrel" grouping for quasideities, which can refer either to gods with very few to no followers or to the product of a union between a god and a mortal. I'm pretty certain they've been assuming I'm in this category, but I think at this point I'm pushing "lesser." Hooray. Based on our ranking, we'll be assigned worshippers from a pool of "volunteers." Adam touches on this part very briefly, but he does include a picture of unhealthy-looking men and women strapped into chairs with glowing, spiderlike devices of metal and glass placed over their eyes. Finemdi determines the best ways to improve their stable of gods through directed belief from these poor people, but we're apparently free to make suggestions. I make a mental note to ask about that head-exploding power.

Then Adam moves on to our responsibilities. Apparently, we're required to aid them with manifestations of our abilities—if appropriate—and go on missions to help capture or recruit other gods. The general goal is to take deities out of the wild and bring them back to Finemdi facilities, with the ultimate objective being the removal of all gods to a safer and more manageable environment. Laid out through a series of slides in this dry, corporate setting, you could almost forget what they're doing is an affront to nature.

"Those are the basics. Now, we'll be covering more in the next few days, but if you have any questions, I'd be happy to answer them," Adam says, clicking over to the last slide, titled *Q&A*. The way he looks at me as he says it gives me the impression he really *would* be happy to do this. How on earth did a naive salesman like him wind up working for a god-hating conspiracy? I resolve to think of a question or two, just so he doesn't feel bad.

"When do we get our belief?" Dionysus asks. It's clear from his posture and shining eyes that he's been listening with rapt attention to every word of Adam's presentation.

"In just a few short weeks," Adam says, smiling. "We'll bring in new thought recruits, set up a belief plan, and review you so they know precisely how to target their conviction. In the meantime, we'll get you familiar with our procedures and make sure you're comfortable here."

"What if we don't want to live here? Where are we, anyway?" I ask, putting up my hand.

Adam nods eagerly. "We recognize that some of our deities have continuing responsibilities in the outside world, and those who do are indeed allowed to maintain outside accommodations. If you'd like to apply for an off-site permit, I can request the appropriate forms for you."

"I'd appreciate that, thanks," I say.

He beams. "As to your other question, we are currently in Impulse Station, an Epsilon-class training and development facility servicing the southeastern United States."

"Okay. So where is that? Like, on a map," I say. It seems everyone here is in the habit of answering questions a little too literally, or assuming too much understanding on the part of the listener. Spell it out for me, people.

"Oh," he murmurs, seeming a little surprised I don't know where I've been taken. "We're in Orlando, Florida, a bit west of the international airport. Just off Landstreet Road." He frowns. "Weren't you . . ."

"I was unconscious," I say, blunt as can be. "But thank you."

His mouth clicks closed, and he appears taken aback. I probably don't come across as the sort of deity who needs to be sedated. "Ah. Well, are there any other questions?"

"I would like one of those forms as well," Dionysus says. "I have business responsibilities to which I must attend. Speaking of which, how long has it been since my"—he glances at me, and I catch a hint of annoyance in his frenzied eyes—"capture?"

"Of course," Adam says quickly. "According to your files, you were both brought in last night."

I glance at the clock hanging over the door. 6:37 PM. That's good—I was worried I might've missed work. I have today and Monday off, so if I can get back sometime tomorrow, I can still make my shifts at the park.

"Where is the man who was brought in with me?" I ask. "I want him released as soon as possible."

"Oh, yes. Nathan, correct? I believe he's expected to regain consciousness sometime tomorrow. Is he one of your retainers?"

"Something like that."

"Not a problem. We'll add him to your guest list." He pauses, looking at us both expectantly, then spreads his hands. "Any other questions?"

"Where can I get some new clothes?" I ask, picking at my medical scrubs—baggy pale blue pants and matching top. I'm glad to no longer be in that perverted backless gown, but hospital chic really isn't my style.

"I'll arrange to have a few options added to your closet. Otherwise, you can fill out a request form and we'll have anything you want delivered directly to your room."

"Thanks," I say, hoping whatever Finemdi has on hand is halfway stylish.

"Anything else?" Adam says.

"When's dinner?" Dionysus asks. "I'm *famished*."

Sure you are. I roll my eyes as Adam glances at the clock and answers with, "Perfect timing, then! The cafeteria starts serving right around six o'clock, so if there's nothing else, I can show you the way now."

"Lead on!" Dionysus says cheerfully, bounding to his feet and knocking his chair away. Coolly, I slide out of mine and make sure I carefully tuck it back under the table. I'm not normally a stickler for manners, but pointing out his constant disrespect in every possible way satisfies my passive-aggressive little heart.

"What's after dinner?" I ask as we head out of the room and begin walking down the halls. Impulse Station is a maze of branching corridors. There was a map included in the information packet I was given at the start of Adam's presentation, but I can't make heads or tails of it. It's like looking at a bucket of rainbow-colored worms. After getting used to the well-designed utility tunnels of Disney, this is like trying to navigate a nightmare realm with Escher as your cartographer. I'd be lost immediately if Adam weren't here to guide us.

"You'll be guided to your assigned quarters—I'll make sure you both have the off-site permit forms waiting for you when you arrive—and given the evening to familiarize yourself with the facility and its rules."

"Are there any other gods here right now?" I ask.

"Oh, plenty," he says, nodding. "Second-largest collection on the eastern seaboard!"

Collection? I'm incensed by the very idea, but I refuse to let it show. I still remember Garen's last words to me, and I'm dead set on proving him wrong. I'll seem like the perfect ally of theirs, right up until the moment I stab them in the back.

A door swings open in the hallway, and I catch the last snippet of what seems to be a heated conversation. ". . . has never been denied," a burly, thickset man in a well-tailored suit is saying, his head turned to speak with someone in the room.

Garen's voice replies, and I'm suddenly a *lot* more interested in this debate. He has a strange tone in his voice, and I realize he's actually *pleading* with the man. "But she's *different*, sir! She has self-control, and that makes her incredibly—"

"I don't want to hear it, specialist!" the man snaps, yelling into the room. "They're all the same! That's rather the *point*, isn't it? Now, get back in the field and do your job!" With that, he spins, revealing a haggard, lined face, a thick gray mustache, and pale green eyes that narrow as they notice me. Those eyes are familiar, but I can't quite place them. "Miss," he says as we walk past.

Garen exits the room, a wonderfully chastened look on his face. It changes to one of shock the moment he notices me. It's painfully obvious who they were just talking about in there. As if he can read my thoughts, Garen grimaces and turns, walking down the hall away from us at a brisk pace. I stop to watch him go, wondering if it's possible to feel any more smug than I do now. The heavyset man holds the door for a few other men in tailored suits, all of whom studiously avoid looking me in the eyes as they file out.

Oh, this is just *delightful*. The more I keep my divine urges in check, the more I'm going to confuse and worry everyone in charge of this place. I'm impressed by how I've been doing so far. Who would have thought such secrecy would be possible for one so lively and vivacious? *Certainly not Garen*, I think, chuckling.

"Are you coming, Miss Freya?" Adam asks, seeming uncomfortable.

"It's Sara," I say, grinning as I fall into step beside them.

A few minutes later, I'm in the cafeteria, realizing I was wrong to label that meeting "strange." It's nothing compared to my new situation. The dining hall we've entered is filled with Impulse staff and gods, all enjoying the night's choices. The hubbub from their conversations percolates through the room, a dull murmur of laughter and gossip. There's an industrial feel to the place. It reminds me of a converted warehouse; a long, high-ceilinged room filled with dull gray tabletops and matching plastic chairs, racks of fluorescent lights above, and cheap speckled linoleum flooring underfoot. A set of double doors yawns to my left, and there's a dry-erase board set on a tripod beside them with the night's specials scribbled in green marker.

As I draw closer, I see the board is divided into two sections: *Immortals* and *Mortals*. Under my heading, there's roasted boar with sage butter and grilled asparagus (poor pig!), while Finemdi's human employees have to contend with the rather depressing option of a potato bar. Dionysus nods at the board as if he expected nothing less, then saunters toward the dinner line.

I look at Adam. "Is everything okay, Miss Frey—I mean, Sara?" he asks nervously. I think he's misread my pity for disappointment.

"Fine, Mr. Carraway," I reply. "I was just surprised by the, um, dinner options."

"Are they not acceptable? I assure you, there are standard menu choices inside that may be more to your liking. This is only the special, after all, and—"

"No, no, they're fine," I say, feeling exasperated. He nearly fell over himself there, seeming horrified by the idea I might be unhappy. I get the feeling most of the staff are expected to bend over backward for their divine teammates. "I was just wondering why the specials were . . . segregated, I guess."

He blinks, confusion rewriting his normally cheerful face. I think he's frantically turning over my words, trying to figure out how this could possibly offend me. I'm not sure who I should have a dimmer view of right now: these people for assuming all gods are stuck-up prima donnas, or my fellow deities for giving them that impression in the first place. "That's just . . . the way it's always been, Miss Sara," he says at last.

"All right, wonderful," I say, deciding I'll never get a straight answer out of him. "Thank you for all your help, Mr. Carraway."

He brightens immediately. "You're absolutely welcome, Lady Sara. Please let me know if there's anything else I can do for you."

"Of course," I say, inclining my head at him and then moving toward the dinner line.

I collect a plastic tray from a large stack just inside the double doors, then turn to take in my options. The room is divided into two halves—on my left, there's a row of stainless steel serving stations, staffed by numerous uniformed chefs. A stenciled metal sign hangs over the line, the word *IMMORTALS* picked out in block letters. I notice Dionysus is already here, loading up his tray with all manner of goodies. On the opposite side of the room, another line of stations, with fewer, less-appealing options and a handful of uninterested staff members, sits beneath a *MORTALS* banner. Finally, there's a do-it-yourself salad bar in the middle, right between the two sides. Blending vegetables and ranch dressing, it seems, is one of the few things deemed acceptable for both groups.

Part of me wants to rebel against this forced inequality, to march right over to the other side of the room and avail myself of their potato bar and maybe a side of sad-looking pasta. This sort of isolation can only create distrust and resentment between gods and their worshippers, and it's a perfect example of Finemdi's corporate philosophy. They see us as intractable, fickle divas, and everything—even their *cafeteria design*—reflects this mind-set. I'd like to think I'm better than that. I'd like to think I can rise above this rather insulting attempt to appeal to my vanity, and take a stand for what's right.

Then I get a closer look at the options on "my" side.

✦ ✦ ✦

I'm not proud of it, but a few minutes later, I shuffle into the lunch-room wielding a tray covered in luxurious treats. Rack of lamb, truf-fle gnocchi, crusty bread slices surrounding a modest dab of caviar, and a bowl of butternut squash soup, all of it weighing down my arms with guilt. I feel more than a little ashamed for giving in, but hey—filet mignon was also available, and I managed to refuse that. I won't indulge until Nathan's back at my side and the two of us are finally sitting down to a decent, uninterrupted dinner. So that means I'm not a complete sellout, right? I mean, *truffle gnocchi*, people.

As I scan the cafeteria, looking for a place to sit, an odd feeling settles into my stomach. I can't say I've experienced this before, but from everything I've seen on TV, it's a high school classic: social anxiety. Every table is packed with cliques. I see research special-ists and doctors chatting away, trying not to stain their lab coats. There are off-duty guards at one table, men in business suits at another. A few Greek gods laugh and shout greetings as Dionysus walks over, scooting chairs around and clearing room for him. He's grinning like an idiot as they clap him on the back and scramble to catch up on old times, treating him like he's some returning prom king at their ten-year reunion.

Is this really happening? Have I been kidnapped and placed in some deviant *Saved by the Bell* remake starring gods and mercenar-ies? This is incredibly strange and off-putting. These gods are born troublemakers, prone to displays of arrogance and egotism that would take your breath away, and now they're acting like frat boys at a cookout? Something's not right. I crane my neck around, looking for other places to sit. Most of the deities seem to keep to themselves,

129

organized by pantheon, and I don't see anyone from mine. There are a few Egyptian gods—I recognize Bast—in one corner, and I think that pack of rough customers a few tables away are from the Tuatha Dé Danann, of Ireland. Native American nature spirits chat amiably next to Slavic deities, and—oh wait, is that a group of Incan or Mayan gods? I've never been very good at keeping up with my kin south of the Tropic of Cancer.

Finally, I spot someone sitting alone in a far corner. I dash over, trying not to look *too* desperate. "Excuse me," I say, feeling surprisingly apprehensive. "Do you mind if I join you?"

The woman, another researcher if her lab coat is any indication, looks up. Her green eyes widen with recognition, and her mouth drops open; it's Samantha Drass, the bespectacled girl who oversaw my admission. "Well, um . . ." she murmurs, looking perplexed. "Freya, right? Hi."

"Hi, Samantha," I say cheerfully, nodding. "You can call me Sara, if you like. Is it okay if I eat with you?" I hold up my tray and give it a wiggle.

She frowns. "I'm sorry, but you *do* know I'm not a god, right?"

Now it's my turn to frown. "Yeah," I say after a moment. "So?"

Her frown vanishes, and she looks pleasantly surprised. "Oh, I thought—um, I mean, certainly. Company is always appreciated," she says at once.

I grin, set down my tray, and sit across from her. For a minute, I busy myself with my meal, cutting apart the lamb and popping a few tender morsels into my mouth. Then I catch Samantha watching with a vaguely envious expression and pause. "Would you like some?" I ask, gesturing at my plate. "It's delicious."

"Oh, no, I couldn't," she says, reddening. I notice her own plate is occupied by salad and a baked potato.

I sigh. "Yes, you can. I don't care about the whole gods-are-better-than-you thing they've got going on here. Now, try some lamb. Or maybe the gnocchi?"

She hesitates but doesn't say anything one way or another, so I push the tray a little closer. "Go on, take something, already," I say, starting to feel exasperated.

Her eyes dart around as if she's about to do something very naughty, then she shrugs and reaches over to spear a lump of gnocchi with her fork. "Oh," she says after popping it into her mouth. "That's *perfect*."

"Not so bad?" I ask, returning to my meal.

"Not in the least," she says. "But we're not supposed to share, you know."

"Yeah, I figured. It's *fun* to do something we're not supposed to do every now and then, isn't it?" I ask with a smirk.

She says nothing, but the little smile on her lips tells me she's not completely hopeless. We pass the next few minutes in silence, enjoying our respective meals. I'm aware of little glances being shot my way from other tables, gods and mortals alike apparently very interested in the two of us. This attention can't honestly be just for me, can it? I might be a god, but something tells me that doesn't quite have the same pull around here. Humbling as it may be to admit, I think this interest probably has more to do with the lady I've decided to join than my own unique nature. On that note, I think I ought to learn a little more about my lonely companion.

"Why don't you eat with anyone else?" I ask. Okay, so subtlety isn't my strong suit.

Samantha sighs and looks away, setting down her fork. She's silent for so long I'm worried I've offended her, but then she speaks at last, a tone of resignation in her voice. "It's my father."

"Why would—"

"They're all afraid of him, so they're afraid of me," she says, still looking away.

"Okay. Who is he?" She stops again, and I can tell exactly why she doesn't want to say. "I'm not going to scamper off when I find out you're related to the Big Bad Wolf, Samantha," I say, rolling my eyes.

"Sorry," she says with a halfhearted laugh. "But when it happens *every time*, you get a little discouraged."

"Spill."

"Okay, okay." She draws herself back and looks at me with those pale green eyes of hers, and in that moment, before she even opens her mouth to say it, I know exactly who her father is. "He's Gideon Drass, chief executive and head of Finemdi Corporation," she mumbles sadly.

"Oh, him," I say nonchalantly. The man in the corridor, giving Garen marching orders—they have the same eyes. Well, well. Now I know who I've dedicated myself to murdering. "We've met."

Her eyes bulge. "What?"

"So that's it?" I say, ignoring the question. "That's why you have to play sad, little loner in the corner? I mean, my dad's the wind and the sea, but I still get to eat dinner with friends."

She cracks a genuine smile at that, and I give myself a mental pat on the back. "He's very protective of me," she says in a small voice. "He doesn't trust people, especially gods. So when he finds out I'm spending time with someone, well, he never says anything to *me*, but all of a sudden they'll just . . . stop wanting to be friends."

"Not right, Samantha," I say. "Well, I'm not going anywhere."

She gives me one of those "whatever you say" looks in response, so I decide to let the subject drop. "Want to try some caviar?" I ask after a moment, now determined to become this girl's friend, if only to rub her dad's face in it. For a brief moment, I wonder how many of my decisions are motivated purely by spite. I decide not to pursue the thought any further.

She makes a face. "Ugh, too salty."

"Suit yourself," I say, scooping some onto a round of bread and munching happily.

After another minute or two, there's a bit of movement nearby and a dark-skinned woman detaches herself from her group and walks over. She's a little heavier than me, but those extra pounds are in all the right places, making her attractively curvaceous. Her face is broad, with wide features that strike me as both beautiful and motherly. Her glorious black hair falls to her waist, twinkling like blown glass, and her eyes blaze like the surface of the sun, glowing orbs of radiant inner fire.

"Hello," she says to me in deep, accented English. I can't help noticing she ignores Samantha entirely. "You are a new god, aren't you?"

"That, or I'm trying to make these fashionable for everyone," I say, gesturing at my scrubs.

"Uh, yes. Well, I'd like to welcome you to Impulse," she says, spreading her arms. "I am Pele, goddess of fire, volcanoes, and dance."

I nod at her. Normally, I'd stand, maybe offer a hand, but I don't like how she's giving my new friend the cold shoulder. "Freya. Love, beauty, and war." I turn to wink at Samantha. "You can still call me Sara, though," I say to her.

She smiles while Pele frowns. "It's nice to meet you, Freya," the Hawaiian goddess says. The way she responds makes me feel like she may have already known who I am, and her next words confirm it. "You're the first Norse god we've seen here, and I wanted to let you know you're welcome to sit at our table, if you'd like."

She turns, holding out her hand to indicate a pair of goddesses looking at us from about twenty feet away. The two are both dark-skinned and majestic. One of them, a young girl who looks very similar to Pele but with cooler, more natural features, waves. Her hair twists around her arm as she raises it, seeming caught in a perpetual breeze. All three of them are dressed in loose, brightly colored, billowy dresses.

"Well, that's great!" I say, glancing at Samantha, who looks miserable. "We'll be right over—I mean, my friend can come, too, right?" I already know the answer, but I'd like to make this uncomfortable.

"Oh," Pele says, her scorching gaze leaving me to glance at Samantha. "Um, it's just—we'd *like* to be able to, but . . ."

"It's okay, Freya," Samantha says softly. "You go ahead."

"Oh, this is ridiculous," I say. "What could her father possibly have done to make you all so afraid of her?"

"Please, I don't—" Samantha begins to say.

Pele grimaces, then leans down and lowers her voice to a whisper. "We all liked Samantha, my sisters and I, but when Mr. Drass found out, he—he sent one of us to another facility."

"Kapo," Samantha says, nodding.

"We miss her terribly, and he'll find some way to hurt you, too, so I just wanted to . . . you know," she says, a pleading look in her eyes.

I bite my lip, looking between Pele and Samantha until the latter seems to make some internal decision, snatches up her tray, and begins moving to the drop-off area by the exits. "It's okay," she says as she goes. "I'm finished anyway."

She marches away, head down, and I look back at Pele, who shrugs. "Fathers, eh?" she says softly.

We both turn to watch Samantha practically throw her tray—still mostly full—onto the drop-off shelf and then dart out of the room. I can feel the hurt and rejection spiraling out of her. "Yeah. Fathers," I mutter, picking up my own tray and going to join Pele and her sisters.

Finemdi: dedicated to perverting the very nature of divinity, to kidnapping the gods of the world, and to commanding us like trained attack dogs, all on the orders of a man who's made a recluse of his own daughter.

I am going to burn this place to the ground.

9

THICK AS THIEVES

Pele and her sisters aren't bad people. They're just terrified. As I eat dinner and chat with them, I find they don't particularly like Finemdi or their overseers any more than I do—they just have a lot more to lose.

"Most of our family is spread across their bases," Hi'iaka (the girl with the eternally windblown hair) says, gesturing with a piece of asparagus on her fork. "We don't know how many facilities exist, but they have at least four in the United States, and several overseas."

"We cooperate because, well, what choice do we have?" Nāmaka, the third sister, says, pushing her food around. Her skin shimmers faintly when I'm not looking directly at it, as if she were part liquid, and her eyes are aquamarine spheres of rippling ocean water. "It's not like we're actually happy here—we want to go back to our islands, to feel the sun through green leaves and wet sand between our toes."

"I miss the sea breeze on my face," Hi'iaka says, closing her eyes.

"Warm lava pools, the flash of lightning over a caldera . . ." Pele murmurs, lost in memory alongside her siblings.

"What about the other gods?" I ask, trying to snap them out of their shared reverie. They're nice enough but also quite erratic and elemental. I'm vaguely reminded of conversations with my father. Like him, these gods are much closer to nature than I am, and easily distracted because of it. Of course, that's just how it seems to me—I suppose one could also say they're not swept up in the worries of the modern world, that they find the important things in life to be in the grass and skies, the waves and sand. For the briefest moment, I stop to consider if I should perhaps take a lesson from these ladies and halt my destructive course. Finemdi doesn't have to be my responsibility. I'll still be around long after its leaders' bones have turned to dust, after all.

Then the battle-maiden in my soul snaps her head up, eyes flashing, and I feel the heat of her disgust as she reminds me what they're trying to do to me and my kin. Sure, I don't *have* to lift a finger. But deep down in the pits of my mind, past the homes of love and beauty, the sanctuaries of fertility and magic, there's an old garrison where a brutal piece of me lies in wait. Decked out in armor and spattered with blood, teeth bared in a rictus, she sharpens her weapons and prepares for the day I need her to unleash the rage of the heavens.

They must *die*.

"Hmm?" Pele asks dreamily.

"The other gods," I repeat. "Do they hate Finemdi, too?"

"Varies, really," Nāmaka says, drawing absentmindedly on the

137

table with lines of water. The stuff just seems to pool on the surface of her skin, though her bright blue dress is completely dry. "Some, like us, have every reason to detest them. We were never meant to be kept indoors, or, worse, away from our family. But take the Greeks," she says, pointing at their table with one soggy digit.

"Please!" Hiʻiaka barks, giggling.

Nāmaka rolls her eyes. "They love it here. The staff fawns over them, their power swells, and they get to pretend this is their new Olympus."

"I hear the suits have Hephaestus making weapons and mystic baubles for them in New York," Pele says, rejoining the conversation.

Nāmaka nods. "They're all over the place, doing all sorts of things for Finemdi."

"Who's the one you came in with?" Pele asks. "The fancy guy."

"Ugh, *him*," I say. "Dionysus. Scumbag."

"Ooh, tell," Hiʻiaka says, scooting her chair closer and leaning in.

I see the gleam in her stormy, typhoon eyes, and recognize the primal need for gossip clawing its way to the surface. Nature deity or not, sometimes you just want to hear some good dirt. "You'll love this," I say in a conspiratorial tone. I tell them all about Dionysus, and it's great. It makes me realize how much I missed having girlfriends to talk to. They gasp at all the right moments, grin as I describe tricking Dionysus to go after Garen, become deadly serious as I talk about the attack in Disney's tunnels, and clap and laugh as I tell them about Nathan's intervention.

"And he looks so cute, too," Hiʻiaka says, giving him a baleful stare. She turns back to me. "Well, we'll make certain all the other goddesses know he's a pig, too."

"If only Kapo were here," Pele says wistfully. "She'd have *really* given him a surprise."

"Oooh, can you *imagine*?" Hi'iaka says, a naughty look on her face.

Nāmaka sighs. "I really do miss her," she mumbles.

That seems to sober things up, so even though I'm immensely curious about what they're referring to with Kapo, I decide to change the subject and look it up on my Mim later. "So what do they have you do here?" I ask.

They exchange looks. Pele turns to me first and says, "Most of the time, it's nothing. Every now and then, they'll have an odd job for us, but they're always little things, you know? Like they don't want us getting bored or thinking they've forgotten about us."

"Why? I mean, you control volcanoes, right? That sounds pretty powerful."

Pele shrugs. "Try to think of how often you come across a problem and say to yourself, 'I've got the perfect solution! *A volcano!*'"

I pause. "All right, you have me there. Still, though—I'm sure that's not your only trick. And your sisters . . . winds and waves, right?" The other two women nod. "So why are they ignoring you?"

Nāmaka shakes her head, sending water droplets flying. "They're not *really* ignoring us, Freya. They're just trying to keep us in check. Most of what we do is already covered by other gods they trust more. That, and there's Ka."

"Ka?"

"As in 'boom,'" Hi'iaka says with a wan smile.

"His full name is Ka-poho-i-kahi-ola," Nāmaka says. "He's the god of explosions."

"Explosions?" I repeat. Then it hits me. "Wait, *just* explosions?"

Pele nods. "He's our brother. Was never incredibly powerful—not like us, at least—but that was before Finemdi."

"They focused a *lot* of belief into him, made him incredibly strong and incredibly good at the one thing he's supposed to oversee," Nāmaka says. "Which basically means he's a walking arsenal now."

"Want something destroyed in a big pillar of fire?" Pele asks, balling her hands into fists and then shooting out her fingers. "Maybe a mountain blasted in half? Makes demolition a snap."

"Call our brother," Hi'iaka says. "He's their living weapon, so we sit around just in case he snaps and decides to blast a facility off the map."

Pele nods. "That's why our whole family is scattered across the world. So he can't blow us out all at once."

"Eesh," I murmur, understanding completely. When gods have many concepts in their portfolios, it tends to indicate that they're more powerful; such diversity is usually a sign they have more worshippers who look to them for help with more things. Every now and then, you'll get a god who's focused on something very specific, yet still wields a lot of power (think Helios, the Grecian god of the sun, for example). More often, though, these specialized deities are weaker. One with a specialization as obscure as, say, *explosions* would probably be very weak. In yet another fine example of deific meddling, however, Finemdi has turned the tables with this Hawaiian god, granting him immense power within a very specific area. I can only guess at the results, but I'm sure they're terrifying. So bad, in fact, that Finemdi's gone to the trouble of capturing an entire pantheon of gods just to keep him in line. It worries me for an entirely different reason as well, because it's probably just the tip of the iceberg. Who knows what other celestial atrocities they've committed?

The Hawaiian sisters bob their heads, looking gloomy. Right then and there, I decide to trust these ladies. I've never been good at picking out liars, so there's every chance they could secretly be double agents for Finemdi, but spirits of nature have never struck me as very duplicitous. Mischievous, yes, but two-faced? That's a decidedly more *human* characteristic than an elemental one. Besides, I've always believed in tit for tat. I assume people are fundamentally good and trustworthy until they prove me wrong, at which point they're dead to me. Sometimes literally.

"So you're here to keep an unstable brother of yours in line, and you don't want to act out because you're worried they'll split the three of you up even more," I say, lowering my voice even further.

They look at one another, then nod. "Sure, they treat us like queens and the food's not half bad, but we're not blind," Hi'iaka says. "We know what they're doing is wrong. We just can't bear to see another of us go."

"And they won't actually do something to *hurt* any of you, because their god of explosions might have himself a little roaring rampage of revenge if he found out."

"Without a doubt," Pele says.

"Then I'll make you three a deal," I say, glancing around to make sure nobody else is close enough to hear. "Help me, and you'll never have to worry about Finemdi again."

Another round of glances passes among the three women, each set of elemental eyes filled with confusion.

"What?" Pele says at last.

"I'm destroying them. Everything they've done is an abomination. I'm going to level this entire facility, and that's just for starters. I need to wipe them off the face of the earth, and I want you to help me do it."

There's a moment of stunned silence, and then Hi'iaka laughs. "You don't think small, I'll give you that!" She looks at her sisters. "I like her. She's *feisty*."

"She's dangerous," Nāmaka says, crossing her arms.

Pele shakes her head at me. "To attack Finemdi is to assault *multiple* pantheons at this point, Freya," she explains. "They're too powerful."

"Really?" I say, giving her a pitying glare. "Since when do you care about *politics*?" I shift my gaze to Nāmaka. "Do the tides change for a handful of depraved mortals? Is that your legacy? To lie down and show throat in the face of threats to your very nature?"

She narrows her eyes at me. "The tides are eternal, barbarian. They will outlast love and beauty, to say nothing of these pathetic bureaucrats."

For a handful of seconds, I pause, staring at her. I realize these words came to me as well, told me I could always wait them out, could trust in time and my own immortality to vanquish them. It was a thought swiftly crushed, of course, dismissed by my outrage at their evil. Why, then, would a creature even more primordial and liberated than myself accept that argument? *This is incredibly wrong,* I think. *What could possibly have changed them so—*

I stiffen as cold, harrowing realization tunnels through me, and I understand at last what's happened here. I see past Nāmaka's waterlogged features and, for a flickering instant, glimpse the hollow soul beyond. Look at her. Look at all of them! These are spirits of *nature*, and they're just accepting their fate—accepting the fact that they've been ripped away from their homes—like it's a minor inconvenience. They don't realize what's been done to them, what they've even lost. *This* is why the cafeteria feels so strange, why all those fickle gods are getting along like they are the best of pals. That "belief" Finemdi offers to lure us in? It's poisoned bait. Those imprisoned dreamers provide power, yes, but at a terrible price. We are what you make of us, after all, and Finemdi knows this all too well. They must think themselves so clever, binding their pet gods with the same resource that empowers them, lacing those oh-so-seductive beliefs with hidden chains of conformity. This is why they trust us, why I'm already walking around like I own the place—because they can *believe* I'll never betray them, and, in time, it'll be true.

They are dreaming their deities into slavery, carving submission into their hearts.

"At what cost?" I ask softly. I must make them see what's been done to them, must force them to acknowledge the permanency of this place's malevolence. "One of your brothers has already been twisted by their machinations. Will that atrocity fade with time, as well? And what other horrors could they engineer while you wait for them to grow old? Their goal is the removal of all gods from this world, Nāmaka—nothing less. You cannot outlast oblivion."

"What would you have us do, little goddess?" Pele asks, eyes afire. "Wage war?"

"*Yes*," the Valkyrie in me hisses. "Bit by bit, you have let them chain you, drag you into complacency with threats and treats. They understand gods—understand how to motivate and manipulate us through belief. *Think* about it. You say you miss the open air, the clap of thunder, the surge of lava on your skin, but in all that longing, where is the *hate* for those who took it from you?"

All three of them are silent now, staring at me.

"They have tricked you. They have molded your personalities while they strengthened your gifts. Belief can move cities, shake the earth, and reshape the world. It can change the nature of men, empires, and reality itself. And it has changed *you*."

I lean back in my chair, eyes moving over them each in turn, searching desperately for some sign of understanding, some sense that they realize what's been done. They say nothing, and the silence drags. I'm about to leave in exasperation, write them off as a lost cause, when Pele looks down at her hands. She flexes them, watching flawless brown skin shift over ancient bones and muscle. "H-how long have we been here?" she asks, her voice cracking. Tiny sparks drip from her eyes, twinkling tears of fire.

Nāmaka's jaw moves soundlessly for a moment before her voice makes it out in a croak. "I . . . I have forgotten."

Hiʻiaka, devastated, looks between the two of them, then back at me. When she speaks, it's in a whisper of wind, a zephyr that carries her voice to our ears alone. "What can we do?"

Deep within me, the Valkyrie screams in triumph at this, my first small victory in the war against Finemdi. I smile, and we begin to plot.

An hour later, the dining hall closes, and we part ways for the evening. My mind whirls with schemes and trickery. *This* is how it's meant to be. I feel more like a general about to lead her armies into battle than a forgotten god in medical scrubs. I flag down a guard and have him lead me to my room, letting him deal with the maze of corridors. I'll need to figure out how to navigate this place some-day, but it won't be tonight. I use the key card that came with my information packet to unlock the door and step inside to find myself standing in a suite that wouldn't be out of place in a luxury hotel. There's a king-size bed, tasteful furnishings, glossy tile floors, and a large flat-screen TV.

My possessions are stacked in a neat little pile on top of the bed, bag cleaned and clothing freshly laundered. There's a handwritten note on top that apologizes for being unable to remove the red wine stains and adds that the room's closet should have a few sets of clothing that might interest me.

I notice a piece of paper on the bed beside my things, picking it up to see it's the off-site permit request form Mr. Carraway promised to provide. I'll need to fill that out later. This room is nice and all, but even if I have to make time in my schedule to play the good little goddess for Finemdi during the day, there's no way I'm staying here overnight—I like my little apartment near Disney, and I don't want to get comfortable in a place I'll be turning to ash. I dump out my bag and look through its contents. There's my Mim, thankfully preserved from Dionysus's wine wave by a closed zipper and water-proof lining. Some makeup and lipstick, a small hand mirror, keys, cash, credit cards, license . . . looks like it's all here. I'll have to get Nathan to go over everything with a fine-tooth comb and make sure Finemdi didn't leave any surprises, but nothing catches my eye.

That brings my thoughts back to my poor friend. I hope he's

okay. The poison is supposed to wear off sometime tomorrow for him, so I'll find out then, but I can't help feeling a little guilty for bringing him into this. One of these days, I promise myself, we'll get a real night out to ourselves. I sigh and shake my head. Regret can wait—there's so much more planning I could be doing, more information I could be uncovering about Finemdi. My eyes dart to the closet door. Then again, there's also new clothing to examine. I glance at my pale scrubs. Yeah, I already know how this is going to end. I'd like to pretend there's more of a struggle between the two options, but I already feel like I lie to myself a little too often as it is.

The outfits in the closet aren't half bad. Most of them are conservative choices, but since today's fashions seem tailored toward women engaged in a blood feud to see who can show as much skin as possible, I can't say I mind. They even have my size. *How thoughtful.* I paw through a half-dozen choices—there's a nice variety in here—before settling on a soft peach top and jeans. I pull them off the rack and quickly slip them on, then head into the bathroom to look myself over in the mirror. If I'm going to snoop around the facility, I'd at least like to look good while I'm doing it. Not that I think I'll seem all that suspicious; there are still plenty of hours left until bedtime, and I spent most of the day resting in a drug-induced coma anyway.

I stare at myself for a minute, twisting to the side to see how my clothes hang, then look up at my head and narrow my eyes. Might as well try to do something about my hair, too. I lean closer, eyes narrowing. No harm in tossing on a little makeup, either.

Half an hour later, I head out of my room, all done up and feeling a lot better about myself. My bag bounces at my hip, filled to the brim with the incomprehensible map, my key card, and all my other possessions. I kneel outside the door to leave the completed off-site permit form on the floor of the hallway, figuring it'll be noticed sooner there. Then I start my journey down the corridors in a random direction, intent on getting a better idea of the facility's layout. As I stroll past stoic guards and soundless security cameras, testing door handles and peering into empty meeting rooms, I quickly get the impression that no one cares where I go. Sure, every now and then I'll run into a door my key card won't unlock, but overall I feel like I have the run of the place.

At first I'm extremely suspicious, wondering what they could be hiding, but as more time passes without anyone stopping me, it all starts to make sense. They pamper deities, treating them like trusted teammates while secretly believing them into an obedient stupor, so why not let them roam freely? I have to admit, I might have been suckered in by their song and dance if it hadn't been for my self-imposed exile at the Inward Care Center. I think all those years spent distancing myself from my divine urges has made me something of a wild card in this place. No wonder Garen seemed surprised when I didn't leap at his offer of believers . . . and no wonder he's so worried about what I'll do now.

Actually, forget worried; I think he's terrified.

Their corporate doctrine allows for gods who only fall into one of two camps: To them, we're either helpful deities they can brainwash and control, or vengeful ones they need to lock away. Since gods are always larger than life, wearing their principles on their sleeves, Finemdi's operatives probably have no trouble sorting us into the right group. At our core, every last one of us is heartbreakingly predictable. Even with lifetimes of wisdom behind us, we'll still make terrible choices if it's what we were created to do, and *they know it.*

Every last one of us . . . except me.

Centuries ago, when I failed my worshippers and proved myself unworthy of my mantle (it's a long story), I never could have imagined I was starting myself on a path that would bring me so low I could actually ignore the call of divinity, the all-consuming addiction of belief. It wasn't my intent, but where I've ended up is the end of a trail Finemdi has clearly never expected a god to tread. *That's* what Garen was trying to tell Mr. Drass—he can't predict how I'll handle all this, because I'm the first god he's met who's clearly in the vengeful camp, yet able to *act* like I'm not.

Speaking of which . . .

I stop in the middle of another featureless gray hallway as a thought strikes me. Where *are* all those vengeful gods? Would Finemdi be stupid enough to lock them all up in a single place? Probably not, right? So they must have a prison at every facility where they stash the gods they can't trust. We are, after all, incredibly hard to kill. Impulse is supposed to be a major headquarters for the company, so it stands to reason there are a few nasties hidden somewhere.

I need to find these miscreants. I pull out my map and start hunting for the word *prison.* Nothing. Ensuing searches for *incarceration, penitentiary,* and *detention center* prove equally fruitless. Finally, a lone wing on the building's highest level catches my eye: *Correctional Ward. Now* we're getting somewhere. I immediately head for the nearest elevator, intent on seeing Finemdi's divine detainees. Unfortunately, this choice puts me up against the stark insanity of the building's lay-out. I thought finding my goal on the map was hard, but doing it in person is a nightmare. I spend—I kid you not—a good *hour* hunting for the place. It's like they designed things to be as confusing as possible. I'm determined, though, and when I finally come to a door with a small plaque beside it that reads *CORRECTIONS*, I pump my fist in the air. Take *that*, stupid architects.

I hold up my key card, wondering if it'll actually work, when the lock blinks green and the door swings open. A white-haired man in a lab coat emerges. He starts when he sees me, a confused look on his face. His name tag says *GOODSON, BARNABY*. I nod at him and reach out a hand to hold the door.

"Oh. Excuse me, sorry," he mumbles, zipping past me.

"No problem," I say. "Have a good night!"

He smiles distractedly, a puzzled tint in his eyes, and waves before turning around and heading down the hall. Well, that was easy. I slip inside the door and find myself in a little waiting room. A larger, more imposing metal door is directly in front of me. There's a guard sitting at a counter to my right behind a half wall of bullet-proof glass. He looks away from a bank of three computer monitors as I enter. One of them appears to have security camera feeds into the various cells beyond—it's split into six different boxes, each showing a different room. The opposite monitor has an overhead schematic of the local area highlighted in green. I can see a hallway with ten small rooms—five on each side—and icons that seem to indicate that only half of them are occupied. The middle monitor has a Web browser open to a social news site I recognize, rows of top-voted links to entertaining articles and images spilling down the page. The guard nods at a slot built into the glass where it joins the countertop.

"Purse, please," he says, sounding bored.

I pull my bag off my shoulder and slide it through the hole in the glass. He takes it, glances inside, then hangs it on a peg on the wall behind him under the number 2. He passes a little plastic token back to me through the slot. I take it and see the number on it matches my bag's peg.

"Remember, ward lockdown's in half an hour," he says, stabbing a button beside him.

There's a buzzing noise from the door in front of me. Catching on fast, I pull the handle, swing it open, and head inside. The room I've entered looks almost exactly like a high-security prison block from a movie. It's a long, low, brightly lit hallway, its spotless concrete floors and gray walls broken up by cells on either side. Each cell looks like a giant fish tank, the stereotypical bars replaced with thick sheets of acrylic glass. All of them have very solid-looking metal doors built into the wall just to the right of the glass, with a locked slot set about waist-high.

Immediately, I feel a sense of menace. The air practically buzzes with mystic energy, and I catch the telltale whiff of wards and defensive spells. On either side of the door I've entered, thick gun racks secured with electronic locks are embedded in the wall. Instead of firearms, however, they contain what look like harpoons capped by jagged spearheads of some pearlescent material. They glow with a faint, reassuring light. I lean in to inspect them briefly, then move to explore the rest of the area. A shiver runs through me as I take my first step down the hall. There's an unsettling urge to turn around and leave growing inside me. I realize this is a bad place, full of very bad things. Maybe I won't check out the entire wing. Yes, just a cell or two before I leave. I only have half an hour here anyway. I turn to my right, looking into the first cell. Its occupant—a large, malnourished black dog—is watching me warily.

I move to examine it more closely and it growls, baring its fangs. Its teeth are enormous; long, daggerlike points that look like they've been carved from obsidian. Waves of heat pour from its mouth, and I notice its paws aren't really canine at all—they look more like the footpads of a gecko, talons of wicked rock capping each digit where a nail should be. It's a scraggly, foul thing, and I realize I want nothing to do with it. I pull back. After a moment, it seems to lose interest in me and resumes pacing.

Across from the dog is another occupied cell. This one has a beautiful young Asian woman in it, her straight black hair falling down past her shoulders to frame a pristine white face. She's dressed in a plain white kimono and sits cross-legged behind a low wooden table. There's a tea set on it, a cup of steaming liquid placed directly in front of her atop a saucer. Scrolls adorn the walls of her cell, every last one coated with intricate Japanese kanji. A woven bamboo mat covers the floor, and a pair of wooden slippers lie near the door.

I walk closer and frown. There's something deeply troubling about this girl, and it's a thorough sense of wrongness that's almost familiar. Then she looks up, revealing eyes of purest midnight. Those black orbs lock onto me, and I see a flash of this girl as another creature entirely, one dead but not dead, her putrid skin split and rotten, kimono decayed and torn, maggots spilling from gaping wounds in her body. It's gone in an instant, but I know exactly who she reminds me of: Hel, daughter of Loki and ruler of the underworld.

"You oversee the afterlife, don't you?" I ask.

She cocks her head to the side, studying me, then inclines it in a little nod. "You are a god," she states in a soft, almost fragile voice. It's practically a whisper, but a hidden speaker broadcasts it into the hall for me to hear clearly.

I return her nod. "I am Freya. I know of another who watches over the dead of our lands. You are both . . . similar."

Her expression doesn't change, but I get the impression she's irritated with me. "And yet not. They can only hope to be a pretender before the darkness of my domain. I am Izanami, queen of Yomi and mother of the gods. Once giver of life, now its destroyer. All others are but pale shadows."

"That's nice," I say, deciding this girl might be a bit far gone for my needs. "Let me know how that works out for you."

I walk on to the next set of cells, and here the sense of anxiety and unease in my heart grows to a fever pitch. I find myself looking at a young man, muscular and fit, with lengthy, unkempt black hair and a tangled beard. His eyes are large and seem to stare too long without blinking. He radiates a palpable aura of alarm and crushing terror, so strong it slips around whatever wards were built to contain him. He wears nothing but a set of gray boxers. He stands as I approach, a frown creasing his features. I narrow my eyes at him. I know who this is; I have unfinished business with his father and recognize the divine horror that clings to him like a shroud.

"Hello, Deimos," I say, pleased to see a creature of fear and misery like him imprisoned. "Any idea what your dad's been up to lately?"

"Should I know you, insolent little girl?" he asks, frown deepening. His voice echoes and multiplies, a thousand susurrations bouncing off the walls, hiding in dark corners, and crawling up my spine.

"She is the Lady of the Slain, Olympian mongrel," a voice snaps behind me, angry and commanding. I turn, smiling as I see its owner, and walk away from Deimos. "It has been a very long time since I have stood in the presence of one worthy of my respect," she says as I approach.

"Too long," I say, bowing at the waist and sweeping out an arm. "Hail, Sekhmet. Most honorable and courteous greetings to the hand of Ra. May your land be an unbreakable sanctuary to its people, and may your claws and vestments be ever soaked in the blood of the unjust."

She smiles, showing off an impressive set of gleaming canines. Sekhmet is ferocious and merciless, easily as dreadful as Deimos back there, but a protector as well as a destroyer. She has the sinuous body of a supermodel—thin, fit, and blessed with perfect olive skin—but her head is that of a lion's; a sleek savanna huntress melded perfectly at the neck with her feminine form. She's missing the bejeweled finery and snake-headed crown I remember from centuries past (little else sticks in my mind like fashion), but I don't think she's even a smidge less imposing or regal for it. She's wearing a sleek red dress accented with golden hieroglyphs, and while I can't fathom ever wanting the head of a cat, I'd be lying if I said I didn't envy the body it came with.

"Little comforts me in this wretched place, Lady Freya, and so I find your words all the more gratifying," she says in a satisfied purr.

She speaks with a thick accent, but her voice is light and wholesome—at least, while her anger is restrained. Few can rage like Sekhmet. "How long has it been?"

"At least five centuries, if I had to guess," I say after a moment's thought. "I remember parting ways after the Ottomans invaded." Wow, where'd *that* come from? I have trouble remembering much of anything past the 1800s. I thought most of my memories had faded along with my power. I'm a little proud of my recall, chalking it up to my returning strength and Sekhmet's presence.

"Ah, yes," she says, lightheartedness descending into menace. "Dark days." She pauses, and I can see the anger begin to rise behind those captivating feline features. "Part of me does not wish to know the answer, but as I see no guards accompany you, I must ask . . . are you an ally of my captors?"

I fix her with a stare that should—hopefully—speak volumes and say in a flat voice, "Yes."

She holds my eyes, and while I can see that anger rising further, there's a wonderful hint of understanding there as well. "They have made you their offer, then?" she asks. "And you accepted it?"

"It was the only way to get what I wanted," I say carefully, still holding her gaze.

"Belief?" she asks, and I can tell a great deal rides on my answer.

"*Revenge*," I reply, nodding ever so slightly at her and spreading my arms.

She keeps me waiting like that for seven terribly awkward seconds, eyes locked on mine as if they could peel the truth from my soul. "I see," she says at last, and to my vast relief I realize she *gets it*.

She was never one to hide her anger, after all—if she truly thought one of her ancient allies had gone over to the dark side, I imagine she'd have lunged at the glass, snarling with fury beyond measure. Her subdued reaction is all the confirmation I need.

I release a breath I hadn't realized I'd been holding and smile at her. "I take it you couldn't bear to compromise your values?"

She grins. At least, I *think* it's a grin. She's showing off a lot of teeth. "Of course. Even if I had, I would never have been able to maintain the charade. This place is *vile*, little fighter."

I give another microscopic nod and then shift myself, preparing to move away. "Perhaps you will get a new chance to prove yourself a useful ally. Perhaps you will not have to spend eternity in that cell."

"One can only hope, Freya," she says softly. "One can only hope."

I give her another bow, then walk to the last occupied room, located just beyond Sekhmet's on the right-hand wall. The rest of the cells are dark, lights turned off and their doors unlocked. I pause outside this final room, a strange mix of emotions barreling through me as I take in its occupant. There's an incredible sensation of disgust, irritation, and . . . *jealousy?*

"Oooh, hel-*lo* there, *chica linda*," the woman in the cell says, getting up and sauntering over to the glass. She's drop-dead gorgeous—a voluptuous, bronze-skinned mirror of myself. Her raven hair cascades around her shoulders, ending in little ringlets, and her features are inviting and pert. She's dressed in what used to be a gray jumpsuit marked with Finemdi's logo, but she's clearly made a few modifications to it, tightening, hemming, and flaring the fabric until it reads as more of a pit crew cheerleader's uniform than a prisoner's. All that's left of the original outfit are a sleeveless, midriff-baring top and very, *very* short shorts.

I hate this girl with every fiber of my being.

She's so like me, yet so *twisted*. They say familiarity breeds contempt, but what I'm feeling is more like territorial rage. It's hard to explain, but there's just something *off* about her, a sense of overloaded excitement that makes me feel like something sinister hides behind that promise of adventure and carefree pleasure. If you take the time to think about it, you realize this girl is not to be trusted. Something tells me she doesn't inspire people to sit back and reflect, however. Everything about her is impulsive, fast, and vaguely deadly. It's like looking at a glittering treasure in the middle of a tomb, knowing it's defended by traps and curses, yet desiring it all the same.

"Well, don't be shy," she says, looking me up and down and biting her lower lip. "I'd love to get to know you better."

"Who are you?" I ask, glaring at her.

She pauses, then tosses her head back and laughs. It's not a pleasant sound. "Shame. You would've been fun. I bet you're full of the most *delicious* secrets." She waits, grinning, for my anger to become visible on my face, then pushes herself up against the glass. "Call me Tlaz," she moans, her breath fogging the acrylic.

"Freya," I spit. I rack my brains, trying to figure out who this is. I'm guessing it's another deity from the southlands, though, which means I'm stuck. I *really* need to get more familiar with those gods.

"No wonder you're so frigid," she says, slithering against the barrier between us. "Give me a chance, child of the Vanir, and I can warm those proud bones of yours."

I must know who this is. It's like she's another god of love, but home to the darkest aspects of the concept—sensual and alluring, yet tainted. "You obviously know who I am," I say, trying to bury my disgust. "So why not make things even and tell me who you are?"

"How is *that* any fun?" she pouts. "What will you do for me in exchange? Or"—she tilts her head and looks up with a coy expression, fluttering her long eyelashes—"what will you do *to* me?"

I'm about to lose it and do something a little drastic, like try to put a fist through the glass, when Sekhmet's exasperated voice comes to me from down the hall. "Her name's Tlazolteotl. She's an Aztec god of sex and filth. Temptress and purifier, able to forgive sins and punish them as she sees fit."

Tlaz lets out an irritated sigh. "Who made you hall monitor, freak?" she yells. "Mind your own damn business!"

"When I am free of this place, I will bury my fangs in your throat, Aztlán savage!" Sekhmet shoots back.

"Brilliant plan! I'll enjoy watching you choke on a thousand infections, you absurd relic!" Tlaz screeches.

Sekhmet replies with a string of curses and the sound of claws against glass. Then Deimos cuts in, saying, "Will you mewling wenches *shut up*? I can barely hear myself think."

Tlaz unleashes a torrent of curses at both of them, and then the dog from the first cell begins barking. The ruckus continues for a few more seconds until there's a crackle from a hidden PA system, and the guard's voice blares out across the hall, saying, "Everyone, calm down immediately or I will activate the current for *all* of your cells!"

Silence falls in an eyeblink. Tlaz bites off the last string of insults, gives me a glare, and stalks back to one corner of her cell. She crosses her arms and sits down, fuming.

"Good," the guard says after a moment. "You'd better come out now, little lady. It's almost closing time, and I don't want them getting any more riled up."

I spare a last glance at Tlaz, who sticks out her tongue at me, and then turn on my heel to leave. Sekhmet's pacing in her cell, obviously worked up, but she pauses to fix me with another calculating stare as I pass her. I don't even give Deimos a look, but I can't help glancing at Izanami as I'm about to leave the hall. She's watching me with that same vaguely irritated expression. I give her a perky wave before wrenching the door open and leaving.

"Gotta be careful in there," the guard says as I enter his little waiting room. "Every one of them's different, but give 'em half a chance and they'll all kill ya."

Really? That's pretty obvious for most of them, but . . . "Even the Aztec fashion plate?" I ask, voicing my curiosity.

He shudders, reliving some particularly painful memories. "Especially her," he says in a soft, distant voice.

10

EYES ON THE PRIZE

Breakfast is, of course, spectacular. Blue corn waffles with bourbon syrup, crème brûlée French toast wedges, blueberry scones, lobster omelets perched on seared fingerling potatoes, and more. It's a fine consolation prize for having to spend another day in this blasphemous labyrinth. As much as I wanted to leave and spend the night in my own bed, I haven't yet gotten my off-site permit and, more important, I'm not going anywhere without Nathan, who's still unconscious. Considering how angry this place makes me, you may be wondering why I'm not fuming over this delay, but that's only because you're not eating these waffles.

I enjoy every last morsel with the Hawaiian sisters, chatting about the modern world and trying to wake myself up with a steaming cup of freshly roasted coffee. I also try to avoid looking at Samantha, who's sitting in her usual corner, sad and withdrawn as ever. I feel immensely guilty, but snooping around the facility is already going to start making Finemdi wary of me—if I want to lie low, I need to avoid other suspicious activities, like hanging out with their leader's daughter.

"So what's the deal with Tlaz?" I ask my companions after our lighthearted griping about modern man runs out of steam.

"Who?" they say together.

"The Aztec floozy in the detention block."

They all make various sounds of disgust. "Better off staying away from those people," Nāmaka says. "They're all trouble."

"I gathered," I reply. "But she's weird, and I want to know more about her."

"You mean she feels like competition and you like to know your enemies," Pele says, glancing up from her pancakes with a shrewd look.

"Or that," I say, smiling.

"Oh, come on—we can tell her," Hi'iaka says. "It's not like it's a secret or anything." Pele and Nāmaka shrug, and Hi'iaka gives me a look that says *See what I put up with?* before continuing. "She used to be a teammate here. Joined about half a dozen years ago after they picked her up in Costa Rica, I think. Everything was fine for a few months. Just another god, right? Then the deaths started."

"The human staff began dropping like flies," Nāmaka says. "Mostly the men, but some of the women, too. All of them succumbed to a terrifying combination of diseases. No rhyme or reason to it. They lost a *lot* of people until they began combing through security footage and put two and two together."

"Right, and by then, the death toll was well into the triple digits," Hi'iaka says, looking disgusted. "I mean, we're talking full-scale lockdown, quarantine conditions, the whole nine yards. Every day, more bodies got carted out. Things were *grim*, let me tell you."

"What did they find?" I ask, appalled and captivated at the same time.

"She was sleeping with them," Nāmaka says. "All of them. Like a kid in a candy store."

"More like a wolf among lambs," Pele mutters. "Most of them were married or in some sort of relationship, too."

"She wasn't even trying to destroy Finemdi, either," Hi'iaka adds. "It was just her nature. She looks for infidelity, leaps on the chance to expose perversity and deviance, and then judges them accordingly. Thing is, she would have been happy to forgive the people who were *already* being unfaithful if they came to her. She would even reward those who spurned her advances. Hell, she could *cure* other diseases they might have gotten, make them the picture of health. But for those who cheated with her?" She shudders.

"Biggest set of fatalities they've ever seen at Impulse Station," Pele says. "We've had gods cut loose on operations, mystical artifacts overload, and summoned creatures go berserk, but in all these years, nothing has done more damage than one wanton goddess."

Until me. "So she's been locked up since?"

Hi'iaka nods. "Straight into Corrections the second they found out it was her."

"What about the rest of the prisoners?" I ask.

Pele waves a hand. "Eh, picked up on various ops. They're all too deadly or unpredictable for Finemdi to just let them wander around."

"And they can't kill any of them because they might have enough believers to regenerate, right?"

"*Tch*. Bingo," Hi'iaka says, making a gun with her thumb and index finger and clicking them together with a wink.

"What about disbelief? Can't they deny them out of existence?" I ask. "I mean, it took Garen all of five minutes to threaten me with that one."

That gets me some frowns. "They've always been a little vague there," Pele says, thinking. "I get the impression they like to hold it over our heads, but actually pulling it off takes some real doing. Easier to just let them rot behind glass, I guess."

"Faith *is* one of the few things in this world that's harder to destroy than create," Nāmaka says. "Ideas are rather slippery in that regard."

"So they're just prisoners forever?" *How awful.* That could so easily have been me, too. Just a little less restraint, and I'd be right there alongside them.

Hi'iaka nods. "Best they can do is teleport them to another facility if anything goes wrong."

"Makes you wonder just how many prisons they have," I say. "How many gods they've captured . . . or destroyed."

She shrugs. "No idea. Probably a lot, though. They have all kinds of tricks."

And I'll need to discover every last one.

The rest of breakfast passes quickly, all pleasantries and pastries, and then I'm off for my first full day as a Finemdi employee. I'm scheduled for something called Divine Calibration in an hour, but my first stop is the Medical wing. I'm really looking forward to talking to Nathan, but when I eventually make my way down there, all I can do is peer at him unhappily through the glass in Recovery. He's still out cold. His chest rises and falls with slow, even breaths, and I watch him for a while, reassuring myself that at least he's alive. I hope he'll awaken soon; it's uncomfortably distressing, the idea that he might be injured. I look away from his sleeping form, confused. I've seen a *lot* of mortals die over the years, some very close to me. Death is nothing new. So why I am so distraught over the possibility of it happening to this one?

I turn back for one more look at Nathan. Maybe it's because he wouldn't be here if it weren't for me. Maybe it's because he's the first halfway decent friend I've had in decades, or maybe it's because he's just a halfway decent guy in general. Maybe it's some weird combination of all that and more. I couldn't tell you. All I know is I want him awake and safe.

With that cheery thought rattling in my head, I begin picking my way through Impulse Station's insane corridors. It only takes me twenty minutes to make it to my assigned room, which I count as a marked improvement. Still, considering it took me thirty to find Nathan, I'm just barely on time.

I enter the door marked *Calibration Suite 7* and find myself in what looks like a high-tech classroom. Sleek plastic desks are arranged in rows, executive office chairs on rollers behind each one. There's a podium at the front of the room, a digital whiteboard affixed to the wall behind it, and a projector built into the ceiling. Adam Carraway, bright and chipper as always, waits by the door. He beams at me as I arrive, clearly pleased.

"Ah, Miss Sara!" he says, sounding thrilled. "Right on time. Please take a seat anywhere and we can get started."

I suppress a groan as I notice Dionysus lounging in a chair on the right side of the room. He looks at me with those dancing eyes of his and grins. "Morning, gorgeous," he says. "Sleep well?"

"Like a baby," I say, pointedly taking a seat on the opposite side of the room from him. "Even had a chance to wander around a bit, see the sights. Did you know there's a beautiful lady in Corrections who'd just *love* to meet a dashing fellow like you?"

"Oh, really?" he says, looking interested.

"Third cell on the right."

"Umm, heh, okay, looks like we're all here," Adam says quickly, clearly uncomfortable with the idea of me playing matchmaker between Dionysus and an Aztec god of sex and sin. "What we're going to do today is put you both on the path to better, stronger believers." He clicks a remote in his hands as he moves toward the podium and the screen behind him lights up with a PowerPoint slide that reads *Divine Calibration: Setting you up for success!* I wonder if these presentations are provided by Finemdi or if Adam makes them himself.

"To do that, we need to get a better idea of precisely who you are." The slide changes to show a stick figure scratching his head while little question marks dance around him. "You see, centuries of competing myths, chronicles, and retellings have left things a little confusing for everyone. You each represent the concept of a deity, and there's only one of you in the entire world. You'll never see another Freya or Dionysus as long as you live . . . but there are hundreds of interpretations for both of you. Isn't that strange?"

The slide changes to a horde of illustrations of Dionysus and myself. I see him in painting and sculpture: a bearded man; a jolly, fat reveler; a lanky, smooth-skinned Grecian playboy; and so on. As for me, they're almost all drawings: warriors and chariot riders, noblewomen surrounded by flowers, and young ladies clutching trees. There are even a few pictures of a Japanese cartoon character and stills of a sword-wielding woman from a video game. It looks like someone did a Google search and pulled any decent image they could find. I glance at Adam, noting the proud look on his face as the images animate into place; I guess that answers the question of who made the PowerPoint.

"Somewhere along the way, enough people worshipped each of you as a deity to bring you into being. As time passed, followers new and old changed that image, adding fresh definitions and altering your appearances and personalities to match. Over the years, you've both been warped to fit a final prevailing mind-set—the last major vision your believers had of you before they vanished."

The slide changes to head shots of the two of us—the same pictures that were used to make our ID badges. "This is who you are now," Adam says, looking up at the screen. "And this is who we're going to have our volunteers believe in. Now, it's not that simple, unfortunately. These days, if someone wanted to start worshipping you, they wouldn't know where to begin. Sure, you'd be empowered by some of their belief—you're both still one of a kind—but it wouldn't be everything you deserve. It's inefficient!"

He clicks his remote and the screen changes to show our puzzled stick figure on one side, next to a bunch of arrows pointing at all the different pictures of the two of us. "What we're going to do is get a precise idea of *exactly* who you are—all your perceptions, desires, motivations, and so on—and use that to build a profile that'll help your believers target you." The slide animates, all but one of the arrows between the stick figure and the pictures disappearing. Then all those misleading archetypes fade away until only our two head shots remain. "See? It's a clear line from follower to god now, which means you'll receive *much* more power out of fewer believers."

He looks at the two of us and smiles, spreading his hands. "At first we'll just work on making you both stronger, but in time, you'll be able to make requests and change things about yourselves! Perhaps you have a crippling vulnerability, like Achilles?" He nods at Dionysus. "Or a weakness to some common element, like Baldur?" He grins at me. "All those chinks in the armor can be removed. Or maybe you'd like a new power? Something to spice up your own set of abilities? Think about it. Weaknesses stripped away and new strengths added in their place!"

Horrifying. I conceal my revulsion at the idea of meddling with the checks and balances with which we were born and glance over at Dionysus. His face is gleeful, mind whirling at the idea of such self-aggrandizement. Can't say I'm surprised.

"Pretty cool, right?" Adam says, going over to the podium and retrieving two packets of paper and some pens. "I'm going to give you both some surveys to fill out. I'd like you to be as exhaustive and honest as possible. The more precise you are, the more precisely we can believe!"

He sets down a sheaf of papers in front of Dionysus and hands him a pen. The god of merriment snatches it from Adam's hands and immediately begins filling out the form. Adam smiles at his enthusiasm, then walks over and places the remaining survey on the desk in front of me. "Here you are," he says, holding out another pen.

Cautious, I reach out and take it. Adam gives me an encouraging nod and then walks back to the podium, where he pulls out a smartphone and begins playing with it. I turn to the survey, filled with apprehension. Whatever they ask, I have to mislead them at every turn. If I'm accurate, it'll be like painting a bull's-eye on my chest. They'll know just who to target for rewards *or* ruin.

The survey's long and doesn't beat around the bush—there are no questions about my name, age, or physical traits. Instead, it launches right into detailed personal information, starting with *What is your purpose?* Then *What are your talents?* and *Describe your dreams.* That last one worries me, because it's one more sign that Finemdi has an uncomfortably detailed understanding of how deities work. I decide I need to be as vague as possible while still hewing close enough to the truth to make it seem like someone who *could* be Freya filled out everything out. Since they already know my specialties, I'll include them, but twisted in all the wrong ways. Question by question, a new version of me takes shape. She's a fickle, bloodthirsty god obsessed with desire and tokens of affection, encouraging rivalries and battle in her name, reveling in the wages of war if they will lead to her exaltation. She smiles on the unpredictable and hotheaded, granting her favors to those who lead with their hearts and always preferring decisions born out of lust and emotion, never rationality.

In short, a clichéd supervillain. They'll eat it up. After the initial battery of questions, there's a multiple-choice personality test, then a series of logic puzzles and hypothetical situations. I Christmas-tree the test, take a halfhearted stab at the puzzles, and answer the remaining questions as if I were a domineering baroness. Finished, I stack my survey, collect the pen, and turn it in to Adam, who seems a little surprised by how quickly I finished it. Dionysus, I see, is still hard at work, taking his time to answer each question as completely as possible.

"Thank you for your participation," Adam says, placing my survey in a folder marked *Freya*. "That's all we need for now, so unless you have any questions, I suppose you're free to go."

"Did you get my permit form?" I ask.

Adam smacks himself on the forehead. "Oh, almost forgot! My sincere apologies, Miss Sara." He rummages around in the pocket of his suit, then pulls out a laminated card with my picture on it.

"It's quite all right," I say, taking the badge and looking it over. It reads *Off-Site Permit* in large black letters at the top. I wave it at him. "Thanks, Mr. Carraway."

He smiles, seeming relieved I haven't decided to rage at him for this minor oversight. I really need to have a talk with my fellow gods about being nicer to mortals. I head out of the room, suddenly left to my own devices. Where to now? I could go and check on Nathan again, but I don't want to seem desperate. After all, if Finemdi thinks I care that much, they might use him against me. Yes, that's why. It's certainly not because I don't want to see him lying there helpless, feeling guilt and a host of other emotions I'm not in the mood to analyze.

That would just be silly.

I have my permit now, which means I can come and go as I please, but since I'm not leaving this place until Nathan can join me, it seems my only option now is to explore further. I turn back to my not-so-helpful map and try to figure out where else I can go. Maybe the research wing? Operations command? Security control? Or perhaps one of these unlabeled areas? There are plenty of rooms on the map that don't have any designations at all, and while I gather a lot of them are just residences, utility closets, and meeting rooms, there might be something juicy hiding in plain sight. After a bit of idly walking back and forth in the hallway, looking down at the map, frowning, trying to get my bearings, and gauging how interested I feel in exploring each area, I decide I'm turning into a stereotypical lost tourist and just pick the first thing I think of: Research. Along the way, I figure I can check out any unlabeled rooms and get the best of both worlds.

This plan seems great in theory. I'll get to cut through most of the complex, ferreting out all sorts of sinister plans and dark secrets. I feel excited, like I'm a private detective about to blow the lid off an evil conspiracy. Several hours later, I come to several stark realizations. First, I've missed lunch. I'm certain it was just as amazing as my previous meals, too, which makes its absence all the more painful. Second, exploring vast corporate complexes is incredibly boring. Nearly every room I pass is mind-numbingly utilitarian. Oh, look, a janitor's closet. Wow, an air-conditioning hub. Always wanted to see a server farm up close. Wonderful, there's the plumbing access. Conference rooms, staff offices, and break rooms, oh my. I swing through the residential areas and thrill to the sight of guest, guard, and god lodgings. As nice as they are, I'm glad for the permit and the freedom to stay off campus. I'd rather not spend any more time here than necessary—meals aside, of course.

I pass random security agents, lab personnel, cleaning staff, businessmen, deities, maintenance workers, and more on my tour. None of them pay attention to me, and they all look like they're actually doing something of value. For the first hour or two, I don't mind this. Around hour three, however, I start feeling a little resentful. I know I don't *actually* want to be confronted by anyone, nor do I really want a job here, but this is killing all my notions of what spying on an amoral company is supposed to be like. Where are the armed guards barring entry to suspicious vaults? The laser alarm systems? The air ducts I'm supposed to crawl through? This place was a whole lot more interesting in my imagination.

Another hour passes, and the sheer scale of the facility starts to dawn on me. I've literally walked for *miles* and haven't seen the end of it. There are multiple stories, and every floor feels like it covers the same area as a football stadium. How did they even *build* this place? It must have taken years. I mean, it even extends down into the basement for half a dozen sublevels, too, and while it's mostly all just maintenance there, it's still—

Wait, what? Confused, I stop in midstride to examine the map more closely. This is Florida. *Nobody* has basements this deep in Florida. The water table here is extremely close to the surface. I look at my map again, trying to make sense of what I'm seeing. This place is gigantic. I don't care how far off the beaten path you are; there's no way you can just build something this big and not have anyone get the least bit curious. I pull out my Mim and go to the local map, telling it to show me where I am. A blue dot appears just off Landstreet Road in the southeastern Orlando area.

"Magic," I say at last, narrowing my eyes at the facility map in my other hand. They have some fancy spells at work here, making the interior a *lot* bigger than it looks from the outside. That's how they can cram so much—including all those subterranean levels—onto a regular parcel of land and not have anyone realize what's going on. I look at my Mim's map again, zooming in to get an idea of how big Impulse Station's lot is. Judging by the little access roads on either side, it's just a handful of acres. Setting aside room for parking spaces, whatever's visible from the outside can't be larger than a basic warehouse—*and oh my gods I know how to destroy them.*

I barely manage to hold on to my phone as triumph roars through me. My lips pull back in a wicked smile, and I stagger against the wall for support. This is too good. If I can pull it off, well . . . it's going to be spectacular. I think I can do it, too. Magic is, after all, part of my portfolio. I just need some time to plan it out, but if I'm right about this, the results will be more than worth the wait.

Satisfied my tedious explorations haven't been in vain, I place my Mim back in my bag and continue on to the Research wing. Plenty of other unlabeled rooms call to me on the journey, but I ignore them—I feel I have what I need from this day already, and I'm not going to waste another second wandering around and poking my head into nondescript office spaces.

It's sometime in the midafternoon when I finally reach the labs. These are spread across multiple floors, but it seems like they share a lot of vertical space, probably to make a quarantine go more smoothly. The section I'm closest to is labeled *Hybridization Control*. Fun. There's another spot on the map called Belief Indoctrination nearby, but I have a feeling any investigations there are just going to end with me staring sadly at a roomful of sedated dreamers wearing creepy helmets.

The rest of the wing includes a few more enticing names, but they're even farther away, and I've already had my fill of wandering, so Hybridization Control it is. I reach the entrance in a few dozen steps, stopping when I notice the name of the section stenciled on the wall beside an unassuming metal door. I frown at the simplicity of the entrance, worrying this will end up just as boring as every other place I've passed today. Only one way to find out, I suppose. I swipe my key card across the access panel and get rewarded with a savage bleep of negation. Locked out. Well, I know how to handle this—all I need to do is wait for some errant worker to come by and charm them into holding the door open for a poor, helpless goddess who just wants to see the sights.

I lean against the wall beside the door, cooling my heels. My plan starts to feel less and less brilliant as the minutes tick by. After what seems like ages, I pull out my Mim and look at the time. Four o'clock? Where did the day go? Someone better show up soon, because I only have an hour left until they start serving dinner. That, and I want to be back in Recovery around six so I can see if Nathan's awake and, if so, hit the cafeteria with him before we head back to the apartment. Another ten minutes crawl by before I hear someone coming. Voices. No, wait, it's a single voice, bouncing off the walls around me, coming from behind me. It sounds masculine, so I put on my "distressed cutie" face—look, gender bias can be useful sometimes—and wait eagerly for its owner to make an appearance.

Moments before my mystery guest rounds the corner, I stiffen as I recognize who's speaking. "—don't care what your excuses are,

I want a full history before I go back out there! I nearly got myself killed the last time, and do you know whose fault it was?"

Garen. He's coming this way. I need to make myself scarce *now*. My shoes skid on the linoleum as I bolt for the far end of the hall, hoping I can make it before he rounds the bend.

"The *what?*!" he yells. "If the requisitions officer knew what I was getting myself into, he wouldn't have given me class-one garbage! *No!* It's *your* fault I didn't have the intel I needed, because guess what: That's the name of your *damn department!*"

I almost fall as I round the bend, flats clacking on the cheap floor as I whip to the side and screech to a halt. Breathing hard, I stagger against the corner and hug the wall, praying he didn't spot me. I can still hear his footsteps getting closer, but did I hide in time?

"Fine!" he shouts. "That's fine. Yeah, I'll just—yes, I'm going to file a complaint!" A pause. "Well, I don't care if there weren't any signs. This is your damn *job*! No, I don't—" He sighs, and I hear a fist smack against the wall. "Look, I have to go. Yeah. All right. *Mm-hm.* Trust me, it's mutual."

He grumbles to himself, followed by the sound of him pocketing the phone. I breathe a sigh of relief. There's no sign I've been noticed. Then I hear the whisper of plastic on fabric and a tiny clatter as he slots a key card into the door. He's actually going inside? I pop my head around the corner in time to watch Garen yank on the door's handle and wrench it open. He stalks inside without a moment's hesitation, letting the door slap against the wall from the force of his pull. It's wide open. *Well, Sara? What's it going to be: Follow your nemesis into the diabolical laboratory or wait outside and play it safe?* I watch the door begin to swing back, closing slowly on its hinges.

What the hell.

I launch myself down the corridor, shoes squeaking on linoleum as I race pell-mell for the rapidly closing portal. At the last second, I catch the handle, stumbling a little against the doorway as I struggle to keep it open and not pitch face-first onto the floor in the process. *Phew.* Reminding myself to invest in a pair of decent running shoes, I stand up and pull the door open. There's no sign of Garen, but a short hallway beckons to me. Quietly, I slip inside.

The building materials here are all noticeably nicer. The floors are made from some sort of glossy tile, the walls have an enameled look, and the lighting is less harsh. I move farther down the hall and see it ends in a T intersection. As I draw nearer, I hear a click from the right side—I guess that's where Garen went. Everything's so sleek and minimalist I feel like I've walked onto the set of a technology commercial.

Nervously, I pad to the edge of the hall and peer around the corner. There's a thick metal door about ten feet down. A sign above it reads *INCUBATION*. Figuring I'm not in any danger at the moment, I straighten up and walk to the door. It's very sturdy-looking, but there's no key card reader, so I shrug and test the handle, which turns without complaint. I open the door a crack and peek into the next area, then immediately slide it closed. Garen's in there, standing in some sort of strange changing room. When I glanced at him, he was pulling on a pair of white coveralls over his gray suit, zipping them up over his chest. The getup looked like something you'd see high-tech painters or asbestos removers wearing. I listen at the door until I hear him leave, then slip into the room.

There are rows of those same white coveralls hanging along the back wall, divided into size categories. The changing table across from them has hairnets, a box of gloves, face masks, and plastic slipcovers for your feet. I take it all in, then shrug and pick out a set for myself. If anything, wearing this stuff will help me blend in. It takes a couple of minutes to put everything on, but when I'm done, there's no way you could tell it was me—with the coveralls' hood up and a surgical mask drawn over my nose and mouth, my eyes are the only part of me showing. That just leaves my bag, which doesn't exactly go with the rest of my ensemble. I stare at it blankly for a few seconds before heading over to the rack of coveralls, moving a few of them to the side, and bending down to shove the bag in the corner. *There.* Once I let the outfits swing back into place, it's impossible to see the bag. That should work.

Hoping I haven't lost Garen completely, I open the inner door to reveal a sprawling laboratory. Researchers in getups just like mine are hunched over workbenches, probably hard at work uncovering secrets man was not meant to know.

At first I wonder how in the world I'm ever going to find Garen here among all these identical workers. Before I have a chance to begin looking, however, his grating, arrogant voice comes to me from just a few rows down. "Wait, this calls for another set to be extracted tomorrow," he says angrily, holding up a clipboard and speaking to another scientist. "Isn't that a bit soon?"

The man, about a head shorter than Garen, is looking up at him and glaring. "I don't recall you getting a say in our schedule," he says, snatching the clipboard out of Garen's hands. "And to be quite frank, I'm sick of you acting like we're just a different set of grunts to boss around. Kindly remember you are here as a *favor*, nothing more, and if I have to put up with one more minute of idiotic posturing from you, I will seriously consider revoking your clearance to enter these labs. Now, if you'll excuse me, *I* actually have responsibilities to attend to around here."

"Dr. Vargleiss, please, I—" Garen begins.

"Save it!" the man snaps. With that, he storms off, leaving Garen sputtering in silence. I try to fight it, but I can't keep an enormous smile from spreading across my face. I turn away on the off chance my attention will get me noticed. That was immensely satisfying. When I look back, Garen's already moving in a different direction, away from the little supervisor with the Napoleon complex. I do my best to follow him without raising suspicion, taking a leisurely walk between workbenches, chemical baths, and lab tables. Every now and then, I bend over and pretend to inspect random cell cultures and whatever else they're brewing. Finally, Garen reaches the far end of the lab, walks to another door, pulls it open, and heads inside. I go to follow, wait a moment for him to get a little farther away, then slip in after him.

I've entered another hallway, and this one makes me feel like I'm in more of a nursing home than a lab. On both sides, there are patient suites visible through large panes of glass. They're all empty, blinds pulled back to reveal identical hospital beds, IV stands, EKG monitors, and other equipment. I walk past a half-dozen rooms like this, glancing into each one, before I have to pull back and hide. Garen's in one near the end of the hall, and I think it may be the only one that's occupied.

I sneak over to peer in the window. He's leaning over the bed, looking strangely forlorn. There's a woman lying there in a hospital gown, a blanket pulled halfway up her chest. An IV snakes into her arm, delivering milky-white poison straight into her bloodstream. She's still conscious despite it, staring at Garen and talking to him in a weakened voice. My hearing is barely good enough to pick up their conversation.

"—like you've had a rough day," the woman in the bed says. *You're one to talk*, I think. She looks like she's been through the wringer; her skin is pale and waxy, her long auburn hair sprawls limply on the pillow, and her face seems taut and pained. Even so, I can see she was once beautiful. Though she looks like she's in her mid-twenties, she has a wise, motherly disposition and firm, commanding features.

Garen sighs and, in a startling display of humanity for such an unrepentant jackass, brushes a few strands of her hair back from her forehead. "Rough month," he replies.

"You ever catch that little Vanir girl you were looking for?" she asks.

He nods. "Yeah, we got her," he says softly.

She smiles, reaching up with a trembling hand to brush his cheek. It's such a warm, friendly gesture that my mind rebels at the idea of anyone using it on Garen. "Then why so glum?" she asks, frowning.

He looks away, turning to the bank of machines that monitor her vitals. "Because you're still here," he says. "I thought she'd be similar enough, that maybe they'd—" He shakes his head. "I don't know why I keep getting my hopes up. No matter how many I bring them, you'll still be here, and—"

177

"Shh," she says, patting him on the back. "Shh. It is what it is. Why dwell on it?"

"Why shouldn't I?" he says, turning back to look at her. To my deepest shock, I see his eyes are shining with tears.

"Well, I've given them hundreds of their little 'hybrids' over the years, and you're the only one who seems to care," she says, shrugging a little.

"That doesn't make it better, Mom," he says, his voice cracking.

Mom? The woman in the bed doesn't get a chance to respond, because I'm so shocked by this that I stumble a little against the glass, making enough noise to draw their attention. The woman just raises her eyebrows, peering at me curiously, but Garen whips around, furious, and fixes me with a stare that could freeze a star.

"Can't you see I'm busy?" he barks.

"I—um, sorry, I just . . ." I mumble, trying to think of an excuse. "Dr. Vargleiss sent me to tell you he doesn't want you upsetting the, um, patient, sir."

This only seems to enrage him further. "*Upsetting* her? That jumped-up son of a—"

"Language," the woman in the bed says, a bit of steel in her voice despite her damaged state.

Garen bites off his words and sighs. "Sorry, sorry." He composes himself, then picks up her hand and holds it for a moment. He looks at her sadly, then nods and turns to me. "Fine, I get it. He doesn't want me around," he says, harsher than I've ever heard him before. "I'll go for now, but you can tell him I'll be back to see her no matter *what* he says. I'll use a *tank* if I have to." With that, he gently sets down the woman's hand and leaves her room, glaring at me as he passes.

"Y-yes, sir," I say, flattening myself against the wall.

I turn to watch him leave. He doesn't even glance back—just reaches the end of the hall, flings the door open with a bang, and marches out. I let out a breath, thankful he didn't realize who I was.

"You're quite the actress." The woman's voice drifts out of the room behind me. Okay, so Garen might not have seen through my disguise, but she, on the other hand . . .

I spin around. "Excuse me, ma'am?"

"The meek-assistant act. It's very good. Hard for a goddess to pretend she's something she's not. I should know," she says, lifting a quavering hand and beckoning me to join her.

"You could tell?" I ask, entering the room cautiously.

She rolls her eyes at me. "Like you can't sense divinity when it's close."

I smile at that. "Fair enough."

"So who might you be?" she asks. "Can't say I've seen another god in . . . oh . . . some time."

I briefly consider lying to her. She didn't rat me out to Garen, though, so I figure I might as well be courteous. "Freya. Though I prefer Sara these days."

"Aah," she says, eyes gleaming. "The famous Vanir. Gave my boy quite the chase, didn't you? According to him, you were very . . . stubborn."

"Yeah," I say, moving closer. "Though in my defense, he didn't really make me feel like I had much of a choice."

"No, I suppose he wouldn't have," she says, sighing. "He's not a bad person, Sara. He's just trying to square things in his life. Make amends."

I sit on the bed beside her. This definitely doesn't sound like the Garen I know. "For what?" I ask.

"Me, mostly," she says. My confusion must show on my face, because she laughs. "Oh, you must be full of questions. But I suppose introductions are in order, first." She clears her throat. "I am Nantosuelta, of Gaul. Nature, earth, fertility, that sort of thing. Just call me Nan."

"Gaul?" I ask.

"Before your time. Celtics and such. We bit it early on, when the Romans came," she says, grimacing. A trembling hand rises toward me. "Pleased to meet you, all the same."

I clasp her hand in mine, feel the weakness in her, thin bones shifting under pale skin. This is a severely damaged god. "And I you," I say, trying not to let my pity show.

"So what do you think of Finemdi?" she asks, returning her hand to the blankets.

I pause, looking around, and she recognizes my hesitation immediately. "Oh, don't worry—they're not listening," she says. "My boy cleared this room ages ago."

"Oh," I say. "In that case, I think they're twisted monsters who need to burn."

She chuckles softly. "That they are, Sara. That they are." She takes a deep breath, a wheezy inhalation that doesn't quite seem to fill her lungs. "And you don't even know the half of it, I'm sure. Well, I can give you your answers, but you know what they say—be careful what you wish for."

"Tell me, Nan," I say, edging closer. "I never was one for warnings."

She grins. "Figured as much. Well, do you know *where* we are? The name of this wing?"

I pause for a moment, thoughts returning to the map. "Hybridization Control, I think."

"Right. Sounds so nice and clinical, doesn't it? Any guesses as to what *kind* of hybrids they're making here?"

I feel myself grow very cold. "You mean . . . *no*," I say, mouth dropping as I look down at her, aghast. "Tell me they're not . . ."

"Of course they are," she says. "Children of the gods receive many benefits: stronger, smarter, limited magic use, all sorts of good stuff. Partially solves the recruiting problem, too. Who needs to worry about résumés and job fairs when you can just breed your own workforce? It's been their policy for centuries now, though they've only perfected it in the past few decades."

I feel like I'm about to throw up. "They *make* you—"

"Oh no, no, not with this vile sludge keeping me weak," she says, gesturing at the IV drip beside her. "Can't carry anything to term like that. No, they just harvest what they need from me, then get a surrogate to finish the job." She pauses, taking in my reaction. "There. Told you it wasn't going to be pretty. Enjoy your righteous anger."

"So Garen—"

"Half god, yes. And so far the only one of my children who seems the least bit upset about it. Interesting boy. That's why he was so keen on getting you—on getting *any* new fertility goddess, really. He hopes he can persuade them to swap me out, put a replacement here. I guess he never got the chance; you decided to work with them after all, didn't you?"

I nod. "Only way I could see to get revenge," I say in a trembling voice. No wonder he was so upset when I took his offer. This also explains his incredibly vile attitude toward me. He was never *really* trying to get me to join Finemdi; he just wanted me so blindingly angry I'd refuse anything, forcing them to take me prisoner. All of it was an act, performed on the off chance he could persuade his superiors to release his mother and put me in her place. I can't say this makes him any less despicable in my eyes, but it *does* put a new spin on things.

"Smart girl," she says. "They're not very nice with the ones who refuse their pitches, as you can see." She gestures at herself with a feeble flap of one hand.

"So this is just . . . punishment?" I ask. "I mean, why else would they *do* this? A male god would be—"

"Much easier, yes. Of course they use them. And yes, this is, to a certain extent, a punishment for some rather"—her lips curl in a wicked smile—"*inventive* acts of rebellion on my part. There are other reasons, too. I believe they like variety in their stock. Perhaps they're trying to breed demigods, as well. It may also be because they are soulless, amoral scum. I don't ask why anymore. The answers never change anything."

"I'm getting you out of here," I snap, feeling the Valkyrie in my heart howl for blood, for death in the face of this mind-boggling injustice.

"*Pfft.* Don't bother," she says. "My time is done. Decades of this filth have left me a shell of what I once was," she says, gesturing at the drip again.

I reach out, aiming to tear it from her skin, but she pulls her arm away, shaking her head. "Enchanted," she explains. "Hercules would have trouble with it. Besides, its work is done. Rescuing me will solve nothing. But . . . if you are dead set on doing me a favor, then there are two things I will ask of you."

"Name them," I say without hesitation.

"If you truly believe you can succeed in razing this place, then please include me in that destruction. I want to die—to be free of this broken shell and this tedious suffering."

I open my mouth to object, but she silences me with a glare. "You can't imagine what it's like to sit and wait, alone, for someone to come and slice you open and remove the very thing you were *created* to cherish, constantly, for *years*. Kill me, Sara, and maybe one day I will have new believers and they will rebuild me, grant me a new body and a new life."

I stare at her, both moved by the gravity of her request and dismayed by how woefully reasonable it seems. *This poor woman.*

"You have my word," I say after a moment, trying not to let her hear the pity in my heart.

She gives me a vague smile, seeming to relax. "My second request won't be as easy to follow, but if you can, well, I'd like you to try not to kill Garen. He's not bad. Just . . . hurt."

I was afraid she might say something like that. But it sounds like she understands what she's asking. To change the mind of a god on the path of vengeance is no mean feat. We are, by nature, more inclined to punish than forgive. "I—I will *try*, Nan. But you're right—it will be hard. He hates gods so much, and if he survives and realizes it was my hand that released you, he will never stop hunting me."

She nods, closing her eyes. "I know. Trying . . . is all I ask."

"*Why* does he hate us so much?" I ask. "Why not Finemdi? They *are* the ones that did this to you, aren't they?"

Her lips twitch. "To Garen, Finemdi is playing the hand it has been dealt. They are doing everything in their power to right what he sees as a terrible wrong—the creation of gods. The fact that I am his mother is, perhaps, part of this view, because as he sees it, if there were no more gods, then there would be no more need for me to be here, to be punished." She opens her eyes to give me a bleak, painful stare. "He blames *you* for this, not Finemdi. For him, every god in existence has played a role in my torture simply by *existing*, by unbalancing the world through their very nature. He believes there will always be a need for something like Finemdi to exist, always be a need for someone to rein in the heavens . . . but he does *not* believe there must always be gods. *That* is why he follows them, and why he despises you."

"That's insane."

She shrugs. "He has been burned, yet rather than blame the arsonist, he has chosen to blame the fire, because once the fire is gone, well . . ."

"No one will ever be burned again," I finish. I'm silent for a moment, trying to add this to what I know of Garen. "Still, to *work* for the people who enslaved his own mother . . ."

"Imagine you are born here, Sara," she says. "Finemdi is all you know. The company is your caregiver, your home, your family. You're raised to believe in their goals, and for years, you hunt dangerous, callous, and depraved gods. You make the world a better place. You feel *complete*. Then one day you wonder where you came from. You do a little research, and you find your mother, and she's right here, at home. She's a horrible, nasty goddess, of course, but you're curious. So you go meet her, and she's not dangerous at all. She's just this broken old woman who still loves you, in spite of it all." She pauses, and gives me a sad look. "Now what do you do?"

"I—I can't begin—" I stammer. *How horrible.* Despite my hatred for her son, I can't help pitying him, just a little. No one should have to be in such a situation, not even him.

"You really have two choices, don't you?" she continues. "Turn your back on everything you've ever known for a mother who's barely been in your life, or keep working for, as you said, the people who enslaved her."

"And he chose the second," I say, feeling a little of my anger return.

"Not exactly," she says with a tiny smile. "He still thinks he can find a way to free me. He thinks he can have his cake and eat it, too—that Finemdi will see reason and he'll keep the mother he loves and the job that makes him feel whole. In his heart of hearts, he thinks he's doing the right thing."

I take a moment to digest that, tumbling it around with my other thoughts, then meet her gaze. "What do you believe?" I ask her.

She holds my eyes for a long time, then shakes her head. "I wasn't made to believe. I've been forgotten and tormented by the ones who were," she says. "All I know is that I am tired, and would like to rest. It was nice meeting you, Sara."

Without another word, she closes her eyes and leans back on her pillow. I stand there for another minute, dumbstruck by what I've discovered, then turn to leave. I must find Nathan. I must get out of here and create a real plan to destroy this place.

I must do many things, but for now, as I move back among the researchers and employees of Finemdi, all I can think is that I must not cry.

11

THE LONG HAUL

I hate waiting.

You see, I never thought about what to say to Nathan when I saw him again—stupidly, I just assumed I could spill it all, bring him up to speed with a whirlwind tale of skulduggery and adventure. What I'm holding on to is basically some of the best gossip I've ever had. The moment I rush to his side in Recovery, I so badly want to tell him everything. Then I remember where I am—remember there are cameras, microphones, suspicious staff—and realize I can't tell him a damn thing. Fortunately, he's still a little groggy, so he doesn't ask too much. I shush him and tell him to rest for now.

I have to wait until we're off-site and certain they haven't bugged any of our things. It is *killing* me. The look in his eyes tells me he understands there's definitely *something* going on, that I haven't lost my mind while he was asleep, but to censor everything I say is completely at odds with my character.

I have to get out of here. I decide to skip dinner, which is, admittedly, another choice at odds with my character, but at this point it's the lesser of two evils. I don't even bother trying to navigate to the exits on my own, either—I flag down the first guard I see and have him escort Nathan and me off the property, flashing my permit and ID badge every chance I get. As we head out, I start to get an idea of their security systems and realize why it's been relatively easy to go wherever I please *inside* the base; they have an outright ludicrous array of defenses, checkpoints, and armed personnel guarding the entrances.

X-ray machines, body imagers, and no less than three biometric scanners (hand, iris, and voice identification) form the frontline defense, but if someone manages to breach them—or trip an alarm—then the turret nests, guard stations, and pressurized bulkheads will probably make short work of any intruders. There's also an off-key buzz in the back of my head, a distant thrum of hidden magic that tells me everything I've seen so far is probably just the technological half of Impulse Station's defensive line. I have a hard time picturing an unauthorized *god* getting in here, let alone a mortal.

It takes us nearly five minutes just to *leave* once we reach these exits, guards checking us to confirm we're not trying to smuggle anything off-site, but at long last, we step out into the waning Florida sunlight, free. I have to admit, I was worried they'd try to pull us back in at the last second. Since he's an official "retainer" of mine, Nathan is supposed to have the same freedoms I've been granted, but I wasn't about to trust Finemdi to keep their word. Now that we're out, it looks like they were telling the truth. It's early evening, the sky is still relatively bright, and only a handful of stars have begun to make an appearance. We're standing outside a nondescript warehouse, clearly not even a tenth the size it would need to be to contain everything I've seen. The parking lot is filled with all sorts of vehicles, and I pray ours is among them. Just how thorough *were* they when they retrieved us from Disney? I brandish the keys to the CR-V like a talisman, holding them high above my head, and give a hopeful click. In the distance, there's a flash of lights and a little beep.

"Yes!" I say, grabbing Nathan and striding toward our car.

"So, about, um, *everything* . . ." he begins, letting me guide him away from the building.

I turn and give him a look. "In a bit," I say, gesturing at our cloth-ing and shaking my bag. "I want to get home and get 'comfortable.'"

He gives me a quizzical stare for a moment, then motions at the building behind us and holds a hand to one ear as if he's on the phone, mouthing *They listening?* as he does. I nod as I give him an expression that says *Obviously!* and then grab his arm and continue my march to the car.

Once we get in, and he navigates out of the parking lot and onto the streets, I lean over and turn the radio way up. Over the din of some heavily Auto-Tuned pop music, I yell at him, "Sorry! I'm just worried we're bugged!"

"I got that, yeah! When can we talk?" he shouts back.

"Let's get home, change out of these clothes, leave the phones behind, and take a walk!" I reply.

"Sounds great!"

It's fully dark by the time we get back, but the apartment complex is in a nice enough neighborhood that nobody looks twice at two young friends out for a stroll. It feels good to be out of Impulse Station, out of their clothes and away from gadgets I'm not certain I can trust. It feels even better to be doing all this with Nathan at my side.

"I was worried about you," I say, giving him a hug.

"I didn't even have *time* to worry," he admits, smiling. "One moment we're knocking out a lousy god of wine, the next I'm waking up in a hospital bed and there's a nurse telling me everything's fine and she's calling your cell phone. What the hell *happened*?"

There are so many incredible things to talk about I feel like I might start drooling. "The organization Garen works for is called Finemdi. It's this huge world-spanning company, and that was just *one* of their facilities back there. They're beyond evil; we're talking twisted, sadistic people, Nathan. Forget about Garen. We have to wipe them *all* out."

"What?" he says, taken aback. "Wait—back up a step. We're killing a whole company now?"

"Eh." I waggle a hand. "Just most of it."

He frowns. "Um, being anticorporate is topical and all, but isn't that a bit extreme?"

"Hardly. You haven't seen what I have."

"Yeah, but . . . it's like you're talking about declaring war here."

I nod eagerly. "Yes! *Exactly* like that."

"Sara, this—I mean, how long was I out? Last I heard, you wanted to get away from these guys, not fight them. What'd I miss?"

"A lot of really sick things, Nate. The world will be a better place without them in it. Trust me. Let me give you the full story, and then you'll—"

"Hang on," he says, fidgeting. "I want to hear it, but I'm going to go out on a limb and assume the spoiler is that they're *really bad* and deserve some serious smiting. Now, are you asking me what I think you're asking?"

I spread my hands, feeling a little bashful. "War *is* part of who I am, Nathan. You don't have to help me if you don't want to, but this kind of opportunity? Oh, it's *good*. Glory, vengeance, and a cause worth fighting for? Take it from a girl who knows: They don't come around often."

He considers this, gauging my obvious conviction against whatever misgivings he might have about getting pulled into a quest to destroy a global corporation. "Whatever happened to Disney princesses and life on the run?" he asks at last.

"They . . . well—"

"Can't we just . . . disappear again?"

I pause, looking at him, feeling the concern and frustration bubble in his heart, and actually consider it. He's not wrong. I didn't start this adventure wanting revenge, didn't intend to go to war with anyone. I wanted to be left alone. We could totally manage it, too, especially now that I know there are other ways to empower myself beyond worshippers. Freedom, power, and adventure. It's all there, just waiting for me to take it, wrapped up in a choice that's safer, smarter, and *way* less likely to get innocent people—like Nathan—killed.

I could do it. The Valkyrie would scream bloody murder, but *I could still do it*. Oh, how I've changed. Turns out I did myself a favor with all those years of apathy and self-doubt: I have free will, maybe more than any god before me, and I really could see myself bowing out of this whole mess to live life to the fullest with my new friend.

Then Nan's room and its pitiful contents flash through my mind, and I know the truth.

"We could, Nathan," I say, feeling like I've been strung up between two trees. "It's certainly the wisest choice for us both. But there's so much evil there, so much hurt. I can't set it all aside, not in good conscience. *This cannot stand*, my priest."

"Yeah, but . . . Sara, the *world* is full of bad stuff. Why does this have to be on us?" He runs a hand through his hair, conflicted. "No, I don't think—"

"Nate, please," I cut him off, feeling tension squeeze my heart. "Really consider this. Think about what's important. Life is more than finding what you can live *with*—it's about finding something to live *for*."

He frowns, thinking it over, and, well . . .

Okay, you know that moment when you're talking about *really important* stuff with a close friend? The one where you lay out your dreams and desires, then watch them as they weigh it all, standing on pins and needles as you dearly hope they'll end up siding with you? That one?

Well, this is one of those moments, and as I'm waiting and worrying, all that anxiety gets the better of me. It's barely a conscious choice, what I do—more a reflex than anything else—but it's enough to change everything. It also makes me a horrible, awful friend, because as I watch him teeter between decisions and face the possibility he might really leave me, I find myself reaching out with my will and giving him the tiniest, faintest *push*. Just a little urging to join me, fight by my side, and risk everything for glory.

I know I could do this without him. He'll be *safer* if I do. So why betray his trust like that? Why make the decision for him? Because I'm a shallow asshat of a goddess filled with selfishness of the purest, most damaging sort, that's why. For all my bluster and arrogance, I'm too weak to let a friend even *consider* leaving me. The damage is done, too. I can see that little impulse ricocheting around his mind, building and snowballing, rising up as a Valkyrie of his own.

Then he snaps his head down in a nod, and I know I've taken away his choice. "Never thought about it like that. Well, all right. Guess we're not hiding anymore," he says, making it clear he's with me. "That didn't take long."

I smile, even though I'm screaming on the inside. In practically the same breath, I've just marveled at how I can actually exercise free will, then stolen it from my only friend in the world.

I'm so sorry, Nathan, I think desperately. *I'll find a way to make it up to you. I promise.*

I give him another hug, hiding my expression over his shoulder in case that little war of emotions made its way to my face. "Thanks, Nate," I whisper.

He hugs me back, then pulls away after a moment, looking curious. "So how are we even talking about this?" he says. "I mean, last I heard, Garen was out for blood and it was either going to be him or you. One mini coma later, and they're letting us walk out like we own the place."

"I'm actually very proud of that," I say, glad for the chance to focus on something else.

I use his question as a springboard to launch into my tale, beginning with the moment I woke in restraints and carrying on through my supremely unsettling conversation with Nan. When I'm done, Nathan looks suitably blown away by all the news, and we've probably circled the apartment complex half a dozen times. The moon is high in the sky, and even though most of the stars are drowned out by lights from the buildings around us, I think I can make out a few constellations. As I do, I feel an unexpected yearning for the old days, when the air was clearer, the night skies glowed with stars beyond counting, and you met your foes on the field of battle and hacked at each other with giant swords like civilized human beings. Now I get to watch myself bumble around in my best friend's mind while my enemies commit crimes against nature and hide behind tailored suits.

"Unbelievable," Nathan says. "Okay, so they're evil squared. I get it. Do you have any idea how we're going to take them down?"

"More than one, actually. It's all a mess right now, but I have time. My official Finemdi schedule doesn't have me doing any real dirty work until my training's complete, and that will take months. Plenty of hours in those days to get stronger and plan."

"Well, I don't have to tell you I'm with you to the bitter end, right?" he says, glancing at me.

"No, but it's always nice to hear," I say with a shrug, trying to be all nonchalant and hoping my guilt doesn't show on my face.

"Great, because when it's time to invade these guys, I want to make sure you're not going to leave me behind just because I'm a mortal."

"When did you get so suspicious?" I say with a laugh.

"Sara, I've seen enough movies to know how this works—and I think you have, too. You're going to need all the help you can get."

I give him a pained look. *I can't do this.* "What if . . ." I grimace. "Nathan, what if it wasn't your choice?"

He frowns at that. "What do you mean?"

"Remember our kiss in the restaurant? That spillover effect I have on the people around me? Well, love's not the only thing I was made to spread. What if you want to help me pick a fight with Finemdi because it's *what I want?* What if I took away your choice just by being near you?"

I mean, I *did*, but I can't bring myself to admit that to him, not so soon.

He shakes his head. "It was still my choice to *be near you* in the first place. Okay, not, like, when you stole me out of Inward, but after, in my apartment? I chose to follow you, Sara. This is just more of the same."

"You don't even know that," I say, feeling miserable. "It's not like I can turn love and affection off like a light switch. There was still a bunch of it left in your brain. You may have never made a truly free choice since you met me. Do you realize that?"

He tilts his head to the side and just stares for a moment. I rub my arms, watching as he weighs it all, and do you know what the worst part is? *I want to do it again.* I want to make sure he picks me, now and forever, even though taking that choice away from him is what started all this in the first place. My self-loathing peaks a little at that, and I turn away, trying to hide the oncoming waterworks. *I suck, I suck,* I suck.

"Nature or nurture, huh?" Nathan says at last.

"What?" I say, turning back to him.

He smiles ruefully and raises a hand to brush away one of my tears. "I'm not the same person I was when we met, I'll give you that—but you're not, either. We all change, Sara. That's life. Everyone and everything we meet has a say in it. Friends, family, advertisers . . . If I'm making this choice because you played a role in it, then good; at least it was someone I trust."

Oh, great. "And if I don't deserve that trust?"

He shrugs. "Not your choice."

"But it—"

"Look, I've made up my mind: I'm helping you," he says, rolling his eyes. "Now tell me *how*."

I sigh. Maybe he's right. Maybe he would've picked me anyway, without my meddling. It's cold comfort in the face of a deeply personal betrayal, but fine. Dwelling on this gets me nowhere, and right now, there is a *lot* to be done. When all this is over and Finemdi's in ashes, then I can sort everything out and make amends . . . right? In the meantime, Nathan is my responsibility, and if he's dead set on helping, then I will *not* have his blood on my hands. I got him into this, and I'm going to make sure he gets out. It's high time I taught him how to survive in a god's world.

"All right," I mutter, wiping away the last of my tears and straightening up. "But you're going to need to train. Get ready, because you're about to learn what it means to be a true priest of mine."

"Can't wait," he says, relaxing. "Though I think it's customary for generals to high-five on the eve of battle." He holds up a hand, expectant.

I can't help laughing. "Is that what they do now? Knew I was out of touch . . ." I say, then haul back and slap his palm with mine.

And that's that. Nathan is at my side, happy to follow me into the fire once again. The only difference is that, this time, we're doing a bit more than starting new lives together—we're kicking off a *war*.

There's a strange routine to the following weeks. I have to admit, those years in seclusion at the Inward Care Center keep coming back to help me. This time, it's in accepting a certain monotony despite every instinct telling me it's time to act. I throw myself into my work at Disney, picking up as many shifts as possible and attending as many special events as they'll give me. I'm going to need every scrap of belief I can wring out of these parks if I'm to have any hope of surviving what's to come. At the same time, I have a schedule to maintain at Impulse Station. There are new "calibration" tests and character assignments to distort and lots of training sessions I need to attend. Every day is a jumbled mix of gleeful childhood innocence and skin-crawling corporate malevolence. Part of me wants to attack immediately, to cut loose and do what I can to bring the place down. It's only through sheer force of will that I keep myself in check. I need to be patient, and, as I may have mentioned before, that never was my strong suit.

Finally, in the evenings after we return to our Finemdi-free apartment, there are the lessons with Nathan. Gods can't be every-where at once, you see, and for times when we need things done in distant places, our most trusted clergy can be sent to do the dirty work for us. To enable them to speak and act in our names, we can empower them with a fragment of our strength. It's kind of like reversing the flow of belief, turning that spark of power back on its source. It's draining, of course, but done carefully, it allows us to represent ourselves around the world. In short, we can grant our worshippers limited powers not unlike our own. For a lowly god like myself, it won't be much, but if he can get the hang of it, it will still give him an edge over any normal human.

Besides these lessons in wielding my gifts, Nathan's doing whatever else he can to help, researching Finemdi and the handful of gods my budding plans revolve around. With all these responsibilities between the two of us, it's starting to feel like the only time I get to spend time with him as a friend is when he's shuttling me around to various locations. Still, it's not like we can step back and smell the roses—our quest is more important than hanging out together, and though it kills me to wait, there will be plenty of opportunities to relax when I've wiped this branch of Finemdi off the map.

I know I'm asking for trouble. I've seen every kind of relationship imaginable, and if I were being honest with myself, I'd focus on how often people come to regret passing up opportunities for fun with good friends. It's just . . . impossible. It's not in me to resist the siren song of adventure and retribution. Oh, I know the lessons, but if you think ordinary people have trouble learning from the mistakes of others, you should see how badly gods get it. We're caricatures of you, after all, padded to the extreme with excessive personalities, vibrant flaws, and conflicting desires. One of the obvious (and unfortunate) results of this extraordinary pedigree is that it tends to set us at odds with ourselves. It's infuriating, too, because we've all lived long enough to be able to tell sensible choices from terrible ones, and yet all too often we must follow our personal philosophies rather than choose what is best for ourselves—or those we care about.

I'd like to think I'm better at it than most, but I can't resist everything. Maybe if I had a chance to distance myself from Finemdi, to spend some time away, I could calm my inner Valkyrie and go the slow and steady route instead of this fiery one, but my constant visits to Impulse Station only serve to reinforce my hatred. It feels like each session brings some new outrage against the divine.

You see, after the personality tests, there were the classes.

Apparently, Finemdi is under the impression that gods need to branch out, intellectually. Dionysus and I end up taking what I can only describe as a senior citizen's community college sampler. Everything is geared toward practical skills and navigating the modern world. There are classes on using computers and the Internet. Current events, pop culture, and world history. Everyday technology (*yes*, I know how to use a microwave!) and financial advice. I have to take driving lessons, conversational etiquette courses, and modern style seminars, including makeup and poise. A rather imposing lady named Patricia Méreaux replaces Adam for the female-oriented sessions, and I thankfully don't have to spend them with Dionysus.

Patricia is very knowledgeable about her areas of expertise, but it's a distant, almost patronizing sense of intelligence. "When did you start doing your own makeup?" she asks during our first Practical Cosmetics tutorial.

"The fifties," I reply. "Met a nice Avon lady who taught me.

Before her, I had it done at salons, and before that, I had the help of ladies-in-waiting. Oh, and I had to learn how to do my own princess makeup for Disney."

She sniffs. "The fifties, yes. That would make your techniques somewhat out of date."

"Well, I'm over a thousand years old," I say, feeling surprisingly defensive. "What's fifty years here or there?"

She fixes me with a shocked expression like I've just asked what was wrong with drowning kittens, then says, "We'll start with foundation."

Don't get me wrong, some of this stuff is actually useful. Learning how to walk in high heels, for instance, was a skill I'd been meaning to reacquire. The last time I wore them was in the French courts—it would have been social suicide not to, no matter how awkward they felt—and it's always been something I've regretted not taking the time to relearn. So yes, Finemdi is helping shore up certain holes in my knowledge. Regardless, it's utterly galling to be treated like a child. I didn't ask for these lessons, and I don't like the implications they bring. I got along just fine before I knew how to use a colorless lip balm with shimmer to create the illusion of larger lips, thank you very much.

I linger outside my classroom after we're finished, stuffing my homework (style guides and makeup tasks, yay) into my purse as I wait. After a few minutes, Nathan arrives. He's here for classes, as well. Some of it is just rules and regulations, but most of his time is apparently focused on making him the perfect mortal representative of the divine.

"How was it?" I ask as he walks up.

He grimaces. "Hope they grade on a curve."

I frown at that. "That bad? You're easily the best high priest I've had in centuries."

That gets a smile out of him, but it's quickly followed by a shrewd look. "Aren't I the *only* high priest you've had in centuries?"

"Well, I'd love to stay and chat, but I have a Corporate Enrichment class starting in a few," I say, grinning.

He rolls his eyes. "It's just . . . apparently I have no idea how to be a priest. I mean, they started asking about your pantheon and things like sacrifices, divine rites, offerings, and on and on, and I was all, 'Dur, she likes chocolate.' You know?"

I shrug and start heading off down the hall. "I'm not big on rules; we were always a fairly lawless bunch. Sorry it's made your classes awkward, but I just want merry little worshippers—all the other stuff is noise."

"So long as you're happy," he says, falling into step beside me.

"With you? Absolutely, Nathan. I mean, you could always stock more ice cream, but nobody's perfect."

"More?" he says, legitimately shocked. "At this rate, I should open a Ben and Jerry's franchise. Could make it the world's first combination Church of Freya and ice-cream parlor."

"Done," I say, actually delighted by the idea. "When do the doors open?"

"Soon as they finish testing the new Freyaberry flavor," he says, and I laugh with him.

We walk in silence for a minute, still smiling, and then he gets a thoughtful look. "What *did* your religion look like, Sara? I mean, your worshippers and everything, back home."

I sigh. "Oh, Nathan . . . you'd have better luck with a historian there. It's been so long and I've forgotten so much. Anyway, even if I did remember it all, what would it matter? I made the choice to leave Europe behind a long time ago, and that includes the old ways."

He looks at me, obviously curious, but I shake my head. I don't mind telling him about my past, but it's not something I want to get into here. "Story for another time. Anyway, I wound up in America and decided to stay put. Seemed safer."

"Okay, that's fair." He frowns as a thought strikes him. "Though it doesn't explain what everyone else is doing here. There's, like, a zillion gods hanging around this place. Did everyone just happen to make their way stateside?"

I stop walking. I hadn't really considered it before, but he does bring up a good point. "No, I don't see why they would . . ." I say after a moment. "Finemdi must have brought them over. Many of their power bases are still in the Old World, after all. It doesn't make sense for them to be here, otherwise."

"Besides Dionysus?"

"Ugh, yes." I sneer. "He must've followed the trail from Euro Disney."

"I guess that makes sense." He looks around the hall, and I can see his mind wandering back to our current situation. "Is the entire place like this?" he asks.

"Boring and confusing?"

He pulls out his facility map and shakes it with a bewildered expression. "That, and a little terrifying. You're not getting a sense of 'death is near'? The whole place feels like a trap."

"No, but I'm also a god. Death is very much a stranger to us."

Nathan stares at me, surprised. "Sara, this place is *dangerous*, even for you. Like, see those plastic blisters near the ceiling?" He points, and I follow his finger to a little black half dome set into the wall. "There are cameras everywhere, guards watching, and freakin' *pantheons*—plural—just itching for a fight. These guys know how to take down *gods*. We have to be careful as hell."

"Huh," I say, stopping to look at the camera. I give it a wave, then keep going. "Never really thought about it before. I mean, you're right—if I actually stop and turn my brain on, it's probably the scariest place I've ever been, but the way it's presented . . . it doesn't really register as a problem."

He shakes his head. "Attack gods, industrialized blasphemy, a global conspiracy to kill or capture you . . . and it feels *dull*?"

I nod. "Profoundly. It's not at all what I expected. I know it's silly, but a part of me still hopes to raid imposing castles on stormy mountain spires. Instead, I get a stupidly large office building."

"You should write a letter. 'Dear Finemdi, please have a more evil headquarters for me to hate,'" he says, miming a handwritten note in the air as he walks.

"Yes, thank you! Would it be too much to ask?" I say, laughing again as we head to our next classes.

I'm glad for the humor, because that Corporate Enrichment session is minutes away, and I need all the lightheartedness I can get to keep my inner Valkyrie locked down. These are perhaps the most infuriating of all my required courses, as their entire purpose is to discern how my powers can benefit Finemdi. Apparently, most of the organization's funding comes from the calculated exploitation of its divine talent pool.

All too soon, I'm listening to Adam tell me more harrowing things about how we can help the company. Dionysus, for instance, is getting tapped for his powers of wine-making and revelry. He will be responsible for producing a series of top-shelf vintages to be sold through a Finemdi-backed corporation at outrageous prices, and all he'll need to do is visit a storage facility once a year to replenish their stocks. On missions, he will be called in to compromise and even topple key structures with a crushing bloom of grapevines, as well as distract guards and enemy staff with euphoria and the irresistible urge for merriment. Listening to these fledgling plans, I feel a strange mix of curiosity and disgust; part of me would love to know the true nature of such "missions," but that's tempered by the certainty that whatever benefits Finemdi can't be good.

At least I'm off the hook for now. Since I'm currently deemed too weak for fieldwork, my responsibilities won't be assigned until I have a few cycles of intensive belief therapy under my belt. Adam is, however, quick to reassure me that my likely duties will be corporate espionage and intelligence-gathering, since I can charm anyone into trusting me.

"Of course, this is just what we've come up with so far," he says at the end of his presentation. "We're always open to suggestions on making Finemdi a smarter, stronger place to work. After all, who better than yourselves to tell us how to use your abilities?"

"Who indeed?" Dionysus says, leaning back in his chair. "Well, no offense to our dear lady Freya, but I, too, am quite capable of twisting mortals around my little finger. I could just as easily perform these acts of espionage as her, *without* the waiting period." He glances over at me and smirks.

Yeah, keep smiling, pal.

"Wonderful!" Adam says, making a little note on his smartphone. "That's exactly the sort of thing we want to hear." He glances up at me, suddenly seeming a little worried. "Er, that's not to suggest you won't be helpful, Ms. Vanadi—we're well aware of your status in the myths as a spell-caster. Gods with full access to even one school of magic are very rare, and we understand you are skilled in enchantment, divination, and more. You may not be at full strength yet, but please understand how appreciated your talents will be in the months and years to come!"

"Of course," I say flatly.

"Now, just to get you focused on other possibilities, we have a little slideshow of some of our deities and the interesting ways they've been able to help us over the years. This is intended to get you thinking outside the box! Remember, there's nothing wrong with a little creativity!" Adam says, pocketing his phone and clicking his presentation remote.

A slide with a picture of a motherly woman appears on the screen. Even captured as a still image, she radiates security and affection. "Ah. Hestia," Dionysus says.

Adam nods. "I thought you might recognize her." He turns to me. "Hestia is the Grecian goddess of home and hearth, associated with the upkeep of one's lodgings and ever-burning fires of greeting and warmth. For Finemdi, she keeps the lights on at all of our facilities. Every time we build a new base, Hestia comes by to bless it with unending 'fire'—which, in these days, equals electricity. Basically, her gift allows us unlimited power consumption at all of our stations, letting us stay completely green *and* off the grid!"

Free energy from the gods. Hubris, thy name is Finemdi. The slide changes, this time to a burly, fair-skinned man with a bob of blond hair that makes him look like a medieval page. He seems like he should belong in my pantheon, but I don't recognize him. "This is Ilmarinen, a Finnish blacksmith and artificer," Adam explains. "Finemdi was able to persuade him to reproduce his most famous work, the Sampo. Though it took the assistance of several deities to provide enough raw materials and the extreme heat needed for the forging, the finished product is a magic mill that produces limitless quantities of grain, salt, and gold."

He clicks the slide again, and an image of a vast underground vault appears, filled with stacked pallets of gold bars. I feel a pang of desire for them. I think of the jewelry collection I could commission from that place, then shake my head and try to focus. Stupid urges. "Essentially, Finemdi may now act as the world's largest supplier of these three vital resources, reaping all the financial and political benefits one might associate with such a monopoly," Adam continues. "Of course, we are careful not to overplay our hand, lest the markets collapse."

Impressive and appalling, all at once. How many artifacts have they acquired over the years? I think back to Garen's magic bracelets and those pearl-tipped spears at the prison and realize it's probably a *lot*.

Another slide appears, this time showing a dark, terrifying man. His stringy black hair is thrown in disarray, hanging in front of savage, almost bestial features. He seems regal in his darkness, a leonine predator in human skin. I could easily see him opening his mouth to reveal a pair of curving incisors. His bloodshot red eyes stare at the camera through greasy lines of hair as if all the world's misery makes its home within. He is rage and destruction personified.

"Even naturally unsupportive deities can be useful, like our friend Ahriman here," Adam says, pointing at the screen. This gets my attention immediately. That was the name Garen mentioned when he threw that little satin ball at me, back at the Inward Care Center. I can still remember the images it burned into my brain. I doubt I'll ever forget them.

"Ahriman is, for all intents and purposes, impossible to restrain. As the embodiment of evil, trickery, and darkness, he has proved capable of breaking out of any prison," Adam says, flicking through a series of slides that show frayed manacles, bent bars, shattered slabs of granite, and similarly compromised means of confinement. "The only catch is that he must be *whole* for this to occur—apparently, his powers of escape function only to release his complete form. As anything less, he's just another god."

"So?" I say. "Wouldn't he just regenerate anything you removed?"

"*Constantly*, yes," Adam says. "And so we in turn must constantly fold, spindle, and mutilate him, if you will." The slide clicks over to show a horrifying room, the contents of which look like a monstrous cross between a printing press and an industrial meat grinder. "Even then, we began having trouble as we realized severed parts of his anatomy over a certain size would attempt to coalesce into a new host for his spirit. This process was nearly instantaneous, and seemed to display a certain low-grade intelligence—we'd see pieces of Ahriman vanish from various repositories, teleporting to appear near larger concentrations of his flesh. When enough got together, the original body would simply die, and the new form would become him." A video begins, showing what I can only describe as a pile of meat sprouting arms, legs, and a head before exuding a layer of skin, growing out a shock of greasy black hair, and opening reddened eyes to focus on the camera with a glare.

"Disgusting," I say, fighting back the urge to retch.

"Incredible," Dionysus says, shifting in his chair. He seems extremely interested in this power. I get the impression he wants it for himself.

"After that, it was a simple matter of incinerating any residue to prevent further reconstruction events, but once we discovered bits of him could teleport, we used some of our more mystically inclined gods to analyze the magic involved. Eventually, we discovered that any detached pieces of Ahriman are attracted to his divine signature—the aura that surrounds him. With the proper rituals and material components, we were able to fake this signature and begin testing its capacity for luring wayward parts of his body to a location of our choosing."

"Why on earth would you want to do *that*?" I ask, now past the point of queasiness and outrage and fast approaching a sense of awed horror. Part of me also wants to ask just what they planned on doing with all those pieces of Ahriman they collected *before* they decided to start incinerating them. That part of me is quickly shouted down by the other parts of me that want to be able to fall asleep tonight.

"Simple!" Adam exclaims, seeming far too pleased with this entire scenario. "Testing showed us that a basic transference spell can be used to piggyback onto the transportation effect, allowing anyone willing to undergo a single quick ritual the ability to teleport alongside the piece of Ahriman to *our* chosen destination! Even better, since these pieces are semi-intelligent and, as a result of the transference magic, tend to regard their carriers as allied flesh, each fragment will act to prevent what it perceives to be fatal injuries to itself. In short, anyone willing to undergo the procedure and carry a piece of Ahriman with them gains the ability to teleport to a safe zone in the event of life-threatening situations!"

My jaw drops at the concept. They're using pieces of a *god of evil* as grotesque "Get Out of Jail Free" cards. Well, that explains how Garen kept escaping.

"I know! It's amazing!" Adam chirps, mistaking my shock for appreciation. "Now, unfortunately, this isn't something we recommend for our divine teammates. Ahriman's aura remains affixed to every part of his body, and while mortals and hybrids are unable to sense it, gods subjected to the field report rather unpleasant imagery and emotions."

I'll say. I shudder at the memories.

"I would like to attempt it, all the same," Dionysus says.

Adam bobs his head. "Certainly, sir! As I said before, it's not recommended, but we do have a handful of gods who are either able to ignore the effects or seem indifferent to them. I'll make sure to set you up with a test piece in a few days," he says, jotting something down on his smartphone.

I don't know what's worse: The idea that any god in their right mind would consider using this vile method of transportation, or the fact that Finemdi employs some who are *indifferent* to the images that come with it.

"Now, like I said, these are just a few examples of what gods have been able to do for us in the past," Adam says, pocketing his phone again. "The point here is to get you two thinking about all the applications your powers might have for Finemdi. Remember, a great idea might take a bit of sorcery to pull off, but as you've seen here, the results can be astounding!"

Dionysus is nodding vigorously, clearly impressed, but I can barely speak. The way Adam's presented it as some sort of infomercial about all the wonderful things gods can do for Finemdi just adds to the horror of the situation. As I leave the meeting, I am, with what's approaching an apocalyptic sense of glee at this point, further convinced that this place needs to be destroyed.

Luckily, Nathan's waiting outside to calm me down, leaning against the wall of the corridor. He makes a face behind Dionysus's back as the god saunters away, off to do whatever professional twits do, I suppose.

I grin at Nathan and make a rude gesture at Dionysus, too. Adam, emerging from the meeting room with his little laptop, notices and gives me a shocked look, then scurries away in the opposite direction without a word.

"Aw, I think you scared him," Nathan says, pushing off from the wall.

I laugh and start walking with him. "He really does mean well, I think. Just happens to be a clueless mouthpiece for Evil, Inc."

"You should see if you can get him a job at Disney. He's always so chipper."

"Hah, he'd fit right in." I smile, imagining Adam giving his little PowerPoint presentation about cartoon characters instead. Honestly, it *would* be a better match. "So, how was class this time?"

He gives a thumbs-down and blows a raspberry. "It's like they're *trying* to bore me. And I have homework. Homework!"

"You'll never get into a good school with that attitude."

"Har, har. They want a research paper on you—minimum ten pages, double-spaced, *with references*! 'A high priest should know their god's background,' boo." He lowers his voice. "Any chance you can destroy this place before next Monday?"

"Nathan, of course!" I say with mock seriousness. "I mean, they're a crime against nature, but now that I know I can *get you out of doing homework*, too, I'll have to pick up the pace."

"So that's a no?"

I laugh, and we joke a bit more before coming to another intersection. I jerk my head down one path. "Dinner's about to start. Join me?"

He shakes his head, looking bummed. "Another training session with that French lady. They seriously want me to be able to help you with makeup and style choices."

"It's actually kind of thoughtful," I say, surprised to be in the position of complimenting my sworn enemies.

"Yeah, no pressure like helping your god put on eyeliner." He waves and splits off in the other direction. "Catch you later!"

I practically skip down the hall, eager to see the evening's menu options. It's not long before I'm going over the specials with gleaming eyes, tummy rumbling in anticipation. When I destroy this station, I'm going to have to figure out how to spare the chefs—I've never seen a place with better meals. Could they have a god of fine dining back there? *Is* there one? I'd ask, but that would only increase the delay before I get to enjoy the food. Tonight's theme for immortals is the Far East, so when I exit the cafeteria line, my tray bears all manner of finely crafted dim sum appetizers, handmade sushi rolls, and a steaming bowl of fresh noodle soup.

I give the place a quick inspection, looking for usual companions and coming up short. It's not surprising—I got to the cafeteria right as it opened, and the Hawaiian sisters are, like all nature spirits, notoriously bad with schedules. I'm about to grab an empty table when I stop short. Garen's here, sitting on the far side of the room with his back against the wall, eating alone.

My first instinct is to shoot him a nasty look and sit on the exact opposite end of the dining hall, but then I think about what I've learned from Nantosuelta and wonder if it might be a better idea to talk to him. I'm curious about the man, and not just because I feel like it's always a good idea to know as much as you can about your enemies.

I'm waffling between the two options when another thought hits: He'd *hate* to eat with me. That tips the balance, and I start heading toward his table with a confident stride. If all else fails, trust in spite to settle a tricky issue. After all, he's ruined at least one of my dinners.

It's only fair I return the favor.

12

UNINVITED GUESTS

Garen lifts his dark brown eyes, fixing them on me as I approach. A mix of confusion and anger passes over his face as he realizes I'm making a beeline for his table. It's wonderful.

I set my tray in front of him and point at the chair. "Care for some company?" I ask, sweet as can be.

He gives me a calculating stare, then glances at his meal like he's trying to figure out if it's worth leaving now—he's barely even started. "What do you want, Freya?" he finally says in a weary tone.

"That's a 'yes,' then? Good." I slide the chair out and plop down, scooting in with some obnoxious screeches.

He shakes his head and sighs. "Come to gloat?"

"Why would I do a thing like that?" I ask, picking up my chopsticks and fumbling with them.

He stirs his soup—he has a mix of dishes from both sides of the cafeteria, I notice—and glares. "Drop the act already. We both know you're smarter than that."

"You really hate me, don't you?" I say, still struggling with the chopsticks. "It's not like I came out swinging. I wanted to be left alone."

He gives me another of his uncomfortable stares, then rolls his eyes. "That didn't change my job, you realize. And no, I don't hate you. I hate what you represent—what you and your kind do to people—but you? As a person?" He shrugs. "I barely know you, and you haven't done anything particularly detestable. Just suspicious."

"Aw, Garen, you sweet-talker, you. What girl doesn't want to hear they're not 'particularly detestable'?" I finish in a gravelly mimic of his voice.

"Plan on telling me what you want yet?" He takes a sip of his soup. "Or are we going to do this dance some more?"

"To be honest, I came by to ruin your dinner because you've been a giant jerk to me," I say, and he smiles a little at that. "But you're dangerously close to being more than a one-dimensional James Bond villain, and I'd kind of like to see how much."

That gets me a very confused look. "Freya, do you have the faintest idea how *strange* you are?" he asks, sounding legitimately curious.

"Nope. Lay it on me."

"There's a *lot* that's wrong with you, actually, but do you know what the worst part is?" He leans in as he asks it, like he's about to share a secret, and I hunch over to listen. "You give people here *hope*."

"Huh? What's so bad about that?"

"You should know—you've been around. Hope can tear a mind apart, make you question everything."

"And what do I make you question, Garen?"

He holds my gaze, then shakes his head, just a little. "You don't get it, do you? Why you're so damnably terrifying? You honestly haven't thought about it."

"Thought about *what*?"

"Freya, if you can act like a person, if you don't *have* to twist people into following you, can accept a normal life like everyone else, then logically, *so can any other god.*"

I think it over for a moment, then bob my head. "Yeah, okay. Makes sense. What's your point?"

"What's my—they *don't*, girl. *Ever.* You're the only god in the history of this company—I've checked—who's been able to do this."

"So you hate gods, but because I can act a little differently, you're . . . what? Worried all those years hunting us down might not be as morally awesome as you thought?"

"In part," he mutters. "Look, do me a favor and slip up, all right? Act like the holy berserker I know you want to be, and quit messing with my head."

"I'll think about it," I say with a wink, and make another try for my sushi.

"Like that!" he says, holding out his hands, exasperated. "You're not trying to threaten me, and this isn't some patronizing attempt at seduction—you're actually having *fun* here."

"'Course I am. The colossal jackass who ruined my life, shot me full of poison, and tried to get me imprisoned for eternity is climbing the walls because I'm being myself." I give him a thumbs-up. "Good times!"

"Glad to brighten your day," he says, drier than a desert. "You think it's so simple. I'm a bad man for doing my job? Fine. Change the job, then. Tell me what I should do about gods, Freya. You're in charge now. What's the plan, fearless leader?"

Ooh, interesting. I set my chopsticks aside and snatch one of the dumplings with my fingers, popping it into my mouth while I think it over. "Some gods *are* evil, I'll give you that," I say, chewing. "So you go after them. Only them."

He gives me a mocking salute. "Great idea, sir. Now all you need to do is define 'evil' and we're off to the races."

"Don't give me that," I say, eating another dumpling with my fingers. "Try a god of pestilence, maybe? God of sin? God of *freaking evil?*"

"God of war?" he asks with a lazy smile. I frown and I'm about to get snarky when he holds up a hand. "Low blow. We'll set that aside for a moment. How about love?"

"Love isn't evil!" I snap.

"The brokenhearted might disagree. Jilted lovers. Adulterers. What's the line between love and lust? Where do stalkers come from? Who decides when love happens? People get hurt, Freya. You know that. Love can ruin lives as quickly as bullets."

"Oh, screw you," I say, legitimately upset. "You're just cherry-picking the worst-case scen—"

"Then who chooses?" he asks. "You? Pick a god—any god—and tell me they don't have the potential for fantastic amounts of harm."

"I'm a god of beauty, too, you know. Where's the harm in—"

"'Was this the face that launch'd a thousand ships, and burnt the topless towers of Ilium?'" Garen quotes with a smirk.

"Ugh." I throw up my hands. "How long were you holding on to *that* one?"

"Have I made my point yet?"

"No! What about nature spirits? They—"

"Name one who can't be associated with a natural disaster. *One.*"

I think it over for a moment. "Forest gods," I say with a defiant look.

"Ecoterrorists," he shoots back. "They'll go to any lengths to protect the land, and you know it."

"Oh, this is ridiculous," I say, feeling flustered. "There are gods of simple things, too! Dance, art, *joy.* Why lock up a god of *happiness*, Garen?"

"Now you're getting interesting," he says, pausing to take another spoonful of soup. "Have you ever known a god with a specialty like that? Just one domain, and nothing else?"

"Yeah, plenty."

"What were they like?"

"Very focused on whatever it was, I guess. *Driven*, really."

"Would it be unfair to say obsessed?"

I feel a trap closing but plow ahead. "No, I suppose not."

"Okay, great. Here's the problem: They come in all shapes and sizes, but at their worst, those gods can be the most insidious of all. People aren't meant to be happy twenty-four seven, and that's one of the nicer fates. I've seen artists so *inspired* they worked their fingers to bloody nubs and passed out from exhaustion. Those gods burn people out, twist them into puppets, and, given enough time, permanently break them. They can't help it—it's their nature. They *have to do it*, and we pay the price." Another slurp. "Except you," he says, looking up from his soup with a very strange expression. "You held back. So are you a reason to find new respect for the gods . . . or hate them even more?"

Huh? "Why would I make you hate—?"

"Because if they could ignore their urges like you can, if they *can* help it, and they *don't* . . ." He grits his teeth and makes a fist. I feel the anger pulse through him like distant thunder. "Then every last one of those miserable sons of bitches can burn."

Ah. "Gettin' a little dark there, aren't you?"

He smiles at that, and for once it's not his oily, practiced one. "You did ask. So yeah, there's your answer. Sorry if you feel like I ruined your life over it, but you know what?"

"Not really sorry?"

"Not so much, no." He returns to his soup, and I feel the anger in him start to evaporate. We both eat in silence for a few minutes, him slurping noodles and broth, me wrestling with my dumb chopsticks.

He looks up, watches quietly for a little. "God of love and war, and you can't pick up a piece of fish?" he says at last, pointing his spoon at my current struggle.

"Fish, I can handle," I say, tossing down the chopsticks with a frustrated noise. "Come to Scandinavia sometime—best seafood you ever had." I hold up a piece of sushi and gesture at it. "This is a little fish burrito, and for some reason, I'm not supposed to use my fingers to eat it?"

He sighs and holds out his hand. After I pause for a few seconds, watching it warily, he snorts and grabs my chopsticks, then reaches over and beckons for my free hand. I narrow my eyes at him.

"What am I gonna do, put your prints on a gun?" he asks, and gestures for me again.

I snort and stretch out my hand. He takes it, fits the chopsticks into my fingers, and helps shape my hand around them. "There, like a pencil. Just use your thumb, index, and middle fingers to wiggle the top one. The other, you don't move."

I try it. He corrects me a few times, and then it clicks. I reach out and pick up a piece of sushi with the chopsticks and smile. "Hey! Thanks!" I eat it, happy with my new talent. "You're still on my list, and I don't know why you did that, but thanks."

He goes back to his meal. "Maybe so when you *do* eventually snap and try to kill me, you'll at least feel conflicted about it."

"Kind of a dick move if that's the case," I say, targeting another sushi.

He makes a little *eh* noise. "Gotta keep up appearances. I know your kind. Too endearing for your own good—or mine."

"It's the cleavage, isn't it?" I say with a grin, crossing my arms and leaning forward.

He snorts. "Seriously? You look like you should be sending applications to colleges."

"Well, excuse me for being dreamt up when this was *middle-aged*," I say, gesturing at myself.

"Look at you, showing off your sense of humor like it's an A on a math test." He drains the last of his soup and tosses down his napkin. "Well, this has been awkward and annoying. Don't make it a habit, if you'd be so kind."

"Call me," I say, toasting him with my water glass.

He makes a disgusted sound, picks up his tray, and leaves.

I spend a few seconds eating in silence, feeling pretty smug about our exchange (other than the fact that I'm going to prove him right when I level this place). Sadly, like all good things, those vibes are not long for the world. A little twitch of movement out of the corner of my eye, a white shape prowling around the table, and suddenly Dionysus is sliding into the chair opposite me, tray piled high with gourmet choices.

"Eating alone? Cruel fate for such a beautiful creature," he says, undressing me with his eyes.

"Did I invite you here?" I growl, good mood thoroughly mangled.

"Did he?" Dionysus says, nodding at Garen, who's just leaving the cafeteria. "Double standards are unbecoming for beauties. Come, sit and spar with me as you did the half-breed." A glass of red wine blinks into existence in one of his hands, and he takes an exaggerated slurp from it.

"I don't owe you anything."

"No," he says with a shrug, picking up a handful of sushi, mashing it into a pool of soy sauce, and eating it. "But then, this isn't quite the sort of sparring I'd prefer anyway." Despite a mouthful of food, he manages to say it in a crisp, unburdened voice. What a weird trick.

"So what makes you think I'm going to sit here for longer than it takes to tell you how much of a scumbag you are?" He opens his mouth to respond, and I hold up a finger. "You scumbag. There." I wrap my hands around the edges of my tray and make to leave.

"Nothing I can say, clearly," he says, and looks pointedly to our right.

I narrow my eyes, then follow his gaze. About twenty feet away, Samantha's having her usual outcast meal in the Forbidden Zone. This time, however, she has a visitor: her father, Gideon Drass. My lips twist, and I set my tray back down.

"You've been listening to them?"

"And you," he says with a sly smile. He pulls an exaggerated sad face and draws a tear down one chiseled cheek. "Boo-hoo, Freya's got self-control, what*ever* shall we *do*?"

"Yeah, old news. What are Samantha and her father talking about?"

He rolls his eyes and takes another crass bite of his meal. "The usual clichés." He mimes a girlish pose. "Oh, Father, I'm torn between familial respect and the need to be my own person!" He frowns and his voice deepens. "Daughter dearest, I love you and can't help wanting to protect you, even if my overbearing choices are driving you away."

"They're people, not tropes," I say, glaring.

"And we are *gods*," he says with a knowing look. "Billions of them, a handful of us. Now tell me whom I should paint with broad strokes."

"Shut up," I hiss. "I can't hear them."

"So Garen thinks you're different?" Dionysus asks, ignoring me. "You frustrate him because you make choices he can't predict, yes?" He tilts his head back and tosses another piece of sushi into his mouth, arcing it like a piece of popcorn. "Hmm. Chablis, I think," he murmurs to himself, and the glass of wine in his hand flickers and refills with what I assume is the perfect vintage.

I sigh noisily and stare at him. "You're not going to leave me alone, are you?"

"Indulge me, and we'll see," he says, smirking. "Come now, fair one. What's the harm in a little *indulgence* now and then?"

I maintain the stare a little longer, then blow out a breath and hold up my hands. "Fine. What do you want?"

"So *many* things," he says, waggling his eyebrows. Then his demeanor changes in an instant, downshifting from lecherous to suave. "But I'll settle for a conversation."

"Why?" I say, picking up another piece of sushi as daintily as I can. "Still hoping to talk yourself into my pants?"

That gets me a full-throated laugh. "Always. But not only for that. Our mutual friend is right: You are different. To Garen, that makes you a threat. I, however, find you a curiosity." He pauses. "A marvelously curvaceous one, at that."

I flip him off. "Get to your point."

"My brash little love, I'm already there. Can't you see? Not long ago, such denials of my astonishing charms were cause for some . . . mild rudeness on my behalf."

"*Mild?*"

He waves a hand. "Do you see me tossing you through any walls now? Or displaying the slightest unease at your baffling prudishness?"

"I assumed you'd given up."

He scoffs. "I would never insult you so. No, I simply realize it is because you are not yourself." He holds a hand to his chest, and those crazed eyes fill with sadness. "You have my deepest sympathies, sweet girl, for you are lost. After all, what goddess of love would deny herself such pleasures?"

One with standards, I barely manage to avoid shouting. "That it?" I say instead. "We done here?"

He sighs. "You cannot see it, can you? Clearly, this detachment was not a conscious choice on your part."

"A conscious—well, *of course* not," I say, feeling like I've missed something. "What, like you can just decide you're going to be a wild card?"

"Yes," he says, fixing lust-filled eyes on me. "Precisely that."

"Nonsense. What god would—"

"None, of course—a god can no more choose to walk a different path than a man can change the color of his teeth." He flashes pearly whites at me. "Ah, but between a path and a brief pause along the way, there exists a world of difference."

"I'm going to miss the rest of their conversation if you don't *get on with it*," I hiss, flicking my head at Samantha's table.

"Very well. A moment, if you please?" He closes his eyes and furrows his brow. "A sane god would never *want* such a thing, no, but—" He grimaces. "With enough—*mmf*—dedication and—*nng*—strength, great things can—can be—" He grits his teeth, tightens his fingers on the table, and twists his face like he's fighting through a briar patch in his head. Then his features relax and he lets out a relieved sigh. He shakes himself, opens his eyes, and . . . my jaw drops. Those eyes—

They're *normal*.

"Achieved," he says in a pleasant, mild-mannered tone.

I sit back in shock.

"Kind of neat, right?" he asks, sounding for all the world like an average guy dropping by for a quick chat.

"What did you *do*?" I ask, leaning in to peer at him. Damn, he's *hot* when he's not insane.

"Shut it off," he says simply. "I don't have worshippers, remember? I have *power*. I serve no one but myself, and that means I can *change myself*."

"Please tell me you're going to stay this way."

He grins, and it's actually endearing for once. "If I could, I think I'd have a shot at those pants of yours after all. The irony is not lost."

"Why can't you—"

"Because it's not me, Freya," he says with a look of *Oh well*. "It's a trick, a show of strength, not a way of life. You can only ignore what you are for so long."

"That's not true!" I say, tapping my chest. "Look what I've done!"

He shakes his head, and that roguish grin turns pitying. "By losing everything? I'd rather not. Give it time, sweetheart. I see in you a goddess on the rise. With that power will come the same urges that define us all. You have ignored your calling for now, but that cannot last forever."

I glare at him. "I am my own person."

"For now," he repeats, and a tremor passes through him. "Ah, you see? It's coming. Why do you think I'm showing you this? We're no different, Freya—the only thing that separates us is time."

The very notion sends a chill down my spine. "Oh, I beg to differ, you hideous throwback."

"I feel the storm," he says, a faraway look in his eyes. "Delirium, delight, the call of merriment . . . they are not far now. So tell me, in these last moments, what do you ask of a god touched by mortality?"

Still feeling staggered, I try to put my thoughts together, to form the most important (and relevant) question I can imagine. "How can you do it? How can you go back to letting your nature control you, to give up free will, even for a second?"

He laughs, and it seems I can hear a hint of madness in it. "I was made, Freya. Made—just like you—for a purpose. I live, breathe, love, kill for it. To have that taken from me? A crueler fate could not exist." He catches my gaze with those human eyes of his, and I'm stunned to see them shimmer with tears. "You ask how I can submit to it, and all I can wonder is how you can stand to do anything but. I am so sorry, sweet girl."

His breath hitches. He shudders, snaps his eyes shut, and grips the table again. There's a pause as the muscles in his arms flex, and then he looks at me, a wretched leer curving his granite lips. Demented dreams swim through those eyes, and my heart sinks as I realize the spark of humanity he summoned is lost somewhere within.

"Come find me when you find yourself," he purrs, dabbing a finger in the soy sauce on his plate. "Then we'll see what *I* can find." He lifts his hand between us, waits a beat, then licks away the liquid with a long, incredibly suggestive stroke of his tongue.

"Gag me," I say, sneering.

He chuckles softly and picks up his tray. "Privacy, as promised, for our little lost goddess," he says, rising. He leaves with nothing more than a bounce of his eyebrows.

I take a moment to mentally scrub myself, trying to wipe the entire unsettling conversation from memory. I don't care what he thinks—even if I gain in strength, draw a little closer to the principles that created me, I'll never be anything like him. Love and war are far removed from the unleashed desire that defines that creature. He's just trying to mess with me. If anything, it's probably all some idiotic scheme to get me in the sack.

I sigh, shake my head, and close my eyes. Time to snoop. The background murmur of gods and Finemdi staff fades. After a moment of searching and sifting, the clipped, tense conversation between Samantha and her father swims to the surface.

"—just don't see why we can't have a nice, normal conversation for once," Gideon is saying.

"Dad, *please*," Samantha hisses. "Look around and tell me how *any* of this is normal!"

"Which is exactly why we need to find it where we can," he says, sounding desperate. "Come on, Sam. Where'd my little scientist go?"

"She's right here, Dad," she says, slapping the table. "Alone in the corner, like usual."

"This again?" he says, and I can hear the eye roll. "Do *not* look to the company for friends—that's all I'm asking! You have a life outside this place—what about your classes?"

She makes an uninterested grunt.

"Hey, I thought you were doing great. Not many teenagers can say they're taking classes at a graduate level!"

"Yes, that's *all* the cool kids care about these days: how many grades I've skipped."

"Well, fine, join a damn book club or something!"

"Oh, right, I forgot it was so easy," she says, matching his sarcasm. "Should I get on that normal-people stuff before or after I review my next delivery of *magical artifacts*?"

"Do not take that tone with me," he says, going into authority mode. "This job is your choice. I've always supported you, but there are rules!"

There's a clatter as she snatches her tray, piling utensils onto it. "Sorry, sir. You're right. I guess I'd better get back to work."

"Sam, come on, you—look, you've barely touched your food."

"Thanks for the chat, Gideon," she says in a dead voice as she goes.

For a moment, there's just the sound of her stalking away. Then, once she's out of earshot, Drass lets out a frustrated groan. I turn my head and crack an eye to see him rub at his mustache, deep in thought, before returning to his dinner. Once it's clear nothing else is going to happen, I tidy up my eating area, pick up my tray, and hunt for the Hawaiian sisters. Smiling when I spot them at their usual table, I make my way over for a bit of *pleasant* conversation for a change. The rest of my meal passes uneventfully, with the exception of Hi'iaka's awesome story about the time she got into a contest of strength with the Anemoi (Greek wind gods of the cardinal directions). I'm not going to get into it here, mostly because I can't do her sound effects justice.

I look at the clock as I head out of the dining hall and realize Nathan still has an hour of class left. I grimace in annoyance, though not because he's missing dinner (the kitchens are open late, so he can always order à la carte); it's that I've just reminded myself what I learned in my own recent lecture. The meal was a nice distraction, but it'll take a sushi roll far better than even the beauties I had for me to quench my rage at Finemdi's perversions. Using the powers and abilities of gods like playthings, dismembering creatures like Ahriman for trinkets, and—

Hey.

A thought strikes me, and I realize it's something that's been bouncing around in the back of my head ever since I left Adam's presentation. I turn it over a few times, looking for problems and liking it more and more. It may not come to anything, but at the very least it's something different from my hate for Finemdi, which is actually very refreshing—I was getting tired of leaving those sessions with nothing to do beyond whining about how much I dislike them.

Now I have a wonderful new idea percolating alongside the ever-present disgust. Hell, it's a good thing I attended that lesson; I need to find a certain place inside Impulse Station, and I'd never have known to look for it without Adam's lecture.

For once, I get to ditch the map. Even if I were willing to spend the ludicrous amount of time needed to scan every floor and hallway, what I want won't be on it. That's fine. All I need to do is follow my nose, so to speak. I wander aimlessly for a few minutes just to put some distance between myself and the other deities leaving the cafeteria, then close my eyes and concentrate. As a divine being, I can sense all sorts of things beyond mortal ken. Gods have an odor all their own, as does magic. It's an aura that ripples under reality, infused with the philosophies and traits of whatever spawned it. Until now, I hadn't really bothered to pay much attention to the auras of anyone or anything in this place; the building's so overloaded with divine creatures and artifacts it's like walking into a scented-candle store for the soul. Now, though, I have something to look for.

The entire place hums with energy. Hestia's everlasting electricity, countless defensive wards, and the trails of dozens of gods all bathe the complex in mystic echoes. Only one of these has what I'm looking for, however—a dull, throbbing ache of calamity hidden among the crowd. I catch the scent and begin moving immediately. It's not hard to remember what I felt when I reached for that piece of Ahriman back at Inward, and even the vaguest whiff of his aura calls to me like a siren. I wander the halls for almost half an hour, sliding against walls, turning away from dead ends, and drifting down stairwells. Finally, I find myself standing in front of an unlabeled door on the first sublevel of the complex: just a boring entrance in the middle of a boring hallway. It doesn't even have a key card reader. Completely unremarkable in every way, except for the aura that calls out from behind it with promises of agony and despair.

I take a deep breath to steady myself, then turn the handle and push the door open. It's pitch-black, the light from the hallway casting a murky pool just inside. I blink at the darkness before me, reach around for the light switch on the interior wall, and give it a flick. Harsh fluorescents snap to life, bathing the room in a pale white light. I cock my head to the side and frown. Instead of the arcane ritual site I'd been expecting, I find myself staring into a storage closet. Metal racks line the walls, filled with spare equipment and office supplies. It might be a little larger than most storage rooms I've seen, but the poured concrete floor in its center is completely bare. There's nothing here.

I'm about to shut the door in annoyance when a thought strikes me. Those racks . . . why are they only attached to the walls? Why not fill the empty space in the middle of the room, too? And when in the history of humankind has a storage closet *ever* had a bare floor? There should be all sorts of detritus—boxes, fallen equipment, forgotten provisions—littering the ground in there. I turn back and step into the room, closing my eyes and focusing on the aura I've been tracking. Yes, it's definitely coming from here. I walk farther, skin prickling from the negative energy that surrounds me. It feels like I should be tripping over Ahriman, or at least whatever they're using to clone his aura.

I bend down to examine that too-clean floor and grimace as the wave of cataclysm swells. *Here.* It's practically oozing out of the concrete. I straighten up, nodding. They must have hidden it somehow, burned it into the floor with a spell and then made the whole mess invisible. If I were stronger, I might be able to overcome whatever illusions they've cast here, but as it is, I already have everything I need to know. When Garen or anyone else toting a piece of Ahriman gets teleported out of danger, this is where they go.

Satisfied with my new knowledge, I move to the door and reach to turn off the lights when everything *flexes* for a split second. It's as if the entire storage closet is a pool of liquid with some deep-sea leviathan trying to thrash its way to the surface. A strange crawling sensation ghosts through my skull, and then there's a dull *whump* of displaced atmosphere as something bursts into existence in the center of the room.

The figure wheezes, inhaling a lungful of air and twitching on the floor for a moment before rolling over. I gasp as I recognize her immediately. Wisps of smoke trail from a singed lab coat, her glasses are cracked, and her hair is plastered to the sides of her head by blood and sweat, but there's no mistaking the girl's identity. I move back into the room to lean over the panting wreck of her body, and pale green eyes focus on me with almost comical alarm.

"Don't tell my dad," Samantha Drass says in a terrified whisper.

13

LITTLE SECRETS

"Excuse me?" I say.

"My dad," Samantha gasps. "He can't find out."

"I'll remember that next time I see him at bingo night," I say, extending a hand. "Can you stand?"

She frowns, then grabs my hand, gathers her legs underneath her body, and pulls herself upright. "Ohhh," she groans, staggering against me for support. Blood spatters against the clean concrete below, along with a beat-up high-tech remote.

"We need to get you to Medical," I say, trying to peek inside her lab coat and gauge how severe her injuries really are. She's holding one hand to her stomach and hunching over, making it hard to see.

"No, no, just . . . let me look here," she mumbles, stumbling away from me and moving to the shelves.

"Duct tape can't solve everything, Samantha," I say as I watch her paw through the cleaning supplies.

"Liar," she says with a half smile, still going through the shelves.

I move closer after watching her leave bloody handprints on a few boxes. "Samantha, you need help. Come on, let me—"

"Ah," she interrupts, pulling a black-and-yellow screwdriver off the shelf. "I knew they'd have one here."

I frown. She doesn't strike me as delirious, but then, psychology was never my strong suit. "Okay, you have your screwdriver," I say, putting my hands on her shoulders. "Now let's take it to Medical and get you all better."

"Wait," she says, fiddling with the tool. "It's not what you think." She opens her lab coat, and fresh drops of blood fall to the floor. She holds the device between shaking hands, tip pointed at her midsection, then gently brings it in to touch her skin.

At first I'm worried she's trying to impale herself on the little thing, but her motion is so delicate and slow it doesn't seem like it could do any harm. There's a moment where it's just sitting against her ragged skin, and I can see something's torn through her scrubs to leave a long, curving wound across her belly. Then the screwdriver flares with a bright golden light. It reminds me of the burst of color from Garen's bracers back at the steakhouse, but it's far less harsh. The jagged edges of the cut in her midsection flutter as if caught in a breeze, then stretch toward each other. They fuse as they meet, and new skin flows between the gaps, filling in the damage and rippling like liquid. Epidermal eddies spread away from her abdomen, crawling underneath her medical scrubs and banishing various other cuts, burns, and bruises. Fresh, healthy pink skin follows in their wake.

She inhales deeply as the light fades, then stretches, rotating her arms and legs to test them. Seeming satisfied, she nods to herself and sets the screwdriver back on the shelf. "So much better," she says, turning to me. The scrubs around her lower torso are still soaked with blood, but there isn't even a scar on the skin beneath.

"Nice trick," I say. "What would you have done if that were not here, though?"

She shakes her head. "Unlikely. They stock these rooms with all kinds of useful gear. I knew there would be something to help me." She sweeps out a hand, pointing at the shelves. "Everything in here is enchanted in some way—it's just hard to tell because the Ahrimaura's so strong."

I pause for a second, trying to figure out what she's referring to, then groan. "Tell me you people didn't name it like that on purpose."

"What? What's wrong with it?" she asks, brow furrowing. "Ahriman's aura. Ahrimaura. We use it everywhere. It's very self-explanatory."

"Forget it," I say. "What are you doing here? What happened to you?"

Her mouth clamps shut and her eyes dart away. "Nothing," she squeaks.

I give her an incredulous look. "Nothing," I repeat.

Her expression becomes pained. "I don't—I can't tell you, Miss Freya, I'm sor—"

"Sara," I interrupt. She frowns, seeming confused. "We're friends, aren't we?" I say. "I'm Sara to my friends."

She groans. "I *can't*, Sara," she says softly. "I've known you for all of what? Half a dinner? My dad will *literally* kill me if he—"

"So who's going to tell him?" I say. "I don't give a damn what he or anyone else here wants."

A look of incredulity flashes across her face. Then she grimaces as some troubling insight hits her. "You're new," she says, more to herself. "Just started training, calibration, all those things, right?" She sighs. "I'm really sorry, Sara, but I can't trust you. Please believe me, I'd like to tell you, to have *someone* I could tell, but you're—" She looks like she badly wants to explain further, but she settles for blurting out, "I just can't."

I'm stunned for a moment until the truth of it hits me: She *knows* Finemdi twists its gods into submissive pets. Samantha doesn't think she can trust me to keep anything from her father, because by the time their trained believers are through with me, I'll *have* to obey him. That also explains why she won't even say *why* she can't confide in me—because it would mean explaining what Finemdi's really doing to its deities. Best of all, though, is the fact that her desire for secrecy means whatever she's been doing is probably very, very naughty. She's up to something, and that could make her an ally. The only problem is that to find out, I'm going to have to be the one to make the first move.

I look her over. *Can I trust you, Samantha Drass?* Once again, I regret not being more skilled at separating the sneaky from the sincere. Overt evil, I can handle. Hidden double-crossers, on the other hand, tend to fool me until it's too late. But I have dirt on this girl now, don't I? I mean, sure, I have no clue *what* she was doing, but by her own admission, it was bad enough to make her terrified of her father ever finding out. Just knowing I can hold this over her head doesn't make me trust her implicitly, of course, but right now it's the little bit of insurance I need to feel comfortable.

Okay. Here goes.

"I refuse to be enslaved, Samantha," I say. "What they're doing to gods goes against everything I stand for."

Her eyes widen. "What? I never said—"

"You didn't have to," I say, spreading my arms. "How else would they keep all their free-spirited gods in check? How else could they trust *any* of us? That offered belief of theirs has to be tainted. Nothing else makes sense."

She gives me a long, hard look. "What are you doing here, Sara?" she asks at last. It's in an entirely different voice from before. In fact, her whole demeanor has changed with that sentence. "When I first met you, you were innocent and fragile, just another god of beauty and love, but the more we speak, the more that seems like a mask."

She's one to talk—I have the sneaking suspicion the "timid lab nerd" routine she's been running since we met is just as much an act as my own.

Well, there was a damn good reason for my duplicity. "Cooperate or die, wasn't it?" I say, making a fist. "Hardly a choice. I *had* to act like any other grateful god who just couldn't wait to have new believers."

"But that's not what you're really after, is it? You've figured out how we . . . 'pacify' our gods, so now what? What will you do?" Her words could easily be accusing, but she seems legitimately interested in hearing the answer. I can't help finding this a little flattering.

"You're actually curious, aren't you?" I ask.

"I'm a scientist," she says, as if that explains everything. "And you're not acting like any god we've ever had. You know what we do, but you haven't tried to take revenge or kill anyone. You could always have tried to run away again, but you're still here. What are you up to?"

"Maybe I just like being around other gods," I say. It's clear from the exasperated look she gives me that she can hear the evasion in my voice.

"I've seen you in the cafeteria," she says, pushing her cracked glasses up on her nose. "The three Hawaiian girls are the only ones you ever talk to."

"Okay, this is silly," I say, crossing my arms. "How about I make you a deal? You tell me what you were doing, and I'll tell you what *I'm* doing."

She frowns, thinking it over. "You first," she says after a few seconds.

Ah, the moment of truth. Can I really just tell her I plan on destroying her father's company? Well, I *can* always kill her if it seems like she's going to rat me out. Still, if they manage to pin *that* on me, I'm done. Best make sure I'm completely in the clear, in case it comes to that. "Is it safe to talk here?" I ask.

"Oh, absolutely," she says, blissfully unaware her answer could be life-threatening. "One of the few places in the entire complex they don't record, actually; magical detection weaves would interfere with the Ahrimaura, and the teleportation effect scrambles electronics."

"Good to know," I say. Then I grimace. "Wait . . ." I pull my Mim out of my bag and try to bring it out of standby. Nothing. The screen is dead.

"Don't worry," Samantha says. "It's just resonance from the translocative field. It'll dissipate in a few hours, though the batteries might be drained. Plug it in to recharge and it should be fine the next day."

"Thanks," I say, returning the poor thing to my bag. "All right, Samantha. You want the short version or the long one?"

"Everything's better with an abstract," she says, leaning against one of the shelves and clasping her hands.

I cock my head at her, one eyebrow raised.

She sighs. "Right. God. Never had to write a research paper, did you? What I mean is, give me the short version to start, and let's go from there."

"That works," I say, wondering if I've just made myself look foolish. Well, this next bit ought to make her see me in a slightly more serious light. "I'm going to destroy Finemdi. What they've done is an affront to nature, to say nothing of the personal wrongs they've committed against me."

Her eyebrows look like they're going to shoot off the top of her head. "Wow," she says, clearly taken aback. "Okay, I'd really like to hear the long version of that one."

I smile. "Bet you thought all I wanted was to steal some artifacts, maybe break out a few gods."

She shrugs. "Well, those would at least be realistic goals. I'm not sure you're aware of how big Finemdi is at this point, but even if you fully understand the magnitude of what you're trying to accomplish, I don't think you quite grasp just how difficult it may be."

I hitch my shoulders up in a shrug. "Reach for the stars. So do I get to hear your side of things now?"

She nods. "I suppose we did have an agreement. I'd still like to hear more about your plans and motivations, though. You're quite unique, you know."

I smile, enjoying her inquisitive nature. "I'd be happy to answer your questions, Samantha. Now, if you don't mind . . . ?"

"Right. Yeah," she says, toying with some of the tools on the shelves. I can see her bearing has shifted in a matter of moments, her face taking on a saddened cast as her thoughts turn to what happened. "It's not all that complicated, to be honest. I've been trying to make a special god. It . . . hasn't been going well. This last time, I really thought I had something, but, well, she snapped and attacked me. I had to destroy her."

She sounds very clinical as she speaks, but even if my gift didn't let me sense emotions, I could tell those words mask a canyon of sorrow and regret. "A special god?" I ask, sensing this isn't the part she's truly broken up about. Best to approach it carefully.

"Someone I once knew," she says softly.

"A friend?"

Samantha looks at me for a moment, her face unreadable. "My mom," she says, quick and sharp.

And she had to *destroy* her? Well. That's . . . ghastly. "Was she a god?" I ask, trying not to let my surprise show.

She shakes her head. "No, but it's the only way I could think to get her back."

I'm at a loss here. I need to know more, but I don't want to shatter this girl into a million pieces with too many questions. "Samantha, I know this is hard for you," I say, picking my words carefully, "but I'd like to understand. I want to help. Can you, um—"

She breaks into unexpected laughter, a high, nervous titter. "I'm sorry. I've never laid it out like this for anyone before. I'm being vague, aren't I? Bad scientist." She takes a breath and composes herself. "I was eight," she says, her voice clipped, emotionless. "Mom and Gideon both worked here, always had. Smart for my age, of course, knew gods were real, but still didn't really understand what my parents did." She looks at me, then shakes her head. "Doesn't matter. I was happy, they *seemed* happy. Everything was fine—childhood. Then one day, Mom didn't come home. Dad said there was an accident at work, and she died. We had a funeral, and right then, *right then*, I should have wondered, because it was a closed casket. No body. I should've stood up in the middle of my father's eulogy and demanded to know what sort of accident didn't leave a body behind. But I was eight. I was a good girl. Good girls don't ask questions like that."

She pulls a carpenter's level off the shelf, turning it over in her hands and watching the little bubble in its center slide up and down. "I was fourteen when I finally started asking," she continues in that same haunted tone. "Can you believe it took me *six years* to work up the nerve? Finally started pulling records, trying to find old security footage. So many dead ends. But then I began looking at my father, sneaking into his files. Everything seemed normal, at first. Then I got to his employment dates. He was hired the day the admission form had been created. Odd, right? They hired him the *exact day* they approved the form to record new hires? I checked other documents and found clues that didn't match up—that implied he'd been working for Finemdi a lot longer than that. So I branched out. His files were a joke, but he had his signature on all sorts of other things. I kept looking, going farther and farther back, and he was always there. I found old, *old* records, and yes, right there, it's my dad, signing off on forms from the fifties, forties, thirties . . . back and back, until I ran out of documents."

"He's a god?" I ask. I'm not the best judge of age, but when I saw Gideon Drass, I assumed he was in his early forties. Most gods project an aura of divinity, though, and I didn't get a hint of it when I met him. Maybe he's half god, like Garen?

She shakes her head fiercely, tossing the level back onto the shelf. "No. No, he's a mortal, if you can call it that at this point. Once I was certain he wasn't a god in disguise, I did some more research into how any of that was possible. Everything was disturbing— really troublesome stuff. It took me a year, but then one day I finally found the security tapes of what happened to my mom."

She looks at me with watery eyes, her professional mask cracking, and I take a step back in shock. It's not her sorrow that surprises me, but the sheer *fury* I see behind that front. "He made a deal. A *deal*. I don't even know who the god was. Just scales, c-coiling in darkness. Doesn't matter—what he *did* is the important part, and I don't think it was the first time. All conjecture." She balls her hands into fists, and it feels like she has to physically force out the next part, the words coming quickly like she's worried if she stops now, she'll never get through it. "He *sacrificed my mother*, Sara. Stabbed her in the chest and drained her blood into a bowl and laid her out for the god in the shadows to take, and I j-just miss her so much, Sara. He took her from me. How many other women has he done this to? Did he ever love her? Did he *have* to love her for it to work? There's so much I don't know."

My skin crawls. I'm not very familiar with human sacrifices, but I know there are some gods who thrive on them, who exult in every ritual death made in their name. I have accepted sacrifices, but always of pleasant things: of honey and ale, fresh-caught fish, and ripe berries. My rewards for these offerings are small but heartfelt, like the gifts themselves. But what of those twisted deities? What would they grant for the death of another human being? Or worse, a beloved wife? For such an atrocity, immortality might just be the start.

"I hated him for it," Samantha continues, "but I'm not like him. I couldn't fathom taking revenge, so I decided I would just undo it. He took her life away, and I would bring it back. Finemdi can make new gods, you know." She pauses. "Did . . . *did* you know that?"

I bob my head, remembering Garen's welcome speech. Just one of many sucker punches he threw my way, trying to get me to refuse their offer.

"Pseudo-gods," she says, nodding. "They're weak, but they're real. I thought if I could take everything I knew of her, all my love and affection, use it to lay the foundation for a fresh deity and slip it into the belief schedule, I could make her live again. That was three years ago, and this was the sixth one. I almost had her, Sara. She was almost back."

"What happened?" I ask, spellbound.

She sighs and flicks the metal shelf, making a light *spang* noise where her fingernail hits. "She came out wrong. Crafting a god is a delicate thing. I've written papers on it. You can sustain and empower yourselves on a wide variety of belief types, but in the beginning, gods must actually be *worshipped*, and this has to be done very carefully. They require an incredibly sturdy underpinning of belief to form correctly. A full mythology, a *reason* to believe in them, a personality . . . imagine how hard it would be to *think* a human being into existence, to get every facet of them absolutely perfect. You had thousands of worshippers and decades of time in which to form, Freya. All I have is a handful of drugged prisoners who can't think for themselves and everything I remember from my childhood."

She hits the shelf with her fist and the supplies jump a little from the impact. "But I was so close this time! She looked right. Sounded like her, *smelled* like her. For a second, she smiled and I could tell she recognized me. Then she . . . she was gone. Destabilized. Just an animal, ravenous, starving for belief and not knowing how to get it out of me." She bends down and picks the remote off the ground where she dropped it, then straightens up and waves it at me. "I was going to hug her when she snapped. Just barely managed to activate the incinerators."

My mind reels at the concept. Samantha is the precocious daughter of an overprotective, possibly immortal executive who sacrificed his wife for dark gifts, and now she's trying to bring that woman back as a tailored god. Worse, every time she fails, she has to destroy her creation, and each one wears the face of the mother she lost.

"How are you even *standing*?" I ask, all attempts at quiet sympathy banished by my astonishment.

She looks at me wearily, then casts her eyes about the room as if she's not quite certain. "Clinical detachment," she says at last. "I'm good at compartmentalizing. Kind of have to be, if I want to hide what I know from Finemdi. My dad."

"I can only imagine, Samantha. I don't know how you can stand being in the same building, let alone *work* for him. He's—well, sorry, but he's a monster."

She shrugs. "I know. And I did hate him. Not just for my mom, either. He stole my childhood, isolates me from everyone to 'protect' me, and runs this horror show." Something like pride sneaks into her eyes. "But I can be *better* than him, Sara. I can fix it all. Where would revenge get me? How can a few minutes of satisfaction make up for a life of pain? Or uplift all the years to come?"

Part of me—the bloody, furious warrior maiden—wants to tell her that *of course it's worth it*, to scream it from the heavens, then help her plan the war she'll need, train her in the ways of vengeance, and, when the day of reckoning comes, exult in gruesome victory beside her.

I tell that part of me to cram it, and listen to Samantha.

"I think it helps that the hate is gone now," she says. "It's all gone. I feel nothing for the man because what he did isn't going to matter. He took something from me, and I'm going to bring it back. *That* will be my revenge, Sara."

And I pegged this girl for a meek lab rat when we first met. She's not wrong, either; in my long life, I've come to understand that creation may always be harder than destruction, but it's far more rewarding. Not that I'm currently following that wisdom. *Ah well.*

"So where does this leave things?" I ask, pointing at the battered remote. "What will you do now?"

"Same as you, Sara," she says. "Reach for the stars. We both have very difficult goals. One day at a time."

I could be disgusted, I realize, by the crime she's trying to commit, yet any anger I might have for her is caught by the gross abomination that is Finemdi. Hating Samantha at this point would be like hating rain before the rushing waters of a flood. Both can be dangerous, yes, but at the moment, one is by far the greater threat. I'm momentarily pleased by this reasoning, as it occurs to me this is exactly the opposite of the way Garen thinks.

In the end, though, Samantha may not appreciate my efforts, regardless of whether I wish her ill. "That's it?" I ask. "Getting what I want would mean wiping out your research here, right? If I destroy this place, what will you do?"

"Rebuild. Start again. I'm not blind, Sara," she says, then laughs to herself. "Well, not anymore, at least. I know what I'm doing is dark. I know this entire corporation is darker still, and my father? Who knows *what* he truly is? I may refuse to take measures into my own hands, to walk this path of violence you follow so readily, but I am *not blind*. If you succeed, our world will be better for it." She smiles. "Unless I get caught up in whatever it is you're doing. I'd kind of like to live, if that's all right."

"Picky, picky," I say with a snort.

That gets me a genuine grin. "What's the plan, Sara?" she asks. "Tell me what I need to know to make it out of here in one piece."

"Fair is fair," I say, nodding. "Here's what I have so far. . . ."

I spill the bones of my scheme, what I've learned so far and what I think will be most relevant to her survival. I hold back a few choice details, but nothing that will put her in danger. When I'm done, she actually seems impressed, which I take as a compliment.

"You're going to make a hell of a mess, at the very least," she says when I'm finished. She pulls the level she was playing with off the shelf and hands it to me. "I'm glad you were willing to tell me all that—I know trust doesn't come easy around here. Good luck, Sara."

"And to you, Samantha," I say, looking at the object in my hands. I hold it up. "What—"

"It's a leveler," she says, moving toward the exit. "Works on the principle that all magic is applied belief. Activate it and it tries to blanket the area with a wave of apathy collected from our 'volunteers.' Think of the worst aspects of modern skepticism, and imagine being bathed in a roomful of it. Tends to shatter spells and dampen gods. It's here in case something follows us through the teleportation effect. You might find it useful."

"Um, thanks," I say, suddenly uneasy about the thing. Concentrated disbelief? I hate to think what that would feel like. "How do I . . . ?"

"Break it open to release the wave," she says, pausing in the doorway. "And thank you, Sara."

"For what?" I ask.

"For not forcing me to use it on you," she says with a wan smile. "And for listening. I'll be in touch. I'd still like to learn more."

She turns and walks out into the hallway. I listen to her footsteps echo as she strides away, then look down at the device in my hands, realizing that even as I was considering the need to kill or incapacitate Samantha, she was doing the same with me.

I like this girl.

14

PARTY CRASHER

I start casting spells that night.

I try to start small, keep them controlled, but I can't help myself—I'm so giddy about the idea of using real magic, about preparing myself for a showdown, that I end up completely exhausted, burning myself out on three meager charms I could have rattled off in my *sleep* back in the day.

I almost take a swing at Nathan the next morning as he wakes me up for work, and it's a struggle to keep it together long enough for the kids at the park to charge me with belief. Even with their help, I feel like I'm sleepwalking through most of the day. That evening, I sit down in my room and try again. This time, I promise myself, it'll just be *one* spell. I gather mystic reagents around myself and get ready to start. That's one thing I love about the modern world, by the way: It's so easy to find spell components. Back in the day, I had to send my followers to scour the four corners of the earth, hoping they would find the strange metals and plants I needed. Weeks, months, and sometimes even *years* would pass before they would return with the supplies I needed. Now I just order everything I need online, in bulk, with free two-day shipping. The Internet's a hell of a thing.

The enchantment comes together like a warm quilt, arcane fibers weaving through the air above me before condensing and settling around my body. I feel a pleasant shudder as the net of energy binds to my soul, and then say the single word that will return it to me when I need it: "Mangalitsa." That done, I lie back down on the floor, drained.

The next time I say it aloud, the weave will activate and I'll have a split second to pick a nearby location for forty gallons of water to appear. Combined with last night's efforts, this is the start of what I hope will be an impressive selection of prepared spells. It's my solution to the problem of being so weak—if I were to start a fight now, all I'd be able to do on the fly is cast one or two pathetic cantrips before running out of juice. Now, if everything goes well, I'll be able to recall dozens of useful charms and enchantments. Each will fade in exactly one month's time, so depending on how long it is before I'm ready to act, I may have to start redoing these, but I don't mind—casting spells is wonderfully cathartic and reminds me of the old days.

Groaning, I push myself back to a sitting position and stand. I walk over to my desk and fish around in the top drawer for a pen, then turn to the piece of notebook paper sitting on top. Below the first three entries, I add *Mangalitsa—creates water.* I've decided to use breeds of pigs for each of the trigger words, as they're both something with which I'm familiar *and* unlikely to say in a casual conversation. I've had some rather embarrassing moments over the years involving forgotten spell triggers and friendly get-togethers.

I look over the list and read the words back to myself, trying to commit them to memory, then move for the door, intent on raiding the fridge for some ice cream. My hand is almost on the knob when I feel something scraping through my brain, followed by a loud *Bang!* from the next room. I wrench the door open and dart into the hall, shaking my head to stave off a sudden wave of dizziness. I spring past the bathroom and open the door to Nathan's room. An expanding cloud of thin white smoke fills the air within, and little chips of plaster and drywall are still raining down. In the center of the room, Nathan's lying on his back, coated in white powder, looking shocked. A dark circle surrounded by a spiderweb of branching cracks has been burned into the ceiling.

"What's going on?" I shout. "Are you okay?"

"It worked," he says in a hoarse whisper. He coughs and brushes some of the larger pieces of the ceiling off his shirt.

"*What* worked?" I say, moving over to him. "Can you stand?"

"I think so," he says, reaching out an arm. I grab his hand and pull him up. "Thanks," he says, shaking his head. Dust rains down as he does.

I pick a large paint chip out of his hair. "So . . . ?" I say.

"It *worked*, Sara!" he says, seeming in awe of himself. "I tried to cast something and *it worked*! I'm actually casting *spells*. I'm a freaking *wizard*."

I laugh and give his hair another brush. "Actually, you're more of a cleric," I say, correcting him, "because if you want to get technical, *I* cast that through you."

"Killjoy," he says, smirking.

"Hey, it was still more than I could manage right now. I'm dead tired—just got done casting a spell of my own."

"Wait, how does that work?" he asks, shaking out his shirt. "If it's all you, then—"

"Magic is just a very special kind of belief, Nathan," I say, shoving some plaster off his bed and sitting down. "It's usually the playground of gods, but I've heard of some mortals who got in on the act through sheer dedication. When you cast that spell, you called on me to help you do it, but there was a part of you in it as well. Together, clerics and gods can become more than the sum of their parts."

"I love this job!" he says. "That was just the fire seed we were practicing, too. What else can I do?"

I adore his enthusiasm, which makes it all the more disappointing that I have to dampen it. "I'm afraid it's not going to be a whole lot for a while," I say, feeling bad about it. "Remember, I'm really, *really* weak right now, and probably will be for months. For now, you'll have to make do with the basics. I'm sorry."

He waves a hand at me, seeming completely unfazed. "No big deal. I'm just glad I actually cast *something*. You want to go celebrate? We *still* need to make up that dinner."

I smile, realizing he's happy to just be able to use a little magic, regardless of how potent it may be. "Not tonight, sorry. I'm completely beat. Maybe this weekend?"

"Sure, so long as you don't have any special events you need to hit at the park," he says, knowing how hectic my schedule has been lately. "Oh, that reminds me—I finally got paid for that last website."

"The one for the real estate lady who kept asking you to make it 'pop'?" I ask. From everything Nathan has said about the field, Web designers must satisfy some of the world's pickiest clientele. I imagine I'd only last a day or two of listening to people spout vague buzzwords while disparaging my efforts before I start trying to take a broadsword to their faces. I don't know where he finds the patience.

He sighs. "Don't remind me. I don't even know *how* the last few were any different, but suddenly she was ecstatic about it, so hey— still a win."

"Congratulations!" I say, getting up and clapping him on the shoulder. "Mastering the mystic arts *and* pleasing clueless clients. This really does call for a celebration." He smiles at me. Then I point a finger straight up. "*After* you fix this, of course," I say, returning a slightly nastier grin.

He follows my finger to stare at the blackened ceiling, and his smile fades. "I don't suppose there's a spell for that?" he asks hopefully.

"How many fat magi do you know?" I ask as I head out.

"What?"

"Magic isn't meant for the lazy," I reply, moving back to my room.

I close the door and survey the remnants of my latest arcane ritual, then groan as I realize I've forgotten my ice cream. I'm about to turn and walk *all the way* to the kitchen, berating myself for my absentmindedness, when I purse my lips as a thought strikes me. My last words to Nathan remind me that I *do* have a minor summoning spell already saved up for something like this.

Shh, don't judge me. Everyone's allowed to be a hypocrite. Especially gods.

"Bazna," I whisper, concentrating on the pint of Cherry Garcia in our freezer.

There's a subsonic hum as the spell activates, detaching itself from my body and burrowing its way under reality. A fraction of a second later, the air ripples around me and there's a cacophonous sucking noise, like a giant trying to slurp a milk shake through a subway tunnel. Then it upshifts to a dainty *pop!* and the ice cream materializes in the air directly in front of me. I hold out my hands and catch it, beaming with glee.

Nathan flings the door open in that moment, obviously wondering what made the racket. He looks me up and down, focuses on the pint in my hands, and gives me an incredulous look. "Really?" he asks.

I give him a guilty smile. "Do as I say, not as I do?" I offer.

He rolls his eyes and is about to return to his own room when I realize something's amiss. "Nate! Wait!" I say anxiously, calling his attention back.

"What? What's wrong?" he asks, suddenly serious.

I hold up the ice cream. "Can you bring me a spoon?" I ask, the smile returning.

"*Gods,*" he groans, stomping off.

He returns with the spoon, of course. I even let him have some.

The next few days fall into the same pattern—collecting belief at the parks, training at Finemdi, and spell-casting at night. My next spell replaces the one I used to snag the ice cream, and the one after that is actually enough to knock me out for two solid hours when I finish casting it, but it's also incredibly important to my plans—believe it or not, I'm going to use it to kill Impulse Station. I choose others based on what I see as I explore Finemdi, or when the whim strikes me. The facility is, as always, a convoluted and dreary place. I don't know how so many gods decide to spend their lives here, though I have to admit I haven't spent much time on the recreation level. Apparently there are an Olympic-sized swimming pool and a whole track-and-field setup, as well as an Internet café, library, arcade, and beauty salon, so maybe I'm missing out. A large part of me hates the idea of using any more of their amenities than I already have, though—it just feels dirty. The meals, however, are consistently spectacular, and they've forced me to admit my urge for rebellion ends somewhere around my stomach.

Eating there also gives me a chance to keep tabs on Samantha, who I never see outside the cafeteria. Even then, it's from several tables' distance as she eats in her corner of solitude. For the most part, I sneak glances at her as I continue my scheming with the Hawaiian sisters and do my best to keep away from the other gods at the facility. I figure the fewer people I have direct contact with, the fewer chances there will be for my plans to be discovered. Besides, the three girls are all right. They may be cursed with elemental flightiness, but they're also friendly, good-natured ladies who share my disgust for those who would control us.

"Here's the key card for the armory," Hiʻiaka says in a fluttery whisper, placing a stenciled plastic rectangle on the table. "Poor guard wasn't paying attention when a quiet zephyr pulled it off his desk and into an air vent."

"Marvelous, little sister," Nāmaka says, sweeping it off the table. "And you're certain they have more of the needles Freya described in there?"

"Of course. You hear so many things when you control the wind," Hiʻiaka says, pointing up with a finger. Locks of her animated black hair lift to twirl around its tip, spiraling in a slow-motion cyclone. "Just be careful—you need to prick someone with mortal blood for it to work, so use it on a hybrid or some other staffer."

Nāmaka nods. "I'm certain I can find someone nearby." She turns to me. "You'll just need to make sure their defensive wards are down, or else the spell will fail."

"Trust me, you'll know when the wards are down," I say. "That will be your cue to move, and for you to start the fireworks." I nod at Pele.

Pele's burning eyes flash. "I can't wait," she says. "It'll be a challenge, this far from the Pacific Rim, but I think I have it in me."

"Remember, we might not have the luxury of timing," I say. "So all of you need to be ready for the signals. Be prepared to improvise." I say this not only because having a date for the attack leaves us open to interception if someone finds out about our plans, but also because these three don't strike me as ladies who live by a schedule. I'd rather keep their actions based on other events instead of a timetable.

"That's always the best part!" Hiʻiaka says, hair billowing at her excitement. Nāmaka and Pele nod, seeming just as happy about the idea of winging it. Yes, I've definitely pegged these women correctly.

"So this is what you four talk about every day?" Samantha says, suddenly occupying a chair at our table.

"What the—" I squawk. The Hawaiian sisters join me in making other sounds of alarm and confusion. I snap my head away to stare at the table in the far corner. Samantha is still there, slowly eating a salad.

"Calm down," the Samantha in front of us says, glancing around. She nods at Hiʻiaka. "Whatever you're doing to the air might not let anyone *hear* us, but everyone can still *see* what's happening." She pauses. "Well, okay, they won't see *me*. But a quartet of goddesses freaking out for no obvious reason will draw more attention than you want."

All of us halt our frantic movements and lean in, narrowing our eyes at her. We do it at practically the same time, and if I weren't still trying to convince the startled Valkyrie inside me it's not time to go into battle mode, I'd be somewhat amused by our synchronicity.

"How are you doing that?" Hiʻiaka asks, voicing the question on all of our minds.

Samantha snorts. "I'm in charge of divine admissions. That includes divine *artifacts*. I get to learn how all the toys work. This is just a bit of illusion dust, a tweaked helm of invisibility"—she knocks a fist against the side of her head, and her knuckles make a metallic *clink* about an inch from her temple—"and a lot of boredom." She sighs. "Maybe some loneliness, too."

"We really *are* sorry we had to stop—" Pele begins.

Samantha shakes her head. "Not your fault." She's quiet for a few awkward seconds. Then she looks at me with a smile. "Did you tell them?"

"Wasn't my place," I reply.

"I love you honorable ones," she says. She glances at the puzzled faces of the Hawaiian girls and holds up a hand. "Personal stuff. Sara and I compared notes a few days ago, told each other a few secrets. I thought about it a lot, and I've decided I'd like to help."

At this, we all break into big smiles, except for Nāmaka, who seems uncomfortable. "As much as I'd truly appreciate it," she says, "there's the little matter of your father."

At the mention of the world's creepiest CEO, my smile curdles immediately. Samantha gives Nāmaka an understanding look. "I don't blame you for being nervous. Which is why this only happens once, right now. I can't get involved in any plotting, both for my safety and yours. But I wanted to help."

"You *do* realize we're trying to destroy the entire facility, yes?" Nāmaka asks.

Samantha nods. "Without implicating yourselves. Tricky, isn't it?"

"Very. Look, it's not that we don't trust you," Nāmaka says. "It's just . . . you've worked for them for years. If you wanted this place gone, why wait? Why turn on them for us?"

Samantha smiles, and I get the impression she's been expecting this question. "Right now, I see Finemdi as a means to an end"— she gives me a meaningful look—"so despite its obvious problems, I haven't really entertained thoughts of open rebellion. If you manage to take this place down, I'm just going to move to another facility and try to, um, finish my work. Who knows? Maybe I'll have more luck there. But the real reason I want to help is because I'd like to make it out of whatever's coming alive. I doubt any of you would be trying to kill *me*, specifically, but if you're planning to annihilate Impulse Station, there's a chance I might get caught up in that."

"We certainly didn't want you getting hurt," Hi'iaka says. "We were hoping to attack at night, when most of the mortal off-site staff would be home, and the real creeps who live here would be asleep."

"Well, I keep some odd hours," Samantha says. "And I realize rampant destruction is one thing gods do *very* well. I just want to make sure I'm well away from here when it all goes down."

"Okay," I say, realizing she wants to pretend our conversation in the maintenance room never happened. Paranoid little thing. "Then here's the deal—when we're ready to move, I'm going to dispel the magical auras defending this place. I'm fairly certain they all run through a central location, so all I need to do is find—"

"Utility closet on sublevel three," Samantha says. I smile at her readiness; she probably researched the location since we last spoke. "Take elevator four-F on the east quad down, go straight ahead until the floor color changes to red, take your first right, and it'll be the second door on the left. No key card entry required—they like to hide things in plain sight."

"Elevator four-F . . . east quad . . . sublevel, um . . . two?" I mumble, desperately trying to copy it all down into my Mim. I still haven't gotten the hang of typing quickly on its touch screen.

"Oh, here," Samantha says, pulling it out of my hands. "Nice phone, by the way. Looking forward to the new version of the OS?" Her fingers dart over the screen as she speaks.

"The what?"

She shakes her head. "Never mind. So you clip the wards some-how, and then what?"

"Then—"

"You'd better get far, far away," Pele says with a dangerous grin.

"I always trust gods when it comes to that," Samantha says, handing my phone back to me. "Okay, let me do my part to help. You're all thinking of this from a magical perspective—kill their spells, use your own to wreck the place—but you're missing the technological one. Impulse Station has computer logs you're going to want to destroy, because as soon as the building looks like it's a lost cause, it's someone's job to trip the emergency backup line and transmit every shred of on-site data to a new facility. Unless you want the blame for all this, you need to get there before they do that. Oh, and trust me: You *don't* want the blame for all this."

"We weren't really worried about that," Hiʻiaka says, grinning. I know exactly why she seems smug about this—we have a plan about how to shift that guilt off our backs.

"Then *be* worried about it," Samantha says. "This isn't even Finemdi's main facility. That's in New York, and they have an additional twelve stations around the world, not counting research outposts and dig sites. You want to strike a blow here, and I get that, but just be aware that in the grand scheme of things, you'll only be bloodying the nose of a *very* potent enemy."

I'd like to tell her I'm not one for hiding in the shadows, but right now, in my weakened state, it's probably my only option for staying alive. Fortunately, Nāmaka is still powerful—and haughty—enough to deliver the message for me. She places dampened

259

fingertips on the table and leans in to stare at Samantha. "We do not hide from bureaucrats. Their days of twisting our minds have ended."

Samantha sighs. "Ms. Nāmaka, please. Think for a moment. If Finemdi has the ability to believe you into compliance, haven't you considered that they might also be able to *disbelieve* you entirely?"

"I . . . oh," Nāmaka says, sitting back. She seems stunned at the possibility, rippling eyes wide with surprise.

"Put yourself on their hit list and evade their teams long enough, and they'll just turn to death by disbelief. They will, of course, consider it a last resort, since it'll require the efforts of most of their facilities to bring down a god of your strength, but they've done it before."

"Hang on, what about the gang in Corrections?" I ask, realizing this could have dire implications for Sekhmet.

Samantha shrugs. "Those gods aren't really threats anymore. They can be kept behind glass with a pittance of resources, and Finemdi doesn't like throwing away potential tools. I mean, what do *you* think would sound better to a bean counter: Spend decades poisoning the minds of those gods with tainted belief on the off-chance they'll crack, or dedicate an absurd amount of power to wiping them out completely so you can free up a cell?"

"Oh," I say, unsure if the explanation actually makes me feel any better.

Nāmaka's silent another moment, then holds up her hands. "All right, we do it your way. We had plans for that 'server' place, regardless. After I'm done at the armory, I'll head to the room with these computer logs and—after a little meddling of my own—destroy it. Water and electronics don't mix," she says with a grin. "Where do I go?"

"Take the—oh, here, this will be easier. . . ." Samantha unclips a pen from the breast pocket of her lab coat and scribbles the directions down on a napkin. "Now, this room *will* be locked, so—"

"On it," Hiʻiaka says. "You can't keep out the wind."

"Great," Samantha says, pushing the napkin over to Nāmaka. The watery god picks it up and pushes it into her bag before it has a chance to get soaked.

"Are you sure you're okay with what we're going to do, Samantha?" Pele asks.

"Like I said, I don't have a lot invested here," she says, shrugging. "Not right now, at least. The closest facility is New York, so maybe they'll move me there. I'd be working with better resources at that location, too, so there's always the chance I can make some real headway on my project."

"But, Samantha . . . your father will be here. He may die. One of *us* might do it," Pele continues, frowning at the girl's cavalier attitude toward the situation.

"That is a *very* poor idea," Samantha says, locking eyes with the goddess. "He is *not* a normal mortal, and he has access to the best weapons and tricks the company can provide. If one of you encounters him, I'm not worried for his safety; I'm worried for yours. Please, if you see him—if *any* of you see him—I strongly advise you to *run*." She looks to me as she finishes saying this, and the message is clear: *These three goddesses might survive him. You will not.*

Judging by the skeptical looks on the sisters' faces, they probably think she's just trying to protect her father. Knowing what he did to her mother, though, I'm inclined to believe her. "Is there anything else you can tell us about the place? Anything else that might be of use?" I ask, deciding to change the subject before one of the other women tries to commit herself to attacking Gideon Drass just to prove a point.

She frowns. "Not really. You're already inside the building, so the hard part's done. I guess in a more general sense, I want you to fully comprehend what you're attempting here. Finemdi's not my father or this facility. It's not a handful of gods or legions of mercenaries, either," she says, looking at each of us in turn. When her pale green eyes settle on me, I get the feeling this isn't the first time she's considered what it might take to destroy this place. "It's a *world-spanning* conspiracy," she says at last, still focused on me. "Their ultimate goal is to eliminate every deity on the planet, and they've been trying to do it for *centuries*. You've all chosen to attack the one organization on the planet that's best-suited to killing you."

"Are you trying to persuade us not to?" Hi'iaka asks.

Samantha smiles at that. "Could I?" She doesn't wait for a reply. "No, I just want you to be *careful*, to actually understand what you're up against. I know *why* you want to do this—they're only the greatest threat to your kind that's ever existed, after all—but I'm not sure if you four actually know *how* you'll be pulling it off."

"Well, we've got to start somewhere," I say. "Impulse Station is as good a place as any."

The other goddesses nod in agreement. Samantha shrugs. "Okay. I don't have the answers, either. I just want to make sure you're thinking about it." She looks over at the false Samantha eating by herself and sighs. "I'm going to head back to my table now. If I don't get a chance to talk to any of you before the big day, I just want to let you know that even though it didn't work out, I'm glad you all tried to be friendly to me. Most of the other gods don't even manage that. Good luck, you guys."

With that, she vanishes. Her chair trembles slightly, then scrapes to the side. I keep my eyes fixed on the illusion of Samantha monotonously eating her salad. It's only because I'm watching intently that I notice the slight hitch as the illusion ends and she picks up where it left off, a bit of salad halfway to her mouth. She gives me a wink as she munches on the forkful of vegetables and greens, then returns her attention to her plate.

"That was kind of neat," Hiʻiaka says, looking back at us. "Do you really think she's on our side?"

"She hasn't called the guards on us yet," Pele says.

Nāmaka sighs. "I don't believe she's out for anyone but herself. It seems that 'project' of hers was her main concern. Freya, do you know what she meant?"

"I do," I say, nodding. "But if she wanted you to know, I think she would have told you. Just believe me when I say it's reason enough to trust her *and* for her to betray her father and everything he's built here."

"Good enough for me," Hiʻiaka says, resuming her meal. She chose the rib eye with smoked bacon brussels sprouts, and seems more than happy to agree if it'll return her to feasting on it sooner.

"I suppose that honestly *was* helpful," Nāmaka admits. "Saves you the trouble of finding out where all their wards were cast, doesn't it?"

I nod. "I wasn't looking forward to tracking them down. This place is saturated with all kinds of magic. Probably would have taken weeks. And now we also know about their computer backups."

Nāmaka sighs. "I hate this modern world. Nothing is what it seems. Now we must be wary of little bits of metal and plastic. Who would have thought you could hide so much on so little?"

"Oh, I don't hear you complaining about that mean ol' modern world whenever it brings you another *Golden Girls* marathon," Hi'iaka says, grinning as only a younger sister can.

Nāmaka huffs, mumbling something about how at least she wasn't "the one hooked on reality television" before returning to her own meal. Pele laughs at their exchange, then turns to me. "So how *do* you plan on breaking those wards of theirs?" she asks. "I know the things my sisters and I can do *are* magic, of a sort, but I can't say that I've ever really thought of myself as much of a spell-caster."

"I've prepared a wonderful time-delayed dispelling hex," I say. "I'll just set it up in the room and give myself a few minutes to get away before it goes off. Should be enough to shut down every spell in the complex."

"And then it's *our* turn," Pele says, showing her teeth. I can tell she's been itching to cut loose ever since we started plotting. I don't tell her this, but part of the reason I want some time to get away is because I have other things I need to do in the building after the wards go down, and I'm worried she might go a little overboard as soon as it's time for her to act.

We finish dinner without further incident, spending the remainder of it on gossip rather than scheming. This suits me just fine, as I realized a few weeks ago that trying to cram too much planning into any given mealtime would result in the majority of it going over the girls' heads. Besides, gossip is fun.

After we're done, I bus my tray and head out into Finemdi's labyrinthine halls. I check the time on my Mim and realize I have another hour to kill before Nathan's supposed to swing by to pick me up. Finemdi actually operates a car service for deities who choose not to drive, but I prefer having Nathan at the wheel instead of some corporate goon. That, and it's a nice chance for the two of us to catch up on our respective days.

Pele's questions about how I plan to defeat Finemdi's spells are still fresh in my mind, so I decide to follow Samantha's directions to that little utility closet where they've collected all of their wards. As long as I don't go over a month, I can set that hex for just about any date I want. It might be a good idea to lay it down now, so I don't forget, time it so it goes off in a few weeks, and adjust as needed. I haven't cast the spell in ages, either—I should probably test it, just so I can be certain it works.

I begin moving through the halls, phone in one hand and my battered facility map in the other. It's nice to actually have directions, for once. After about ten minutes, the elevator doors open with a dull beep, revealing the letters "B3" stenciled into the walls on either side in bright yellow paint. The hallway continues straight ahead, studded with unremarkable doors at regular intervals. There's a dull buzz of machinery in the air, and beyond that, I can sense the deep thrum of magic. It almost feels like it's been pooling here, collecting over the years like water in a cave system. I put the map back in my bag and stick with the phone from here, walking the deserted corridors as Samantha described. I pass numerous side hallways and offshoots, but ignore them all, my attention focused entirely on the color of the floor under my feet.

It shifts from dark blue to orange to . . . red. *There we go.* I see the entrance to another corridor ahead on my right, just past two nondescript doors, and I'm about to take it when my curiosity gets the better of me. What in the world is behind all these other doors? I mean, the map labels huge swaths of these lower floors with dreary tags like *Maintenance*, *Supplies*, and *Utilities*, but how often is a janitor really going to hoof it five minutes down a creepy corridor for some floor wax? And take this door on my right, for instance— how would they even *remember* what the closet labeled *B3-X-5E-36* had inside? They must have either minds like steel traps or a phone book–sized directory of the place. On a whim, I try the door handle, expecting to find the standard setup of metal shelving, cleaning supplies, and—if I'm *really* lucky—an upright vacuum. Instead, the door swings open on another hallway. This one's a bit more brightly lit than the one I'm in, and its floor is light brown instead of red. I stick my head out, glancing left and right, and notice it extends a few hundred feet in either direction. *Hmph.* Not what I expected, but in the end, it's just a different kind of boring.

I step back into my own hall and pull the door closed. I walk another twenty feet over the red floor and I'm about to take my first right, just like Samantha said, when I stop, something tickling the back of my mind.

Wait . . .

I whirl around and look at the door I just opened. Twenty feet away. An increasingly puzzled look growing on my face, I walk back, open the door again, and take a step in, then look to my left.

Yeah, I *thought* I saw the hallway in there going a *lot* farther than twenty feet. I dash back out into the red hall, zip down twenty feet, and stare into the right-hand corridor I was about to take. There's no sign of the other hall with the light brown flooring.

"Oh, you clever people . . ." I murmur, looking back at the door. So this is one of the hidden tricks of Impulse Station. "'B3-X-5E-36,' eh? And what level am I on? B3?" I've passed *how many* nondescript doors on my wanderings? I think I'm starting to understand how Finemdi's staff gets around this place without spending hours of their day. The whole building must be laced with teleportation magic. Who knows how many different links there are throughout this facility? I should probably start trying to map these out—it could prove very useful.

One thing at a time, though. First, I'm going to find this roomful of wards. I head down the right-hand turn. I quickly pass one door on my left, and it's not long before I come to a second. This one is apparently *Utility Supply #204*. I feel an odd sense of vertigo as I approach it, like I'm teetering on the edge of a vast precipice. Tiny ripples twitch and scrabble in the air around the doorframe, but I know they're not real; even when I close my eyes, I can see them. It's as if reality were leaking gas. Whatever's behind this door is definitely something a little more powerful than Formula 409. I test the handle and find it turns easily, just like Samantha said it would. I open the door a crack and peek inside. The room's single light flicks on as I do, illuminating a space not much bigger than a walk-in closet.

My vision swims and I'm forced to blink back tears as a wave of dizziness staggers me. To me, the room is in flux, constantly jumping between two states. It is at once a standard supply room like any other, yet I also see it as a writhing nest of incandescent snakes, a Gordian knot of living spells. There are so many wards, abjurations, and enchantments gathered here I can't pick out an individual one—they're all blending together in a bedazzling hive of energy. My deific senses are going into overdrive, like my soul's been given a jolt of smelling salts.

I pull the door closed and lean my head against it, taking some deep breaths. *Wow. Okay*, so they have a *lot* of spells running through this place. I'm a little confused as to why they would pick a single room to be the source for all of them since it's a bit like putting their eggs in one basket, but then I realize the only one who could even *see* these things is another god, and if there's a god wandering free inside the building, the automatic assumption is that they're friendly. Besides, I'm getting a migraine just standing here. If these were scattered throughout the complex, they'd probably have gods tripping over them left and right.

Well, one more spell won't go amiss. I'll just add my time-delayed disjunction magic and be on my way. I can only imagine the chaos that will result when it eventually goes off. The shattering of dozens of wards alone will probably make things very hectic, but I know there has to be one spell in here in particular that's going to cause some *real* problems for Impulse Station when I kill it. I steel myself and fling open the door, facing down the madhouse of magic beyond. The trigger word is on my lips when I hear a sharp whistle to my left.

I spin and my jaw drops. Garen's standing there, grinning at me with that disgusting smirk of his. He's in his standard gray suit, but his right hand is clasped around a new accessory: a gorgeous trident plated in gold and polished to a razor shine. He's not alone, either; there are a half-dozen Finemdi mercenaries in full assault gear behind him, machine guns pointed at me. He raises his trident and tips it toward me like it's some demented fairy godmother's wand.

"Gotcha," he says softly.

15

WANT OF A NAIL

"Didn't we go through this already?" I say, turning to Garen and putting my hands on my hips.

"Thank you, Freya," he says, spinning his trident in one hand. "I was going out of my mind wondering when you'd slip up. Knew it was just a matter of time."

"I wasn't aware exploring storage closets was a crime."

"Just happened to pick *this* closet, did you?" He rolls his eyes. "Not that it matters. I have enough evidence to put you away even *without* prowling around our warding nexus."

"Is that what this is?" I say, jerking a thumb at the roiling mass of spells to my right. "And here I was looking for more shampoo."

He laughs. "It is my great pleasure to report that, per standard protocol, you will now be detained until an executive is able to review my evidence and make a formal judgment," he says, lowering the trident to point at me. "It is my *even greater* pleasure to add that, because of your belligerence and disorderly conduct when confronted, I was forced to take you down."

Energy begins to gather between the prongs of the trident, glowing white-hot. I glance at the closet beside me, its door wide open, and whisper, "Chester White." I visualize the knot of magic as the epicenter of my spell and repeat *two hours two hours two hours two hours* in my head, hoping I'll be conscious by that time.

Garen frowns, and the flow of energy on his trident ebbs for a moment. "What?" he says.

An awkward silence descends. "It's a breed of pig, sir," one of the mercenaries behind him says after a moment. Judging by his physique and tanned skin, he strikes me as someone who probably spent some time on a farm at one point.

Garen turns to glare at the man, who shrugs. "Is that supposed to be an insult?" he says at last, returning his gaze to me.

I hold up my hands. "Sure," I say. "Why not?"

He sneers. The trident's energy blazes back to full strength, a flickering strobe of power. It stays like that for a moment, casting epileptic shadows on the walls around us, before lashing out at me in a scintillating flare of light. My world gets very bright for the briefest of instances and then, shortly thereafter, very dark.

When reality swims back, I find myself in that same gray-tiled holding room I saw when I first awoke in Impulse Station. Once again, I'm lying on a gurney, restrained by thick metal bands. At least the IV drip is gone. I've been ratcheted up to a forty-five-degree incline this time, and the first thing I see when I open my eyes is Nathan, lying directly across from me in a similar setup, unconscious.

Then Garen's head leans into view, smiling at me with that intensely punchable grin of his. "Sleep well?" he asks. I notice he still has his trident in one hand.

"Been raiding Neptune's footlocker?" I say, ignoring his question.

"Oh, this?" he says, giving the trident a spin. "Another toy from Hephaestus, actually. I think he just likes the shape."

"So is there a particular reason I'm back here, or do you also 'just like the shape'?" I ask, glancing down at myself. They didn't take the time to put me in one of those weird backless hospital gowns again, so I'm in the clothes I was wearing when they knocked me out: a teal chiffon blouse and gray jeans. I'd normally consider it quite flattering, but I've just started the countdown clock to destruction— if this is really going to turn into my final assault on Impulse Station, I'm annoyed I don't have the tactical catsuit I specifically ordered for it. Now I'm going to look like a high schooler at her first job interview instead of a deadly commando. This is just embarrassing.

Garen rolls his eyes at my comment. "Yes, yes, you're a very pretty goddess. We're all *so impressed*. No, you're here because of *this*." He reaches out of view to my right and pulls back a thick manila folder. Then he leans his trident against my gurney and removes a glossy color photo from the folder, holding it out at me. "Look familiar?" It's a security camera shot of me speaking to Sekhmet.

"Or this?" he says, pulling out another. This time, it's me getting into the white coveralls in the Hybridization Control changing room. "Stop me whenever you see something you recognize." He flips through more, showing a bloodied Samantha Drass leaving a supply closet and me heading out shortly thereafter. A shot of me outside Incubation, hiding around the corner from him. There I am opening random doors on various levels, making notes in hallways on my Mim, deep in conversation with the Hawaiian sisters (key card on the table in front of us, of course), and other generally suspicious snapshots.

"Can't blame a girl for being curious," I say lightly.

"Actually, we *can*," Garen says, slapping the folder closed. "You're obviously a god on a mission—the simple fact that you're acting unlike any other deity we've ever recruited would be cause for alarm, but these things you're doing? They're downright strange, Freya. Finemdi doesn't like strange." He jabs me in the ribs with one finger. "And *you're* not going to like what's coming."

I glare at him. "Well, Garen, what could they possibly do to me? Maybe tie me down and cut out bits of my body to spawn new minions?" His grin fades, and he just stares at me. *Ooh, yes, that hit home.* "Where are the pictures of me and Nantosuelta?" I say, trying to see how many of his buttons I can press. "All those years of poison make her a little too grim for your evidence packet?"

"That will be enough, Freya," he says, clearly strained.

"You're the son *of a god*, Garen. Nothing you ever do will change that," I say.

"I don't care," he snaps, leaning in close. "Your kind are a blight on this world. Do you realize the wars you've caused? The bloodshed and suffering? So you met my mother. Bra-*vo*. You must be tickled pink by all that *amazing* detective work. But in between patting yourself on the back and deciding you've found one more reason to hate us, did you ever consider that if it wasn't for you, she *wouldn't be there?*"

"That is *Finemdi's* doing and no one else's," I reply, narrowing my eyes at him. "*Their* poison, *their* bonds, *their* knives. You're working for the people who tortured—"

"You think you're so damn *clever,*" he spits, cutting me off. "Centuries in age, magic, the belief of fools . . . you think all that gives you some great insight, you arrogant *parasite?*" He pushes away from me and stalks into the center of the room, standing in front of Nathan. "My mother's life, her fall from glory, her punishment . . . *all* of it is because of the meddling of gods. Who destroyed her pantheon? Who hounded her over the centuries, ripping away her worshippers one by one? You think *Finemdi* tore her down?" He slams a hand onto the table beside him. "You will never stop your war with each other, Freya. You will never stop hungering for belief, and my mother and the rest of humanity will never stop suffering for it. Am I to blame the only people in the world who see you for who you truly are?" He sighs, seeming exhausted. "If I were that shortsighted, I'd have no one left."

I don't suppose I ever really thought he'd listen to reason. He's too far gone, lost in the back alleys of revenge and despair, and I don't have the strength or desire to pull him out. I shrug as best I can in the restraints. "Do you honestly have anyone now?"

He looks at me, and for one fleeting instant, I see the haggard son who's just trying to do right by a mother who's almost faded from this world. Then his expression hardens. "I don't have the luxury of needing others, Freya. That, I believe, is *your* specialty," he says, and shoots a hand back to indicate Nathan. "I have a goal, and a means to reach it. That's more than most can say."

Insults and boasts. No surprises there. "Well, let's talk about what else you have, Garen," I say, deciding to lead the conversation elsewhere. "Specifically, do you have the time?"

He frowns at me, then looks down at his watch. "Just after four," he says, suspicious.

I left the lunchroom around two o'clock, so if I had to guess, my spell is going to activate sometime in the next half hour. Good. At least I'll be conscious for it. "Thanks," I say. "Wouldn't want to miss dinner."

He snorts. "You really think you're getting out of this, don't you?"

"Those pictures don't prove anything," I lie, knowing in my heart Finemdi is far too paranoid about its gods to let something like this slide.

"Believe it or not, your opinion doesn't count for much," he says. "You and your friend here will be confined until an executive can review the evidence"—he leans in and gives the manila folder a mocking wave just inches from my face—"and then you'll be locked up forever, like you're supposed to be."

"Right. So we just wait here until your 'executive' decides to make an appearance?" I make a face. "This can't be much fun for you, either."

"It most certainly can," Garen says, laughing quietly. He checks his watch again. "And he was supposed to be here at four, but I'm not surprised he's late—executives are busy people."

"Must be a full-time job, dissecting gods," I say.

For a moment, he looks like he's going to rise to the bait, but then he just shakes his head and moves away, setting the folder back down and taking his trident with him. He starts to pace the room, giving the weapon in his hands an occasional spin. A few minutes pass like this before the silence is broken by Nathan, who inhales deeply and opens his eyes with a moan.

"Ow," he says, looking around unsteadily before focusing on me. "Hey," he murmurs, a smile on his lips. "Fancy meeting you here."

"I know, right?" I say.

He winces. "I'm glad to see you. I had this awful dream. Thugs broke into our apartment and knocked me out."

"Did they drag you to their evil lair and clamp you to a gurney?" I ask, returning his smile as I let him know exactly where we are.

"How did you guess?" he says, chuckling weakly. "So what's up?"

"This and that," I say. "I'm pretty focused on this whole 'getting captured and interrogated' thing right now. Garen seems to think I'm plotting something." I tilt my head in his direction.

"Oh, hey, didn't see you there!" Nathan says, looking at the man with a big smile. "Nice to officially meet you."

"A real treat, I'm sure," Garen says.

"So you're the bad guy?" Nathan asks.

"This isn't a movie," Garen says, smirking at him. "Is there a man on earth who actually *thinks* he's the villain?"

"All in the eye of the beholder, I guess," Nathan replies.

"Has to be," Garen agrees. "Am I the bad guy to you, kid?"

Nathan looks him up and down. "You still want to hurt Sara?"

"I'm not a sadist," Garen says. "I want her locked up, gone from this world, sure. Whether she gets hurt in the process is entirely up to her."

Nathan smiles at that. "Up to her," he repeats. "Right. So, on the off chance she'd actually prefer to be free . . . would you hurt her to keep her here?"

Garen nods. "In a heartbeat."

"Then yes, absolutely," Nathan says, his smile vanishing. "You're the bad guy."

"I'm crushed," Garen says, sounding anything but. He moves to another table on the far side of the room, and I notice my bag is lying on top of it. He opens it and begins to poke around, frowning as he pulls out the carpenter's level. He holds it up and looks at me with a puzzled expression.

"The television in my room was crooked," I say.

"Sure it was," he murmurs, returning the level to my bag. He looks down at his watch again, clearly frustrated by the executive's delay.

"Maybe your boss had better things to do," I say. "Tell you what: Let us go for now, and we can always catch up another time. It's not like I'm guilty anyway."

"Wow, a cocky god," Garen says, smiling. "Let me get my camera."

"I'm just saying this is a waste of time for both of us," I reply. "Besides, don't you get tired of fighting? Ever want to take a vacation? See some fjords or something?"

"What, do you get paid every time you plug Scandinavia?" he asks, seeming amused.

"Enjoy the midnight sun, hike the mountains, go kayaking . . ."

I say, playing along. "Ask me about travel packages and group discounts."

He gives a genuine laugh at that, and I'm surprised how different it sounds compared with when he's trying to make me mad. From my chat with Nantosuelta, I know Clichéd-Scumbag Garen is an act on his part, but realizing there's a sense of humor beneath that mask is kind of shocking.

"You know, I honestly wish I could," he says, staring absently at his trident. "Finemdi's great with annual vacation time, but being on call twenty-four seven really forces you to stay close to home."

"Careful, you might actually start making me think of you as a human being," I say.

"Half god," he says softly. "No worries there."

"Yeah, how do you square that with your whole 'Grr, gods bad' shtick?"

He shrugs. "You're supposed to know the hearts of man. How many people actually make it through life without the occasional hit of self-loathing? I just have a head start."

"I'm not sure why I'm asking my evil captor this," Nathan says, speaking up, "but have you ever tried therapy? Sounds like you have a lot to deal with."

"Eh. This works pretty well, to be honest," Garen says, giving his trident another spin.

I'm actually enjoying this little verbal sparring match of ours, so it's a mild disappointment when the door swings open, interrupting the conversation. Gideon Drass, CEO of Finemdi, strides into the room.

"Specialist," he says, nodding at Garen. He turns to me and

walks closer. "And this is our troublemaker?" I wasn't all that impressed when I saw him in the hallway a few weeks ago, but now that I know who he is—and what he's done—I take the opportunity to examine him a little more closely.

On the surface, he's rather plain. I could see him fitting in with the crowd at a football match or tipping back a pint at a local bar. But if you know to look deeper, a sense of deliberation and skill becomes apparent. His movements are economical and planned, as if he's keenly aware of his body. He's dangerous, I realize, perhaps far more than Garen, because unlike my gray-suited nemesis, he's extraordinarily good at hiding it. I lock eyes with him, staring into those pale green irises of his, and feel like I'm meeting another god. He has that same sense of age and detachment, like nothing can surprise him anymore.

"Freya, yes?" he says, staring at me. "What has she done now?"

Garen slips around him, grabs the manila folder, and holds it out. "We think she's planning something, sir."

Drass begins riffling through the photos, pausing every so often to look at me. "What's this with my daughter?" he asks at last, flipping around the one of Samantha leaving the supply closet.

"Lab accident," I say immediately. I'd already thought about what to say if anyone asked me about this, though I never expected it to be her father. I figure staying close to the truth without actually describing it will be most effective, though I'm still terrified of implicating her. "Something she was testing went off, activated her little Ahriman teleport effect. She seemed annoyed but managed to fix herself up with a screwdriver in the supply closet."

"Yes, Ms. Drass turned in a report to that effect, though she left out meeting Freya," Garen says. "I don't have it on hand, but apparently an artifact from one of our dig sites overloaded somehow. More to the point, I'd like you to note how this incident fits into Freya's pattern of investigations. When we picked her up today, she was in front of the complex's warding nexus. She's clearly trying to discover the inner workings of Impulse Station."

"And why is that?" Drass asks, directing the question at me.

"I'm just exploring, sir," I say, using an airheaded, flattering tone for him. Over his shoulder, I see Garen shake his head. "I wanted to know more about this place—that's all."

Drass grunts at that and begins shuffling through the photos again. "Just exploring, eh?" he says as he finishes. "That was a security pass on the table between you four. And you looked like you were trying very hard to *hide* from Specialist Garen, there."

"She's never even been to the rec level, sir," Garen adds.

His eyes widen. "Really. All that time for 'exploring' restricted wings and prison areas, and none for diversions?" He snaps the folder closed. "I think you may have been right all along, Specialist."

"Sure, take his side," I say, dropping the act.

He chuckles at that. "She has a sense of humor, I see."

"Oh, I'm well aware, sir," Garen says drily. "What do you recommend?"

"Impulse Station is primarily a staging facility," Drass says, rubbing his mustache with a thumb. "She being such a unique case, I think our only option is to send her somewhere better equipped for deep analysis. Meridian One in New York, or Coriolis Labs in Austin, I'd say." He turns his gaze to Garen. "Is there a need to expedite things?"

Garen shakes his head. "No, she's harmless. Quasideity status. We haven't even started her belief regimen."

Drass rolls his shoulders and stretches. "All right. Put her in a holding cell for now. I'll weigh my options and make a formal decision next—"

There's a little *snap* in the back of my mind, a mystic twinge that provides my only warning something's about to happen. Then the floor heaves, sending the two men pinwheeling into the walls and our gurneys crashing to the tiles. The overhead fluorescents flicker briefly before cutting out in a burst of sparks as the building around us creaks and groans like a dying animal. Everything begins to shake, walls rattling and swaying like we're on a massive fault line. A titanic surge wrenches its way through the structure, accompanied by an earsplitting deluge of scraping and blasting sounds. Ceiling tiles fall, equipment shatters on the floor, and the yells of the two men are lost in the din.

"*Harmless?!*" I scream, laughter mixing with the sounds of bedlam.

Far below us, my spell has activated, slicing through the mystic weaves and enchantments around it like a pavement saw through tissue paper. Magic can be an incredibly fragile thing, depending on the circumstances. Permanent spells like the ones I've just disrupted are almost always tenuous constructs, buoyed by belief and emotion and, as a result, highly vulnerable. Countering a direct spell in the heat of the moment, on the other hand, is nigh-impossible. It's the difference between breaking an arrow while it lies on the ground and snatching it from the air midflight.

The mayhem I've unleashed is due to the destruction of a single spell—my primary target all along. Sure, I may have clipped their alarm cantrips, wards against unauthorized teleportation, force barriers, and gods know what else, but those were all bonuses. My true goal was the one enchantment I realized they *had* to be using, a clever little dimensional warping spell that made the inside of Impulse Station a *whole* lot bigger than the outside.

Basically, I've just forced a multistory, industrial-strength juggernaut of a building to assume its normal size in the middle of a dinky warehouse.

It's all headed straight to hell now, Impulse Station wracked by insane stresses on every level. I'll never know exactly what it looked like on the outside, but in my mind's eye I see the warehouse blasting outward as it gives birth to a gargantuan structure, pieces of debris sailing in all directions. I envision the parking lot shearing off in waves of asphalt and twirling cars as the subterranean levels suddenly burst into being, displacing tons of rock and earth. I can see those floors filling with sand, water, and twisted debris as the weight of the enormous building above them crushes downward. Support columns will buckle, entire wings will collapse, and utter pandemonium will be the order of the day. In spite of all this delightful anarchy, I'm not naive enough to expect Impulse Station to fall apart completely; I know they've built this place to last, hardened it against every conceivable form of divine and military assault, and though I've blown it back into reality, that alone won't be the end of it. Even now, the tremors are dying down, the hail of falling objects is dwindling, and the awful sounds are receding to a dull roar.

But that's okay—it's exactly how I planned it.

Emergency lamps kick on, shining into the wrecked chamber

from just above the doorframe. They illuminate a sea of fallen ceiling tiles, upended tables, and scattered equipment. Somewhere in the mess, I can hear the other men groaning.

"Mulefoot," I whisper. The spell flares to life, instantly transforming my body into an ethereal shade. Everything fades as if I've been plunged underwater, my vision blurring and the sounds around me becoming hollow and distant. I push myself forward, more an act of will than muscle, phasing through my bonds. I manage to roll away from the gurney just as the spell runs dry, my corporeal flesh snapping into being once more. There's a clatter as my suddenly weighted body crushes a few ceiling tiles. Just long enough. It's a little sobering; I used to be able to spend days like that. I was hoping to save it for a locked door, too, but I didn't see any other option.

"Are we under attack?" Garen yells, shifting aside a piece of rubble. I notice his trident shining dimly in the glare of the emergency lights, its prongs sticking out from under a small heap of broken tiles.

"Yes!" I exclaim, lunging forward to snatch it. He tries to scrabble free, to leap at me, but it's too late. I tear the weapon out of the debris, spin it above my head with a flourish, and jab it straight down into his chest.

There's a wonderful moment of resistance as the prongs slice into his flesh and for a heartbeat, I dare to dream my revenge has come at last. Then the teleportation effect rips him away, denying me the kill. The rubble his body was supporting caves in as magic compresses his form and snatches him from danger. I grimace and hold the trident up in the dim light, watching Garen's blood glisten dully on its tips. Well, it's not a total loss—I actually have a spell

I can use with this vital fluid. I wipe one of the tines on my sleeve, staining the fabric. Then Drass groans from somewhere in the rubble. I whip my head in his direction, a murderous grin stealing across my features. I wasn't expecting him to be here, honestly, but this is too good to pass up.

I stalk forward, weapon at the ready. Samantha's warning plays in the back of my mind, but it's overwhelmed by the drumbeat of adrenaline and vicious opportunity. There, in the gloom ahead: Drass is moving, shoving aside pieces of construction material. It looks like half the wall and a hunk of the ceiling have collapsed on him, but he's brushing off large pieces of concrete and rebar as if they were cardboard. I move forward, raise the trident, and try to bring it down on his head, hoping to brain-damage him before that infuriating teleportation trick can whisk him to safety. I do it silently, refusing to give him the slightest warning despite the diverse array of quips on my tongue. It's actually very hard to resist saying something—gods *love* to crow.

The razor-sharp barbs flash through the air, right on course to give him an involuntary lobotomy. Then, in the blink of an eye, Drass snaps his head up, frowns, and thrusts out a hand to stop their descent. The trident jerks between my fingers, there's a splash of blood, and I look down in astonishment to see the central tine has passed straight through the palm of Drass's left hand. With incredible strength, he clasps his fingers around the spike and pushes me back while levering himself to a standing position. I yank at the trident, trying to free it from his grasp, but it feels like it's been embedded in solid cement.

"This is all your doing, then?" Drass says, disgusted. He takes a step forward, shoving me back as I try to maintain my hold on the weapon. "Your arrogance is astonishing."

"What *are* you?" I ask, struggling with the trident.

"A simple man with a complicated life," he says, moving toward me again. There's not much space in this room, and I feel like I'm going to bump into the far wall any second now. He gives me an appraising look. "You are interesting, but no longer worth the trouble, I think."

He slams forward with his arm, and I lose my footing in the debris, tumbling onto my back as I fight to keep my grip on the trident. He kneels down, reaching forward with his right hand, and I'm moments away from screaming and trying to escape when I glance up at that other limb of his, impaled on the gleaming spike of my weapon. His fingers close around my throat, and in that instant, I focus my will into the trident, pleading with it to give me its strength, to come to life and unleash the magic it was forged to contain. White light bursts into the room, a frenzied strobe of energy pooling around Drass's injured palm.

His grip around my throat loosens as he looks up in confusion, and just as he pulls back, I command the trident to fire.

There's a tremendous flare of lightning, and my vision goes stark white. I feel Drass's weight ripped away as he's caught by the blast, followed by the sound of him colliding with the far wall, roaring in pain as he does. I blink rapidly, trying to clear the brilliant spots from my eyes. The room swims into hazy focus, and my sight returns just in time to see Drass detach himself from the new pile of rubble he's created and stagger toward me, cradling the cauterized nub of his left forearm to his chest. I've managed to blow off his hand.

My elation is short-lived, however, as Drass snarls and lunges forward with his good hand outstretched. He grabs at my chest, gathering up a fistful of blue fabric, picks me off the floor, spins me around, and hurls me at the same wall he just hit. I have only enough time to throw up an arm to shield my face as I collide with the shattered concrete. There's a moment of intense pain, and then I'm sailing through the air again in a cloud of gray dust and debris. I hit the tiled floor of the next room with a cry, dazed.

He's just tossed me through a wall. I recognize with no shortage of discomfort that this is becoming a semiregular occurrence in my life. I roll onto my knees, groan, and pick myself off the floor. Still woozy, I lean over and peer into the room I've left just in time to catch a glimpse of Drass pounding out of its doorway. I'm confused at the notion of him actually retreating, but then I realize I've been pushed aside. He simply doesn't want to deal with me anymore. Clearly, he has more important things to worry about. I want to feel insulted by the idea that he's abandoning our fight, but I'd be a fool if I thought I could stand toe-to-toe with him. Besides, I have plenty of other things I need to be doing, too. My work here is just beginning, though it's off to a fairly good start.

"Who has the upper hand now?" I rasp, smirking at my own joke and giving my left arm a mocking wave.

"Sara? That you?" Nathan's shaky voice comes to me from the other room.

"Nate?" I say, picking my way back through the hole I made on my recent flight. "Where are you?"

"Under the pile of junk that looks like a Web designer!" His muffled voice comes from a large mound of ceiling tiles.

I run toward him and begin to dig, tossing away fistfuls of wreckage until I reveal my friend. He's still strapped to the gurney, lying on his side and coated in dust. "What did you do?" he says, coughing.

"Tore Impulse Station out of its extradimensional foundations," I say, pulling at his straps.

"What does that mean, and since when can you *do it*?" he asks, a little cloud of dust billowing in front of his face as he shouts the last words. It sends him into another coughing fit, and I wave the particles away.

"It's all in the wrist," I reply.

He waits a beat, then says, "You've secretly been all-powerful the entire time, haven't you?"

I shrug, freeing the bands around his arms before moving on to his midsection. "Pretty much. Just lazy."

He brings his hands down to help with the remaining restraints. "A goddess after my own heart, then," he says as he works.

"Or the other way around," I say, starting on his legs.

"What?"

"Worshipping a god can tweak you a bit," I say. I pull the last band free and roll him out from under the toppled gurney, then take his hand and drag him to his feet. "Belief changes everything, Nate. Even the believer."

"Huh," he says, dusting himself off. "Well, no complaints here. And thanks." He reaches over and gives me a hug. "I didn't like the way things were looking."

I hug him back. "Well, they're looking up now."

"I'll say," he murmurs. "So how do we get out of here? Do you have a spell to—"

He stops as he sees the too-wide, nervous smile spread across my face. Well, *this* is awkward.

Somewhere deep down, the tactician in me is stunned, mouth agape, eyes darting over the various blueprints of obliteration she's drafted since I joined Finemdi. You see, Nathan's just made me realize that after weeks of scheming, there remains a rather large hole in my plot to eradicate Impulse Station: how the hell we're supposed to leave it.

"You . . . don't have a spell prepared?" he asks slowly, trying to figure out what's wrong.

"Worse," I murmur through gritted teeth, still smiling as my thoughts race. I'm furiously trying to formulate a decent, spur-of-the-moment exit from this place.

He pauses for a moment, considering me, before his eyes widen and I see comprehension take hold behind those bright blue irises. "We don't have a way *out*?" he asks bleakly.

"Er, no," I say. "Not . . . at all." Okay, so I may have left an escape route out of my finely tuned war plans. In my defense, gods can be a bit single-minded. I've been focused on fatalities since I got here. How I was going to leave once I was done with them just didn't come up.

Nathan squeezes his eyes shut. "Right. That's, um, not so great, then." He sighs. "Well, I guess we're just going to deal with that later. So what's next?"

"What do you mean?"

"In your plan. What do we do next?"

"Oh," I say, realizing I hadn't really worked Nathan into my strategy yet, either. Man, I'm bad at this. No point in letting him know that, though. "We head for the prison wing. There's a friend there I'm going to recruit."

"Cool," he says, apparently intrigued by the idea of meeting one of my allies. "Lead the way."

I nod and decide to focus on our departure issues later. Stick to the plan, Sara. Before we head out, though, I'd like to get my weapon back. I scan the room for the trident and smile as I notice its shaft gleaming from under some debris. I pull it free with one hand, but my happiness spirals away as I get a good look at it—its tips are mangled beyond repair, the central one melted down to a gnarled stump. "So much for that," I mutter, tossing it aside.

Nathan shoots a curious look at me, but I just shake my head. I settle for reclaiming my bag, picking it from the floor next to the fallen table and looping its strap over my head so I can wear it across my body. Then I move for the exit, pausing in the doorway to peer out into the corridor. Yells sound in the distance, echoing beside the panicked noises of Finemdi's staff racing for the exits. More emergency lights reveal a delightful spread of ruin and rubble, but no immediate threats. I cross the threshold, intending to head for the nearest stairwell, when the building shakes again.

It's not as heavy as the first round of tremors, but it's enough to make me grab the wall to maintain my footing. Nathan steadies himself on the doorframe and looks at me. "What was that?" he asks.

A long, low hissing noise, like steam escaping from a giant cauldron, answers him from somewhere far below. Then there's a distant explosion, and the building shudders again. The hissing continues—in fact, it seems to be getting even louder. I turn to Nathan, face paling as I realize precisely what it is. "We're going to need to hurry," I whisper.

"Why? What's going on?"

"Well, do you remember when I told you I made friends with a few Hawaiian goddesses?" I say, pulling him into the hallway.

"Yeah," he says. "Three of them, right?"

"Right. There's Nāmaka, Hi'iaka, and . . . Pele."

"Okay, so what does that have to . . ." He pauses, frowning. "You didn't," he says after a moment, and I can tell he's just realized their most famous sibling's specialty.

"I did," I say.

"Okay, we need to *move*," he says, breaking into a run.

Together, we race for the stairs, that distant hiss building with every step. Time is suddenly very short. When I planned things with the sisters, I asked Pele to do something as soon as the wards were clipped, something to ensure nothing remained of Impulse Station. You have to understand, I wasn't thinking about escape at the time. I was just looking at the building's hardiness as a particularly difficult problem.

And to Pele's great satisfaction, I realized she was the solution. She was right, what she said back when we first met: Her gift isn't something you'll need very often. Once in a great while, though, it's the perfect answer. Right now, those ominous sounds echoing from below tell me she's begun to do her part. Far beneath Impulse Station, the Hawaiian goddess of fire has unleashed her strength.

There's a volcano brewing under our feet.

16

HOTFOOT

Our destination's not far—the tiled cells are only three levels down from the top—but Nathan is turning red and dripping with sweat by the time we reach the twelfth floor. I'm dry as a bone, of course, though I can still sympathize. With the power knocked out, the building's central air-conditioning has been shut down, and Florida is not kind to those without electricity. To make matters worse, there's a heat rising from below that's deadlier than any tropical summer. Every few minutes, the building shifts as more of the lower floors melt into the lava pool Pele's created. Panting Finemdi workers stumble past us as we race upstairs, paying absolutely no attention to anything more complicated than putting one foot in front of the other on their way out.

I race for the detention block, Nathan wheezing at my side as the squeals and groans of stressed metal echo throughout the complex. I'm forced to find my way around two impassable corridors. One is filled with caved-in ceiling debris and what I think are pieces of a satellite dish, while the other's not even there anymore—just a long drop down four levels into a pit of jagged wreckage. When I finally turn the corner onto the hall leading to Corrections, I'm immensely proud of myself.

That sense of satisfaction is short-lived, however, as I notice we're not alone. There are four mercenaries standing just outside the door. They're wearing the same assault uniforms as the men who were with Garen earlier. They raise their weapons, training them on me and Nathan, and we both put up our hands. One of them begins speaking into a radio clipped to his right shoulder. "Another one, sir," he says. "It's a woman."

Garen's voice crackles over the com, sounding unstoppably angry. "Blue blouse, blond hair?"

"Yessir," the man says, gun never wavering.

"Knew it," Garen says. "Her friend with her? Reddish-brown hair?"

"Right beside her, yeah," the man replies.

"Great. Shoot him first, then fill her with enough rounds to keep her unconscious. I'll be there as soon as I can find a safe route." The radio clicks off.

"Copy that," the man says, finger tightening around the trigger of his gun.

I'm about to scream out, to try to dodge in front of Nathan, when all of a sudden each of the men sways drunkenly, eyes rolling up into their heads before they collapse to the ground in a heap. I frown, utterly bewildered, and turn to Nathan to ask if he did anything when I realize he's lying on the ground as well, unconscious. All of them are fast asleep.

"Nate? You all right?" I ask, shaking him. Nothing. He's out cold.

I'm still confused a few seconds later, when Garen comes back over the radio. "Report," he says. "Is she—what the . . . ?" His voice is distant now, as if he's not talking directly into his receiver anymore. "Roberts? What are you—ah, hell. Wake up! Wake up, damnit!"

"Oh!" I say with a start, realizing what's happened; Nāmaka must have made it to their armory, stolen a magic needle, and found someone to prick with it. Every mortal in the building will be in dreamland. "Serves you right," I say in the general direction of the radio before turning my attention back to my friend, exasperated.

Please don't think I'm ungrateful. This *has* prevented the two of us from getting shot, after all, but it does leave me with a new problem: What am I supposed to do with Nathan? I can't just leave him here. I have to admit, I didn't think through the full repercussions of several parts of my plan. I look around anxiously for a moment, then shrug and pick him off the floor, tossing him over my left shoulder with a grunt. I shuffle down the hall to the pile of snoozing mercenaries and snatch up one of their assault rifles with my free hand. I haven't fired a gun in decades—I'm far more comfortable with swords and other melee weapons—but I won't deny their lethality. This could prove useful, especially if one of the cells beyond has been breached.

I reach out to test the handle on the door to Corrections. Locked. I know all the key card readers have internal batteries they'll use if the power goes out (thank you, Hi'iaka, for that little tidbit) and

I already spent my phasing spell, so I'm going to need to find a card with the proper clearance. I carefully set Nathan back on the floor and begin to search the sleeping mercenaries. I come away with a 9mm pistol, which I slip into my bag, a beautiful black fixed-blade combat knife, which I strap to my right arm, and one key card from their leader. I try it on the lock; the device gives a pleasant beep, and I hear a click from the door. Excellent. I take another minute to gather some extra ammunition clips from the men, stuffing them into my now-bulging purse, then hoist Nathan back over my shoulder and head into Corrections.

Besides the new emergency lighting and the guard snoozing in his little glass-walled office, the entrance looks the same as before. Then I realize there's something else that's not quite right: the door to the prison ward is ajar.

I move closer, pull it open just enough to stick my head in, and peer into the hall beyond. A few pieces of rubble have fallen from the ceiling, but overall it seems untouched by the chaos I've created. That's not surprising—this place *was* built to withstand angry gods. I glance around, trying to see who opened the door, and freeze the moment I spot the intruder. Midway down the hall, standing in front of the last occupied cell, is Dionysus. He's pacing back and forth in front of it, seeming very agitated.

"The vines won't come!" he yells, thudding a fist into the glass in front of him.

Carefully, I pull my head back and weigh my options. Taking on Dionysus was *not* included in my plans. In fact, I hadn't intended to face off against any deities. No way I can see to avoid it, though. First I guess I'll need a place to stash Nathan. I look around and my eyes settle on the guard's cubicle. That could work. I move toward it and try the mercenary's key card on the door next to the half wall of glass. The lock gives me a happy beep. Smiling, I pull the door open and take Nathan inside. There's not a lot of space in here, plus I don't want my friend trapped with an angry man if the spell wears off early, so I drag the security guard out and carefully set Nathan down in his chair. I'm so focused on what I can do about Dionysus that I almost miss the computer screens—they're still on, flickering in the harsh emergency lights. Looks like the prison has backup power. I lean in, squinting at the monitors. There's Dionysus in the hall, still trying to break into one of the cells. The other imprisoned gods are watching him with great interest. I see Sekhmet, prowling back and forth, clearly looking for a way out. Every time the building shudders and sinks a little, she jumps. If I can figure out how to unlock her cell, I'll have an ally against Dionysus. Problem is, I don't have much time, and I've never been all that great at technology—besides the standard keyboard and mouse, there's a control panel here for the cameras and the cellblock, and I have no idea what any of its numerous buttons and switches can do.

Another shriek of metal cuts through the air, and I hear the distant rumble of falling masonry. I grit my teeth and begin trying controls at random. I need to free Sekhmet anyway—might as well do it now. The hall's lights turn on and off as I mess with one bank of switches. I move to another bank, and large steel shutters begin slamming down in front of the chambers. Nope. I reverse those and focus on a row of bright red buttons. There's a loud whine and several imprisoned gods scream as arcs of lightning blast through their cells. *Whoops.* I stop pressing those buttons. The gods are looking around wildly now, confused. On the monitor, Dionysus glares down the hall at the entrance door, says something to the cell beside him, and begins stalking toward me.

Crap. He must think the guard is messing with him. Hurriedly, I move to another row of controls. The first one doesn't seem to do anything until Izanami, the pale, terrifying Japanese girl, rises to her feet, walks over to her door, and pushes it open. Dionysus stops in his tracks as she steps into the hallway. He says something to her I can't hear, and then she stretches, raising her hands above her head. Long shadows creep out from underneath her kimono, stealing across the floor. Even on the camera, I can see their edges are made of thousands of grasping hands and writhing tendrils. Dionysus takes a step back, but the shadows are already on him, moving over his skin as if he's been caught in a personalized eclipse. He screams, and I can hear it clearly through the open door. Great weeping sores open on his body, patches of his skin blackening with necrosis before they slough off in sprays of blood. He crashes to the floor, trembling in pain as his body continues to heal and die in an excruciating cycle. Izanami turns away, walks to the block's entrance, and pushes the door open. Her shadow lengthens as she moves, twisting unnaturally so it can remain on Dionysus.

I look up as she enters the room just beyond the glass. She glances at me, then walks over to the sleeping guard and places her hands on either side of his head. The barest smile touches her lips as she says, *"Anata no shi wa watashi no yume desu."* Then the man *melts*, his body disintegrating from the head down as black lines of corruption race across his skin. A cloud of flies bursts out of his withering carcass, and the rest of his soft tissues spill away into a pool of tarry ooze, revealing a filth-encrusted skeleton. Then even the bones crumble and decay, until all that remains is a black smear on the concrete.

Izanami rises to her feet, seeming pleased with herself. The swarming flies descend behind her, extending from her back like a pair of buzzing wings. "I am in your debt, Lady of the Slain," she says in her soft, childlike voice. She stares at me with those fathomless black orbs and bows. "I would see it repaid. Consider your choices with the greatest of care, for a favor from the queen of Yomi is not given lightly." She straightens, and then a column of darkness rushes around her, splashing against the ceiling like a velvet waterspout. It unravels as quickly as it appeared, whipping away to reveal an empty room. She's gone.

I hear a shuddering gasp from the cellblock and look to the security cameras to see Dionysus panting on the ground, wounds closing. The shadows have left with their maker. I return my attention to the control panel, trying to extrapolate Sekhmet's cell trigger from the one I pressed to release Izanami. Why these aren't labeled is beyond me—are the guards really so well trained that they're not even the *slightest bit* worried about releasing the wrong god? Or maybe this is intended to make it more difficult for an intruder to do precisely what I'm attempting. If that's the case, it's working. I sigh and stab what I hope is the right button. Out of the corner of my eye, I see Dionysus roll onto his side, groaning. He looks almost completely healed.

Then Sekhmet's cell door swings open and she strides into the hallway, seeming pleased and surprised. Another tremor shakes the complex and she breaks into a run, heading for the exit. She aims a kick at Dionysus as she passes him, sending him sailing into the glass wall of Izanami's former cell with a cry. Laughing, she walks into the entryway and looks to me. Her leonine features brighten immediately.

"My old friend!" she cries, extending an arm. I rush around the corner and clasp her hand in mine, kissing her once on each cheek as I shake it. "This is your doing, then?" she says as we separate.

"Impressed?" I ask, grinning.

She nods, golden eyes flashing with delight. "I was right to trust in you, dearest Freya," she says. "Never did I think you would join them, though I feared they would prove too dire a threat."

"Every foe has a weakness," I say.

Sekhmet's about to respond when a haughty voice from the doorway cuts her off. "I beg your pardon, ladies," Dionysus says, a weary smile on his face. "But I'm in a bit of a hurry. If you don't release my darling Tlaz, I'm afraid I'm going to need to strangle your high priest over there." He points at Nathan, still asleep in the guard's chair. Grapevines have burst through the wall behind him, and loops of greenery are wrapped around his neck.

"Let him go *now*," I thunder.

He rolls his maniacal eyes and laughs. "Mine first."

I take a step toward him, and he shakes his head. "Ah-ah-ah, no. You'll do as you're told," he says with a smirk. Out of the corner of my eye, I see the vines tighten around Nathan.

I back away, glaring. "Good," he says. "Now, get in there and open the cell, and be grateful I lack the time to ask for more. I considered having you parade about naked. His life *is* in my hands, after all."

Sekhmet looks at me, and I give my head a tiny shake. There's no way we can disable him before he could kill Nathan. "What is she to you?" I ask as I move toward the security room.

"What is she to me?" he repeats, laughing. "How can you not know? *You* introduced us!"

I stop. "What? I most certainly did not!"

"'A beautiful lady in Corrections who'd just *love* to meet' me is, I believe, how you put it," he says, crossing his legs and leaning against the doorframe. "I was suspicious but curious, all the same. Imagine my surprise when you turned out to be correct. Lively, lustful, and lovely. I had to have her, and the feeling was mutual."

I turn to Sekhmet, who sighs. "It's true. He's been in nearly every day to speak with her. They say the most despicable things to each other."

Dionysus chuckles at that. "Oh, sweet Sekhmet, how I enjoyed your company as well. I do so love an audience." He motions to me. "Go on, then. Release her."

Feeling incredibly irritated with myself, I stomp into the little office, hunt for the correct button, and press it. How was I supposed to know he'd actually take my advice? And that Tlazolteotl would intrigue him? *Stupid, stupid, stupid.* On the camera, I watch as the chosen cell's door opens and Tlaz saunters into the hallway, still in the eye-catching remains of her jumpsuit.

Dionysus turns to watch, an enormous grin on his face. He strolls down the corridor to meet her, the vines around Nathan loosening and falling away as he does. When they meet, they wrap their arms around each other and lock lips, losing themselves in a passionate embrace. Sekhmet watches them from the open door, somehow managing to look like a scandalized cat. I roll my eyes and haul Nathan onto my shoulder once more.

"Come on," I say to Sekhmet as I step out of the security office. "Let's get the hell out of here."

She frowns, and I can tell she wants to race down the cellblock to gut Tlaz. I can't say I blame her, but we have more important things to do. "It's not worth it, not when this place is about to collapse," I say. "Can you help me with the door?"

I don't think she's entirely convinced, but then the building shakes again, and she snarls and turns away from the entwined gods, opening the door for me. We step out into the hall, almost tripping over the sleeping mercenaries. I'm a little confused by them, as I didn't think everyone would be out for this long—I told Nāmaka she might have to keep pricking mortals. When I escaped the Inward Care Center, Nathan was unconscious for only a few minutes. The only explanation I can think of is that the effect must be tied to the needle; when Garen vanished, he took the thing with him, ending the spell prematurely. I doubt Nāmaka's left Impulse Station yet, so maybe everyone will be sleeping a bit longer than I expected.

Sekhmet glances down at the snoozing men and gives me a questioning look. "Magic needle," I explain. "Every mortal in the facility is in dreamland, just like Nathan here."

She nods and loots an assault rifle from one of the men, slinging it across her back. Then she grabs another, checks to make sure the safety is off, and fires a round into the head of the nearest mercenary. His body jerks once, then goes still.

"What are you doing?" I say, surprised by the loud noise.

Sekhmet moves to stand over the next man. "I will not leave a potential foe alive," she explains, shooting him. Her voice is so calm I'm a little taken aback—was she always this methodical and cold-blooded? "Nor should you. How long have you been adrift, Freya?"

"Adrift?" I ask, jumping a little as she looks down her rifle's sights and fires again, killing the third mercenary.

"Hidden away, lost without purpose of love or battle, holding tight to the few worshippers you can find," she says. She raises the weapon and points it at the head of the last man. "You are soft," she hisses, watching me intently as she executes him.

"Excuse me?"

Sekhmet raises her gun and checks the clip, then reloads it and flicks the safety back on before resting it against one shoulder. "It is not intended as an insult, dear friend. It is merely an observation. You have lost yourself." She places an olive-skinned hand against my cheek and gives me a toothy grin. "But do not despair. Among the righteous carnage you have unleashed, we will find your place anew. Now, what is our goal?"

That gets my thoughts back on track. "Incubation," I say. "I have a promise to keep."

"Ah," she says. "More vengeance?"

I shake my head. "Mercy."

The heat increases as we head down the nearest stairwell, staying close to the route I mapped out weeks ago, after I made the decision to fit Nantosuelta's death into my plans. I realized I couldn't leave her to be crushed under rubble or burned in the ruins, kept alive by whatever embers of belief Finemdi had provided. I needed to ensure she died an honorable, painless death—a true, just release from her tortured existence.

Nathan's still unconscious, but I can tell by the beads of sweat dripping from his brow that things are getting uncomfortably warm. There's a surging pulse of noise all around us now, a rhythmic hum composed of rising lava, collapsing floors, and liquefying metals. Impulse Station is falling apart. I can feel the ground shifting under our feet now, and even though I have no way of knowing for certain, I feel the lower levels must already be slag in central Florida's first active volcano.

When I push open the door to the research wing, I expect to find another empty ruined hallway. The corridor we enter is certainly wrecked, but to my surprise, it's also home to a half-dozen heavily armed mercenaries. The men raise handguns the second they get a good look at me, and I barely manage to haul the door closed before they unleash a hail of gunfire.

"What are they doing here?" I say over the sound of bullets pinging off the dense metal behind me. "And how are they awake?"

"Hybrids. Allow me," Sekhmet says, gently pushing me to one side.

She backs up, flips the safety off her assault rifle, and runs full tilt at the door. At the last second, she jumps into the air and flings out her legs, crashing both feet into the metal with bone-jarring force. The door crumples inward, its hinges flying off in little puffs of concrete, and Sekhmet rides it down into the hallway, firing as she falls. I watch around the corner as two mercenaries drop, spurts of blood shooting up to take their places as they crumple. Then Sekhmet rolls off the door, springs up, and launches herself down the hall, clearing the space between her and the men in one inhuman leap, gun blazing. She lands among the confused and injured mercenaries, drops her weapon, and sprouts hooked, razor-sharp claws from her fingertips. Spinning and slashing, she dances between the men, claws sending them to the floor with quick, brutal sweeps. It's over in moments.

Sekhmet straightens in the middle of the hall, standing in victory over the butchered remains of her foes. The corridor around her is covered in bright, sticky swaths of blood, her fur is matted, and her red dress is completely ruined. She shudders in bliss, bringing one blood-soaked hand to her lips and giving it a long, happy lick. Her claws vanish under her skin as she cleans herself. "Exhilarating," she says as I approach. "It's been so long."

I grimace at the display, though I can't deny that some part of me wishes I could have helped create it. "Impressive," I reply, motioning at the door labeled *Hybridization Control*. Sekhmet nods and retrieves a new rifle from one of the fallen, moving to stand beside me. I reach out with my key card and try it in the reader. Once again, it beeps green and the door unlocks. Handy thing.

I move in beside Sekhmet, encountering the same glossy, high-tech architecture I remember from when I was here last. The building rumbles again as we walk down the hall, but it looks like this area has resisted most of the damage—there are only a few cracks in the walls, and it even feels cooler in here. We pad through the bright white corridor, now bathed in the harsh glare of emergency lighting, listening to the sounds of Impulse Station dying around us.

I take the right-hand turn, move through the changing room— coveralls litter the floor and one of the tables is overturned—and open the door to the Incubation laboratory. I'm about to head in when I feel Sekhmet's hand on my shoulder.

"Stop," she whispers. Her nostrils flare, and she shakes her head. "They are waiting."

"How many?"

She bows her head, concentrating. "Dozens," she says under her breath.

"What? Why? What are they doing here? How could they know I was . . . ?" I trail off, confused. This isn't a critical area, is it? I expected the place to be deserted. Who would want to stick around with a volcano underfoot? Then I gasp as the answer comes to me in a flash. "*Garen*," I snarl. Of course. Why else would someone station those guards out in the corridor? He's come here to save his mother, and I'll bet he brought every hybrid warrior he could get his hands on to help.

Now what do I do? Should I really try to keep my word to kill this woman if it means plowing through her own son to do it? I believe a promise should mean something, but I'm not blind; I will not compromise myself in the name of the law when the situation has changed, and to be honest, this feels like it's shifting from a mercy killing to an assassination attempt. I'm really not liking that idea. Besides, I still have someone else I must eliminate—my final task in Impulse Station. I sigh, letting go of this goal. "Bring her peace, Garen," I whisper. "And another day, I will find you to collect the death I am owed."

I turn to Sekhmet. "New plan," I say. "I think you'll like this one."

She cocks her head to the side, an unspoken question.

"*Revenge*," I say, grinning at her. Immediately, she breaks into a smile, revealing long incisors. I pull the door shut, close my eyes, and focus on the image of Gideon Drass as I last saw him. I think of his demeanor, the clothes he was wearing, the outline of his body, and the way he moves. Then I say a single word: "Berkshire."

The spell blazes to life, and in my mind's eye, I see Gideon standing in what looks like a hospital corridor, red with anger, gesturing with the stump of his left arm. This is one of my favorite kinds of magic. Divination has always been a specialty of mine, and the speed with which I've found my prey is a testament to that legacy. I concentrate on the image, pulling away and trying to place it in the world around me. "Where are you, Mr. Drass?" I say as I tease apart the vision. It wavers in my mind for a moment, skipping a beat like a piece of film straying from the projector before snapping back with a wider angle. He's standing on a tiled floor, surrounded by scattered pieces of glass and concrete. Broken viewing windows line the hall on either side of him, and I can make out empty beds and toppled medical equipment through each one. There are probably a dozen mercenaries in the room, standing in a rough circle around Drass and . . . Garen?

What the hell?

Wait, I recognize this place: This is the patient wing where Nantosuelta was being kept. In fact, I think they're right in front of her room, or near enough. The angle isn't quite right for me to tell for certain, but Garen's presence all but confirms it. There's something else in there, too—a large black upright chamber on wheels that looks sort of like a high-tech iron maiden. One of the mercenaries is holding on to a pair of handles on its back, keeping an eye on a set of monitor readouts bolted to the side. A thick glass plate set into its front reveals an interior filled with churning shadows, a rippling sea of night. I peer closer, willing the view to contract, and make out a form in that murk. Then the tube's occupant pushes forward, placing dainty white hands against the glass and leaning in for a better look at the two men yelling at each other in the corridor.

I frown, unable to put a name to the face. I thought it might be Nantosuelta in there, but this woman is different. I don't think she's a god, honestly—she's pretty, but it's not the flawless sort of beauty you see worshippers creating. Then she smiles, laughing silently at the argument before her, and her eyes widen in amusement. Whatever humanity she had vanishes in that moment. Those are dead eyes, reptilian and cold. She pulls down a loop of flat brown hair, smirking, and twirls it around her finger as she watches.

And I recognize her.

Those large front teeth, her too-long features . . . I look between her and Drass, putting the pieces together. "We have to go in there, Sekhmet," I say, banishing the vision with a shake of my head.

"But I thought—"

"No. Everything I seek is beyond that door. Are you prepared?"

"Such a question!" she says, throwing back her head and laughing. "Always!"

"Then I'd be honored to join you in battle, my friend," I say, setting Nathan down and readying myself.

"Words I can never tire of hearing," Sekhmet says, checking her weapons.

I reach out for the handle, look at her, and nod sharply before flinging the door open. I do not know what Drass and Garen were arguing about, or the purpose of that strange machine, but I do know what it holds. There is something vile in there, and worse still, it wears the flesh of a human like a suit of armor. I have to face it, to understand what's happened, because I recognize that shell. Seeing that creature and Gideon Drass together was all it took for me to make the connection.

Samantha may have her father's eyes, but she's the spitting image of her mother.

17

TWISTED ROOTS

I'm not sure how I feel about this.

Only a handful of minutes have passed, and we're both soaked in blood. The laboratory is in an even greater shambles than it was when we entered, filled with bullet holes, vivid splashes of crimson, and dozens of bodies. Sekhmet did most of the heavy lifting, and while I was certainly no slouch, I'm mildly troubled by what I've just done. Maybe she's right about me going soft, because slaughtering a roomful of men—half-god, brainwashed abominations, no less—felt . . . awkward. My portfolio includes *war*, doesn't it? Why did this seem so strange to me?

I hold up a hand to Sekhmet, motioning her to wait while I reorient myself. Large-caliber exit wounds in my back and sides are still closing, and part of my right arm hasn't regenerated yet, so she won't suspect I'm also having a miniature crisis of conscience. I certainly wasn't expecting one. Maybe it's because these are the first people I've actually killed in decades? You might be surprised at my, well, surprise here, but you have to look at this from a god's perspective: Once you see centuries pass and generations live, die, and live again, you start to get a bit detached from the value of a single life. It's even harder when a significant part of who you are is pure battle, worshipped for ages in all its deadly splendor.

Then again, do I really want to be comfortable with murder? It's not exactly like riding a bike, nor should it be. Maybe it's a good thing I'm feeling a little conflicted right now. *Hmm.* You know, at some point, I need to take a moment and figure out how thoroughly I want to be Freya, and how much simpler things got after stepping into Sara's shoes. For now, though . . .

I shake my head and mentally shove those misgivings back down. This is not the time to feel out of place. Focus, Sara. Focus on why you're here: Revenge. Destruction. Glory.

You know—what used to get you out of bed in the morning.

Regrets are for after the battle ends, I think, crushing the last of those strange worries.

I straighten up and start moving again once the wounds finish healing. All those weeks at the parks have dramatically improved my ability to regenerate, but more important, the guards weren't prepared for gods. I saw to that when I sent Nāmaka and Hiʻiaka to ransack their armory; all our foes had were their mundane weapons.

Ineffective or not, there's one thing those assault rifles can still do: make a *lot* of noise. There's no way Drass and his team missed hearing the gunfire, to say nothing of the screams. "So much for stealth," I mutter, wiping my bloodied combat knife on the hem of my frock and returning it to its sheath.

"Only the weak hide in the shadows," Sekhmet says with disdain. She looks like something out of a hunter's nightmare, a lion-headed murderess completely coated in blood. Her dress is a tattered mess, torn by dozens of bullets and barely hanging on to her sleek body. I glance down and sigh; my clothes aren't in much better shape. I really liked that outfit, too.

"Where is our prey now?" Sekhmet asks, already hungry for more.

I point at the door to Nan's little hospital wing. She nods and strides toward it, seeming utterly ecstatic at the thought of shredding more hapless mercenaries. I look around the room, taking in the devastation we've caused. Another tremor sends a block of tiles falling from the ceiling, covering the mutilated remains of some of the men in dust and debris. No wonder they had her locked up—I'd forgotten just how vicious she was.

Sekhmet kicks the door in with a single savage blow from her leg. "The judgment of the gods is upon you!" she yells in the shattered entryway.

A brilliant flare of scintillating green energy blasts out of the hall, and Sekhmet rockets back into the laboratory like she's been launched out of a cannon. She plows through three different stations before coming to a rest atop a heap of ruined building materials, dazed.

"Who let you out of your cage, little kitty?" I hear Garen say from the corridor. Carefully, I pad around to the side and flatten myself against the wall near the broken doorway.

"Please deal with her, Specialist," Drass says. "Then perhaps we can settle this ridiculous argument, yes?"

"Don't you dare touch her while I'm gone," Garen says sharply, and I can tell he's not talking about Sekhmet. Then, in a louder voice: "Come on, boys. Let's see how many ways we can skin a cat."

I move farther from the entrance as footsteps approach, slipping around to the other side of a large piece of rubble. Moments later, Garen strides out of the entrance, a glowing amulet clutched in his right hand. I don't get the best look at it, but I think it's in the shape of a stylized eye. The men fan out around him, moving deeper into the laboratory, and I notice Sekhmet has already vanished from the mound of wreckage she made in her flight.

Then there's a blur of movement and I catch a glimpse of the Egyptian goddess in midleap, soaring through the air toward a stray mercenary with claws outstretched. He screams, firing wildly as she crashes into him. Talons rip through Kevlar and fangs sink into his neck. The men converge immediately, rifles ablaze, and Garen begins running in the direction of the conflict. I take the opening her distraction has made to dart into the waiting hallway.

Drass's eyes widen in surprise the moment I enter. Now it's just him and the mercenary monitoring the chamber. The occupant of that tank—the creature wearing the skin of Samantha's mother—looks at me with unsettling interest as I approach.

I nod at the woman. "Bags all packed, I see." Outside, I hear more screams and gunfire. Somewhere even farther away, another explosion rocks the complex.

"The station's a lost cause," Drass says, swaying a little as the ground rumbles. "The volcano was a nice touch."

"Thanks. I'm proud of it." I walk a little closer. There's another bright green flash from somewhere behind me, throwing my shadow down the hall for an instant. It's followed by crashing sounds and yells.

Drass chuckles, moving in front of the chamber to face me directly. "Pride. From a god. How surprising."

"How can you judge me for anything?" I say, frowning as I draw the knife from its sheath on my arm. "You sacrificed your own wife for dark gifts, and now . . . now I couldn't begin to guess what's going on. What *is* that thing?" I shoot a finger at the creature. It grins at me.

Drass glares. "You don't know what you're talking about," he snaps.

"Enlighten me."

"I'd prefer to kill you, if it's all the same," he says, withdrawing a small platinum cube from his jacket. He glances at it, turning it over in his fingers, and I see it has little markings on each of its faces. Drass picks one side and holds out the device, pointing it at me. I have no idea what it's about to do, but I refuse to stand around and find out. I coil my legs beneath me and leap out of the corridor, crashing through a damaged pane of glass into one of the empty patient rooms as the cube activates. It emits a dull tone as it hums to life, like an elevator of ruin arriving at its destination. I feel a wash of heat behind me, and the room turns stark white as the thing unleashes an enormous beam of incandescent light into the corridor.

"Nimble thing, aren't you?" I hear Drass say. His footsteps sound in the hallway, drawing nearer. Before he gets a chance to corner me, I get up, flip the knife around in my hand, and lean out the broken window. He's just ten feet away, holding the cube in front of him.

I launch the blade at him before he can turn it on again, and I'm rewarded with a cry of pain as the weapon blurs through the air and embeds itself in his remaining hand, knocking the cube from his grip. Behind him, the woman in the chamber laughs and claps.

"Sir!" the remaining mercenary says, moving toward him.

"Keep your damn eyes on the readings!" Drass yells, motioning him away with the stump of his left arm. In the distance, there's more shouting, following by another cry of pain and a bestial roar. At least somebody's having fun.

I walk back into the hall as he grabs the hilt of the knife between his teeth and yanks it out, spitting it away from him. He flexes his injured palm—I notice it's not bleeding nearly as much as it should be—and sighs. "What is it with you and my hands?" he asks, eyes darting over the floor. He's looking for the cube.

In response, I pull the 9mm handgun from my bag and shoot him in the chest. He staggers backward, wincing in pain. "Agh, that *stings*," he says, reaching up with his remaining hand. He tugs at the hole in his suit, and his fingers come away with a flattened lump of metal.

"Really?" I say, confused. "A blade cuts you just fine, but you're bulletproof?"

He shrugs, flicking the slug away. "Skin's enchanted to have the *exact* properties of Kevlar. Magic can be annoyingly literal, at times. It's not going to stop a knife, but it usually gets the job done."

"How about an eye?" I say, lining up a shot and firing. He throws an arm in front of his face to block the bullet, but I'm already moving.

I dash forward and drop into a slide, shooting across the floor like a runner going for home—Drass looks down just in time to see me sweep up the platinum cube and come to a stop right beside him, aiming at him with my gun in one hand and the artifact in the other.

In response, he kicks me in the ribs with enough force to pick me off the floor and send me sailing into another nursing suite. I clip the edge of the divider as I crash through the glass, denting the metal window frame. I refuse to count this as getting knocked through another wall—that's been happening to me too much as it is. Drass rushes in after me, but he's too late. I'm already staggering to my feet, and I've managed to hold on to both my gun and the cube. I fire a warning shot into his abdomen, then brandish the platinum device at him.

"Fine," he wheezes, pulling the new bullet out of his suit and holding it up in surrender. "What do you want?"

"That's simple: I'm going to kill you for what you've done, Gideon," I say, furious.

"Kill me for *what I've done*?" he repeats, seeming amused. "You haven't the faintest idea what that is, little goddess."

"I know enough."

"Do you, now? And what will killing me accomplish, exactly? Do you think I am somehow special? That my death will deal Finemdi a blow? I'm a *figurehead*, my dear, elected by a board of directors who have done *far* worse than even *I* will ever know, to say nothing of their chairman."

"And who is that?"

He laughs, shaking his head. "As if they'd tell me. You've never had to fight a bureaucracy, have you? So used to a world of black and white." He puts out a hand to steady himself on the doorframe as the building sways again and some very loud rumbles shake the wing. "I'm an *employee*, Freya."

An uneasy feeling slides into me. My goals, once so clear and indisputable, suddenly seem as unstable as the building I've ruined. I feel the need to reignite my anger, to justify it to myself. "Then explain the woman—explain what you did to your wife!"

"She *agreed to it*, you presumptive parasite!" he yells at me, beyond frustrated. "She sacrificed herself for the greater good, to keep that monstrosity chained! It has no true form, so we had to give it one before we could seal it away. And now your idiot scheme has threatened everything. We need to get her out of here *immediately*, and I need her cage reinforced before we can. To do *that*, I need a god's energy, so if you're not going to volunteer, how about stepping aside while we use *hers*?" He jerks his head at Nantosuelta, still lying in her bed across the hall.

I look from her to the creature and back to Drass. "I don't believe you," I say at last. "Why not kill it? Disbelieve it?"

"Because we *can't*," he says, gritting his teeth. "It's over *four thousand* years old, reinforced by *celestial mechanics* and tough as nails." He holds out his hands—well, hand. "You want to give it a go? Be my guest!"

I look at the woman in the chamber with a wary glance. She smiles and crooks a finger at me in a "come hither" motion. "What is it?" I say at last.

Drass sighs and looks away. "A mistake. Okay, look, Garen thinks you have autonomy, so let's see how different you really are: I don't want a fight. Go, run, hide—I give you my word I won't follow. Yeah, you're on our list, but you're not a threat to the world." He points a shaking finger at the thing that used to be his wife. "That one *is*."

I pause, taken aback. This is not the way things are supposed to go. Honestly, here's where he should be telling me his evil plans. "There's no possible way I can trust you," I say, steadying my grip on the gun and artifact.

He shrugs. "No, there's not. But seriously, between you and this atrocity, which do you think I'd rather set free?"

I roll my eyes. "Neither. But I see your point."

That gets a tight smile out of him. "Great. So what's it going to be, little god?" he says, taking a step back and raising his arms. "I'm offering an olive branch here—turn around, march your immortal ass out of my facility, and let me clean up the mess you've made."

I waver for a moment, wondering if there's even a chance he's telling the truth. Then the Valkyrie in me screams that it's a *trick*, to strike now, destroy him before he can make the first move. She tells me this is my moment, that leaving now wouldn't just mean abandoning Nantosuelta—what of my glory, my vengeance, my principles?

Nathan also flashes in my mind, telling me I could still walk away. Every step down this path is one further from the happiness and friendship we set out to find. This is just a building, Drass but one monster among many—I may win this battle, may survive it along with my friends, but what of the war? In this moment, I see with heartbreaking clarity the two roads that stretch before me and understand that no matter which I choose, I'm certain to lose something along the way.

The question, then, is simple: Who am I, right now? The

beaten-down little girl in a mental hospital who just wanted to be left alone, or a world-changing goddess on the rise? Getting to this moment has been so easy, so thoughtless. At every turn, I held true to my principles, and now I stand surrounded by hate and ruin, risking real friends in the name of mythical beliefs. Is that my future, too?

I abandoned my legacy once. I could do it again.

"You're right, Drass," I say in a soft, grateful voice as I realize the truth, realize that I've been down this road before. "I have a choice."

The woman in the chamber cocks her head to the side, looking confused.

"Thank you for helping me see myself for what I truly am," I say, raising the gun a little a higher. "There will be no deal. Not because of what I can and cannot do, but because of what I *want*. I choose divinity. I choose the mantle. I choose *war*."

He grits his teeth at that and glares, but when he replies, he doesn't sound furious or frustrated—just disappointed. "It was worth trying," he says, more to himself.

His features tense, and I'm readying myself for another attack when a clatter from the hallway interrupts us. Garen walks in and flings Sekhmet to the ground. A handful of mercenaries are still with him, all glaring at the Egyptian goddess, who looks like she's been through the wringer. Smoke rises from singed fur and broken limbs, and her regeneration somehow seems to have been halted. Groaning, she raises her head to take in the corridor. Her golden eyes widen as she focuses on the chamber and its possessed occupant.

"*Apep*," she gasps from the floor. I frown, unable to place the name. She obviously recognizes the creature, but I always thought Set, the Egyptian god of deserts, disorder, and violence, was the Big Bad of her pantheon.

The woman in the tank takes a bow. Garen shrugs at that, then moves a little farther into the hall, dragging Sekhmet with him.

"Drass?" he calls. "Where are you hi—oh," he says, spotting the two of us in the side room. He glares at me, then raises his amulet without saying anything else. It flares green, and I know I only have heartbeats to react. I thrust the platinum cube before me, and will it to activate.

In the split second before it answers my call, I see Drass's eyes lock onto the cube and take note of the face I've picked at random. His mouth forms a soundless *NO*, and then everything is lost in a monumental *crack* of lightning. The ceiling splits open as a tremendous wall of electricity descends from the heavens, blasting through the unstable edifice and shearing it in two. We're both flung backward by the explosion, and to my great dismay I feel the numbing thumps of weakened masonry giving way before my body as I rocket through several walls. Impulse Station lurches, the entire structure veering to one side as thousands of tons of reinforced supports and retaining walls give way. Both halves of the colossal complex sink into the lava pool at its base at awkward angles, and I feel myself roll across a concrete floor as everything is tilted to the side. It's like I've just unzipped the building.

Shaking my head to clear away the brilliant flash, I use the nearest wall for support and lever myself to a standing position. Emergency lighting cuts through the haze of dust, but something else illuminates the disaster area, as well. A dim red glow suffuses everything, seeping up from below. I stagger toward the rift I've created, and the building's new upturned angle lets me catch a glimpse of dark storm clouds gathering beyond the shredded rooftop of its other half. I reach the ragged edge of my side and look down. Perhaps fifty feet away, an enormous pool of molten rock churns, devouring the structure's foundations. Accelerated by the unnatural change in temperature, sharp winds tear through this artificial valley, carrying away vast clouds of debris and loose paper.

On the other side of this hellish fissure, about thirty feet away, I can make out the mangled bodies of the mercenaries and Sekhmet's unconscious form perched just beyond the obliterated remains of the hospital corridor. That means Nan, Drass, and the woman in the chamber must be on my side. I look around, trying to find some trace of them. I think I've been tossed away at an angle. I'm just on the edge of what looks like a standard utility corridor. Several boring doors are set into the nearby walls.

I catch a glimpse of some movement from the opposite side. I'm about to head closer to see who it is when a hand clamps onto my neck, picks me bodily from the ground, and starts walking me toward the building's edge.

"Fancy a swim?" Drass grates into my ear.

The drop is barely five feet away, and I can tell he's about to throw me in before we even reach it.

"Mangalitsa!" I choke out, legs kicking. I don't have a destination—don't have time to choose—so the 40 gallons of water materialize right over my head. The miniature deluge engulfs us both, sending us rolling back into the building. It's no more than what a moderately sized aquarium could hold, but with the slanted floor, it's enough to knock Drass off his feet. He loses his grip on my neck as we both tumble against the back wall of the utility hallway.

Sputtering in shock, he lunges for me again, but I scamper away, moving deeper into the hallway. There's a gaping hole in the wall where I burst in, but things are a little more intact here. Doors are set on either side, though I have no idea where any of them lead. My first instinct is to fight back, but I lost my handgun and the cube in the blast, and there's nothing left in my bag besides the leveler, which would probably do more damage to *me* at this point. Then I get a look at the plaques set beside the doors and realize they're not going to help me escape—they're more of those shortcuts, and I have no idea where they lead.

Drass pushes himself to his feet with his good arm and staggers toward me. Silhouetted by the glow of the lava pit, he looks terrifying, like a mutilated demon in a business suit. Only he's not fireproof. The realization makes me wish I had some way of tossing *him* into the pit, but even if I could tackle him over the side, I'd probably end up going in with him, and that's a fate I'd dearly like to avoid. I can regenerate, but not that fast. It would take a *long* time before this place cooled enough for me to re-form, and longer still for them to dig me out.

The man flexes his remaining hand and smiles at me. "Starting to regret that little trick now, aren't you?" he says as if he's read my mind. He bends down and picks up a long piece of rebar. "Is that fear I see? Come on. Isn't this what you *chose*?"

"Still is," I spit, eyes darting in search of a weapon.

"*Why?*" he practically screams, slashing the air with the rebar.

I shuffle back a few steps in surprise at the fury in his voice. "If you can deny your dogma, you can be *more* than every other empty-headed god!" he continues, sounding unhinged. "You could be free! Why embrace what *you know* will take that from you?"

"Because it's *the right thing to do*," I hiss, backing away another step. "Y'know what, Drass? Forget gods and philosophies and all the crap you tell yourself when you're trying to fall asleep at night. End of the day, you hunt, cage, and torture a group of people you *hate*, you bigoted—"

"*You're not PEOPLE!*" he yells, flinging himself at me.

I flinch away, stumbling in the tangle of concrete and ceiling tiles at my feet. There's a *whoosh* as the rebar zips past my left ear, and then the building shifts again, sending a small avalanche of debris tumbling between us. A cloud of dust billows around me, shot through by the terrible blush of the lava like it's a dying sunset. I regain my footing, hoping he's been caught in the downpour, but as I straighten up, my heart sinks. Rebar twitching in his only hand, Drass emerges from the haze, sidestepping the small mound of rubble and planting himself in front of me.

"I'm sorry," he says, gesturing with his stump. "You were saying?"

I give him a bitter laugh. "Yeah. *I'm* the single-minded one. If fighting you means following my birthright, then *cool*. The world is not a better place without Freya, but it *will* be one without you."

"What a waste," he says, voice dripping with contempt. "Brave enough to face me, but not your own flaws. You're a coward, Sara Vanadi, and unworthy of your gifts."

He steps forward and beckons to me. Another gust of wind

streams through the canyon, peeling the dust away to reveal the bubbling lake of fire, rising still. Drass tilts his head at it and lifts his eyebrows, telling me where I'm headed. Heart pounding, I edge back another foot. I can't best him in a physical contest, and we're about five seconds from one. There must be a way of taking him down, but he's layered in enchantments and dark magic and every instinct is telling me I should have listened to Samantha and just run for it, no matter what plans of mine hinged on his death. He raises the rebar over his head, and the time to decide on a course of action is suddenly gone. I ready myself for his attack, hoping I can hit him somewhere it hurts, like the eyes, before he bludgeons me into unconsciousness and tosses me into the molten lake.

Then an odd tremor runs through my mind, and in the same instant, flames mushroom around his head, blazing up from nowhere to form a localized sphere of fire. It's gone in a split second, but it is enough to set his hair ablaze and stun him. He lunges forward, but he's swinging blind, and I'm able to sidestep the blow and shove him to the ground with one kick to the back. In the distance, across the canyon, I hear Nathan whoop. "Yes! Sara, *I got him!*" he yells.

I'm elated, but it'll all be for nothing if I can't use this to my advantage. Drass is already picking his way to his feet, so I'm going to need to act fast. I have no weapons, and even if I could muscle him in, the lava is still too far to reach. I can't make a thirty-foot leap, either, and my only escape route is down ruined hallways he knows better than I do, or through teleportation doors that aren't going to lead anywhere useful. If I knew they could get me to the other building, that would be great, but as far as I can tell, they all go to the sublevels, and those are currently filled with—

A brilliant smile lights my face as I realize there's a solution I haven't yet considered: If I can't take Drass to the lava, then I need to bring the lava *to him*.

As all this runs through my head, the man staggers upright and spins around, soot-streaked features contorted with rage. He roars and charges me without another word, long past the point of banter. Even though the corridor's tilted at an awkward angle, he manages to move terrifyingly fast, and we're about to collide when I jump up, grab the handle on the door to my left, and haul it open. The door is hinged so it swings toward me, and thank the gods for that.

An enormous column of liquid rock and metal pours out of the opening, engulfing Drass and splashing into the corridor as the magic in the portal connects this door to a preset location somewhere deep inside that volcanic lake. Flecks of burning magma spatter my skin and clothing and I scream as it burns me, but it's nothing compared with what's happening to Drass. He's completely coated in the flow, a man-sized lump of glowing rock thrashing around in an unending cascade of molten ooze. I run for it, scampering up the incline to the edge of the divide as the stream eats through the wall below it and sinks down into the building, taking the remains of Finemdi's CEO along for the ride.

"Sara! Sara, are you okay?" Nathan calls out from across the fiery chasm.

"Did you see that?" I yell, overjoyed.

He shakes his head. "Was too far in! What happened? Did you get him?"

"Hell yes, I got him!" I reply. "We did it!"

He cheers, throwing a fist in the air. I'm about to join with some victory shouts of my own when something moves in the ruins behind him. I stiffen in shock as Garen walks out of the shadows, bruised and bloodied, an assault rifle in one hand and the glowing amulet in the other. He points his gun at Nathan's back and calls out to me. "I'll make you a deal, princess!" he yells, his voice hoarse. Nathan whirls at the sound, turning to face the man. "Throw yourself into the lake, and I'll let him live!"

"Nate!" I cry, furious at my inability to reach either of them.

My friend puts his hands up. "Please don't shoot," Nathan says.

Garen rolls his eyes. "Shut up," he mutters. "Well? What's it going to be?" he yells in a louder voice. "Lava bath, or one dead mortal? I know you care about him."

"And I'm supposed to trust you?" I scream back.

He laughs. "Why would I care if he lives?"

"I have no way of knowing that's true," I reply. "And hasn't he seen too much? Wouldn't Finemdi make you kill him anyway?"

"Thanks, Sara, that's really helping," Nathan says, sounding very worried.

Even across the burning crevasse, I can make out Garen's oily smirk. "This is a trade I'd be more than happy to make! And you know what? Right now, I think Finemdi might have more important things to worry about than whether a lowly mortal escaped. Just a thought."

I sigh, shaking my head. I'm trapped. There's no way I'm throwing myself in, but I can't see an alternative that will save Nathan, either. Maybe I can aim for the edge of the pool and pull myself out when he's not looking? I glance down, watching as clouds of caustic gases dance on the surface of the lava. Those might hide my landing. . . .

"Enough," a soft, quavering voice calls out from my left, carrying over the divide. Garen's eyes go wide as he spots the source, and the muzzle of his weapon dips. I tip out, looking around a flapping piece of insulation, and see what's gotten his attention. Nantosuelta is standing on a broken spar of concrete not ten feet away, leaning heavily on her IV pole. Her platform juts out above the canyon like a broken bridge, and it looks like it's taking all her strength just to remain upright. Even as I watch, her wizened feet slide ever so slightly in the loose scree of crumbled rocks scattered atop the concrete.

"Mother, please, you must—" Garen begins.

"Stop," she says, silencing him with a glare. "Let the boy go, Garen."

"I—but I can't just—" he stammers, looking pained.

"This is over," she says, struggling to hold on to the metal pole beside her. "If you can't release your hate for my kind, then at least concede the battle for this day. It's done."

"But—"

"*Drop your weapons*," she hisses, the malevolence in her tone surprising me. "If you ever loved me, you'll do this favor, Garen."

"I—Mother, it's not . . ." He trails off and hangs his head. He gives it a little shake, and then his chest heaves in a sigh. "Another day," he mumbles after a moment. Then he tosses the amulet and gun away from him, out into the divide. They land with distant *plop*s, vanishing beneath the molten flow. He looks up at me, glaring. "Another day," he says louder, and I know it's a promise.

Nathan backs away, skirting around the edge of the building and putting a little distance between Garen and himself. Nantosuelta nods. "Good boy," she says, utterly exhausted. It seems even this short exchange has drained her of whatever strength she had left. "The only one. You were the only one, Garen. I'll always love you for that."

"Mother . . ." Garen says, his voice uncharacteristically soft. "I know it's hard, but please, I can help—"

"You have. You've helped me so much," Nan says, smiling. "But I'm not strong enough. I'm so very, very tired, Garen."

"Please . . ." His voice cracks, and he sinks to his knees.

"Don't be sad, my boy," she says. "I'm free. Remember that. Remember *me* like that. Free."

Then she lets go of the pole and leans forward. She clips the edge of the concrete and topples over, spinning once before she hits the lava. I see her hospital gown catch fire, and then the liquid closes over her frail body, burying her forever. Just like that, she's gone. I pull back from the edge, feeling an odd mix of shock and relief.

I hope she finds her peace, and I hope one day, when she is ready, her believers will return to give her life in a better world.

Garen looks stunned, eyes locked on the spot where his mother disappeared. He's still on his knees, hands splayed on the ground in front of him. Tears run freely down his cheeks. Nathan looks between him and me. "Now what?" he asks at last.

That breaks me out of my reverie. "I . . . can you see a way down from there?"

He glances around, then shakes his head. "No—I can't go much farther along the gap in either direction. Do you have a spell for this?"

I grimace. "Nothing useful."

He sighs. "Well, that's just great."

A light rain begins to fall, misting down from the gathering clouds. It hisses when it hits the lava, sending up wisps of steam. The lake is a lot closer now, maybe twenty-five feet, and the heat is incredible. "At least we won't have long to wait," Nathan says, looking down.

"Sorry, Nate," I say, shoulders slumped.

He glances up at the building tilted above him. "Maybe I can climb it?" he says halfheartedly, putting out a hand on one crumbling wall.

I nod, looking up at my own half. It's a long shot, but . . . "It's better than noth—"

A raging gust of wind takes away the rest of my words. High-pitched laughter echoes out of the clouds, and something glints in the sky above us. "Woo! Need a lift?" Hiʻiaka's voice cries from the heavens, echoing in the wind. The glinting metal resolves into a car, a cherry-red convertible held aloft on a furious current of air. The machine zooms down from the skies, pulling level with me. Pele, Nāmaka, and Hiʻiaka are all crammed in the front seat, beaming. The trunk is jam-packed, overflowing with an incredible assortment of divine artifacts held down by bungee cords.

"Not bad, eh?" Pele says, motioning with her head at the lava lake.

"Get in!" Hiʻiaka calls out, reaching back to pat the rear seat.

I grin at them, then point across at the other half of the building. "Nathan and Sekhmet first!" I yell over the wind.

Hiʻiaka nods and the car veers away, rushing to the other side of the divide and stopping just below Nathan's floor. My friend looks at me, then leaps into the backseat with a cry of happiness. The car lurches forward, and Pele reaches out to grab Sekhmet's unconscious body, which she shoves into the backseat with Nathan's help.

"What about him?" Hi'iaka says, pointing at Garen, who's been watching the proceedings with traumatized dismay.

"Leave him," I reply. "'Another day.' Isn't that right, Specialist?"

He glares at me through red-rimmed eyes. "You're all dead," he croaks. "Hunt you down. Every last resource I can get my hands on. It'll all be for you. Enjoy this. Really. Because you are all royally—"

"Ah, actually, I believe you're the one who's in trouble," Nāmaka interrupts.

"Yeah, see, before we picked up this sweet little number, we had some fun in your computer core," Hi'iaka says. "Nothing special. Just sent some emergency broadcasts about how this 'Specialist Garen' guy had snapped, taken out the whole complex because of his mom. Easy stuff."

"I think there was supposed to be a whole lot more transmitted, all sorts of important files and records, but they had a little flood," Nāmaka says, shrugging. "Shame."

"I had a spell ready to impersonate you, just in case," I add. "Even had some of your blood on hand for the illusion"—I point at the patch on my shoulder that's his—"but it never really came up, and the only one who'd know any better is currently melting along with his facility."

"Oh, you got him?" Pele asks.

"Your lava!" I reply. She grins at that and laughs.

Garen looks completely shell-shocked at this point. "They . . . they won't—"

"C'mon, you know better than that," I say. "A whole facility down the tubes and the *only* evidence they have is a secure transmission naming the culprit? Oh, they are *never* going to believe you, are they?"

It looks like he's going to reply, to fight back, but then he seems to deflate, head sinking to his chest. Hi'iaka shrugs and spins the wheel of the car, giggling. The movement is just for show—all it does is turn the tires—but she has her winds move the convertible back across the rift at the same time, rocking to a halt when it's next to me.

I hop in, landing in the backseat beside Sekhmet, who's still completely out of it. Nathan, grinning from ear to ear, gives me a thumbs-up. The car shifts, veering away from the side of the building. Garen glares at us as we go, eyes burning with promises of vengeance and destruction.

As we move forward, past the concrete spar with Nan's fallen IV pole, I see into the rest of the hospital corridor and feel a stab of worry. Just beyond the open door to her room, the black chamber is sitting against one wall, listing on its side. The mercenary in charge of monitoring it is sprawled on the floor in the middle of the hall, his skin completely gray. The chamber's hatch is open, and the creature it once held is nowhere to be seen.

That's coming back to haunt me, I think as the car rises into the clouds, pulling away from the devastated wreck of Impulse Station.

18

BEST INTENTIONS

"Pan-seared Spam with pineapple glaze and rice!" Pele shouts, shoving aside various dips and a vegetable platter so she can set down a tray covered in little bowls.

"Spam?" I say, feeling cautious. I glance at my friends, and Nathan and Sekhmet seem to share my trepidation.

The other two Hawaiian sisters nod vigorously. "Don't knock it till you try it!" Hi'iaka says, reaching out and grabbing a bowl.

I shrug and take one of my own. It's been three days since Impulse Station sank into an enormous lake of burning metal and rock, and we haven't heard anything from Finemdi since. With their data center's computer records destroyed before they could be backed up off-site, we've all been under the assumption that it will be a long time before they get around to finding us again. I'd be an idiot to think Garen died in the building, but I doubt I'll be seeing him anytime soon, either.

After we were certain Finemdi wasn't about to retaliate, we decided to celebrate. It's just a little potluck get-together—certainly not like the parties we all remember from our heydays—but it's a nice change of pace. I have a feeling Sekhmet, after years of imprisonment, is especially happy to have a chance to relax. I provided the chips, veggies, and dips (I'm a terrible cook), Nathan whipped up some pot stickers, Nāmaka mixed drinks, Hi'iaka made pulled pork sandwiches on sweet rolls, Sekhmet brought baklava for dessert, and Pele, of course, has her Spam dish.

. . . Which isn't bad, to be honest. It tastes salty and deliciously greasy, like a bit of homemade fast food. I can understand how it could become a guilty pleasure, though you have to see this from my perspective: It is completely impossible for me to gain weight. Or die from a heart attack. I know, I know, gods get all the perks.

"So what's next?" Hi'iaka asks before shoveling Spam strips and rice into her mouth.

"We lie low," I say. "We gather our strength and see what they do. I don't know about the rest of you, but I need worshippers badly. I can handle humans just fine, but the moment someone starts throwing magic around, it's over."

Pele sighs and nods. "I think we all need a better source of belief than what Finemdi was providing."

Sekhmet grimaces. I can tell she wants to get out there and crack some heads, but she knows we're not prepared to take on the rest of the company right now. "I agree," she says, though she doesn't sound pleased. "I will try to find out more about our enemies, as well. We must also consider the fact that Apep is loose in this world."

"Yeah, who is that?" I ask. "I thought Set—"

"Set is the product of many years of conflicting mythology," Sekhmet says. "He was worshipped as a god of foreigners and the desert before mortal politicking placed him in shadow, and even at his worst, he was somewhat balanced by this upbringing. He is no friend of mine, but I can understand him. No, Apep is a literal god of evil. He is the personification of darkness and chaos, of all the things man fears in the night. His only goal is to cover the world in shadows and devour humanity. He is a threat to creation itself, and we were all his enemy. Set fought him daily, before the myths changed his role."

She spears a piece of Spam with one claw and holds it before her beautiful golden eyes. "You know, sometimes I think Apep himself was responsible for that. I believe he wanted to hide, to make mortals forget him until it was too late. My people did not worship him, after all—they simply believed in his existence and the need for his destruction. He is a god with no followers. He exists to be hated." Her mouth opens wide, showing off a terrifying array of teeth, and she tosses the meat in and chews thoughtfully. "I like it," she says at last, nodding at Pele with a little purr.

"Well, that's cheery," Nathan says. "So how do you kill a god without worshippers? How does he even exist?"

Sekhmet shrugs. "Strange, is it not? What brings him back if he is injured? We destroyed him countless times, and each night, he would spawn anew. Our past is filled with his demise, yet he always survives."

I think of what Samantha said in the supply closet, about how gods can live off all sorts of belief once they're formed. Then I remember what Drass said when I questioned him about killing Apep: *reinforced by celestial mechanics*. Those were his exact words, weren't they?

"Night," I say, putting two and two together. "When man fears the dark, Apep grows stronger. He's tied to shadows, and even if it's daylight outside, it's always night somewhere."

"There aren't any other gods who do that?" Nathan asks.

Sekhmet shakes her head. "Your history is littered with gods of darkness, but I know of none like him. You either have mythical creatures of shadow that wish to destroy the light, such as sky dragons or great wolves"—she nods at me—"or humanlike gods with dark natures that still draw worship. You may believe some gods 'act' evil, but there is almost always a duality there, a hidden trait to be praised, or some need for them. A god of the underworld, for instance, may be brutal and merciless, but without them, the dead might roam free. In his heart, man believes in redemption and balance, a reason for everything to exist. Yin and yang, life and death. Apep is nothing like this. He is simply darkness and destruction, a waiting threat that must be battled and broken."

"So he's just . . . pure evil? Death for everyone? How boring," Hi'iaka says. "At least he'll be easy to track down; follow the bodies, right?"

"If only," Sekhmet says, showing off her fangs in what I *think* is her version of a wan smile. "Apep's goals may be apocalyptic, but his threat is one of corruption, calculation, and intelligence. I would not expect to meet him on the battlefield—chaos and sorrow will follow in his wake, but always from behind proxies and mortal fools. In truth, this makes him far deadlier than some mindless, howling destroyer."

Nathan groans. "All that, and he can't die. Which brings us back to the main problem: How do we stop him?"

His question is met by blank stares. "I think we file that under 'bridges to be crossed later,' Nate," I say at last, feeling as if there really *isn't* much we can do. I may have screwed up letting that thing out, but it's a big world and I'm still a small fish; even if we *could* find him right now, what good would it do?

Nathan looks equally unsettled, but then he gets a curious look. "All right. Table the whole 'unkillable god of evil' thing for now. What are you going to do about Finemdi?"

I frown. Is that a trick question? "Uh, destroy them?"

"Right, but *how*? You keep talking about that like it's on the grocery list between 'milk' and 'bagels.' These guys are *bad news* and all of you seem totally 'whatever' about them." He pauses, thinking. "Always have, actually."

We look at one another for a moment, then Sekhmet speaks up. "It is . . . hard, I think, for us to take them seriously. Even after everything they have done, they are still mortal."

"I think we're kind of hardwired to not see humanity as a threat," I explain. "Apep? Yeah, we can see the danger there. Finemdi, though . . ."

"Seriously?" Nathan says, setting down his food and looking at us like we've grown extra heads. "Did you *see* the look on Garen's face when you left him there? I was already terrified of the dude, and now his mom is dead and he's got nothing to lose? And that's *one guy*! Finemdi probably has a zillion more just like him, and their *only mission* is hunting you all down. How does this not register any higher on DEFCON God than 'mild inconvenience'?"

I'm about to reply with more static about how immortality changes your view of the world, but then I stop myself. He's right. These creeps turn divinity inside out, bend gods to their will, and collect us like very dangerous stamps. I don't need more reasons to hate Finemdi, but maybe it's a good idea to fear them, too. Just a little. "Mortal's got a point," I say, smiling. "If we go into this with blinders on, we could fall right into their hands. They know us, right? They'd *expect* us to underestimate them."

"Still not sure how being afraid helps us, but all right," Nāmaka says, seeming unconvinced but not particularly interested in arguing.

"No, no, I think I get it!" Hi'iaka pipes up. "We know we're awesome, and *they* know we know that, so they might get the drop on us because they think we *won't know* that they know we know that!"

"Uh. Yes. Probably," I say, then turn back to Nathan. "Thank you. If we ever start ignoring obvious stuff like that again, just pipe up. Godhood has its blind spots."

He grins at that, clearly pleased with the compliment, then nods and returns to Pele's dish.

"So . . . big baddies are great and all, but what about the important stuff? How are we going to get new worshippers so we can deal with all this nonsense?" Pele asks, clearly trying to change the subject.

"The parks," I reply, grateful for the chance. "I have a job there."

"You need a job?" she says, surprised.

"Well, no. My job gets me my worship." Quickly, I explain the relationship between the heartfelt belief of the children at the parks and our own divine natures.

"Can you . . ." Nāmaka begins when I'm done. She seems caught between amazement at what I've found and embarrassment about having to ask for help. "Can you get us jobs like that?"

I look around, and the rest of them nod eagerly. "I think so . . ." I murmur. "There are more than enough tourists to go around, and I'm pretty sure there are even a few Hawaiian characters you can play. That, and I can always try to whip up some illusions to help you land more roles."

"Might be a good idea for all of us. I mean, *she's* probably going to raise some eyebrows," Hi‘iaka says, pointing at Sekhmet.

"Honestly," the woman says, rolling her eyes. Her brow furrows for a moment, and then the air shimmers and her face warps. A new head snaps into existence atop her shoulders like a slide clicking into place on a projector. She's completely human now, a Nile princess with brown almond-shaped eyes and strong, chiseled features.

"I never knew you could do that!" Hi‘iaka exclaims.

"What, you think I just walk around town as a lion-headed woman and no one's the wiser?" she says, seeming amused at the idea. "Ages ago, Thoth gifted me with an enchantment to let me change my appearance. Useful for times when I wish to be less conspicuous."

"I always loved that trick," I say, watching in fascination as her features slide back to their former leonine glory. "Okay, well, you're all set, but if the rest of you need an illusion, I can probably figure something out."

"That, or we start going through the trunkload of artifacts you stole," Nathan says, smiling at Hi'iaka.

"Hey, good idea," the windy goddess replies.

"Jobs, new belief, and careful plotting," Nāmaka summarizes. "Seems like we have everything well in hand."

"Hear! Hear!" Pele says, raising her glass for a toast.

We all join her, sipping on some of Nāmaka's island punch.

"So where are you ladies planning on staying?" Nathan asks when we're done.

They all share guilty looks, then turn to me.

"What?" I say, caught off guard.

"Just until we get some finances. Won't be long," Pele says.

"Wait, really?" Nathan asks. "You're all homeless? Homeless gods?"

They nod in unison, and I sigh. "Fine. Sure. We'll figure something out. Invest in some sleeping bags or something."

"Ooh, I want a hammock!" Hi'iaka chirps.

Groaning inwardly, I return to the meal. Don't get me wrong, they're all very nice, and I've known Sekhmet for centuries, but this is a two-bedroom, two-bath apartment. Things are going to get incredibly cramped in no time at all.

A few hours later, as our new houseguests are cleaning up, I take Nathan aside. "I'm sorry we didn't have a chance to discuss that," I say. "Priest or not, this is your house, too."

"Seriously?" Nathan says. "Don't worry about it. I just keep it all in perspective."

"Perspective?"

"A few months ago, I was stressing out over a job. Now I'm trying to figure out how four goddesses are going to be able to crash at our place. Before that, it was how to escape an evil corporate headquarters that was sinking into a lava pit. Trust me, this is *much* more exciting than I ever could have hoped for, Sara."

I smile at that. "Okay. Just let me know if it starts getting to you."

"Will do," he says, giving me a friendly salute.

"Nice move with the fire blast, by the way. Not sure I ever got around to thanking you for that. Remind me to start teaching you some new spells."

He beams at me, seeming utterly delighted by the idea of learning more magic. "I'm really glad it helped," he says. "I was worried it'd explode in my face again."

I'm about to reply when I hear a crash from the kitchen and shake my head. "Speaking of which . . . I'd better check on them. Want a refill?" I ask, pointing at his glass.

"Sure, thanks!" he says, handing it to me.

I take it and walk back.

"Sorry!" Hiʻiaka says, using a burst of air to sweep pieces of a broken plate off the floor and into the trash can.

"No worries," I say, heading for the fridge. I guess I can expect a lot more of this to come. *Ah well.* I spent decades without seeing the barest hint of another god, and now I'm sharing an apartment with four of them. I suppose I was due.

"So clumsy," Nāmaka says to Hiʻiaka, giving her a rueful smile. "You remind me of that poor girl, Samantha." She turns to me. "What do you suppose happened to her?"

I frown. "No idea. I hope she made it out, though. I mean, she's probably okay, right? Smart girl."

Nāmaka shrugs. "A lot of smart people probably died there, Freya."

My frown shifts to a grimace. "I should try to get in touch. Maybe send her an e-mail or something? Just to make sure."

"She'll be fine," Hi'iaka says. "She was smart *and* paranoid. And fun! Those types don't die off camera. Now, help me find any splinters from that plate. Don't want our mortal stepping on one, do we?"

Surprisingly enough, I find myself reassured by that. We bustle around the kitchen and living room, using our various gifts to put the house in order, then set about planning our new living arrangements—grocery shopping, chores, cooking, and so on. A small part of me is irritated by the new chaos in my life, but overall, I finally feel like things are heading in the right direction, that my existence is back on track. After all, I have a brand-new, miniature pantheon of my own, complete with one dedicated worshipper and a never-ending wellspring of believers. Even better, I have a colossal enemy empire I need to bring crashing down. For a creature of purpose, I have been without accomplishments and goals for far too long. Now I have them in abundance.

I can do this. I can toe the line between divinity and humanity, can overcome my foes while retaining the wisdom and free will that let me challenge them in the first place. I will reclaim my birthright—the mantle of Freya I lost all those centuries ago—*and* find where I belong in this modern world . . . without losing myself to either.

My name is Sara Vanadi, and I finally feel like a god again.

+ ◆ ◆

Samantha Drass stretched in her chair and sighed. She was still in Florida, in a small apartment her father kept a few miles from where Impulse Station once stood. It was, objectively, a nice place. All the updated appliances and glossy countertops in the world couldn't make it feel any less empty, though. She already found herself missing the sense of purpose and crowds of Finemdi. They could be stressful, sure, but they also helped her ignore all the nasty side effects of an overly dramatic past and formulaic loneliness. Not for the first time, she wondered if she should get a cat.

Her laptop sat open on her father's desk, the most recent e-mail from Finemdi glowing on its screen. It was a mass e-mail, simple and to the point: *All employees of Impulse Station. Please report as soon as possible. Thank you.* They didn't even know how many had made it out alive.

Ignoring the request wasn't even a consideration for Samantha—what would be the point? She had no desire to escape Finemdi, and in fact, depending on where they transferred her, this could be the breakthrough she would need to resurrect her mother at last. The thought gave her pause, as it led to her wondering if her father had survived. Even after all those years of grief, the thought of losing him was surprisingly painful. His crimes were unforgivable, but he'd always loved her, always cared about her safety and success. That old hurt rose to the surface, showing on her face. Half a decade spent distancing herself from the man, and somehow there were still feelings there.

Samantha gave her head a shake and tried to stop thinking about it. There were plenty of better things to focus on, and finding pain in the past was dangerously close to becoming her official hobby.

Pushing her glasses onto the bridge of her nose with a practiced nudge, she set her fingers on the keyboard and began to type. She'd barely finished the first sentence when a twitch of motion caught her attention, a shifting of light in one corner of the darkened room. Hand shaking, she slid open a desk drawer and withdrew a gun she'd never fired.

She stood slowly, bringing the weapon before her, and called out, "Hello? I know you're there! Please leave now and I w-won't have to shoot you."

In response, the shadows moved again, the outline of a figure becoming distinct. A footstep clicked on the wood floor of the living room, a light, tentative tap. Then another, and another, the figure walking out of the gloom toward her.

"Please, I don't want to have to—" The rest of her words were lost in a gasp as the intruder stepped into the little circle of light cast by her laptop, its dull glow illuminating features that, for Samantha, were achingly familiar.

A face she'd had to memorize a thousand times, trying to get every freckle, every wrinkle perfect. The smile exactly as she remembered it. Each hair in its proper place. Everything. It was *her*. It was really, truly her.

"Mom?"

ACKNOWLEDGMENTS

Before I thank the people who helped this book exist, let me thank you, awesome person, for reading it. It's one thing to put together words and ink and ideas, but by reading them, you make it real. Freya and her friends live every time you open these pages, and I can't tell you how grateful I am to you for this. Now, on to the myth-makers!

Laura Nevanlinna and Ilona Lindh, thank you for taking a chance on a random game designer who wanted a little publishing advice. While I'm at it, let me thank everyone at Rovio Books for their help and support, and Rovio Entertainment as a whole for taking a new world under their angry, mischievous wings.

Christopher Cerasi, thank you for being a ridiculously amazing editor and an even better friend. To Elina Ahlbäck and your team of incredible agents, thank you for bringing this book around the globe, and to Erin Stein and the fantastic folks at Macmillan, thank you for believing in it right from the start.

Finally, thank you to Danielle, my very first reader and, most important, the first person who told me she wanted to see more. I hope to always have new adventures for you.